W9-BXM-689

CHRISTOPHER AND HIS FATHER

CHRISTOPHER

Hans Habe

AND HIS FATHER

Coward-McCann, Inc.
New York

c . 2

To Licci

I

My Name Is Wendelin

Christopher Wendelin tried to atone
in his own life for the fact that his
father was forced by the Nazis to make
an anti-Semitic film called "Ritual
murder".

*H*E hoped they would condemn his father.

It was almost six. They had expected the verdict in the early afternoon, and now it was already evening. The park was covered with snow.

Why did father call me and why did I agree to come? It's fifteen months since I last saw him, yet he whistled and I ran like a dog. I didn't expect a bone. He must be that certain of being acquitted. All he can really be sure of is that they won't arrest him again. Pickpockets and safecrackers and drunken drivers get locked up, but political criminals are released. Political is a flattering adjective, an extenuating circumstance that turns criminals into gentlemen. If you have money you're out on bail. If you have none, others will put up bail for you, and once you're free you can live on forgetfulness.

Christopher stood in front of the framed photographs. Only the desk lamp was lit, but he knew the pictures from childhood—his father surrounded by famous actors and actresses looking at him like at a magician. You were there, friends; you cannot deny it. His father in the studio with a green shade over his eyes; his father at a costume ball, in tails, pleased with himself. His father, always his father.

Many photos had been destroyed or had disappeared into the cellar. Perhaps they had been seized and were among the documents of the trial: the photos with the Führer and sub-führers, taken at the premiere of the film *Ritual Murder* in Berlin, at the reception after *L'Aiglon* in occupied Paris, at the Christmas with the soldiers on the eastern front.

I knew all of them, the Führer and the sub-führers. The propaganda führer had gotten me out of bed at ten one evening. "You always wanted an electric train, didn't you?" The car with the swastika rode through the night, Leipziger Strasse, Berlin. The shop opened. We take the lot, including bridges, tunnels, signals. What were they celebrating? *Ritual Murder*? Or *Michael the Ancestral Farmer*? Anyhow, I always wanted a train with bridges, tunnels and signals.

The white marble bust on the mantelpiece was of his father, too. Young, slick, dead, the head of a giant; perhaps his father liked the bust because he always suffered from being short. The kind of man who only has pictures of himself. When everything breaks down, vanity remains.

The butler had come in and was busying himself at the desk. "He should have been back long ago," he said. "Perhaps we ought to call up." Christopher did not move. "It's a long time since you were with us," said the servant.

The servant hasn't abandoned him. It would be surprising if his friends had. Were all of them Nazis? Had anyone ever been a Nazi? Memories cut off like an electric light. Ghastly deeds switched off, the good times switched on.

The butler had left. Some snow had slid from the roof. Otherwise all was still.

The occupying forces had left the house untouched, and so had the new government. Perhaps they too had memories. The teachers were so careful not to ask Richard Wendelin's son certain difficult questions. As a Hitler Youth, a long trip on the miniature cruiser *Admiral Hipper*—what splendid times! When I was fifteen I was supposed to go to the front, but of course they didn't send me. Father saw to that. Now people say that men are ungrateful, but it is sickening how grateful they are. I don't want to remember and I don't want to be grateful.

He looked at the time. Had they arrested his father after all? Crimes against humanity. One ought to know first what that really means. So what, you can rely on the judges. They, too, have their memories.

Wasn't I within an inch of becoming one of them myself?

The last years of the war, at Uncle Bertram's. Baron Boderode, who hid Poles and liberated Jews. BBC. If someone comes we can say the boy was tinkering with the set. BBC and Radio Moscow. That's where I heard "Richard Wendelin, an assassin behind the camera." A light had dawned on me. But when?—that's the question. Am I proud of myself because of the last year? Aren't I switching memories off and on, like the others? He suddenly thought of slipping out through the garden door.

Suppose they do arrest him? "How's your father doing in prison?" they'll ask. Do I care? I inherited his name as I might have inherited a disease, or a face. Only that isn't quite so. We have the same disease, but not the same face. We are both called Wendelin, but his name is Richard.

"I've been acquitted!" said Richard Wendelin, spreading his arms in expectation. But his son did not approach him. Quickly Richard Wendelin lit all the lights. His face was red, and in spite of his gray hair, he looked young. Like someone without a moment to lose, he went to the desk and brushed the top of it with his short, strikingly white hands.

Christopher observed his father as he might an actor he had once admired who had suddenly revealed himself to be a ham. Not that the actor was acting less well, it was merely that the public had now been to the theater more often. Back in Hamburg, when Richard Wendelin was released from prison, he had not spoken of the past. The past was a venereal disease you caught in your student days; there was no need to tell your son about it. Instead he had given the son a copy of *Faust*, with his own stage directions in it.

"Justice has triumphed," said the father, and the son didn't know whether his father was acting badly or whether such a line was simply impossible to deliver.

The court was apparently retired for an hour and a half, but the verdict was a foregone conclusion. The statements made by the Jews and the Gypsy woman had proved how decently he had treated them in Hungary. How lucky that some of the Jews and Gypsies were still alive. If all the German witnesses had behaved equally well the previous verdict of the De-Nazi-

fication Court would have been sufficient. They finally admitted to *Notstand,* higher orders one had to obey, "Goebbels'
threat of a concentration camp." The young lawyer fortunately
had shown a staggering knowledge. "We need young people
like that. Now you can hold up your head again and look
people straight in the eye. I think you should finish your studies. We'll have a long talk about that."

Sometimes, when scolded in his childhood, Christopher had
determined to win his case by silence. You could gain your
rights by stubborn silence. The same stubbornness overcame
him now; he would stay silent and leave in the middle of the
performance, a disappointed spectator.

What was happening onstage seemed to favor his intention.
The butler came in, carrying a bottle of champagne with two
glasses on a tray. Richard Wendelin pretended that the second
glass was for the servant. "Let us drink, Josef!" "Congratulations, Herr Staatsrat, from Rosa too!" The father loosened
his tie; he looked as he did in the studio, wearing the green eye-
shade. The telephone rang, and while Richard Wendelin was
speaking his face came to life, came to life and grew old, because the red of the cold winter evening turned into the hectic
red of old age. "The press," said the father. "All of a sudden
they've discovered me again." But Christopher was still standing in the wings, making no move to applaud.

And the monologue went on, wordy and ad lib, the speech
of an actor waiting for his fellow actor's entrance, but his fellow actor hadn't even put on his greasepaint. Why had he asked
Christopher to come? It wasn't about his studies, not primarily.
His son was now mature enough, he said, to understand that
he, Richard Wendelin, was human, with all the contradictions that implied, not good, not necessarily bad, but full of
contradictions. He didn't spare himself. He accused himself,
not so much because he had failed as because he had become a
failure. He had wanted to give his son the inexhaustible treasure of a good name, and had burdened him with the curse of a
tainted name instead. "Give my love to your mother," he said,
as though, the recipient of many gifts, he wanted to distribute

some. "Tell her how sorry I am for what I have done to
her. But I have done most to you." He had tears in his eyes.

Suddenly—perhaps it was the easy tears—Christopher was
glad he had come.

I was afraid he would touch me, but he doesn't touch me.
He could weep when Snow White was laid in the glass coffin;
that's why he knew how to touch the hearts of his Germans
when little István Balla, in *Ritual Murder,* comes down the
village street where the Jews are waiting with sharpened knives.
I've known his Snow White tears since I was four, and now I'm
mature enough to understand them.

"Why don't you say anything?" asked his father. "Is my butler
the only one to congratulate me?"

"What am I to congratulate you on?" said Christopher. In his
childhood he could never stick to his plan, and now again he
couldn't remain silent. "Who has acquitted you? Not me."

The reply came in a mild voice. "Have you suffered that
much?"

"Hell, I'm of age. I could have changed my name."

"It's not a question of name."

"Of what, then, blood? I only see blood when I cut myself
shaving."

"I'm an artist, Christopher. That means that I am more
sensitive to the times than others. Artists and children are the
first victims of the times."

He knows that art can always seduce me. Art and his charm.

"I'm not a child anymore," said Christopher. "You have remained an artist. You are incurable."

"Are you trying to be more intolerant than the court?"

"In a moment you'll be talking about the people's infallible
instinct like your friends did, with their People's Courts. The
men who acquitted you sent Hans and Sophie Scholl to the
scaffold."

"Baron Boderode has incited you. And your mother."

"I have seen *Ritual Murder.*"

"You thought it was marvelous."

"I was too young to know better."

"Millions thought it marvelous," said his father. "I refused to do it as long as I could."

"Everyone refused and everyone did everything."

His father spoke as though to himself. Was he guiltier than others? Collective guilt had been acknowledged, but he had been singled out to be persecuted. Weren't seven years of suffering enough? *"After you have watched yourself die/And walked beside your own coffin . . ."*

Now he's quoting Grillparzer. In a moment he'll quote *Faust*. After all, he was only a "little man." Nothing but a little man. How I hate them, these little men. It is easier to finish a discussion than a monologue.

"They showed the film to the SS guards in the concentration camps," Christopher said. "Perhaps one of them would have refused to push Jews into the gas oven, but after *Ritual Murder* none of them refused—in with them all! You don't have to apologize to me. The Jews have forgiven you—those, that is, who are still alive."

The champagne glass which the butler had emptied was in his way; he pushed it aside. He was going to say that he remembered the Christmas Eve when the crates of champagne were brought, "Happy New Year," signed "Dr. Goebbels," probably it's still the same champagne, Happy New Year, Herr Staatsrat! But he didn't say it; he didn't want to give his father a chance to speak, he didn't want to hear about higher orders and suffering and justice. He left the room.

Charm is a matter of practice, and Richard Wendelin's charm had grown rusty. He had no time to think over his son's visit; he had to polish up his charm like old silver.

They all came: the journalists, the radio reporters, the press photographers. Although for years he had considered them only as enemies, Richard Wendelin knew how to handle them. He sent for champagne; Rosa made little sandwiches. But physical pleasures could, at best, create only the right atmosphere. These were inquisitive young people; champagne and salmon were not enough to satisfy them. There wasn't one whom Richard Wendelin, almost as though he were an inquisitive re-

porter himself, didn't ask how his newspaper was doing or
about his personal position with the radio. As to the photographers, he inquired about their cameras; after all, this was a
field in which he could have shone. He did no such thing:
Here the moment had come to captivate by humility. He joked
about his ambitious but faltering efforts at becoming a successful amateur photographer. However, when they asked him to
be photographed in front of his own bust, he refused. "Little
as it may be to the liking of my enemies, I am not yet a monument to the past."

This was the cue. What plans did he have? asked the reporters. Now he had to be cautious. Seven years of total inactivity
had been imposed upon him—"I have refused every offer,
partly to save producers and theater managers embarrassment,
partly so as to be able to reappear before the public with a clear
conscience." Incautious sentence! A young man with a crew
haircut and rimless glasses seemed to be the leader of the group.
Richard Wendelin believed he knew these young intellectuals
who, as though at a word of command, had taken the place of
the young Siegfrieds. What happened to the conscience of a
man who had just been legally and definitely acquitted? the
reporter wanted to know.

"I'm glad you raised that question," said Richard Wendelin.
It always made a good impression to praise the inquisitor's
inquisitorial abilities. He sat down at his desk as if turning his
gaze inward. "For seven years I have been fighting," he said,
"because I possessed ample proof that I had been forced to
make my films. Yet I couldn't expect a moral acquittal. I still
don't construe the verdict like that. No, I certainly don't feel
morally acquitted, not even today, today least of all. I have
been given an opportunity for active repentance, that's all, a
probation period. All I hope for is to be allowed to place my
modest abilities at the service of active repentance."

He was slightly put out by the fact that the reporter with the
crew haircut was not writing down these words. Another one
had set in motion one of the modern tape recorders about whose
technical construction he had likewise duly inquired. He started
to elaborate on the German film, the German theater. Although

this certainly had nothing to do with his involuntary absti-
nence, he said, both of them were in a parlous state. To the
best of his conscience and ability he wanted to devote himself to the rebuilding of cultural life in Germany. Conscience—
there it was again, the incautious word. Did he dare to hope
that new Germany wanted to make use of his talents, considerable as they were? questioned the reporter with the crew haircut. Were there no serious grounds for suspecting—he was only
asking—that Herr Wendelin had acted, admittedly under du-
ress, but also opportunistically? After all, *Ritual Murder* was
the film specially shown to the guards in the concentration
camps.

He had protested to Goebbels against this misuse of his film
most vigorously, even if unsuccessfully, Richard Wendelin
retorted. And as to opportunism, couldn't the word be replaced,
with some goodwill, by "misguided idealism"? "Eighty million opportunists, or seventy or sixty million, if you like.
That's a very improbable figure." Quite true, there had been
people on the other side of the fence, better men than he had
been—"Don't forget, I was never anything but an artist"—and
it was high time to erect a monument to these people who had
saved the good name of Germany. "To be allowed to collab-
orate in doing so is my dearest wish."

It was past ten when he was left alone. But he did not remain
alone, for there was the inquisitive telephone. If only news-
papermen had rung up, Richard Wendelin would have been
happy, for since his release from Allied arrest he had stared at
the silent instrument with disappointed hatred. From the re-
ceiver now came undesired applause. His former mistress, Hermine Moellendorff, rang. For seven years she had been "prohibited," and therefore no doubt had aged by seventy years.
"Congratulations," she said, but it sounded like "I hope we
shall soon be working together again." Then a roommate from
college rang who only a year ago had avoided him in the street.
Suddenly someone cried "Heil Hitler!"—whether with conviction or irony, it was hard to say. He answered awkwardly,
vaguely, hung up abruptly, not only because he assumed that
his telephone was tapped—governments come and go, but

eavesdroppers remain—but also because he could not explain
to his well-wishers how serious was his intention to break with
the past. The past belonged to the past, once and forever.

He was tired; he felt the heavy burden on his chest. The
air smelled of magnesium flashes, champagne, cigarettes and
paste. The ashtrays were full, the glasses empty; burned-out
flashbulbs and crumpled black strips of film lay all over the
place. All this offended Richard Wendelin's almost superstitious sense of order. He wanted to pour himself a glass of
champagne—as much champagne as possible, the doctor had
advised—but he couldn't remember which glass belonged to
him, and he was nauseated by the thought of touching other
people's glasses.

Charm was a matter of practice, and you needed practice to
assess its effects on the audience; audience was everyone who was
not you yourself. You could develop too much charm—charming, more charming, and most frivolous in the end. He was
afraid that this time others might have spotted the false notes
which normally he alone perceived. The reporter with the crew
haircut and the young lady from the radio station, under
whose eyes he had grown older and older, and the fat lout of a
press photographer—was this the younger generation that was
waiting for him at the prison gate? A skeptical generation, so
skeptical that they had competed for the Iron Cross to the rim
of the Führer's grave, and were now as innocent as the prosti-
tute who never fails to mention her first seducer. A generation
of clever idealists who were proud never to have been assailed
by temptation, though this was not due to them but rather
to temptation. Temptation is short-winded and always takes ten
to twenty years to get its breath back before making a fresh appearance. Guilty generations those in which it walks abroad;
innocent those in which it rests. They were a hostile generation
that had declared a quarantine between fathers and sons. But
why such strict precautions if these clever idealists considered
themselves so immune to the disease that had infected their
parents?

Why had he not thought of Christopher till now? He had
always felt that work was a form of intoxication and diligence

an escape from misfortune; perhaps he had only been trying to dull the pain that Christopher had caused him. Timing was also a matter of practice. He had obviously called Christopher too soon. What are the Jews and the Gypsies to Christopher? If he hadn't left Christopher's mother, his son could never have given a damn for Jews and Gypsies. He didn't desert her on account of Hermine Moellendorff but because Gertrude had brought him bad luck. Bad luck was contagious. It now seemed clear that he shouldn't have sent Christopher to stay with a fool who listened to the BBC and freed Jews from concentration camps. Who would believe him if he said now that he had recognized the coming of a new era and had wanted to help his son cross into the future? What were the Jews and Gypsies to Christopher? Christopher hadn't forgiven him for the divorce and for Hermine, or for the mockery of his schoolfellows and the spinelessness of his teachers. Parents forgive their children, but children do not forgive their parents. Well, he would practice the virtue of forgetting. After his first new successes, Christopher would see everything differently. Sons, too, see their fathers with the eyes of others. And then one day the son would come to the father of his own volition, and he, the father, would say: "The day on which I was acquitted? I don't remember."

This prospect calmed him. He opened the drawer of the desk, which, like most of the drawers in the house, contained some sleeping tablets. He did not touch them. He wanted to try to sleep without sedatives on this first night after his acquittal.

Christopher stopped in front of a toy shop window that was decorated for Christmas. It was a suburban shop, and the toys looked as though wealthier children had played with them already.

I lost my head, he thought. I said either too much or too little. But the words my father uses, like *justice* and *head up* and KZ, that frivolous abbreviation for *concentration camp*— how else can one react to them? The *catastrophe*. He calls *catastrophe* what was the end of the catastrophe.

A teddy bear and a Monopoly set and a wooden railway engine were standing in the window. Dr. Goebbels' train had a dining car and a sleeping car. His photograph used to stand on my desk: "To my dear Christopher, Dr. Goebbels," and a year after the catastrophe it was still standing there. I must face this and stop lying to myself. After all, I don't go up to the others and stick out my tongue and say, "I don't acquit you, not me!" Of course, they're not my fathers. Everyone else was entitled to misbehave, but not him, he's Christopher Wendelin's father. I should be fair. Why should I be fair? My name is Wendelin.

He turned up the collar of his coat, tried to avoid the puddles on the sidewalk. It had begun to thaw. It was good to worry about the weather.

A butcher's shop. White marble, empty hooks, everything removed, only a pig's head on a clean plate. We are a clean people, we Germans, at least as far as pig's heads are concerned. We extracted the gold teeth cleanly, too; only the piles of corpses were unclean. But then, those were Jews, Jewish corpses. I wept when Uncle Bertram hid the Jews, not out of pity, but because I had to sleep under the same roof with them. But he took me into his trust, and I didn't betray it. I know Baron von Boderode is also a German, only he did something, and that's what matters. Not merely intentions. They say my father tried to join the army when they offered him the material for *Ritual Murder*. The film was supposed to incite not merely Nazis, but Christians as well. The Jews hate you, they kill Christian girls. So you hate the Jews. So you kill them. Richard Wendelin, an artist, a little absentminded, tried to join the army, but he didn't join it. Instead, I got the train set and he made *Ritual Murder*. All the same, he did save me from dying for Führer and fatherland. The hero's death he was always talking about in his films was for other people's sons. Why didn't he want me to die a heroic death? Other fathers did; a nation of heroic fathers and heroic mothers.

He felt he was getting sentimental; one more minute, he too would be weeping Snow White tears. Like father, like son. I walked all the way to Hamburg on foot, and he gave me the scenario of *Faust*, and I have kept it, until today. And yet

I had long ago seen the pictures from the concentration camps, from the KZ, as he would say. "I've been acquitted!" he said. Of course they acquitted you. After all, you have wrapped their conscience neatly in cotton. Moreover, they have their memories. They were just on leave from the front when *Ritual Murder* was showing. They sat in the movies necking with some girl while up on the screen Jew Lefkovics was being executed. Didn't I have to hurt him? Now he is sitting alone in his study; Josef is pouring out champagne for him. Congratulations, Herr Staatsrat, from Rosa too.

He could not explain to himself why he felt all this bitterness. His mother should have forbidden him to go. Didn't she suspect him of loving his father?

His mother was not at home.

When you opened the door of the apartment you found yourself in the big studio from which the two bedrooms and the little kitchen led off.

Christopher had never been so conscious of the difference between the house in the Munich residential quarter of Bogenhausen, and the studio in the artists' quarter of Schwabing. The studio in which the painter worked, dealt with her correspondence, received guests, gave artists' parties, spent the evening reading, played music and occasionally fell asleep, fully clothed, on the divan, was always in disorder. The party must have been particularly good that afternoon, because the tables, chairs and sideboards were littered with used glasses and plates with remnants of food; someone had left an umbrella on the settee, and a crumpled hat hung on the easel as though part of a Surrealist painting.

He saw nothing but contrasts. The marble bust of his father and the half-finished self-portrait of his mother. Christopher had paid little attention to the picture; he had never thought much of his mother's art. Now he was struck by the merciless rage which she had turned against herself. She was not beautiful; in his childhood, when he had compared her with the mothers of his friends in school, he had often felt ashamed of the little woman with the over-large head and the fuzzy, disheveled hair. Yet there was no need for her to portray herself as an ugly gnome with matchstick-thin legs stuck into holes in a palette. The picture, so modern that in the Third Reich it would have been burned as degenerate art, and so representational that modern artists would have thrown it into the dustbin, seemed to Christopher a true symbol of the dillettantism of his mother. At the same time it occurred to him how strange it was that he did not resemble either his father or his mother; for all he knew, he might have been a foundling. He was tall, with the almost hairless body of the Greek Discobolus, he had soft, light blond hair and pale blue eyes that were slightly asymmetrical, a nose that was not too small but almost bridgeless. Oh, how he hated this illusory dream image of the healthy Aryan! How he hated it in his childhood when his father proudly paraded him around, a living Aryan certificate! How much and how often he had wished since then to be a Jewish foundling, with black curls, dark eyes and a hooked nose.

The key scraped in the lock. His mother's hair was covered by a scarf which she did not take off, although it was wet from the dripping snow. She threw her coat across an armchair, looked round the room, and sighing, began to carry glasses and plates into the kitchen. She had taken Frieda home, she said. Frieda was her blind friend whose dog, Wolffi, was an excellent guide, yet not quite so reliable that he could drag her home when she was drunk. "Frieda was stinking drunk again."

The door between the kitchen and the studio was open. Gertrude Wendelin had turned on the tap, and the running water drowned the babble of her voice. Christopher sat down on the sofa among rugs, paint pots, forgotten plates. He buried his head in his hands. Didn't she understand him, or had she merely forgotten him again? When Richard Wendelin had been sent to prison seven years ago, she had fetched her son back like a forgotten object. Richard Wendelin had no way to protest. Now she owned her son and could forget him.

She knows that the trial came to an end today; perhaps she actually heard the verdict on the radio. It's pure chance that the endlessly chattering radio happens to be turned off. She knows that I've been to see him. Anger seized him at such thoughtlessness.

He rose and went into the kitchen. "I've been to see father," he said.

"So they've given him back his purity. Like a clean shirt from the laundry."

"Is that all you have to say?"

"Why did he want to see you?"

"He never got around to that. He only said I was mature enough and could now hold my head high. It sounded like one of his productions of Schiller. He probably wanted to suggest that I should take up my studies again—with his money."

"You could dry these plates," she said. She didn't look up. "You look miserable. Why did you go?"

"Why didn't you stop me?"

"I'm not your nursemaid. And besides, I couldn't have stopped you."

"You think he's irresistible."

"No, but he is your father."

"I just managed to stop him from talking about the 'voice of blood.' "

"But seeing him again has stirred you up."

When he protested, she ignored it.

"Either you believe in the 'voice of blood' and similar rubbish," she said, "or you don't. If you don't, then please stop feeling responsible for your father. It's pure chance that I married him. I might just as well have married my dentist. When I was sixteen I was so in love with him that I had two perfectly healthy teeth extracted. In that case, your name would have been Müller. Incidentally, he joined the SS later, so you wouldn't have been any better off with him, either."

They went back into the studio, where Gertrude Wendelin collected the forgotten plates.

How am I to explain to her that I don't give a damn whether my name is Wendelin or Müller? Everyone looks for some sign of a father complex in me. If I tell her that it wasn't meeting him that stirred me up, but his acquittal, she will say: Poor boy, he is repressing his complex! No one wants to believe that you can be stirred up by a dirty deal. You ought to be used to that, they'll say. In *Ritual Murder,* the Hungarian Jews bake their Passover bread with the blood of an innocent Christian child. Isn't that enough? And in *Michael the Ancestral Farmer* there is the conspiracy between Jews and Gypsies. Isn't that enough? The Theodor Körner film, his last and at the twelfth hour, has the call to young Germans to perish as heroically as Lützow's Rifles—*We'll Die for You.* Isn't that enough?

On the Führer's birthday, at the Vienna Burgtheater he turned the Black Knight Florian into a Nazi hero, the peasants into party comrades and Geyer's trusty followers into the Old Guard. Isn't that enough—do I need a father complex? The films were masterpieces and the plays shattering, and I was delighted. And now they have acquitted him because a few former concentration camp inmates, from among whom he got his extras as he got his celluloid from Berlin, stated that he had been "humane." He was always humane. He could write letters like no one else, with colored pencils. And when he came out of prison he made me a present of *Faust.* Obviously, I have a father complex.

"I must get out of here," he said. "If I'm not to suffocate I must get out of here. Can you lend me the money?"

His mother was standing in front of the self-portrait that looked like a gnome. "Where do you want to go?" she asked.

"I don't know. Out of here!"

"Running away won't change anything."

She sat down beside him and took his hand. "You can't run away," she said.

"Why not?" He thought: Old people can only think in clichés.

"Because it doesn't help," his mother said. "You have talent. Everything you have written shows a great gift, and you know I'm not a doting mother. Here you can be of some use."

"Who for?"

"We weren't all Nazis."

"No, of course not. The Nazis simply raped you all, and unfortunately you came to like it. And anyone who didn't like it kept his mouth shut, because it isn't nice to lose one's virginity that way."

"You should talk to Boderode."

"Uncle Bertram is old and wants peace and quiet."

What's the use? In a minute she'll start talking about new Germany. She likes it because she is allowed to paint as she likes. She can portray herself as a gnome with his feet in a palette and there are actually people who will buy it. They fatten their bellies and call that the new Germany. The champagne business has never been so active, the newspapers say —we have to be proud of something. We all got through by the skin of our teeth, so we have to celebrate. Though beer would do as well, with our highly sophisticated conscience we have to have champagne. Soon my father will be hanging new photographs of new führers in new frames. Today I can hold up my head, and tomorrow he will go further and expect me to be proud of the name Wendelin.

"It's late," said his mother. "Sleep on it. We can talk about it tomorrow."

In February nineteen hundred and fifty-three Christopher packed his suitcase, and with the money his mother had given him, he was ready to leave for Israel.

At first, his plan had seemed utterly hopeless. Germans were forbidden to enter Israel. The country had no consular representation in Germany, and the consulate in Paris had answered with a printed form, cold and polite. Christopher did not permit himself to be discouraged. Indecision was his natural state, and any decision came over him like a fever that changed his nature into its opposite. Baron Boderode had connections with the president of the Zionist World Congress, dating from the time he had aided Jews and Poles. He put Christopher in touch with Dr. Aaron Weinstein, a short, thickset American who looked like an athlete and behaved like a perpetual-motion machine.

The first discussion in Dr. Weinstein's hotel room began at seven in the evening and ended at two in the morning. Even a man in such a position of authority had to obtain the consent of the Israeli Government. He confronted Christopher with surprising conditions. "We are operating on the fringes of legality," he said after midnight. "Even if the Government decided to make an exception, you as Richard Wendelin's son would be stoned in Israel. But the Government is not the people. I believe it thinks differently and looks ahead." If Christopher took a Jewish name to demonstrate that he intended to remain in Israel for good—"Israel is not a zoo where you go to look at Jews"—the Government might one day accept the responsibility for having "smuggled" him into the country. "I use the word intentionally, Herr Wendelin. You need not change your religion, but you must change your identity. Once you enter Israel you become an Israeli, with or without citizenship. Think it over carefully . . ." Six weeks later he saw Dr. Weinstein for the third time and received from him an Israeli visa. In Israel his name would be Abraham Avni.

He packed his case twice and emptied it again. The choice of the few books he was going to take with him worried him. He owned the *Selected Poems* of Heinrich Heine, newly published as an act of restitution, no doubt. His friend Ferdinand had given him the India-paper edition for Christmas. Quickly he put the book back with the others. If he took it out in the kibbutz they would think he was trying to use Heine, his favorite poet, as a key to the hearts of the Jews.

He went over to the window. The late afternoon was glass-blue; the Föhn was blowing the precocious spring into the city. The picture outside his window had become as familiar to him as his own room. Down below lay the anemic gardens in front that separated the two blocks of houses from each other, and opposite stood the four-story square building that had been erected on a bomb site. Brick by brick it had grown under his eyes; the dust had drifted into his room, the noise of the drills had shaken his walls; on the scaffold the workmen had drunk their beer. And then the new neighbors had moved in, with their children and their desk lamps and their radio sets. The girl with the long blond hair had stood half naked by the window. They put up the cheap lace curtains, and now the building seemed to have been there for fifty years. He had not seen the girl again, and the windows resembled each other like bathroom windows. He thought of the blue sky of the Middle East, of orange trees, olive groves and the kibbutz.

Why can't anyone understand that I chose Israel? Only Ferdinand seems to understand. "You want to clean your father's name," my mother said. She can't think logically, but this, at least, prevents her from being calculating. You don't clean a name by discarding it, though my mother does not know that. And anyway, why do people always have to ask me why I'm doing anything? *People, people, people,* no word is as powerful, so stupid. If I stole, I'd be acquitted; they would say I was only venting my frustration. And if I wrote a brilliant play, they would say, "He was just trying to outdo his father." Maybe I should have gone to Paris, instead. Mother with her romantic ideas about Montmartre and the Quartier Latin and all the other tourist attractions. "Paris is nearer." Nearer to what? To the new Germany, with its ever increasing consumption of champagne and its bathroom windows. In Paris they would simply take me for a German, and if I didn't talk too loudly and compare Nôtre Dame with the Gedächtniskirche, they would say, "*Voilà,* the Germans aren't so bad." But I'm not out to become a traveling salesman for the German way of life. I'm not interested in cleaning my father's or Germany's reputation. I want to breathe.

The front garden on the other side of the wire fence came to life. The men were coming home, some of them with empty briefcases under their arms, the sandwiches eaten, others with briefcases filled with work. All of them with briefcases. Leather gloves, briefcases, Volkswagens: the emblems of the German miracle. The fat city editor, the limping teacher, the bearer of the Knight's Cross with the Rommel cap, all were swallowed up by the front door. Behind the milk-white glass doors the elevator moved upward and downward.

Dr. Weinstein forced me to burn my bridges. Many thanks, Herr Doktor! Eighteen Israeli pounds a month, full board, a roof over my head, free postage for two letters a week. I don't think I will be writing many letters. In Paris I would have been asking my mother for money. I shall write a play. Twenty-two years old and I have never earned a penny. "You must change your identity." Many thanks, Herr Doktor! Where else could you leave your identity at the border? Don't worry, I won't claim it again, they can keep it locked up in storage. Abraham Avni! The first name I chose myself, the family name was Dr. Weinstein's idea. "It's a neutral name, people won't ask where it comes from. They seldom ask questions in Israel." In *L'Aiglon,* which my father directed in the same heroic style as he did *Florian Geyer,* there is a line that runs: *"On n'a pas prononcé le nom de votre père."* But maybe Dr. Weinstein was not an honest broker, either. He wouldn't have bothered about me, had my name not been Christopher Wendelin. A tooth for a tooth, the sins of the fathers, the wrathful God—centuries had made the God of the Jews into a God of vengeance. I love the Jews, but I know nothing about them. The hell with it: People hate them without knowing them. "The Jew cheated me." Every day Germans cheat one another, only that is an experience which doesn't count. Experiences are like merchandise in a department store; you take what you need. The Jews haven't sat down at the table with the Germans, like the French, haven't waged a Boer War, like the British, haven't produced a Quisling, like the Norwegians, haven't invented thumbscrews, like the Spanish. Maybe all that will come eventually, if they have a government long enough, but that isn't my business. They're young and I belong with them.

The first lights went on in the windows opposite. Goodbye, Frau Lehmann, goodbye, blond girl, goodbye, you twins with the long plaits.

It struck him that his goodbye to his friends annoyed him, like having to answer a troublesome letter. Should he sleep with Inge once more? Inge was the most comfortable girl he had ever known, with a full bosom and a one-and-a-half-room apartment. She worked as a photographer with a firm that manufactured cameras, making so-called amateur photographs for the advertising leaflets. Children bathing, champion skiers, sunny landscapes. Inge was sunny, and as remote from problems as the mountain ranges in the background of her pictures.

Her emotional demands were as modest as her physical appetite was robust. There was nothing vulgar about her; she was simply comfortable. After only a few sentences she always came to the real point. While they were still at the front door she assured him of her love; a few moments later she accepted the assurance of his love as though it were expected. She will shed a few expected tears.

Christopher watched the architect's wife busying herself at her desk. Strange, how with every woman you remember a certain movement, a certain peculiarity, a certain gesture. A singer, a friend of his mother's, always used to sit up in bed and sing her arias. A female medical student scared him by proving her virginity, then reassured him with her gratitude; astounding what subtleties she was capable of under the pretext of anatomical studies. The young wife of an old orthopedic surgeon had a knack of always having a dream handy which she insisted on instantly translating into reality. If love was more than the occasional desire for another's skin, more than planned intoxication, a party for two, coupled egotism, then in twenty-two years there had been too much emptiness.

The thought of his half-packed suitcase nagged at him, but he could not drag himself away from the sight of the building opposite. It was a doll's house in all its repellent obviousness and regularity. The twins with the plaits were doing their homework; the architect, in shirt sleeves and braces, was reading his evening paper; Frau Lehmann was scrubbing away her loneliness; in one apartment four men were sitting at a card table. Heine wrote the lines: "And as I stood on the St. Gotthard Pass, I heard Germany snoring. It slept below in the gentle care of thirty-six monarchs." The thirty-six monarchies were dead, the last monarch was dead, and the last Führer was also dead. Only Germany was still snoring on.

Perhaps everything that happened happened because the country slept so well. Six million Jews murdered, three and a half million Germans killed—how many lie awake thinking of it now? No dreams, only nightmares. I watched and the others snored, so why say goodbye? Only Ferdinand is different, but then he is almost paralyzed, and sits in a wheelchair by the window. It's no coincidence that my only friend is a cripple. I am afraid of men. To men I am always Christopher Wendelin, to women, simply Christopher. Women never ask my name. Men don't ask that often, either, but when I tried to get into the university I had to give my father's name, and they didn't take me. Women took me. My father was a success, and I was only a success in bed. At least I should have been Don Juan, but all I leave behind is Inge, with a full bosom and a one-and-a-half-room apartment!

Behind most of the windows the curtains were now drawn. Christopher turned around and began sorting out the useless. Even so, he knew he would still be burdened with the useless.

II

My Name Is Abraham Avni

CHRISTOPHER had been in the kibbutz Ani Omer in northern Israel, where the Jordan originates and feebly gropes its way southward, for one year and two months. In summertime you looked down on a yellow carpet of sunflowers and up at the snow-covered peaks of Mount Hermon. A hot wind blew in from the desert over the hills, and forts stood between the fields, only a few miles from Syria's threatening frontier.

He had learned Hebrew, and a good deal more. His hands were calloused from the hard labor on the land, his body was steeled against heat and cold. He drove the tractor, carried crates from the little jam factory, felled trees and could recognize their diseases. He had learned how to build a house, how to make a table and a bench. For a year he had lived in the men's dormitory; for the last few months he had had a room of his own. He sang the Jewish songs and danced the hora. Sometimes he looked after the children, carried buckets from the kitchen, and helped the women with the washing. On the Sabbath, which was scarcely sanctified here, for the work was great and belief in God was small, he sat with the others at the long, cleanly scrubbed table and listened to their stories and discussions. He spoke little, but he learned much. He no longer believed that all Jews had dark hair, dark eyes and a hooked nose. Nor did he any longer believe that they were all wise and sad and kind. He read a great deal; no one with a hunger for books remained hungry here. When newspapers came from Germany—they came rarely and were as old as newspapers can be that grow a week old in a day—they were given to him, but he put them aside until they had become even older. Christopher talked politics with none but the head of the kibbutz, the only one who knew the truth about Abraham Avni. Moshe Dzwonicki had organized the rising in the Warsaw Ghetto and belonged to the radical leftist party Hashomer Hatzair. But like a good soldier, Moshe rarely spoke of his past experiences; he built on the present and trusted in the future.

Christopher received only eighteen pounds a month and rarely went to Haifa, which he could reach in two hours by truck. When he did go, he sat outside at a café and wondered at the growth and vitality of the white city. He became accustomed to the fact that Jews living together were like all other people. The waiters were deaf, the taxi drivers cursed, the old swore at the young, old and young stared after girls, the girls wiggled their bottoms. Like the Israelis, he disliked the American Jews in Israel, falling over themselves with enthusiasm and leaving quickly. When he heard German spoken he turned away. He never went down to the port. Every now and then he bought a recent German paper, which was sold at just one kiosk, read it surreptitiously, looking for his father's name. He wrote long letters to Ferdinand and was angry with himself because he had painted everything in rosy colors. He received long letters in return, swallowed them like a medicine against homesickness. From his mother, who for weeks seemed to forget him and then wrote him three letters in one week, he received hectic letters. Gradually, these became the only ones he read. He began to write a novel and a play, but he was too exhausted to continue working on them. He wrote a few poems and showed them to no one.

He felt esteem for everyone in the kibbutz, tenderness for some, but he had no friend. Without honesty there can be no friendship, and he could not reveal the truth. In the beginning, he was afraid of being discovered and wondered who the others took him for. But people came here from everywhere and nowhere; the younger ones didn't want to hear about the past and the old spoke of it in a hush. Memory was not switched off and on, it was wiped out. They knew he had been baptized, but they did not inquire about his religion. What they wanted to know about was the strength of his hands. "We're a foreign legion and we're at home," Moshe Dzwonicki once said to him, and did not wait for Christopher to ask him how the two things went together.

Nothing here went together. There was a lawyer from Dortmund who had been in a concentration camp and was the only one of his family who survived. There was the former owner of a men's clothing shop in Berlin whose Christian friends had kept him hidden during the Nazi years. For six days of the week the two of them worked together in the kibbutz; they learned how to handle a gun and laughed when they hit the bull's eye. But whenever the conversation came round to Germany, they found nothing to say to each other. The lawyer could not overcome his hatred, the store owner could not overcome his gratitude. There was the head of the kibbutz, who had been the last to escape from the Warsaw Ghetto, a former coppersmith who lived only for what he could bring out of the earth, the harsh soil of Israel. There was a young American whose father had made millions and supported the Zionist movement. The Harvard student worked hard and the leader of the kibbutz praised him, but on the Sabbath they found nothing to talk about because the leader was an Israeli, the student a Holiday Jew. There was an old couple from Poland— the children were allowed to bring their old parents with them, and the kibbutz looked after them; the old couple spoke Yiddish and only prayed in Hebrew. And there was an elderly refugee from Algeria who was teaching his young wife French. Six days a week the Algerian and the young Englishwoman, who had only intended to stay here a few weeks, worked for the kibbutz, but on the Sabbath they retired with their baby into their tiny quarters and spoke to no one.

The work was apportioned and carried out according to the sun. Discipline in the fields was as iron as in barracks, but no one grumbled and few laughed. Everyone did his duty, often working into the night and sometimes on the Sabbath. Anyone who did not do his duty had to go. The deserters were not condemned, they were scarcely despised; they were forgotten. Free time was apportioned; it was respected like work, no more, no less. It seemed to Christopher as though the heart too had its hours. Never had Christopher met such solidarity, not even during the nights of the air raids. Never, he thought, would a Jew have stolen an iron from his neighbor's burning house. But he learned that the Jews were as hard as the harsh soil of Israel. Even when the children were sick the mothers still went out into the fields or into the factory. The sick were watched over not by their relatives, but by those whose job it was, and when a man died they carried him to his grave without complaint and looked after his widow until she could go back to the fields or to the factory. During the first year, men and women slept in separate dormitories; only the elderly couples had their own room. In the warm nights the younger couples met in the fields among wild bushes, and young men lay with young women; but love did not flourish here, and only rarely did the eyes of two lovers meet across the Sabbath table. It seemed to Christopher that duty had laid its heavy hand on the kibbutz Ani Omer; love between man and woman had suffocated under it.

It was that way after a girl lay down with him one night— Esther, the only survivor of a thirteen-member innkeeper's family from Lemberg. They met where the untilled field behind the one-story factory ran down to the Jordan Valley; and later, when Esther had a room, he went to her. She was nineteen, had a full bosom and reminded him of Inge, only she never spoke of love. Perhaps she had never heard of it. He wanted to tell her who he was because he was used to talking frankly to the women he slept with, even if he didn't love them and would never see them again. He wanted to tell her that he had nothing in common with the blond conquerors who had murdered her family. But in the kibbutz people did not ask about the past, not even on nights when the summit of Mount Hermon gleamed like a second sickle.

After a year and four months, Christopher still wondered what would happen if anyone discovered that he was Richard Wendelin's son. Once the daily press reported that there had been questions in Parliament about protests because two Germans had been allowed to enter the country. They talked about

it at supper, and Christopher had the feeling that one or two of
them were looking at him. Another time they were talking
about films, and a German Jew who had only recently immi-
grated mentioned *Ritual Murder*. Everyone became silent and
a woman began to cry. Someone quickly started to talk about
another film and Christopher thought it was on his account,
but perhaps it was only because of the woman who was crying. His fear seemed to him senseless. He was Abraham Avni,
not a German and not a Holiday Jew; they had accepted him.
But why had they accepted him? Moshe Dzwonicki treated him
like anyone else, because the leader of the Warsaw Ghetto
rebels had lost the ability to love one person more than another. Most of them, however, Christopher thought, were
friendlier toward him than toward one another. Were they
trying to prove to him that the God of Israel was not a God
of vengeance? Were they embracing the son of Richard Wendelin, or the blond Christian with the blue eyes? They
looked upon him as a man serving a life sentence among others
serving a life sentence, but he wasn't sure whether he would
be able to fulfill the contract. At such moments he asked himself why he was here. Wasn't the world larger than Israel? The
Wandering Jew had gone forth from Jerusalem and was driven
about on the face of the earth; Abraham Avni could have been
driven about in the world if he had not found peace in Israel.
The harsh soil of Israel was his peace.

In June of the second year a great crisis was announced, as
is the way with great crises, by a small crisis. Parliament had
permitted a few non-Jews to come to Israel. Among them was a
young German, Horst Stettin, and he too came to the kibbutz
called "I Say," Ani Omer. Horst Stettin, not much older than
Christopher, was the son of a Hanoverian engineer and Nazi
party member. He knew why he was in Israel: he wanted to
help rebuild a few Jewish lives. He had taken the Jewish religion, planned to become a Jewish farmer, and had changed
his name to Abraham Salomon—they called him Salomon,
perhaps because two Abrahams were too many for one kibbutz.
Abraham or Salomon, who never wished to set foot on German
soil again, who never received a letter and never wrote any,

refused to speak a word of German. This Paul of the Jews offered Christopher his friendship. Christopher would not accept it, perhaps because he feared it would reveal his identity. But perhaps he resisted only forming his first friendship in the kibbutz, after a year and four months, with a man whose name used to be Horst.

It was a small crisis, the flash of lightning before the storm.

He saw the dark girl at the evening meal, but Martha Kohorn must have arrived in the course of the day, for she was already wearing the high-necked Russian blouse worn by the women in the kibbutz, white with a green band around the neck. She was sitting at the far end of the long table, not far from Moshe Dzwonicki, between the former wine merchant from Algeria and the mother of three Palestinian sons.

He eyed her with a hostility which became all the greater the more the conversation at the other end of the table centered on her. What annoyed him most was her sense of freedom. One is never so alone as in a community which existed before one was there and will exist after one has gone, but although Martha Kohorn was only going to stay in the kibbutz for a few months—Moshe Dzwonicki had welcomed her in a friendly manner but with few words—she seemed to be at home. She had an unusual and unusually high forehead, so that Christopher couldn't help thinking that she was offering her forehead to the world around her, not provocatively, but rather as a mirror: as you look into it, so you will see yourself; I don't want to catch you, but you won't escape me.

Was he being unfair? She is a Holiday Jew. They don't make much fuss here about these pilgrims who empty out their conscience as if it were a crate of oranges. Kohorn. Moshe hadn't mentioned it, but naturally everyone had read in the newspaper that Misha Kohorn, the great pianist, perhaps the the greatest of all, was giving concerts in Israel. She must be his daughter. It's possible, but not certain. He can't be less than sixty and she is probably a little more than twenty-two. The youngest child of the family, a spoiled girl from a good family

—the Kohorns survived the Thousand Year Reich in London
—and now her loving parents have sent her to the kibbutz, as
girls of good family are sent to a finishing school. It will do you
good to eat vegetable soup, white cheese and gray bread for a
change; caviar will taste twice as good afterward. It isn't her
fault that she bears a famous name of which she can be proud,
and I, a no less famous name of which I am ashamed.

Martha Kohorn helped herself to the gray bread and
homemade jam—there was neither vegetable soup nor white
cheese—but she made no attempt, as most newcomers did, to
praise the simple meal. She jokingly asked Moshe Dzwonicki
whether they had enough jam left over for "export" if they ate
such a lot of it themselves.

A glance from the other end of the table, and once again
Christopher was overcome by disquiet. It had nothing to do
with the name Kohorn; he suddenly thought of the Trojan
Horse. This time there were no Greek soldiers inside it, but
rather beautiful Helens. Yet at Ani Omer, unrest was prohibited from entering.

Only a few of the older people remained behind in the dining room after the meal. They read or wrote letters or, now that
they were safe from the disparaging remarks of the youngsters,
indulged in reminiscence. The others had pushed toward the
door, for eight o'clock had struck and a delivery of oranges was
expected early next morning.

The night was warm and the sky full of stars. All the stars
were close to one another, and all of them were far from the
earth, and all seemed to be circling slowly around the earth.
Through the open door light fell upon the dry soil. It had not
rained for a long time and the sand smelled like hot grass.
Usually the young people went off in all directions; tonight
they hung about like the audience after a movie show in a
small town.

Esther approached Christopher, touched his hand. "Shall
we go for a walk?"

"I have to be up at five," he said impatiently.

Then the girl, who had been surrounded by young men,

came up to the two of them, shook hands first with Esther, then with Christopher. "My name is Martha Kohorn," said the girl.

"My name is Abraham Avni," said Christopher.

"Have you been here long?" asked the girl in German, the language she had been speaking at table.

"Sixteen months," said Christopher.

"Martha is staying half a year," said a young man, as though it were something special.

"I know," said Christopher. He felt angry because Esther was still holding his hand.

In his dark room he sat down by the window. The lights had been switched off. Only in the hospital a light was still burning. "My name is Martha Kohorn." "My name is Abraham Avni." There had been a pause between the two sentences. For the first time I wanted to say, My name is Christopher Wendelin. Did I want to challenge her? Are you the son of the director of *Ritual Murder*? she would have said. Yes—what of it? Why did she speak German to me right away? Because I look the very picture of the German murderer? I'm exaggerating. I'm sure she only speaks German and English; they don't learn Hebrew in English boarding schools. I shall avoid her; the kibbutz is large enough. Am I afraid of giving myself away? My name is Abraham Avni and it used to be Christopher Wendelin, like the others used to be called Kohn and Rosenbaum and Torczinski. Only with me it isn't the same. The others have become their new names, but I have split myself. I am like an accordion. One part is fixed, ivory, black and white, stops and keys, but there is also the bellows, completely black, which moves, closes, opens, comes near to the keyboard, moves away from it. For sixteen months I have been drawing near to the fixed point, drawing away from it, coming close to it again. Sometimes Abraham Avni is at one with Christopher Wendelin. Or is it much simpler? The Trojan Horse. Love is forbidden in the kibbutz like electric light after ten. You lie in the grass and a girl comes to you, but even so we are a single great courageous community. Until a dark girl comes from

outside and shakes hands with you, and suddenly you're not
sure what your name is anymore.

He could not avoid her. Moshe Dzwonicki had told him to
instruct Martha Kohorn in farming. Moshe Dzwonicki never
gave orders, but his word was obeyed in the kibbutz as it had
been in the Warsaw Ghetto.

There were not many tractors at Ani Omer, because it was a
poor kibbutz. Wealthy American Jews, who gave the tractors,
gave them to the old kibbutzim where religion was still very
important. In Ani Omer the Hashomer Hatzair was in charge,
and you couldn't be sure it didn't sympathize with the Communists.

Christopher drove a tractor. At the same time he helped with
the harvest. He stood beside Martha, and when she took on
more than she could manage he helped her to raise the fork.
Their hands touched. On the tractor he looked around at the
other working women. Martha had rolled up her sleeves; her
arms were brown and her neck was brown. He hoped the work
would be too hard for her, but it never was.

At times she walked along beside the tractor. "I imagined
that the Jordan would be wider," she said.

"It is wider further south," he said.

"Is there always snow on Mount Hermon?" she asked.

"The whole year round," he said.

She looked up at the hills that ran along the Syrian frontier, so gently, as though nature knew nothing of frontiers. "Is
that an Israeli fort?" she asked.

"That's our frontier fort. The mountain range is already part
of Syria. Never go beyond the bushes. In December they shot
two of our women. We went across and burned down a village."

"Were you there?" she asked.

He blushed. "No, I wasn't there."

Once she followed him from the fields into the kibbutz. He
parked the tractor in the shed. "Why haven't you got a gun?"
she asked.

"Why should I have a gun?"

"On all the other tractors there are submachine guns."

"I don't need a submachine gun."

Moshe didn't give me a gun and I didn't ask for one. Would they have given it to me? Of course they would. Nobody distrusts me and if I have no friends, it's because I've kept to myself. They don't want to know about the past; that unites us. They make plans; that separates us. I haven't thought whether I'm a Socialist or not. I hate politics, since it was politics that ruined us. Am I a German who is afraid of politics, am I a German who mustn't think? I haven't yet written any of those things that I wanted to write. I have only learned to be a Jew. So a Jew is something different from what I am—and that's wrong. There is no one in the kibbutz whom I hate or despise or oppose—and that's wrong. I work like a horse because I want to make good what I have done, but I haven't done anything. I think of what has been done to the Jews, not of what has been done to me—and that's wrong. I wanted to breathe freely, but the free think of the future; I have built myself a prison in freedom—and that's wrong.

He was thinking all this for the first time, but when the suspicion arose in him that he was only thinking it because Martha Kohorn was in the kibbutz, he found a thousand reasons to disprove it.

He suspected something else: that Martha Kohorn was asking about him. Two or three times he found her in conversation with Moshe Dzwonicki, and thought that they stopped talking as he approached.

One evening, as he was walking toward his house, he heard footsteps behind him. He swung round; he had learned to recognize her footsteps.

"Have you anything to read?" she asked calmly.

"The library is full," he answered.

"I've read the German and English books already, and I can't read Hebrew."

"I only read Hebrew," he said.

She laughed. "You write your own books."

"Who told you that?"

"There's nothing to be ashamed of in writing books."

She sat down on the bench outside his house. He hesitated but he sat down beside her.

After a while he said, "You're spying on me. What do you want to know?"

"I'm not spying on you. But I'm curious . . ."

"For example?"

"Why are you here?"

Like a stubborn child he said, "Why are you here?"

"My father is giving concerts in Israel. He thought it would do me good to think about something else. He thinks I'm too serious or not serious enough. I don't know."

"That's just what I imagined."

"You haven't answered my question, though," she said.

"Why do you ask me? Why are the others here?"

"They're Jews."

"Do you want me to produce documentary evidence that I'm a Jew? I'm sorry, but my Jewish grandmother's birth certificate was burned."

It was beginning to grow dark. A hot wind was blowing from the Syrian frontier. When night fell the desert wind fled across the frontier to Israel. Christopher remembered Italy, through which he had wandered after getting his university entrance, and he was surprised that he remembered it for the first time. The fields that sloped down to the Jordan were no different from the fields north of Naples; the hills on the Syrian border resembled the undulating countryside of Tuscany. He had avoided the similarities like the port of Haifa.

"How long do you intend to stay here?" she asked.

"Forever. Why, can't you imagine that?"

"I was nine when we went to London. I grew up with English people. It may have been because of my father's name, but I never suffered any persecution."

"There's nothing for you in Israel, then," he said.

"I admire a great deal in Israel, but not everything. There are Jews who come to Israel as Catholics go to Lourdes."

"What you don't like is the hard life here."

He was surprised when she replied, "That's possible. I'm

not a Socialist, and Israeli Socialism is as alien to me as Russian or Italian Socialism. Are you a Socialist?"

"I don't think about it. We're building a home."

"Were you driven out of yours?"

Irritated, like an accused defending his character in court, he said, "I was born in Berlin. On the tenth of December nineteen hundred and thirty."

"You're four days older than me. A Sagittarius."

"A Sagittarius. And a German. And an Aryan. An Aryan-German Sagittarius. I came to Israel although Israel is closed to Germans. I gave up my German passport. I changed my name. And now you know more about me than anyone else in the kibbutz except Moshe."

"You were fifteen when the nightmare came to an end," she said.

"But I was a Hitler Youth," he said, and he felt as though the truth were creeping round him like a tempter.

"Everyone had to join the Hitler Youth."

"You went to an English school and now you feel yourself to be English. What one was at fifteen is very important. Do you remember who gave you your first doll?"

She laughed. "My first doll wasn't a doll but a cloth rabbit. I've still got it."

"Dr. Goebbels gave me my first train set."

"All right, but you're twenty-three . . ."

"And my whole generation nauseates me. They show off their birth certificates the way people used to show off the proof of their Aryan origins. People were once proud of not being Jews. Now they're proud of not being murderers."

"Have you come here to vindicate the Germans?"

"I am here to avoid Germans."

Over in the hospital a few lights flared up. In another house, where the old couples lived, the lights went on and a few figures could be seen running past the windows.

"Why don't you write about that?" she asked.

"About what?"

"I don't know. The things that bother you so much."

"The Jews bother me. But a Jewess who thinks she is English wouldn't understand that."

"So you think the Jews are a race?"

"No, a people."

Her question had struck him harder than he would have admitted. So he began to talk about the history of the Jews. He spoke of Jacob and his family, of David and the capture of Jerusalem. "Hundreds of years before the Teutons ravaged Europe the 'cowardly Jews' were warriors and conquerors." He spoke of Egyptian corruption and the Jewish religion, of the kings and of the Omri dynasty—"Almost a thousand years before the birth of Christ, Shalmaneser III took that land over there from the Syrians"—of the miracles of the deliverance that occurred as regularly as though they were no miracles. And they weren't miracles, for the Chosen People had to survive. He spoke of the epoch of Jeroboam II and the close connection between rulers and prophets, for at that time there arose Amos and Hosea, Isaiah and Micah. He spoke of oppression and persecution and of Babylon. "Here, in the valley of the Jordan, Zedekiah was taken prisoner by Nebuchadnezzar and his sons were slain before his eyes, and his eyes were put out. It was six hundred years before Christ and two thousand five hundred years before Hitler." He spoke of the Persians and of Ezra and of the Temple in the desert of Sinai, of Greek and Roman rule and of Judas Maccabeus's victorious march on Jerusalem, about Pontius Pilate and Caligula and the revolt of Bar Kochba—"When it was put down only every tenth Jew was left alive, and nineteen hundred years later Israel rose again." He spoke of the Diaspora and of assimilation. "In the fourteenth century they were on the Rhine. I have no idea what my ancestors were doing at that period." He spoke of the persecution of the Jews in the Middle Ages and of Paul IV's ghetto, of Moses Mendelssohn and Heinrich Heine, of Spinoza and Ehrlich, of Wassermann, Einstein, Meyerbeer, Halévy, Freud, of Theodor Herzl and Chaim Weizmann.

The light in the hospital had long since gone out. Although it had grown cool there was sweat on his brow. He rose to the surface from the history of the Jews as though coming up from the stormy depths of the sea, and was surprised that the surface was so calm. He had forgotten that Martha was sitting beside him, and now he thought that she would talk about the overzealous proselyte. This word too came from the history of the Jews and described opportunistic heathens. But she said nothing. For a long time she had been holding his hand, and he had not noticed.

From that day forward, Christopher's life changed. In the morning his first thought was that he would see Martha again; if he hurried he could sit next to her at breakfast. When Dzwonicki wanted to give her a different job, he said she did two people's work and he couldn't manage without her. He found an American book which she hadn't read in the library and took it to her. When Esther approached him he found all sorts of excuses and was glad when she went out into the evening hand in hand with the Harvard student. He too went out into the evening, lay down in the grass and discovered the scent of the bushes. The fields were no longer dry ground from which one wrestled treasure; they were like the fields around Boderode Castle. When he looked up at the sky, it was not merely to see whether it was going to stay fine or rain. He did not fight the unrest that was growing within him; he embraced it. His thoughts were not mathematical formulas; they did not end in a result; they were a path along which he went without asking where it led.

Once on the afternoon of the Sabbath, he summoned up his courage and asked whether she would go out with him to the fort. They had talked about it and he knew the commandant.

It was a hot day at the end of July. The birds were visiting from tree to tree. In the fields work had ceased; the kibbutz goatherd was sitting in the shade of a tree. He was over seventy, his name was Gabriel Pollack, and he had once taught geography in a Viennese school.

The footpath in the middle of the fields, so narrow it looked as if the cultivated land was too mean to leave a wider space free, ended at the fort, just under the mountain ridge. The bunkers, not very different from those built around Berlin when it was besieged by the Russians, only smaller, formed a semicircle, and the round gun turrets rose up out of the earth like large toadstools. Two girls in uniform marched up and down, came to a halt, looked down into the Jordan valley or up at the hills, where Syrian soldiers were sitting with their legs drawn up, guns cradled in their arms like children. When you turned around you saw in the valley the elongated buildings of the kibbutz. The evening sun lay gentle over the harsh soil of Israel.

The commandant of the fort received them in the command bunker, a bare, damp room lit by a single electric bulb. The bulb swung slowly to and fro with the rhythm of a clock pendulum. He was a young captain, not yet thirty, of gigantic stature, with blue eyes and a thick reddish-blue moustache. He had served in the Jewish Brigade under Montgomery of El Alamein, and sun-bleached British medal ribbons were attached to his open-necked shirt, which revealed a thick, dark throat. When Christopher told him that Martha Kohorn was from England he spoke to her in English, Oxford English, as Martha later said. He offered them orange juice, led them through the bunkers, showed them the gun emplacements and the sandbags and the tank traps. They were made of old railway tracks driven vertically into the ground, a track from an earthly terminal into hell. Outside, leaning against a small tank, he gave them a telescope, but since he was a soldier, the fields, the valley, the river and the hills became a maneuver area under his pointing hand. "We have no secrets," he smiled. "The Arabs know what we have and they know that what protects us are not tanks and tank traps." Christopher pretended to understand, but he understood only a few words, because he had never learned any foreign language but French.

While Martha and the captain were talking, as though they had always known each other, and he walked now beside one, now beside the other, he was once more overcome by misery.

In the kibbutz he was jealous of all the young men to whom Martha spoke, but that was not the feeling he had with the young captain. He had once spoken French with the captain, and they would now have spoken French for his benefit, too. They were not shutting him out. He had created the island around himself because they're Jews, he thought, and I'm not a Jew, even if I can recite the list of kings of the Omri dynasty by heart. Do the two of them belong to the same race, the same people? Or don't they, rather, belong to a people that is far bigger than the Jewish people, the truthful people of the earth. I have learned Jewish history, but I have forgotten truth. I feel like a spy because I abuse the trust of the others, because I don't tell them who I am and that I am not Abraham Avni but Christopher Wendelin, son of Richard Wendelin, who made the film *Ritual Murder.* How can they forgive me for my father when I conceal from them who my father is? They trust Abraham Avni, who wouldn't have existed without Christopher Wendelin, and I even cheat them of the freedom to forget Christopher Wendelin. Thus he walked along, smiling when they smiled, serious when they were serious. When the captain stretched out his hand and said "Shalom," he pretended not to have seen the hand.

It was growing dark. Christopher took the girl's arm. He knew that now she would return his kiss, but he had no longing for her mouth. He felt a painful longing to talk to her.

When they were down in the valley again, Martha said, "You're very quiet. Is anything wrong?"

He did not reply. Only later did he say, "You wanted to know who I am. Before I came to Israel my name was Christopher Wendelin."

Her arm rested in his arm. "Why is that a secret?" she asked.

"Don't you know who my father is?"

"Yes," she said. "I can imagine."

"Shall I let go of your arm?"

She stopped and let go of his arm. "You're crazy," she said. "I think you're really crazy, Christopher."

And she ran her hand slowly over his hair.

*   *   *

In Italy the summer was hot and rainy. Richard Wendelin suffered from the heat and rain, suffered from the weight of his heart. Most of all he suffered from his work.

The subject of his first film since the war was not of his own choice. During his seven years of silence, he had developed the idea of making a film on the twentieth of July plot, on the officers who had plotted to kill their Führer. But, bit by bit, the theme had slipped through his fingers. First the Lohmeyers, Herr and Frau—"the production mates," the papers called them—had objected to the scenario. People abroad would say the Germans were trying to gain by glorifying a revolt which they, the Germans themselves, had drowned in blood. Inside Germany, on the other hand, it would scarcely be possible to gain sympathy for men who had stabbed the fighting troops in the back. Finally the Lohmeyers came out into the open. If the name of Wendelin was to be restored to its old splendor, one had to proceed cautiously and not start off with such a thorny subject. When Richard Wendelin refused to understand, he was accused of "lacking instinct," he who owed all his successes to his unerring instinct for what flattered the public without rising above its horizons—or did the Lohmeyers mean by lack of instinct lack of taste? They had made their fortune in potatoes and had kept their noses clean solely because potato merchants had not been asked for a confession of political faith. Did they think you had to be in the Resistance in order to make a film about it? The next subject Richard Wendelin had suggested to them was the story of the Persian monarch Shah Abbas I, 1586–1628, a great conqueror, and Maecenas. *Isfahan*—an evocative title, an exotic spectacle, sex in historical costumes, a great male role, and everything perfectly calculated to distract a harassed public from its memories. Richard Wendelin had to listen to all sorts of excuses. Frau Lohmeyer even went so far as to say, "Persia—most people don't even know where it is!" But this time he saw through it. The producers were fighting shy of the high investment—after all, you could never tell how the Government, how a virginally democratic press, would take Richard Wendelin's first postwar film. The experiment might be worth a few hundred thousand marks, but it was not wise to invest millions in potato money in the name Wendelin. Richard Wendelin gritted his teeth, but the Lohmeyers knew that no other producer would trust him with a film. So they were left with the story of the miracle worker of Paestum, the true story of a young Italian girl whose miraculous cures, or what were regarded as such, had transformed a drowsy little village into a witches' cauldron of envy, ambition, alcohol, sex and greed. Not a bad subject; it might even provide for some artistic work. It was thoroughly acceptable to the Church, and if the Lohmeyers were not too stingy, one might make use of Paestum's spectacular Greek ruins as a background. Richard Wendelin planned to set the market scenes by the sea, among the shattered columns of the temple of Poseidon. Nevertheless, it would still be a "minor film," without stars, insignificant compared with *L'Aiglon, We'll Die for You* and *Ritual Murder.*

Insignificant—but how difficult it would be he had not foreseen. His former cameraman, having belonged to the SS, had sought refuge in Argentina; two other cameramen had declined with regrets. To save money, few technicians had been brought from Germany. Richard Wendelin had to make do with Italian lighting technicians, makeup artists, assistants, who were quite unwilling to adapt themselves to the German tempo. Half the actors were Italians with whom he had difficulty in communicating, the other half unknown Germans who assumed an irreproachable political record was a substitute for talent; these too he had to treat with kid gloves, because a difference of artistic opinion would naturally be exploited against him.

It had been raining for two days. The blue sky of Italy turned out to be a picture-postcard myth for tourists. As though the sky were the roof of a theater with a thousand curtains, one curtain after the other; the endless sand beach of Paestum turned into a brown sea and fused with the brown sea; the hurriedly erected awnings were soaked through; the rain poured down viciously on the wooden stalls that stood between the temple of Poseidon and the temple of Ceres.

The heat had not diminished, it had merely become damp

and soggy. Marina Bertolini lay naked on the bed and complained of fever.

Richard Wendelin had been gazing at the desolate beach. Now he turned away from the window. Although Marina complained of having pneumonia, there was a tray of empty plates by her bed. She eats too much, he thought; she eats as though she were already a world-famous star. The full bosom was astonishingly firm, but the hips would have to be reduced by the use of lighting; this Neapolitan child of the slums had devoured too much macaroni. What a beautiful, wild face, what expressive eyes! From where did such a stupid woman get so much expression? He had no wish to go to bed with her now. She was too naked and he was put off by the way the hair in the triangle of Venus reached to the middle of the flat belly, almost to the navel. Only southern proletarian children have such an opulent growth of hair. He had made Marina Bertolini his mistress because he had not slept with a woman for a long time, and he feared that worry and failure might have robbed him of his virility. He slept with her because nights of love were necessary to the days' work, created the right contact between director and actress; because he was superstitious and in his heyday had always slept with the leading lady. Work was a temptation, career was a temptation. He should have withdrawn, proudly and bitterly. He still had his house, his pictures, his books. If you fear to be forgotten, you humiliate yourself; if you need applause, you are already humiliated. He had wanted to spend his time reading Diderot in the original. Instead, he was making a film. What would Hermine Moellendorff say if she saw him now, in this cheap hotel, which the Americans had left a shambles after their landing, surrounded by incompetents, beside the bed of a naked girl with an obscene growth of hair? He ought to have answered Hermine's desperate letter, but the letter had made unreasonable demands. He was having trouble enough steering his own ship into port. He couldn't take Moellendorff in tow as well.

"Cover yourself up," he said in his broken Italian. "You'll catch cold."

He went into the next room and sat down at the desk, a

ludicrous piece of furniture with one leg too short. There lay the letter to Christopher that he had started ten days ago and up to now had not finished. Should he read it through? It was easier to write lies than to read them. "I think you would like the film I am making here after the well-known novel by Enrico Capodaglio. I have managed to avoid Capodaglio's vulgarity. Not a word about politics, but the drama of temptation is always a political drama; people will understand, I hope, why I set out to castigate the corruption that unfailingly follows in the wake of mass hysteria." Why these lies, he asked himself, why the lie about the great endeavor, about his own desire to work with amaturs—"Neo-realism, certainly, but not in the cheap manner of the young Italians"—of the great expectation felt "back home" about his fresh start?

He had discovered Christopher's address through Gertrude, indirectly, although nothing gave her greater pleasure than telling him Abraham Avni's address in the kibbutz. "My dear Christopher," he had written, but he would have to put the name Abraham Avni on the envelope. It was because of this truth, not because of the lies, that he found it so hard to end the letter. He could not write "Mr. Abraham Avni" on the envelope and not speak about where his son was living or the name he had taken.

His son's decision had greatly upset him. For the first time he had been overcome again by the famous rage which had once made film studios tremble, but he had long since mastered it. Now he, too, had something to forgive, which the other had done. Perhaps he should latch on to mass hysteria as the explanation of Christopher's behavior. He himself had been the victim of mass hysteria, and now his son in his turn was a victim of this orgy of German masochism. But he would not accuse him of that. Christopher's flight to Israel was not yet known to the public. "I respect my son's decision," he would tell the reporters. "I wish him well. I wish I were young enough to do what my son has done, to some extent, on my behalf."

His eyes fell on the neatly sharpened colored pencils. He had once written to the boy in seven colors and illustrated his letter with all sorts of funny animals—a pity it was no longer that easy! If he succeeded in winning over his son, this would mean a good deal for his own future. Who knew how many friends Christopher had made among the Jews and other irreconcilables already, how many he would make in the future? Who better than his son to build a bridge between past and present? But it would be too late for a reconciliation, once the public had proclaimed Christopher. He must end the letter now.

"Come and give me a kiss," he heard Marina call out from the next room. "I'm hungry for kisses!"

He was about to snub her roughly when the impudent waiter, who never knocked, came in and said there were visitors to see him.

The Hotel Nettuno had no lobby. Richard Wendelin had to receive the Lohmeyers in the dining room. The rain had herded holidaymakers and film people into the room. They filled all the tables, talked loudly, shouted weather reports across the room, ran out, forgot to shut the door. Richard Wendelin had to squeeze his way with the Lohmeyers past tables at which assistant directors, technicians and bit players had spread themselves out, most of them in raincoats. "Is it going to rain tomorrow?" an old Italian woman called out to him, as though he were Poseidon, whose temple ruins stood outside the window.

They found a table in the center of the room. Herr and Frau Lohmeyer drew together. Richard Wendelin was used to the woman speaking, calculating, deciding. The man—gaunt, cantankerous, a bookkeeper who won quiz programs—seemed to be there only to accompany his wife. Richard Wendelin observed to his astonishment that this time Herr Lohmeyer conducted the conversation.

"Everything's topsy-turvy. Fine weather in Munich, rain here."

"It's a pity Signorina Bertolini is ill."

"It's lucky we didn't send any fresh tents."

The blond woman, in the loden costume with the Tyrolese hat, played the part of a silent Lorelei. She could not deceive Richard Wendelin. His sure instinct told him that Herr Lohmeyer, unused to carrying out such a mission, was stalking him.

Should he ask the two of them why they had made the long journey? Surely not to talk about the weather.

His first assistant director came to the table. "I've just been talking to the priest, Herr Wendelin. If the bad weather continues, we can film in the church tomorrow."

"Excellent," he said, rose slightly from his chair and beckoned to the chief electrician, who was sitting with his wife and three children at a distant table. "Guiseppe," he said, "you must try to get the church lit today. Have a curtain put over the rear windows. We'll shoot the first take from the organ stool." Superfluous instructions, but he clung to them. He was a busy man; the potato merchant and his Lorelei must understand that. From all sides people were looking at the commanding general's table, and the producers resembled more and more the other wet little bourgeoisie in their summer disguises. The rain was drumming on the windowpanes; it was coming down more heavily and seemed to be spending itself in a final effort.

Now Herr Lohmeyer could have started talking about the weather again, but an imperious look from his wife forced him to pick up the hot coal. He began speaking about the political situation in Germany, criticizing the cowardice of the distributors and movie house owners. "You sign contracts, but do you think these people stick to them? It's enough for a movie owner in Essen to get cold feet . . ." As he spoke he looked for help to the silent Lorelei, but she only nodded sadly, as though hearing all this for the first time. Heine: "I don't know what it means . . . I think in the end the waves will swallow up boatmen and boat."

Herr Lohmeyer was struggling with the waves. "It's my fault," he said. Richard Wendelin could positively hear the bedroom discussion: *Do be a man, Albert!* "My wife warned me I would be in trouble. But I have found a solution which I hope will be fair to all concerned."

There it was. Richard Wendelin was being asked to withdraw his name from the film—"without the slightest financial loss, of course." The film would run without a director's name— "a modern idea, it might start a school"—unless Herr Wendelin was prepared to let the young assistant director sign in his

place. Frau Lohmeyer finally intervened. "We must bow to circumstances, my dear Herr Wendelin, we must play the others'
game and not try to be fairer than they are. In a word, I am
thinking of this solution just for the moment, up to the premiere—we're planning a tremendous premiere—and then, if
it's a smash hit, as it will be, we shall appear before the press
and say, 'The film you have greeted with such enthusiasm is the
first postwar film by Richard Wendelin.' "

He looked around. He saw the tables at which the nonentities
were sitting who didn't dare to push aside the china and cutlery.
He wondered what would happen if he now got up and swept
the china and cutlery from the tables; so much beautiful, broken
china, so much tinkling cutlery, so many gaping faces. He did
the opposite. He straightened up, immediately felt taller,
smiled for the benefit of the spectators, put his fists on the table
and uttered a single word: "No!"

"But my dear Herr Wendelin!" exclaimed Frau Lohmeyer,
while Herr Lohmeyer began to polish his thick horn-rimmed
spectacles, as though the quiz program were over for him.

"No!" repeated Richard Wendelin. "Another word and I
shall stop shooting the film right now. This may be a matter of
indifference to the movie house owner in Essen, but it isn't to
me and I shall soak you for damages." He decided to talk the
language of potato merchants. "If you're counting on the corruption of the German courts you're making a mistake. Those
times are over. Contracts are contracts, there's equality before
the law now, and my acquittal by three courts should have
proved to you that there are judges in Germany again." The expression on their faces told him that they had taken a calculated risk but had left a way open for themselves to retreat. And
now that he had played the democratic card he played a second
—let us not forget the masses who had greeted *Ritual Murder*
with such enthusiasm, and those masses were not dead. "You
didn't put me under contract because of my lovely blue eyes,
but because you know that for the broad public my name is
associated with the unforgotten films. All I need do is appeal to
this public and you'll see whether you can entice so much as a
dog into the cinema with all your nonsense." That should have

been enough, but he had a third card in his hand and he had no wish to hold any trump. "Don't the distributors think I have any sympathizers? Perhaps not today. But just let me announce that the road to repentance that is being kept open for millions of others is being closed to me, and that it's not the victors who are preventing me from my comeback but Germans —film distributors and cinema owners, or whatever they're called . . ."

That's it, he thought. They are cowards and only worried about finding the way back to a civilized goodbye and the next installment after this unfortunate chapter. Now was the time to behave with magnanimity. He looked out of the window, and remarked that the storm over the sea was clearing. A victor helping his wounded opponent to his feet, he assured the producers that there was no need to send tents from Germany. He had already ordered them from Rome.

He provided the defeated army with an escort. He stopped at an extra's table, slapped the astonished man on the back and said: "Come along tomorrow. I've got a part for you." As he passed the technicians' table he said: "What are you doing here? Mordasini is already in the church." In the doorway a fat, soaking wet woman ran into his arms, and he said, "The rain suits you, my child." Everyone not himself was an audience.

He opened up the red peasant umbrella standing by the entrance and conducted Frau Lohmeyer to the waiting car. He kissed the hand of the lady in loden with the *grandezza* of a marquis bidding farewell to a visitor to his castle, but he merely extended the tips of his fingers to the quiz wizard.

Upstairs in her room, Marina Bertolini had meanwhile dressed.

"Supper!" she cried. "I feel perfectly well again."

"Go by yourself," he said. "I've got to finish a letter."

One day after their visit to the fort, Martha went to spend an evening with her parents. When she came back she told Christopher that she had talked to her father about him and that Misha Kohorn would like to meet him. She said it with the same ease he had envied her on the first evening and which he

came to admire. She hadn't asked him whether she might talk
to her parents about Christopher Wendelin. He was ready to
flare up, but then accepted it, realizing that Martha could do no
wrong.

A few days later, Moshe Dzwonicki sent him into Haifa to do
some shopping for the kibbutz. Martha was given permission to
visit her parents the same evening. They arranged to meet at
the hotel.

Before going to meet her, he sat on the terrace of a café in
Herzl Street, wondering what Martha had told them about
him. Did she say she feels more for me than for the others in
the kibbutz? Is Misha Kohorn interested in the director of
Ritual Murder or in the son who has come to Israel to expiate
for his father's crimes against the Jews. Am I here to demonstrate that although my hair is blond I'm not a beast? Or did
Martha merely tell them about a curious young German, like
an object to be exhibited, a freak show, a good German?

Suddenly he felt a hand on his shoulder. "Bull!" he said.
That was what they used to call Karl Melchior at the Munich
High School. "What are you doing here?"

"You can ask that again." Karl Melchior laughed. "Believe
it or not, I'm the first German journalist in Israel. I thought up
a terrific scheme. I'm accompanying a senator from Hamburg
who is planting some kind of peace tree here." In a few headlines he told the story of his career. After graduation he worked
on the newspaper of the American occupying power, temporarily
in the sports section, then took a dive into politics, was now
chief reporter on a daily paper in Frankfurt. "I imagined I was
the only German on this hot soil, apart from our tree growers,
of course. What are you doing here?"

"I'm working on a kibbutz," said Christopher.

Another mighty slap on the back. "You've got to have luck,
says my boss. You might as well chuck a reporter who doesn't
have luck straight off. Richard Wendelin's son in a kibbutz—
man, that's news."

"That's news you're going to keep to yourself," said Christopher.

Karl Melchior, looking like a bulldog, let his jaws hang the way bulldogs do. "Even at school you were a bit odd, Christopher, but what an idea! How long have you been here?"

"A year and a half."

"For God's sake, man, how can you stand it? If I had to stay another three days I'd go off my nut."

The headwaiter strolled past them and, with his hands behind his back, remained standing by the table of two chess players.

Karl Melchior lowered his voice. "They look at you here as if you were a leper."

"Does that surprise you?"

"I haven't done anything to the Jews. On the contrary . . ."

You needn't produce your birth certificate, thought Christopher. "You're a German," he said. "Who here knows whether your father didn't gas Jews?"

"My old man worked on the railways."

"I'm not talking about your father. It would look silly coming from me."

"Is that why you're in Israel?"

"It doesn't matter why I'm in Israel. You won't write about it."

"Christopher, you can't ask that of me! I've been trying for a week to find something interesting."

"Israel is interesting enough."

"To Germany you're more interesting than the whole of Israel."

"Let's change the subject."

Like most ex-schoolmates they had nothing to talk to each other about, so they talked about school. "Have you heard anything of Zieselsberger?" Zieselsberger had been their Latin teacher who had been in the habit of inviting the boys to evenings of chamber music. He had seduced minors and received nine months with probation. No, Christopher hadn't heard anything of Zieselsberger. What about Jahoda, whom they used to call "Dustbin"? No, nothing about Jahoda, either.

There they sat in Haifa outside the café in Herzl Street, behind them Mount Carmel, the white houses, the dark cypresses. Green buses and creaking taxis drove down Theodor Herzl Street; to their right two Israeli officers, to their left an American couple with a young man, probably their son, probably in a kibbutz; an Arab trader went from table to table offering carpets . . . and they talked about teachers, schoolfellows, school pranks. "Do you remember Huber, who used to smell so awful? He fell under a tram." They talked about girls and school reports and "Dustbin," and all the time Karl Melchior seemed to be thinking only about his article, while Christopher Wendelin was thinking only of how to prevent the article from being written.

"When are you going home?" Karl Melchior asked out of the blue.

"I'm not."

"Christopher, you're not news anymore. You're not normal. You don't know what's going on at home."

"I sometimes read the paper. They've knocked down tombstones in the Jewish Cemetery in Cologne again."

"A few hoodlums!"

"In other countries hoodlums draw sexual pictures on bathroom walls."

"They'll be locked up. Take our editorial staff. All young men. I swear, there isn't one among them who isn't anti-Nazi."

"But you can't stand Israel."

"Please stop trying to make a Nazi out of me. I came here without prejudices. I have nothing against the Jews. The Jews have something against me."

"We were in the Hitler Youth together, Bull."

"What of it?"

"Do you think the Jews don't know that we prayed for victory?"

"Should we have prayed for defeat? And besides, we used to pray for the Bavarian football team, too."

"The Jews are funny that way," said Christopher. "They don't think of the Nazi Party as a football team."

What the hell—why should I try to explain to Bull? I left Germany so that I would not have to explain to Bull. The bad Nazis were at home and gassed Jews; the good Germans were at the front and fought the war. And we were the best Germans of all, we only prayed. Surely a Jew can understand that! The

Jews are famous for their intelligence. They must know: this
one was infected by his father, that one wasn't; this one was already sixteen and defended Führer and fatherland with a *panzer-
faust*, that one was only fourteen and besides, he happened to
have the flu. Can't the clever Jews distinguish one from the
other?

"So you feel thoroughly at home in the kibbutz?" asked
Karl Melchior.

"Are you interviewing me?"

"I suppose I'm allowed to ask. What's the name of your kibbutz?"

"You take me for more stupid than I am, Bull."

Karl Melchior shrugged his shoulders. He changed the subject, or rather returned to the starting point. Christopher had
lost contact with his homeland. Sure, there was nothing to be
done about the old people, but they had no say in things, fortunately, they were slowly dying off. "Not that I mean we only
think of the past." Most of the young people were still sceptical.
"No wonder, after the mess the old ones have left us. A few
years and you won't recognize Germany. We've had enough.
If the Yanks want to stick us in uniform again they'll have something coming to them." Youth nowadays really had a chance
to do something, he went on. "Look at me—I can earn what I
like. If I don't like it in Frankfurt I can go to Munich or Hamburg. They need people now with a clean record. You have to
take the future in your own hands."

Christopher looked at his watch. It was six; offices and shops
were closing their doors.

"Terrific girls," said Karl Melchior. "Terrific girls. I would
never have believed it."

Terrific girls, on that point they could agree. On second
thought, no, they couldn't agree on that, either because to
Bull Melchior from Frankfurt it came as such a surprise.
Christopher gazed after the passersby. They're on their way
home, to their wives whom they love or with whom they quarrel,
honest men, cranks, an upright craftsman, an old Israeli, a young
immigrant, a virgin, a swinging chick. There isn't one among

them who has murdered an innocent child. Shall I tell Bull that is why I'm in Israel?

Then Karl Melchior said, "You were always the best at German essays. Don't you write anymore?"

"Now and again."

"You've no idea what possibilities there are now. We're hunting for good contributors everywhere. We even advertise for them. You could send us something every now and then. It can be as pro-Israeli as you like." He gave Christopher his card. "I'd like to make a note of your address."

Christopher rose, smiled, shook hands with Karl Melchior. "You may not believe it," he said, "but we might meet again sometime. If you write so much as one line about me, I shall break every bone in your body. Even at school I was stronger than you, Bull."

"I'm glad to see you, Herr Wendelin. My daughter has told me a lot about you."

Misha Kohorn was a small man, much smaller than Christopher had imagined him. Although he must have been about sixty, he reminded Christopher of the young shepherds on Meissen porcelain. He was almost diminutive. His movements, not unmasculine, nevertheless possessed a musical grace, and the snow-white hair encircling his high forehead—Martha had inherited her forehead from her father—resembled a powdered wig. He had a rosy face and bright, impudent eyes. When he spoke he seemed like a young man.

Christopher was greeted by Mrs. Kohorn, a good fifteen years younger than her husband, even more cordially than he had been by Misha Kohorn himself. This, however, may simply have been due to her temperament, which Martha had described so well. She was possessed of a dynamic busyness which Misha Kohorn watched with amusement, like a ceaseless circus act.

Christopher had never met a more stimulating conversationalist than Misha Kohorn. He gave an account of his concerts in Israel—"a triumph," commented Alice Kohorn—emptying out a cornucopia of anecdotes to go with it. "The more famous you become the more schoolmates you have. I was four when my parents left Russia and came to Berlin, and that is where I grew up. Israel is full of people who went to school with me. I don't argue with them, although I practically never went to school at all. At seven I was a prodigy. It's an absolute wonder that I don't make too many spelling mistakes. Incidentally, my German has become a bit rusty—you must forgive me."

Involuntarily, Christopher compared the maestro with his father. They had long since sat down at table and Misha Kohorn was still talking about Misha Kohorn. His association to Misha Kohorn was Misha Kohorn, and although he had the gift of self-mockery, his anecdotes always ended with a humorous victory for Misha Kohorn. The pianist's aversion to other artists was also familiar to Christopher—even the dead Paderewski, whose name Christopher had incautiously thrown into the conversation, he tore to shreds. "He was a genius," Kohorn said deprecatingly, "an unparalleled genius, because he hadn't the slightest talent for the piano and achieved his world fame solely by hard work. Can you imagine what it means to practice for ten hours a day and then have to give a concert with bleeding fingers?" The two fathers had their similarities—and yet, how dissimilar! Misha Kohorn radiated the gaiety of a perfect life, whereas even at the height of his career, Richard Wendelin had been trying to prove something. Misha Kohorn conveyed the impression that he was illustrating with mild caricatures something long since proved. Richard Wendelin's eyes seemed always to be directed toward a mirror. True, Misha Kohorn hardly let anyone else get a word in until halfway through the endless meal—it was sumptuous and the little man, to the accompaniment of his own commentary, devoured incredible quantities of food, all the while gulping down champagne as though it were pure water—but his eyes watched over his table companions with bright attentiveness, carrying on a continual dialogue even while he alone was speaking.

The further the evening advanced the more complex Christopher's feelings became. Martha's mother heaped one kindness after another on him. The zealous woman with the alert nose that swung up into the air like a miniature seesaw not only cared for his physical well-being but also took an astonishingly personal interest in him. "I hear you are working on a play, Herr Wendelin"— "Martha says you speak fluent Hebrew" — "If it hadn't been for you, Martha says, she would never have been able to live up to the demands of the kibbutz."

Martha spoke little, but her eyes rested on him and she never missed an opportunity of praising him. "Christopher has a bad conscience when he spends an evening outside the kibbutz"— "Christopher can tell you the shortest route"— "Christopher has heard of Beethoven's Concerto in G Major before, Papa. You don't need to explain to him." Christopher's distrust had vanished long ago; he felt to a frightening degree at home. But they didn't seem to understand his presence in Israel any more than Bull Melchior had. The question bothered them, yet they didn't dare put it to him.

Then, at last, Misha Kohorn said, "And how do you like it in Israel, Herr Wendelin?" The pianist had risen, had uncorked a bottle of champagne with his skillful, short hands, strikingly muscular for such a frail figure, and had asked the question, seemingly in a casual tone, as he stood with his back to the others, but the perfectly natural, long overdue question caused Christopher embarrassment.

"I came to Israel with great expectations," he said, "and I have not been disappointed." Anyone who speaks of Israel, and everyone in Israel speaks of Israel, speaks in clichés, but then, the purpose of clichés is to bridge awkward situations. "I'm happy in Israel," he said.

And as though to defend him, Martha immediately added, "To Christopher, Israel is identical with the kibbutz."

To Christopher's relief, Misha Kohorn did not inquire further into his reply, but spoke of himself again. He too felt happy in Israel, although he had never been a Zionist and knew the dark side of the founding of the State. There were still no more than twelve percent of all the world's Jews in Israel and yet people spoke about the "Jewish people," when really they should be speaking of the Israeli nation—a welcome pretext for the anti-Semites of the world to regard the Jews living in their midst as members of an alien people. "They didn't get very far with the concept of race, my dear Herr Wendelin. How extremely convenient now to be able to replace it with that of a people, to the applause of the Israelis and the silent acceptance of the other Jews."

"Israel has other worries besides anti-Semites," Christopher objected. Martha was looking at him encouragingly, and it seemed to him that she was pleased by his ease. No Jew could have spoken less self-consciously.

"The word 'anti-Semite' is out of date," said Misha Kohorn, "even if what it means is not. As far as the Arabs are concerned, for instance, we ought to talk about 'anti-Israelism'; with most Germans it is a matter of 'anti-assimilation.' If that were not so, there wouldn't be so many German anti-Semites who are basically well disposed toward Israel. The more natural it becomes to speak of the 'Jewish people,' the more acceptable it will be to regard eighty-eight percent of Jews as foreigners, and then the Germans will be able to say that they hate the Jews 'only' as they hate the Italians, to whom they have no objections either, so long as they stay in Italy. Hate will have found a cushion on which to rest. Incidentally, anti-assimilationism also makes it easier to be anti-Semitic where there are no Jews. Anti-Semitism has been unmasked as a product of hatred, whereas anti-assimilation as a theory is still respectable."

"But the Jewish people is a reality," said Christopher. "The many thousands of years of Jewish history . . ."

"About which Christopher knows more than any of us," Martha interrupted.

"No one denies it," said Misha Kohorn. "I merely ask myself why nowadays there is so much talk about the history of the Jews as a people and so little about their history in the Diaspora. Before Hitler, most Jews were so completely a part of the countries in which they lived that they felt the word 'assimilation' to be insulting, and after the collapse of Hitler and his absurd theories the natural process of assimilation would have continued, for it is perfectly natural that, thanks to the Diaspora, there should be more than one single Jewish history. But then the State of Israel was founded. Out of stubbornness, hurt feelings, disappointment, German, British, American Jews claim to belong to the Jewish 'people,' although they feel perfectly at home in Paris, London or New York."

"Can you be at home where you are not welcome?" said Christopher, pleased by his own courage.

Misha Kohorn's cheeks had reddened. "An excellent question." Christopher had the feeling that the pianist cast Martha an approving glance. "A feeling of belonging has nothing to do with popularity. If it had, the Dutch Jews would be Dutch, and the German Jews would not be Germans, which is obviously nonsense." He admired the Israelis, he continued. Herr Wendelin must not misunderstand him. "The kibbutz experiment appeals to me, particularly because it gives the Socialist a chance to live as a Socialist within capitalism, but my son did not die either for Israel or for some 'Jewish cause.' An individual experience, you will say, but what is conviction but the result of individual experiences?"

While Misha Kohorn was speaking—they had gotten up from the table and sat down in a corner of the lounge, close to the open window—Christopher wondered whether, without suspecting it, he had ventured onto thin ice. If what the pianist said was only true to some extent, if even a minority of the Jews felt like Misha Kohorn, he would have come for the wrong reasons to the wrong country. Whether he had wanted to clear his name, as his mother asserted, or whether he merely couldn't look the Germans in the eye, in either case he was concerned with the Jewish people, whose existence was questioned by a Jew, Misha Kohorn. Or was the ice even thinner? He remembered that Karl Melchior had come to Haifa with a "tree-planting group." Eight years after Auschwitz the Germans were planting a peace tree in Israel. Suspicious, highly suspicious! Was he, Christopher Wendelin, so German that he had anticipated the German plan of making restitution for the crimes committed against the Jews, or rather, against Jewish Poles, Hungarians, Czechs, and Germans to a state that had not existed at the time of the gas chambers? Better the peace tree than the gas chambers, but at the same time, a fatal confusion had arisen, convenient to the Germans, and who knows, acceptable to the Israelis—but not to him, Christopher Wendelin, who was not yet an Israeli and was no longer a German. Might he not be obeying a deeply rooted anti-Semitic instinct, which made him choose Israel because, as Misha Kohorn had said, it was extremely convenient to confuse the living Israel with the dead Jews?

These thoughts entered his consciousness only in a vague and confused manner, because at the same time he was pre-occupied by a question which as yet he dared not ask, when Alice Kohorn intervened and commented, as was her way, on what her husband had said. "You might misunderstand Misha," she said. "His temperament often runs away with him—he wouldn't be an artist if it didn't. He managed to make himself very unpopular during the state reception in Tel Aviv . . ."

"You needn't worry about Christopher," interrupted Martha. "He isn't a Holiday Jew. He knows why he is here."

Christopher's malaise grew. They will go on talking about me, and in a minute my father's name will crop up. Oh, no, of course it won't. Even here they are displaying unwonted compassion. Astonishing views for the son of Richard Wendelin, they will say after I've gone. Why don't they say it right away?

"May I ask you something, Herr Kohorn?" Christopher said. "Go ahead."

"If those are your views, why do you refuse to give concerts in Germany?"

"The time is not yet ripe," said Alice Kohorn.

Misha Kohorn shook his head. "It's not as simple as that, Alice, and you know it. I can give you only a very banal answer —an answer you have heard often enough. When I shake hands with a German, I don't know whether he killed my brother."

"I don't want to compare myself with you," said Christopher, "but I had similar reasons for leaving Germany." He tried to smile. "I don't know either who killed your brother."

Misha Kohorn stood up, went over to the window, looked out across the lit-up harbor, came back. He seemed to Christopher curiously changed; wit and vanity had vanished from his features, and you could hear a certain excitement in his voice. "But you of all people should know, Christopher. I doubt whether the Germans are a great nation, in spite of Beethoven, but you won't dispute that Germany is an important country. Perhaps because I was born in St. Petersburg, grew up in Berlin, and spent my most important years in Paris and London, I am a European, and Germany lies in Europe, lies, as they say, in its very heart." He ran his hand over his hair. "What I wanted to say is that I would give concerts in Germany if you were there to show me who murdered my brother. No, don't repeat that you don't know. You do know. I have forgotten how to read German eyes, but you can't have forgotten yet. And if you don't know, then you should try to find out. In short, I share Martha's esteem for you, but I don't think much of desertion in peacetime. The Germans should have deserted during the war. Then there would have been sense in it."

"Don't you think," said Martha, turning to Christopher, "that that was why I brought you to my father? You don't know my father. It's pure chance that we happen to agree."

Her naturalness freed the conversation from the oppression that had been hanging over it. Misha Kohorn did not appear to expect an answer from Christopher, and Christopher did not reply. They talked about tomorrow's concert in Haifa. "It's a pity tomorrow isn't the Sabbath," Kohorn said. "I would have liked to invite you."

This was the signal for the party to break up, although Misha Kohorn had not intended it like that. "You musn't listen to my wife. She thinks I need nine hours sleep, and yet I do splendidly on five, and I certainly won't practice, firstly because the piano is rotten, and secondly because my concerts keep me in good form. You know—Paderewski's bleeding hands." He laughed, as though perfectly aware of his own maliciousness.

It was past midnight. Martha and Christopher ran across the street. They had promised to meet the truck driver who was to take them back to the kibbutz on the dot of midnight at the corner of Plumer Square. Martha helped Christopher with his parcels. Only when these had been stowed away and they were sitting close together beside the driver did she ask, "How did you like my father?"

"I envy you your father," he said.

They talked and talked, as though they had been living for a hundred years and now had to draw up the balance sheet. Martha got to know about Christopher's friends; about his love of horses and ships; about his mother and Baron Boderode; about his enthusiasm for French poets and Spanish painters; about the singer who had seduced him; and about Ferdinand, who sat in an invalid's chair and could laugh like no one else. Christopher got to know about Misha Kohorn's moods; about Alice Kohorn's zealous excesses; about the school of interpreting which Martha had been through in Geneva; about the job at a French airline that awaited her in Paris; about her inborn lethargy and musicality; about her brother's death in the RAF, about her mother's annoyance because she refused to think of marrying; and about the young Englishman whom she had loved and who had married someone else. They talked about Christopher's plans. He told her of the play which he had wanted to write about the rising in the Warsaw Ghetto, and one evening he read her his poems. He made a promise that he would devote all his free time to his play, and when they parted in the evening she said with a smile, "You should have been working . . ."

Christopher treated his happiness as a childless couple treat a child that has come to visit them for a few hours. He tended it and did not know what to do with it. What he was experiencing was something mature and complete which had never begun, had not grown, had just happened. He was overcome by a great disquiet at the thought that a man and a woman cannot become one if their bodies do not become one. He desired Martha as a man desires a woman whom he has possessed and looks for again and finds again. But how could he find her "again" when he had not found her before? Ever since he had begun to think, he had feared impurity, and now he was frightened by the purity of his feelings, his inability to imagine his relationship with Martha as other than complete and final.

One moonlit night they went out into the fields that sloped down to the Jordan. At their feet lay the silver river. The moon shone as coldly, as if it were searching for a living being. The false peace that had lain for thousands of years over the land of Jacob was breathing among the bushes.

Martha lay down on the grass and crossed her arms behind her head. She was sunning herself in the moon. He sat with his legs drawn up, and looked sideways at her face that was as peaceful as the landscape. Now they were alone and fear came over him, unlike any of the fears he had ever felt before.

He bent down over her and her arms came to meet him. "Do you love me?" she asked, and he said, "I love you." She said, "I love you," and he kissed her.

He thought that now everything around him would fade, but instead everything took on a sharper outline, harsher and more hostile than the light of the moon. In the silence there was a voice he did not know, a voice from outside. It was bright and noisy and belonged to someone he did not know was present.

Sweat broke out on his brow. He knew that he desired her, knew it with the clarity of the light and the voice. Had he been interested for too long in bodies as bodies, instead of as the communion between a man and a woman? Once he had begun to ask himself these questions, he would not be able to stop asking them. "I love you," he said. If he repeated the words he would forget everything, but instead of that, pictures from near and far raced toward him: the house opposite, Zieselsberger, the voyage on the *Admiral Hipper*, a letter from his father, Moshe Dzwonicki, Inge's front room, His longing had fled from his body into his brain and was now ground into a thousand grains.

She put her arms around his neck, drew him close. Anger welled up in him because she knew nothing of his fear. He overcame the anger, but the fear remained. He kissed her forehead, but his tenderness was like a defeat.

"Lay your head on my arm," she said.

He laid his head on her arm, and this too was a defeat. Was she sorry for him? Pity could redeem but not help him. And again anger rose in him, for only experience knew pity, and he hated her experience. He was afraid that she would get up and go. In silence he begged for her to be patient, but what would change if she was patient with him? He longed for darkness and silence; it was bright and noisy around him.

"Are you happy?" she asked.

"Yes," he said, and had never been more unhappy.

She sat up and bent over him. "I don't think I have ever seen your face so clearly," she said, running one finger over his eyebrows. He drew her to him; they kissed, and he wished she would stand up and go and leave him forever.

Now she was sitting beside him in the grass, leaning on one arm. He turned over on his stomach and buried his head in his arms. He didn't know whether to cry or to pretend to be crying. Whoever it was who was speaking to him, couldn't he help him? If the Devil had tempted him with an offer of help, he would have sold his soul to the Devil. What was she thinking? What did she imagine he was thinking? He believed her capable of the horrible thought that he could not sleep with a Jewess, and he wanted to tell her that he had lain in the grass with the girl from the Lemberg Ghetto and had been happy. He wanted to tell her that he desired her, but the admission of his longing would have been an admission of his weakness. His body was bathed in sweat. He tried to think of other women and of the first evening, when she had offered him her forehead, and of his own body, which was young and healthy and strong. He tried to flee from reality into fantasy and imagine the woman as though she were not sitting next to him. He tried to conjure up all sorts of obscenities, but when the Devil came to him, he assumed the face of an angel.

"It's getting cold," she said. "Shall we walk a little?"

He wanted to revolt against so much understanding.

They walked down into the valley, where the moon was playing among the sunflowers.

"Do you think Adam and Eve walked across these fields?" she said.

"Yes," he said bitterly. "You're Eve and you want to teach me to eat of the tree of the garden, that I may distinguish between good and evil."

He laughed, as though he had not meant it bitterly. Why did

she act as though something had happened which had not happened? *And Adam knew Eve his wife; and she conceived, and bare Cain, and said, I have gotten a man from the Lord.* A couple only existed when they had known each other. Tomorrow, in the bright daylight, they would walk across the fields, and what had not happened would stand between them. Filled with fear, he had counted the days till her departure, and had wanted to hold back every passing day. Filled with fear, he now counted the days till her departure and didn't know whether he would be able to bear the agony of her still being there.

"Do you remember when I first came up to you on my first evening in the kibbutz?" she said.

"Yes."

"I was much cleverer than you. I already loved you then."

He stopped, drew her to him. If he pulled her down into the grass now, the light would go out and the voice would become silent, and he would take her and love her, and the rising sun would find them asleep. But the fear returned.

They approached the kibbutz, close together.

At the end of August a documentary was shown after the kibbutz supper. The old-fashioned projector had been set up in the dining room. It was a silent film; the only sound in the room was the voice of the man operating the machine.

He was just describing the excavations by the Red Sea when a young man hurried down through the rows of spectators. He was looking for Moshe Dzwonicki. The head of the kibbutz left the room; the film continued.

From outside a shot rang out. A woman said in a loud voice, "What was that?" No one answered. A few men rose and went soundlessly to the door. Christopher let go of Martha's hand. The man was still talking about the excavations. There was a salvo of gunfire.

The light went on. The projectionist, taken by surprise, had forgotten to stop the projector. You could see Moshe Dzwonicki walking toward the front in the beady light of the projector. There was a deathly hush.

"The Arabs have attacked our truck," said Moshe Dzwonicki. "Please keep calm, everyone. Group A will assemble fully armed by the rear entrance, led by Zvi Mendel. Group B under Yallon Aleichem will guard the kibbutz. The rest of you will go quietly to your houses. You will remain there until further notice."

Even now there was no panic and almost no excitement. The older women stood aside, the men went toward the door. Only one woman called out across the room, "Take care, Yitzchak." Two young girls followed the men. And a few old women shook their heads, as though to say, You can't even watch a film in peace.

"I must go," said Christopher to Martha, although he belonged to neither Group A nor Group B.

Then he was standing outside in the night. The searchlight on the factory roof, which had only been used once or twice in Christopher's memory, was working according to plan. The light swept across the flat-roofed houses, the sandy soil, the old people's benches, over the heads of the men who were hurrying past Christopher. Shots rang out from the direction of the fort. Christopher remembered pictures of prisoners of war and concentration camps.

One of the buildings, just behind the hospital, was now brightly lit. That was the armory where ammunition, pistols, rifles, submachine guns, a machine gun were stored. Christopher saw figures moving behind the window.

He told himself that he had no business out in the yard. Group A consisted of trained soldiers; Group B was made up of volunteers, elderly men. He drove a tractor, carried jam crates from the factory, helped the women with heavy work. He didn't even have a gun.

Because I'm a German, I detest guns, but would this apply to even Israeli guns? Or have I been waiting for them to press a gun into my hand? Why didn't Moshe call me and say, "Here, Abraham, take a gun"?

Group A left the lit-up building on the double. Yallon Aleichem was assembling the men of Group B outside the factory. Old men and women passed Christopher on the way to their houses. He thought they looked at him. Although the yard was full of movement, he felt alone. In a moment, Martha would come out of the dining room. He ran toward the armory. He was aware that for the first time he was not obeying an order, was, in fact, defying an order. "No one will leave their houses until further notice."

As he entered the armory the last member of Group A ran past him. It was Max Nagy, from Budapest. In his late twenties, only three months in the kibbutz, he had not taken a Jewish name yet. He was carrying a gun.

The armory was a long, narrow room. It lay in a yellowish light, like a hospital ward. The room was empty. There was not a single gun in the rack that stood in the middle of the room. The nameplates showed the owners: Yallon Aleichem, Zvi Mendel, Israel Torczinski, John Jackson, Rachel Kohn, Dov Gipner. Max Nagy also had a nameplate. The weapons were gone, but against one wall stood a few crates of ammunition. One crate was half full of cartridge belts. Christopher took a few bandoliers full of cartridges, threw them over his shoulder, hurried out.

There was no one left at the rear entrance to the kibbutz. The night was vast and empty and dark. The false peace that had lain for thousands of years over the land of Jacob lay over the land. And Christopher stood there and childhood dreams came into his mind. He wasn't afraid, or rather, he was afraid nothing would happen. Childhood dreams of saving a girl from a burning house, battling with a dragon, sailing in a boat through the streets of a flooded town, victory over a power a hundred times stronger than himself. He wished armed Arabs would emerge from the bushes; he would defeat them with his bare hands. The night was vast and empty and dark and silent.

An attack on the truck could only have happened on the way from the fort. Just before the film had started, a small truck carrying provisions had set out for the frontier. That was about two hours ago; the attack must have taken place on the way back. He no longer cared about Moshe Dzwonicki's orders. He ran past the factory and along the narrow road linking the kibbutz with the fort.

The glow of the flashlights appeared, glowworms that grew larger and larger. He heard voices. There stood the truck, surrounded by men. The side was riddled with holes, the windscreen smashed. The driver was hanging out of the truck with his head on one side and one arm over the door. The blood that had run out of his mouth was beginning to dry. The men carefully lifted him out of his seat. They had no need to be careful anymore. He was dead. In the glow of the flashlights, Christopher recognized a few men from the kibbutz. Next to him stood the gaunt gynecologist from Krefeld. He was much too old for Group A, but he was carrying a gun over his shoulder. He bent over the driver, his gun tilted forward, and almost fell on the dead man. The gynecologist was excited and spoke in German. "He's dead," he said.

Shots rang out; everyone straightened up.

Then figures emerged from the darkness. "Who goes there?" shouted someone. "Me," said Moshe Dzwonicki angrily. Followed by a few men, he came from the direction of the hills. His thin mouth was thinner than usual. "We caught a couple of Syrian soldiers," he said. "They're dead. Go and fetch them." And he pointed into the darkness.

Christopher thought that Moshe Dzwonicki recognized him. He stood there like a boy caught stealing, the cartridge belt over his shoulder. He wanted to offer some excuse, but Moshe Dzwonicki walked past him in the direction of the kibbutz. The others followed him. There was no stretcher at hand; a broad-shouldered young man carried the dead man on his shoulders. Christopher walked behind him. He was the last.

A few flashlights lit the way ahead. You could hear footsteps ringing out on the stony ground. Small pebbles jumped aside from under the men's boots, and when they fell by the side of the road, it was like the patter of raindrops. No one spoke. They walked in a long column, in two's, a long column of Jews. They walked as they had walked in Egypt, in Babylon and in Auschwitz. They were carrying a dead man as they had always carried the dead. They walked in silence and with bowed heads, their eyes on the ground, on the harsh soil of Israel.

III

My Name Is Christopher Wendelin

$\mathscr{T}$HE little hotel where Christopher was staying in Marseilles was situated on the Quai du Port, at the corner of the Avenue St. Jean. The crossing had been stormy; even now a cold autumn wind was sweeping over the harbor. Just across the cobbled street the fishing smacks lay hull to hull, once painted in bright colors, now a monotonous gray-blue. Washing fluttered from the lines; there was almost no sign of life on deck. That morning, there must have been a market under Christopher's narrow French window, for a few abandoned stalls were still standing there. The wind flapped the black awnings; the wind carried lettuce leaves, remains of vegetables, sheets of newspaper over the cobblestones. Outside the door of the hotel, children were chasing a mangy dog. The metal sign of the hotel banged against the wall. A whore had been arguing with a Greek sailor. Together they turned around, together they put out their tongues. It was bizarre, and had Christopher been in the mood, he would have laughed. But he didn't feel like laughing.

The port looked exactly as he had pictured it. He wouldn't describe it to Ferdinand. It hasn't changed; he can read about it in *The Count of Monte Christo*.

He left the hotel, left the port, strolled up the Cannebière. The Cannebière, too, was exactly as he had pictured the main street of Marseilles. In a café near the Church of St. Peter and St. Paul he sat down by the window, asked for writing paper, began his letter to Ferdinand.

"I don't know," he wrote, "when and why I made up my mind to leave Israel and come home to Germany."

The expression "come home" is wrong, but I can't weigh every word in the balance.

"It may have been that evening when the Syrians came over and attacked our truck. Why hadn't I asked for a gun? Did I feel throughout that year and a half like a monk in a hair shirt, different from the Israelis, who had not come to Israel to repent but to build up and defend a country? And why didn't Moshe Dzwonicki give me a gun? Because he knew who I was? I don't think so. He didn't want to force a gun on me; he was waiting for me to ask him for one. Or did my conversation with Misha Kohorn make so deep an impression on me? Or my conversation with that fool, Bull? Even that is not impossible. The more I thought about what Misha Kohorn really meant, the clearer it became that fundamentally, all he was saying was: All well and good, my lad, but the Israelis don't need you."

On the wall of the building opposite a neon sign lit up. *Dubo-Dubon-Dubonnet.* I put down the pen because I now had to write about my father.

"And then came the letter from my father, which I've mentioned to you. Meanwhile, the premiere of his film has been arranged in Frankfurt; I read about it today in a German paper. When I went to Israel, I couldn't imagine that a year and a half later his name would shine in lights over the entrance to German movie houses. One more reason for avoiding the land of my father? It would be, Ferdinand, if I didn't care about that country. *Blut und Boden?* It is, rather, that something is happening to my name and no one has asked me whether I consent to it. It is no longer your country, you will say. You know, I now understand why married couples who hate each other nevertheless stay together. Does not hate link just as much as love? When the others in the kibbutz read that at home"—"at home," I won't cross it out—"they are giving fat pensions to generals who in the very last hour had deserters put up against a wall and shot, they merely nodded their heads and went off to work. I felt the blood rise. Now you will laugh and think I'm coming 'home' "—I'll put that in quotes—"to change things. I know I can't change anything. But my face was burning with rage and I couldn't lie and say it didn't concern me. I had lied too often as it was. Dr. Aaron Weinstein helped me come to Israel, and he helped me leave, but I'm not sure that I am grateful to him. Everything might have been different if I hadn't been lying from the very first moment I landed in Israel."

Outside, it was misty. Shops and offices were letting out. He thought of Herzl Street. He was never quite at home there, and he would probably never be quite at home anywhere else.

"We will talk about it and you will help me to understand."

What the hell, Ferdinand can't help me. A friend is someone to whom you tell the whole truth, and yet you never tell the whole truth to anyone. I'm full of highfaluting declarations, a drop of philosophy, a drop of world history, and I'm not even sure if it isn't merely an excuse, for I'm ashamed of personal explanations. I think them petty, yet it may be that I only fled on account of Martha. Not because she left earlier than planned—it was probably the attack, her mother was scared —not because she is in Paris, not because I want to see her again. I won't throw my life overboard for any woman, not even Martha. But I have found a hundred explanations and in the end always accused the kibbutz. Martha isn't Esther, she isn't a girl who should be laid in the grass and the bushes. For Martha it would have been an adventure, and for me it couldn't be an adventure. But that isn't certain, either. The only thing certain is that I wanted to discover the truth, and I realized I would never discover it in the kibbutz.

"The worst is behind me, but I feel none of the relief you normally feel when the worst is behind you. I am speaking of the parting. It was so difficult for me because they made it so easy. There was a great sadness in Moshe Dzwonicki's eyes that seemed to say: I knew it. If a single one had tried to hold me back, I would have stayed. I think I was a great disappointment to them. They organized a goodbye party for me, and the whole time I was there, there had never been such a party. They never considered me a Holiday Jew. Those they let go without any farewell. But they had not said farewells to those who belonged to them, either, because none of them had ever been unfaithful. The girls danced the hora, and I had to dance too. The choir sang and Pollack, the goatherd, recited 'The Cranes of Ibicus.' He probably didn't know anything else by heart, or he wanted at all costs to recite a German poem. Only Moshe Dzwonicki said nothing. The Israeli authorities made it easy for me, too. Perhaps they were quite glad I was going before anyone found out that I was Richard Wendelin's son. But . . ."

Shall I tell Ferdinand? *Dubo-Dubon-Dubonnet.* The café opposite looks like a drawing by Toulouse-Lautrec. I won't tell Ferdinand. Because the worst was not saying goodbye to the kibbutz, but the afternoon with the immigration officers. How can he understand at this point I did not change my mind? "Ah, yes, you want your German passport back? What is the name? Christopher Wendelin? Let's have a look. When did you deposit your passport? Right, you took the name Abraham Avni. And now you want your passport back? Now you want to be called Christopher Wendelin again? No, no, there's no difficulty, Herr Wendelin. We've had a call from the Ministry of the Interior. Dr. Weinstein has been in touch with them." A hunt through the papers. "Cigarette? You speak excellent Hebrew, Herr Wendelin." Stress on the name; Abraham Avni was not mentioned again. "Well, here's your passport. Lucky you changed your mind in time." No irony, a simple statement of fact; the passport would have run out in five weeks. "It hasn't run out, everything is in order. At least, as far as we're concerned. The German authorities may be different. That's your problem. When do you intend to leave? Have a good trip, Herr Wendelin."

"I didn't have any trouble over my old German passport, either, Ferdinand. I got it back without difficulty." A friend is someone to whom you tell almost the whole truth. "I thought you could leave your identity at the border, say goodbye to identity forever. But, of course, that's a fallacy. They keep your identity on file, well stored, and you pick it up again before it runs out." Ferdinand won't understand that, but it doesn't matter. New paragraph.

"I am going to Paris tomorrow. It's not much of a detour, and I want to see Martha. I may only stay one night. I haven't any money. That brings me to my immediate problems. When I entered the kibbutz, I left the little money I still had in a bank. It's just enough for the trip home. Do you realize that I shall soon be twenty-four and never have earned an honest penny? Except in the kibbutz. Perhaps that is another reason why I deserted. Not because the pay was too little, but because it was too simple to earn it. Eighteen pounds—no more, no less."

Now I'm embellishing my motives. I could cross that out. Ferdinand won't misunderstand. Not Ferdinand, but everyone else. So you didn't like it in Israel, Herr Wendelin? Well, there's no place like home. The first person who says that to me will get it on the jaw. You can choke on your damned home. Then why didn't you stay in Israel, Herr Wendelin? Because I have the right to call myself a German, but you haven't. Why haven't I, Herr Wendelin? Because we can't both be Germans, you and I. Anyhow, my return has nothing to do with the Jews, if that's what you think.

"I want to see whether I shall starve. I must look for work immediately. Don't tell me that's easy. I've read the advertisements in the newspapers, Germany's ridiculous advertisements. 'Wanted: managing director, annual salary one million, to start at once, no experience necessary.' Or something like that. I don't want to be rewarded for starting a war or importing slave laborers from Poland or inventing the practical little mobile gas chamber. I don't remember doing any of these things, so I have no claim to a reward. I want to see whether I can earn enough by my pen"—that sounds pretentious. I'll cross it out—"by my writing to keep myself from starving. Maybe in the end, someone will publish something that makes some sense."

Now for a few optimistic lines, so that Ferdinand won't be afraid of me. Ferdinand's laughter is the only thing I'm looking forward to. If only I could find out how he manages to laugh!

The coffee was cold. He drank it up, sealed the letter, and went out into the mist that was rolling in from the Château d'Iff and the old port over the Cannebière as in the days of the Count of Monte Cristo.

Martha fetched him from his hotel on the Left Bank of the

Seine in her little two-seater. Two weeks after he had left Ani Omer, he had written to tell her of his decision. She had replied that she would be glad to see him, but she had not encouraged him.

They drove up Avenue Hoche, to the Kohorns' *pied-à-terre*, where a "little party" was being held. Misha Kohorn lived in London, but he had a *pied-à-terre* everywhere—in Paris, Rome, New York. "My parents will be tremendously pleased to see you." What's that to me? One night in Paris, I told Martha. I had just enough money to pay for the hotel. Off to Munich in the morning at ten thirty-two. It isn't true that Martha absolutely had to be present at the "little party." It isn't true that her parents absolutely insisted on seeing me.

Martha inquired about the kibbutz. Had Abraham, the other Abraham, found his bicycle? Was Moshe still angry with her for suddenly leaving? Did Gabriel receive the *Larousse* she sent him? Is Sarah really pregnant?

He answered like a schoolboy, and wouldn't have been surprised if she had asked after Zieselsberger. He looked out into the evening tumult of the Champs-Elysées; the kibbutz seemed further away than his school days, but he clung to it. Seven o'clock. Now they would be sitting around the long table. Moshe was talking about next day's work; Esther had tears in her eyes because the Harvard student was leaving soon; Max Nagy was eating his fourth slice of bread and jam; the old people were nodding and waiting for the young to go and leave them to their memories; outside, the cloudless sky and the harsh soil of Israel. I am sitting beside Martha and driving to a "little party" in the Avenue Hoche. Nothing binds her to me but the country from which I had fled. I'm good at that. First I fled Germany, then Israel; first there was homesickness for Germany, now there is homesickness for Israel. "Herr Wendelin and my daughter were together in the kibbutz," Alice Kohorn would tell her guests. When I was around, people always had reasons to lower their eyes considerably. Now they have one more reason.

He looked at Martha, but she was staring straight ahead. I should have said, "Don't you understand that I want to be alone with you?" But I am too much of a coward. I wouldn't say it. We were alone often enough in Israel, and what good had that done? In Israel she had said, "I love you." That was no more. I don't want to go to her party. Are you perhaps proud because you have found the bridge between love and friendship? I no longer gave a damn for friendship; friendship had been good enough for Israel.

"Are you going to write your play now?" she asked.

"Yes, I suppose I will."

"There will be some interesting people this evening," she said. "My mother has invited Kasimir Nessor especially for you. She's taken a liking to you."

"Thanks!" he said.

"You know, it costs me almost nothing to fly on the airline I work for. I shall come and see if you're really working."

A slight hope, because of the free trip. "Do you enjoy your job?" he asked. They were circling the Arc de Triomphe.

The *pied-à-terre* really was a *pied-à-terre,* not much more than a drawing room of imposing dimensions. Ten or twelve people were already assembled, and new guests were still arriving. Alice Kohorn took Christopher under her wings. She introduced him around as a "young writer—Herr Wendelin was in the kibbutz with Martha." The conversation went on in German, French, English. Most of the guests had friendly words for Christopher. They were used to helping young artists whom Alice Kohorn helped. With unerring strategy the hostess steered Christopher toward Kasimir Nessor. "Well, now you know all our friends, Christopher. I'm sure you'll find Kasimir interested in talking to you."

It is strange to meet a man who became world famous the same year I was born. Kasimir Nessor was the author of the great First World War novel, *Front Line.* The most widely read novelist in the German language, his books had been banned and burned; a German who had never set foot inside Germany again; a famous collector, the owner of a château on the Île-de-France, almost a legend.

Kasimir Nessor turned away from the actress from the Comédie Française to whom he had been listening with ill-concealed boredom. "I'm glad to meet you, Herr Wendelin. How is your father?" And before Christopher could recover from his amazement, "There's something strange, which you perhaps don't know. Your father and I used to get on very well together—how old is he, exactly?"

"Fifty-three."

"Is he really five years younger than I am? Yes, that's right, when *Front Line* came out he was not yet thirty, a very promising young director. He had only one desire then: to film my book. Fortunately for me, and perhaps for him, too, Hollywood got it first. Really it's my fault he didn't become a refugee."

Christopher stared at the novelist in wonder. There stood this man, an impressive man, *un grand monsieur,* as the French would say, talking quite naturally about Richard Wendelin. Was hypocrisy strange or only too uncomfortable to him?

"I hear you're on your way to Germany," said Kasimir Nessor.

"I was in Israel for a year and a half . . ."

"I know." But he didn't seem in the least interested. How strange to meet a man who uttered the name of Richard Wendelin without slapping Christopher on the back, without saying, "Good boy, so you did a year and a half in Israel!"

"You're right to have a look around Germany. I'd like to talk to you about that."

"You haven't been back to Germany since the war, have you, Herr Nessor?"

"I don't feel homesick. I'm not a Jew." This he said with a laugh, and his laugh, too, captivated Christopher, for it was a laugh such as he had never heard before. The eyes were laughing, and the folds round the eyes accompanied the laughter of the eyes with a little dance, but the mouth, although it joined in with a smile, remained on this side of laughter.

"People long only for those places from which they've been driven," Kasimir Nessor said. The Nazis had tried to change his name, to reverse the letters and make the Jewish name Rosen out of it, and the Jews actually welcomed this. The Germans couldn't bear to see the son of a Westphalian civil servant desert from their own ranks, and the Jews did not know what to make of the voluntary refugee. It was not hostility to

Germany that persuaded him to remain far from Germany.
"Anti-German—that's too easily said." In Christopher's place,
he too would go and have a look at Germany. But in his case it
was different: they no longer spoke the same language. "There
is a language that says something, and a language that conceals
something." For a writer that was doubly difficult. "Moreover,
writers and refugees have something in common. They are liked
best when they are nicely put away."

Alice Kohorn interrupted the conversation. She was leading
a slender, dark woman, dressed with discreet elegance, from
group to group. "My dear Bettina," said Kasimir Nessor,
spreading out his arms. "Herr Wendelin—Frau Professor von
Benda," said Alice Kohorn, but the woman did not shake hands
with Christopher. In fact she turned pale, seemed to wince, and
instinctively took a little step back.

When the two of them had moved away there was a brief
silence. Did Nessor notice, will he pretend not to have noticed,
shall I pretend not to have noticed?

"Don't worry about that," said Kasimir Nessor. "Professor
von Benda, a great Austrian doctor, died from the strain of a
mission which he took in an effort to save his Jewish compa-
triots. Frau von Benda never quite got over the shock. Furthermore, Germans don't have a monopoly on injustice. We *émigrés*
demand our share of it, too." He put his arm around Christopher's shoulder.

Supper was ready. The guests—by this time there were over
twenty of them—crowded round the buffet. Martha introduced
Christopher to a young American who wrote a column for the
Paris edition of the *New York Herald Tribune*. The interest
William Steele showed him, as he strained to bring out his
halting French, irritated Christopher, but he did not know
whether this was because he feared that his name had roused
the journalist's interest, or because he suspected something
between Martha and "Bill." He looked for help from Kasimir
Nessor, who had been buttonholed again by the elderly actress
from the Comédie.

What am I doing here? Let me go, I want to go back to the
kibbutz. We're sorry, Herr Wendelin, you have collected your

passport; we can't smuggle you into Israel for a second time.
Let me go, I want to go to Germany; at least there I know the
walls of the houses with the lavatory windows. So you didn't
like it in Israel, Herr Wendelin? Misha Kohorn is sitting in a
corner with Frau von Benda, talking to her persuasively; they're
talking about me. Richard Wendelin's son, but he was in the
kibbutz. A German, but a decent lad. I didn't murder your
husband, Frau von Benda. I only prayed for victory, like Karl
Melchior, like the others. If you can't understand that, Frau von
Benda! *Émigrés*, Kasimir Nessor said. The Israelis, to whom I
don't belong, and the Germans, to whom I don't belong—I'm
very capable, one evening in Paris is enough for me to find a
third group to which I don't belong.

"You're not eating anything," said Martha, touching his
hand.

"I'm not hungry, I guess."

Bill came over to Christopher and said that he himself had
been in Israel a year ago. "Martha—*c'est une fille merveilleuse*,"
he said. "Yes," said Christopher, "she is a wonderful girl."
"What are you talking about?" asked Martha, as though afraid
the conversation might be about her. Don't worry, no conversation at all. Christopher was then left alone by the piano, leaf-
ing with feigned interest through the scores. Alice Kohorn noticed it, came over to him, and began to talk about Martha's
job. She stayed longer with Christopher than with any of the
other guests. Very tactful. She had probably noticed the em-
barrassing incident. An old lady took over from Alice Kohorn,
a Frenchwoman. Her gushing conversation proved that she did
not know who he was. Martha brought Bill a whiskey. Thank
you, he was only interested in scores. "Have a drink with us,"
she said to Christopher in passing. Again he looked for help to
Kasimir Nessor, but he was surrounded by women. The folds
around his eyes performed their merry dance. Have courage,
they seemed to say, even a party comes to an end, eventually.

At ten to midnight the guests were leaving. Now I can leave
too. Would Martha give me a lift? Where does she live? She
hadn't said a word about where she lived. She had no need to

worry that he would say, Let's go to your place. There was a little café in his hotel, but what would they talk about? Do you remember Zieselsberger? No, that was at school; she was a kibbutz comrade. Do you remember the night in the fields behind the factory? I'm sorry, my mind was wandering; it was the kibbutz that did it. Did you come to Paris on my account? No, I only came because of the interesting people. Goodbye till Munich! I'm living with my mother. But that won't worry you, and the flight costs next to nothing.

He wanted to say goodbye to Misha Kohorn, but the host had disappeared; he had probably gone to bed. Now Frau von Benda walked past him. Alice Kohorn was sorry he had to leave the next day, she said. "But we won't lose sight of each other, Christopher. Martha always knows where you are." Many thanks. I won't get lost.

Martha was standing in the doorway. "Don't be angry. I have to help Mother."

"I'm not angry."

Then someone touched his arm. He looked around. "We two will disappear together," said Kasimir Nessor, not even troubling to lower his voice. Turning to Martha, he said, "Don't worry, I'll bring him home safely." Martha quickly kissed Christopher on both cheeks.

"Can I give you a lift home?" asked Bill Steele.

"Thanks, but Herr Nessor has been so kind."

"I'll definitely see you in Munich," said Martha. "I've got your address."

"Yes, my mother's address."

"Please write me straightaway."

"Yes, I will."

Kasimir Nessor's big sports car stood outside the door. "The only youthful thing about me," he said. "I still like uncomfortable cars."

In the hotel's little café, Kasimir Nessor ordered two pernods. He picked up the conversation where he had broken it off as they left the car.

"I'm giving you advice which I am not following myself,"
he said. "There is no exile's return, because the refugee remains for the rest of his life stamped as a refugee."

"It's not a bad title," Christopher objected.

"It's the same as saying there's something special about being
a Jew. Philo-Semitism is a variant of anti-Semitism. The philo-
Semite is an anti-Semite with a clear conscience. The one puts
the Jew on a pedestal, the other locks him up; both lock him
out. In both cases it is a matter of isolation. If you want to iso-
late someone you have to give him a name. Since it is temporarily unpopular to talk about Jews, people talk about refugees. Why, still? The penal law protects the criminal from
being persecuted once his sentence has been completed. Only
the *émigré* remains an *émigré* after his 'release.' For myself,
it doesn't worry me that people speak ill of me behind my
back—they do that about anyone who is read in Germany.
But it does worry me that no one speaks ill to me about anyone.
In Germany I'd have the choice between a silence which would
burden my conscience, and protest which would burden my
conscience, and protest which would burden the conscience of
others. You, at least, are not a refugee."

"But I could become one. You know that they are preparing
for the premiere of a Wendelin film in Frankfurt."

"Does that surprise you? That it should have come about is a
highly complicated process. The past cannot be 'overcome,'
because the Germans fail to make a break where they ought
to make one, but draw a line where it is out of place."

"Do you mean the difference in the generations?"

"I'll come to that in a minute. For the outside world, you
see, there was never such a thing as a National Socialist government, but merely moral chaos that lasted for twelve years. To
the Germans, National Socialism was a form of government,
good or bad, depending on their viewpoint. What to the world
outside is chaos is to the Germans an episode, glorious or shameful, depending on their outlook. The problem is insol-
uble because, alongside the murder of the Jews, there was a war.
Let us suppose that the government had murdered six million
Jews, but had not waged a war."

"Do you mean that the world would have forgiven the Germans the six million Jews?"

"Let me develop my hypothesis. Few Germans would have identified themselves with the murder of the Jews in peacetime—more than are willing to admit today, but still only a minority. Let us further assume that the bloody regime that murdered Jews but did not make war finally collapsed. For example, as the result of internal quarrels within the leadership —as I have said, this is only a hypothesis. A new Germany would then have expelled the assassins and their accomplices, thereby 'overcoming' the past. But Hitler led his people into war. I don't say that the German soldier waged war in order to prevent the enemy from liberating the concentration camps, but he stood between the concentration camps and the enemy. He defended his fatherland, they say—a double lie, because to begin with, he only attacked foreign countries, and his fatherland was not a fatherland at all, but chaos. As the war ended, schizophrenia took over. Think of the former soldier who today detests the National Socialist past—the average case, I hope. He repudiates the Hitler regime, but he is proud of having defended the fatherland that was identical with this regime. Not content with that, he hates Germany's former enemies because he thinks they were fighting not only against the regime but also against the fatherland. What makes him think that? And how could the world have fought the regime without fighting Germany? Perhaps because I am concerned with language, I find in grammar the answer to the question of why the Germans cannot come to terms with their past. In every language I know, 'past' is a noun that only exists in the singular. The word 'pasts' doesn't exist, because there is only one past. The new Germans are the inventors of a double past. They look back on a concentration camp past, of which the majority are ashamed, and on a war past, of which the majority are proud."

"But how can you punish millions of German ex-soldiers? The Germans punishing them would be only ex-soldiers themselves."

"No one is asking for that. Furthermore, the law can only do so much. What people do is merely the consequence of what they feel. Therefore, the German can only overcome the past in himself. But it must be the whole past, whole and indivisible. So long as a single German mother has the photograph of her dead son in uniform standing on her chest of drawers, the past is the present. Don't misunderstand me. Naturally the photograph of the dead son will stand on her chest of drawers. But if we are to believe that Hitler forced the Germans into uniform, then they were wearing prison clothes, and though a mother loves her son whether he's in prison clothes or not, whether he was sent to jail justly or unjustly, she won't put his photograph where he's in convict's clothes on the chest of drawers. She'll have a picture of him in civilian dress. Even sentimentality is schizophrenic in Germany—half love, half uniform. And that's only possible because no one has had the courage to separate the two."

The waiter brought another round of pernod.

Perhaps my coming to Paris has served some purpose, after all. Here he is, talking to me, telling me, of all people, the things he has thought about during endless, sleepless nights. He is not talking to me, not to the son of Richard Wendelin.

It seemed as though Kasimir Nessor no longer knew that he was talking to Christopher. "There is no break between past and present and because of that, the situation is hopeless. You won't achieve anything. But there is a break of sorts—in the wrong place. When Germans come to see me, the phrase about the two generations immediately crops up—your generation and mine. The word 'generation' has become an excuse for everything. They say I don't understand the young Germans. They don't dare to say that I don't understand the Germans; they refer to my gray hair. Do you notice the cynical game? Your father and I belong to the same generation, and in telling you not to listen to your father, they are telling you not to listen to me. To escape from collective guilt—or collective shame, which would be more accurate—the Germans have fastened on the collective guilt of a generation. And this, then, abracadabra, immediately includes the refugees. The word 'generation,' however, unlike 'past,' is a noun with a plural, and not only in the sense that one generation follows another, but also in the sense that people within the same generation are different. The dividing line is drawn horizontally, separating the years, but it ought to be drawn vertically to separate convictions. You are my son, not your father's. There is nothing unusual in that."

Christopher gazed into the milky-green liquid. He feared Kasimir Nessor might notice his emotion.

"The bad fathers on the one side, the good sons on the other," Kasimir Nessor continued. "But it's not as simple as that. I don't think the youth of today would build concentration camps, but there are many reasons which explain this, not all of them moral. For instance, bitter experience. People say 'yesterday's generation,' and automatically think of old men. But yesterday's generation means yesterday's young men. Being young is no more a guarantee today than it was yesterday."

Christopher smiled. "You are sending me to Germany with a lot to look forward to."

"Perhaps not a lot to look forward to, but with hope—perhaps. All I wanted to say was that while with many wines, vintage is a sign of quality, it never is in men."

"You're right. My father was young in those days . . ."

"That's not the point. Millions of Germans would have made *Ritual Murder*. They didn't happen to be film directors. We are a nation of opportunists, and are thus even capable of doing good, provided it is profitable. Stop complaining that fathers are not examples of good behavior. If you look back at history, you will find that one generation is not entirely different from the next, but that it is distinguished from it by a process of wear and tear. The good gets worn out, but fortunately so does the bad. The fact that your father is no shining example for you does not of itself make you good, and if you should happen to have driven out the bad in yourself, you're going to be pretty lonely. You are a young German and therefore in some way not entirely free of your father's sickness. But no hereditary disease is as virulent as the one you have acquired yourself. Most hereditary diseases are curable. And although German youth—" he stopped, as though afraid of betraying his full concern "—although German youth," he continued hurriedly, "is not as

spotless as it thinks it is, although the break between the generations is artificial, your generation might set an example to the
next."

"If I could be sure of that . . ." said Christopher.

"There can't be any certainty," said Kasimir Nessor. "But
nevertheless there is a hope."

There was no one else in the café but the waiter with a disgruntled look that meant closing time.

Christopher accompanied Kasimir Nessor to his car.

"If you need anything, let me know," said Kasimir Nessor.
"Martha Kohorn has my address."

There was a note on the door: "Letter and key with Frau
Winter." Frau Winter lived on the floor above. "Oh, Herr
Wendelin," said Frau Winter, "back home again?"

"Yes, back home again," he said.

"You've spent a long time traveling, Herr Wendelin," said
Frau Winter. "Won't you come in?"

No, he said, he had to unpack. He went down the stairs. Obviously mother hasn't said anything about Israel.

The studio was cold and tidy. Of course, it was Saturday,
the cleaning woman had been in. On the easel stood an unfinished picture, a symphony of ears, almost abstract. She is moving
with the times, he thought.

He put down his case, sat down, opened the letter. How
sorry she was, wrote his mother. She had had to go to Nuremberg for an important exhibition. She would be back tomorrow
evening. "We will celebrate. The refrigerator is full." There
was a hundred-mark note in the envelope.

The door to his room, as always, was half open. He looked in
through the door. He hesitated, for only when he had crossed
the threshold to his room would he really know that he was
back. He entered the room and put the case on his bed. He did
not open it.

It was five in the afternoon and because it was Saturday, the
house opposite was alive. The limping schoolmaster stood in
front of the bookcase and took a thick volume from the shelf,
probably a dictionary. There was a new lamp hanging from

the ceiling in the apartment of the fat editor of the local paper
—six glittering arms, a glittering spider of brass. In the twins'
flat a teenage party was in progress and the twins no longer had
plaits.

Shall I phone Ferdinand? The telephone is next to the wheelchair. In a minute I shall hear Ferdinand's laughter. I won't
call, though. Letters don't blush. The telephone doesn't blush.
When I talk to Ferdinand, it must be the whole truth.

He went into the bathroom, washed his hands, combed his
hair. He used his mother's soap and comb and brush. He still
didn't touch his case.

It was a gray, raw October day. The streets were full. A cart,
drawn by heavy Pinzgau horses, drove past. It was the first
Saturday in October, the last Saturday of the October Fair. He
suddenly felt like going out to the fairgrounds. He had never
liked the fiesta, but if he had to be alone it was best to be alone
among a lot of people.

It was not yet quite dark when he entered the fairground, but
all the lamps were lit, thousands of bright-colored electric bulbs.
Like the wagons in a medieval camp, the stalls formed a circle
round the vast annual fair. The human flood forced Christopher
into the meadow. Shooting galleries on either side, guns banging, paper flowers falling under the bullets, roses and tulips,
storks and paper sailors, three shots a mark, hares and deer running round in a circle, little targets in their bellies—everything twirled, everything whirled, empty eggshells rose on jets
of water. Don't use your elbow for support! Give me a gun.
He didn't use his elbow for support; he stood upright, the gun
pressed between his shoulder and his cheek. One glass tube
shattered after the other, deer and hares fell over, feigning
death; in a moment they would stand up and race round in a
circle again. "Another three shots?" Yes, another three shots.
Tulips and roses and storks and sailors fell to the ground. He
put some money down and turned to go. "Won't you take the
flowers, sir?" No, he wouldn't take the flowers. He made off,
hearing laughter behind his back.

Everything twirling, everything whirling. A scenic railway
pitched downward amidst shrill women's screams; the ghost

train emerged. In the last carriage, Death was standing, holding tight; Death was afraid of falling off. "This way, ladies and gentlemen, Mr. and Mrs. Smith on the motorcycle of death." Mr. and Mrs. Smith wore leather suits, black leather—does that remind you of something? The entrance to the fools' wheel: only fifty pfennigs. People turning head over heels, heads banging against the wooden barrier amid howls of laughter. The merry-go-rounds looked forgotten, remnants of turn-of-the-century fairs, pink horses with golden manes, turn of the century and Surrealism. But this was 1954, jets rising and falling, women screaming, their bosoms bouncing up and down, chocolate hearts flying. The main streets of the fair with stalls to right and left; between them the huge timber buildings known here as tents: Hackerbräu, Löwenbräu, Pschorrbräu. From the tents the music of brass bands, singing and laughter; a gigantic wooden lion moved its head forward and backward, emptied a lion-sized quart jug. Chickens were turning on the spit, hundreds and thousands of crisp, fat-dripping, headless creatures, brown and gleaming, turning on the spit, some this way, some that, six marks, seven marks, eight marks, "for every purse," for every appetite, a bit of salt that makes you thirsty, the chicken makes you thirsty, the thirst makes you jolly. The sausages in front of the stalls like a curtain; the blocks of cheese piled up in mounds; a smell of beer and roasted nuts and Turkish delight and fried fish.

Ani Omer, thought Christopher. The hand in his pocket became a fist. With broad shoulders he forced his way through the crowd, men in Lederhosen, Negro soldiers, women in loden costume, dangling chocolate hearts, an elegant gathering, ladies and gentlemen arm in arm, rocking and swaying, blocking the path, the heavy cart horses of a beer dray, policemen in correct uniforms, their hands on their rubber truncheons, American Military Police. Ani Omer, thought Christopher, and for the first time he was glad that he had broad shoulders and was blond and blue-eyed. I hate you and I have a right to hate you. Though I look like Christopher Wendelin, I am Abraham Avni. The immigration officer, the little man with the sour bureaucrat's face, had given him back his passport, five weeks and it would have expired, and thought he was giving him back his identity—an error, my friend, you have restored to me a passport for Christopher Wendelin, and I have become Abraham Avni.

He walked and walked, spilled away by the flood. He stepped aside for no one, not even the drunks. Everyone stepped aside for him, even the drunks, and he was sorry that they did, for he was looking for trouble, a quarrel, an argument, someone he could knock down. I'm being unfair, people have fun everywhere, mobs are ugly everywhere, everywhere they booze and guzzle and are ugly. But what do I care? I don't want to be fair.

There was a crowd around the strength-testing machine. The men rolled up their sleeves, took the heavy wooden mallet in both hands; women laughed as if someone was tickling them, the mallet fell on the anvil, a piece of iron on a steel rail shot higher and higher; it seldom reached the highest point. "Try your strength, three goes for a mark!" He pushed a mark into the hand of a man in a leather apron, took hold of the mallet, swung it over his shoulder, brought it down with a thud on the anvil. The piece of iron shot upwards, hit the top with a noise like crushing glass; there were shouts and cheers from the girls. He forced his way through the admiring throng. That's right, stare at me, you bastards; keep your traps shut, or I'll tell you why I'm in such good shape. The sun was hot and the soil was hard, the harsh earth of Israel.

His throat was dry. Swaying, as though he had already drunk five quarts of beer, Wies'n beer, extra strong, 16 percent stock wort; he strolled to a tent. At first he saw little, because clouds of smoke and the haze of sweat hung so low, were so dense, that they actually had turned the colossal hall into a tent. He saw little, heard only the din that assailed him like a noisy army: thousands of voices, yelling and singing and laughing; shouts for the fat waitresses who hurried to and fro, sweating, carrying mugs of beer; jokes thrown from table to table; even the music was drowned in it: *Who's gonna pay, who can say, who's got all that dough to throw away* . . . A drunk slapped Christopher on the back, took his arm; he had difficulty in shaking him off; a man had fallen down and was lying on his back, drowned in beer, lying with his eyes open, moving his fingers and calling out to passersby; Christopher stepped over him. He didn't look for a table, ordered a quart of beer, gripped the earthenware mug as though it were the mallet which he had just swung, did not put it down until he had drained it. The orchestra, on a raised podium on the other side of the room—two dozen men or more, in leather shorts and stockings, Tyrolian hats on their heads—had just had their rest; now the jolly peasants reached for their instruments again, trumpets, bass tuba, trombone, kettle drum and chimes, the conductor raised his baton . . . Christopher listened and thought that the alcohol had robbed him of his senses. "We raise a cheer and fire our guns, / The Frenchie turns and off he runs. / And if you ask the lads in black: / That is Lützow's fearsome pack." He knew the song. In *We'll Die for You* the battle song had been played by the Reich's best military band. "But never tremble hearts so bold, / The Fatherland we safely hold! / And if you ask the dead in black: / That was Lützow's fearsome pack." He grabbed the fat waitress by the arm, took a second quart of beer from the struggling girl, drained it without putting it down. Then he fled the tent as though thousands had risen and were crowding after him, hundreds of women carrying quart mugs in front of them like guns; the men and women walked faster and faster, more and more ominously they clung to his heels, he ran faster and faster; they didn't catch up with him; only the music, he thought, caught up with him. "From father to son let the word go back: / That was Lützow's fearsome pack."

He stopped and gasped for breath. He looked up at the dark October sky, but only saw Eros sitting on a pot with his bow in his hand, the arrow pointed towards the urinal. He began to laugh, laughter shook him, he laughed till the tears ran down his face. He had to lean against the pillar on which Eros sat relieving himself, shooting his arrow in the direction of the urinal.

"Don't you want company?" he heard a voice beside him.

He saw a girl standing there, a slim, blond girl with a face that reminded him of death, although she was a pretty, very fair girl. Only her eyes were so dark that they looked like two cavities, and her mouth was painted so dark that it looked like a dark hole.

"Are you going to buy me a beer?" said the girl.

"I haven't any money," said Christopher.

"Then I'll buy you a beer," said the girl, taking his arm.

He paid for the beer which they drank at the counter, since there was nowhere to sit. "What's your name?" she asked.

"Christopher." The girl laughed. "Mine is Christa."

People pushed past them; the whole place seemed to be in motion. Christopher though he was merely imagining this because he had drunk too much. "We must go," said the girl. "Closing time. They close down at twelve here."

The river of people was flowing towards the exits. The policemen were walking along behind the merrymakers like circus attendants, sweeping up the horse manure. A gigantic Negro in an American uniform was vomiting. Two drunks were playing football along the stalls with an empty tin can. The lights went out. Out of the October mist loomed the figure of Bavaria, the province's patron goddess. A few more shots rang out from the shooting galleries, then the guns were cleared away. The iron shutters rattled down over roses, tulips, storks, deer and sailors.

"You can drink a glass of wine at my place," said the girl. "On the house."

He didn't know why he called a taxi, climbed in, embraced the girl who had put her hands on his knee. He didn't know where the taxi was going, why the driver was cursing; he only noticed the lights flitting past; at a red traffic light a few drunks knocked on the window. The girl waved to them with one hand; with the other she played with the buttons on his shirt. When the taxi jerked forward again Christopher thought he would vomit. The girl paid for the cab.

In the dark hall, he asked for the bathroom. She opened a door and switched on the light. Standing at the toilet he began to get his bearings. He was apparently not in the apartment yet; the bathroom was in the corridor. It was a relatively large room in which there was relatively little space, because it served as a junk room, too. There were brooms and brushes and buckets, and in among them two dog whips, a cane, a vacuum cleaner, a few lengths of rope, a whip with knots at the ends of the leather thongs. If I'm smart I'll be able to dodge out without her noticing; perhaps the apartment door is shut.

But it was open; Christa was standing in the doorway. "Are you scared? she asked. "Why should I be scared?" "You know." A bottle of wine was standing on the table, open. She sat on the arm of the chair and undid his tie. He drained the glass. "You look as if you can do it without whipping," she said. "Most of them need whipping."

The room spun round. I'm the man on the revolving floor; in a minute I shall bang my head against the barrier. Most of them need whipping, but I can do it without whipping. How old can she be? Twenty, twenty-one? Why did I think she looked like death? "And if you ask the lads in black: / That is Lützow's fearsome pack." Martha, her father a pianist, perhaps the most famous of them all. "Martha, a wonderful girl." Mother has no time, there's an exhibition in Nuremberg. I should have rung Esther, no, not Esther, Inge.

"I haven't any money," he said.

"You're a luxury item," she said, untying his shoes.

He poured himself a second glass of wine and had the feeling that the wine was sobering him. She opened a cupboard, took out bed linen, and covered the couch with a sheet. She spread a second sheet over the embroidered cushions. "Now you can undress me," she said. He took off his trousers, began to undress her. Her warm skin stuck to his body. He pulled her onto the couch; the linen smelled fresh. She laughed as he made love to her so violently. "You must be starved. I hope you can do it again." He fell asleep on her breast, woke up, made love to her a second time, felt drunker than before, fell asleep again. "You look like an angel," she said. "You can ring me, if I've got time. I've got a phone."

Dawn was beginning to break when he left the house. He was quite sober. Only now did he realize that the girl's house was close to the main station. He was hungry; he hadn't eaten anything since lunch the previous day. He caught sight of a sausage-seller's stall, right by the station. "Two," he said, "with mustard."

The morning people loomed up out of the mist. A young man in a leather jacket stopped by the sausage stall. "Well, I'll be damned," said the young man, "If it isn't Christopher Wendelin."

He hunted through his memory. Then the name came to him, Siegfried somebody. He had met him at Inge's, a colleague of Inge's at the camera factory. "Morning Siegfried," he said and, as though apologizing: "I've been away for a long time. How's Inge?"

"No idea," said the young man. "I'm not with the firm any more." He exchanged a glance with the stall owner, asked: "Still at the university, Herr Wendelin?"

"No," he answered. "I quit long ago."

"Where have you been?" asked the young man.

"Abroad," said Christopher. The young man nodded, as though that was all he had wanted to know. He shook Christopher's hand.

Christopher paid. The man looked at the coins hesitantly, did not put them in his pocket. "Excuse me," he said. "Did I hear right? Is your name Wendelin?"

"Yes," Christopher said impatiently.

The man leaned forward. "Excuse me, are you related to the director of *Ritual Murder*?"

Instinctively Christopher said, "My father."

The man's head came still nearer. "Give your father my best wishes. Tell him he should make another fine film like that soon again." He pushed the money that Christopher had put on the counter back to him. "Take it," he said. "You can have a few sausages on me any time you like."

Christopher left the money where it was, turned around, and walked quickly away toward the station. A drizzle was falling. He opened the door of a taxi. I've saved money, he thought. At Christa's. Almost at the sausage stall, too. He looked out into the morning. I'm at home, he thought. My first day at home.

*   *   *

His mother came back from Nuremberg and pressed him to her heart. The room next to the studio became his home again, his familiar, alien home. He knew again when the railway official went to bed, and heard that the man with the *Ritterkreuz* and the Africa cap had been arrested. He worked at night on his play, and tore up in the morning what he had written the night before. He wrote articles about Israel, took them to Munich editors, and was surprised that they were accepted. He said his name was Caesar Wendt and signed the articles "C.W." The articles were printed, and he didn't understand why the fees he received were so high. He no longer accepted money from his mother and she was proud of him. She asked why he didn't take a job, but he thought he could earn more as a free-lance journalist. In fact, he did not want to tell the editors his name. When they told him that they had had enough on Israel he wrote miscellaneous reports—about the men who slept in the station, about the women in the food market, about carnival balls in a suburban café. Editors praised his feeling for local color.

During the night he worked on a novel with Martha as hero-ine, and in the morning he tore up the manuscript. He heard nothing from her. Every day he wanted to write her, but he knew that he would tear up the letters as he had torn up the manuscripts. One day, when he brought in an article on truck drivers, the editor said, "Why the hell don't you give us your phone number? There was a serious incident on the Israel-Syria border. You're an expert on that subject. Write something for us quickly." He sat down at a typewriter and wrote an article on the Israel-Syria border. "It's a bit one-sided," said the editor. "That's why I've signed it Abraham Avni," Christopher answered. Next morning he cut out the article, put it in an envelope and sent it to Martha.

Two or three times a week he went to see Ferdinand. They sat by the window of the little villa where Ferdinand lived with his mother. The leaves fell from the trees, the gardener swept them up into neat piles, the rain fell, the heaps became wet, and the wet heaps looked like little coffins. Snow covered the garden and Christopher pushed Ferdinand's wheelchair up and down on the verandah.

"You shouldn't visit me so often," said Ferdinand. "You should look for other company."

"What company?" asked Christopher.

"Young people."

Christopher thought about Kasimir Nessor. "I've been away too long," he said.

When he had earned enough money there were times he never left his room for days on end. "The money is lying in the street, waiting for you to pick it up," said his mother, but she understood his staying in bed, because often she herself only got up to cook something for her son and herself. He read books from the lending library, stared at the wall of the house opposite. He made up his mind to write a book about Moshe Dzwonicki.

One evening, in a faintly bohemian tavern two men were talking at the bar beside him. One said, "They didn't gas enough of them."

"Who are you talking about?" asked Christopher.

"The Jews, of course," said the man.

Christopher grabbed him by the collar. Although he was a heavily built man, he seemed to Christopher as light as a feather. He threw him over the bar like a shuttlecock. The man fell with his face in the bottles; green liqueur ran over his face; his face was red and green with blood and liqueur. The customers, young people for the most part, took Christopher's side, and he managed to escape before the police arrived—he ran away to avoid having to give his name. For days he was in such a good mood that his mother asked whether he had a girl.

"Fists are no argument," said Ferdinand.

"Fists are the only argument," said Christopher.

"You said yourself the young people were on your side," said Ferdinand.

Christopher thought about it and remembered what Kasimir Nessor had said. This time he did not throw away what he had written during the night. Some days later he read in the paper that people were awaiting "with interest and very mixed feelings" the premiere of *The Miracle Worker of Paestum*. The same morning there was a letter from Paris in the letterbox. "Your article is wonderful," wrote Martha. "It made me feel I was back in Ani Omer. I am longing for you. At the end of the month I may fly to Munich. Would you like me to?" He wrote her a letter, tore it up, ran to the post office and sent a telegram. The end of the month might mean in fourteen days, or twenty-five.

In the middle of April, late in the evening, the telephone rang. It was Frankfurt; Bull was on the line. "I'd rather tell you myself," said Bull. "Tomorrow, or the day after at the latest, you will read it in the paper. I had to write your story. It's because of the film. The premiere is in Frankfurt."

It was superstition, mere superstition, that had made Richard Wendelin visit Hermine Moellendorff. Like all those who live in a tangle of convictions without belief, Richard Wendelin would not have been able to explain this one particular superstition. He could not have said whether he finally yielded to Hermine Moellendorff's telephone call because he feared she would put a curse on him, or because he wanted to pacify fate by an act of charity, or because in his great days he had always spent the last few days before a premiere with her.

He had only been in her house for an hour; and already he regretted it. Hermine Moellendorff still owned the villa near the Starnberger See which she had bought after the success of *Michael the Ancestral Farmer* to escape from bombs and robbers. She still talked about "her" *Michael,* although the wrought-iron plaque with the name of the house on the wall facing the street had been carefully removed during the regrettable days of foreign occupation.

The older he became the more importance Richard Wendelin attached to keeping both feet firmly on the ground, so he was doubly irritated by this house which no longer seemed connected with reality. He could hardly believe that he had spent so much time here. It seemed so long ago. "You see, nothing has changed," said Hermine Moellendorff, but he found it difficult to believe that every day he had sat in this salon. What difference does it make, he told himself, whether Louis Seize furnishings are seven or eight years older? But even the slender Gobelins furniture decorated with La Fontaine's fables seemed so old that they were no longer the old ones: they had been antique; now they had become old. Hermine Moellendorff had become old, too, by more than the eight years during which he had met her only fleetingly. Incredible that she was only forty-five in January! If only she didn't try to hang on to youth at any price which, like a thief, runs all the faster the more ardently it is pursued. An intelligent woman, and an actress, too, should have known that too much makeup would emphasize the wrinkles she was trying to conceal; that a flowing hostess gown was all the more unbecoming the more theatrical it was; she should have known that youth hides bashfully when you talk about it, and that nothing links people less than memories. "I know, I know," she repeated whenever he spoke of his work, of the new film. She wanted to ingratiate herself with the present by this "I know," and yet with every "I know" she moved further away from the present. "I know"—and she sat in her house by the lake and gazed out onto the pine forest as though the past were hiding there among the trees and one morning would come toward her, smiling.

For days Richard Wendelin had been preoccupied, not so much by the film's premiere—in any case he had promised the producers he would not attend—as by the article about Christopher, which had appeared in a Frankfurt paper and had spread all over Germany. The newspapers, he thought, must have known long ago about his quarrel with his son, about the stay in Israel, and perhaps also about Christopher's return, but naturally they had saved the "sensation" for the opening night, a hand grenade, an ambush. Did they want to play the son against the father? Would they succeed? Like everything else, this was a question of addition and subtraction. They could number the son's virtues—for naturally that was how Christopher's actions would be presented—among the father's qualities; and then his own repentance would appear in a new light.

Or else they might subtract the son's actions from the father's virtues; then the public would respect these virtues even less. What about Christopher? Was he merely obeying his conscience? Conscience was grossly overestimated by the young. They probably thought it comes from science, from knowledge, while conscience, in reality, was a feeble conspirator, who could be convinced of anything. Or had Christopher himself suggested or at least inspired this wretched newspaper report, in order to destroy the first, still insecure and already dilapidated bridge which he, Richard Wendelin, had erected with such laboring effort? All this was unpleasant, but not half as bad as the third possibility, that the son had definitely broken free from his father, and was now acting as if his father were already dead and he was going his own way, not discarding but forgetting the name of Wendelin.

Richard Wendelin had wanted to talk about all this to the woman with whom he had shared his best years. She spoke as if they had parted yesterday. Like a good pupil trying to prove that she has done her homework, she named the stations of his past, now rather distant, life. The wound he had inflicted on her by his love for Christopher did not seem to have healed. She did not mention Christopher's name, she avoided all conversation that concerned him.

"I would go to Frankfurt, all the same," she said.

"What would I gain by it?"

"It's time you stepped out of the legend that has been woven round you. They have turned you into a symbol."

"I'm afraid one does not turn into a symbol by accident."

"You must defend yourself against it," she said.

"And how am I to do that?" he asked wearily.

"You haven't changed."

"I'm afraid that's true," he smiled.

She crossed her legs. The legs were slim, but the knees under the long skirt were pointed and bony.

"You know what I mean," she said. "Your personality, your charm are still irresistible. If the film is a success, the triumph should be associated with you."

"And if it isn't . . . ?"

"It will be a success. But if there's a scandal, as those who pull the strings want . . ."

"Whom do you call those who pull the strings?"

"The Jews, of course."

"Nonsense!" he said harshly. "The Jews are . . ." He was going to say, "The Jews are dead." "The Jews have gone," he said.

"You don't mean that seriously?"

"You're living on the moon."

"No, you're the one who is living on the moon," she said. "You talk about the presence of the Jews—as though that mattered! That's the Jew's strength, that he doesn't have to be present in order to exercise his influence. He doesn't want to be present, he's far too much of a coward for that. If I had been with you"—a brief pause—"if I had been with you, I would have sent a few people to Frankfurt. They would soon have found out who was stirring up trouble. The public have nothing against you. It's only the Jews who are forever stirring up trouble . . ."

He looked out at the garden that sloped down to the lake. The evening mist was dancing over the water, the opposite bank was no longer visible. He wondered what excuse he could find to leave before supper—the dining room with the mirror-lined walls, candlelight, the old housekeeper who had found it difficult not to greet him with a wink. "Nice to see you again, Herr Staatsrat." Candlelight, lace tablecloth, there were bound to be oysters, his favorite dish. "Nothing has changed, Richard." And then she would want to show him the bedroom, in which nothing had changed, either. There is no room that changes more than a bedroom that remains unchanged for eight years. Perhaps he had been wrong. The idea filled him with panic. Perhaps he had been wrong, perhaps it had not been Gertrude who brought him bad luck, but Hermine. That at the beginning everything had gone well, then, better and better, proved nothing; after all, in the end everything had gone badly and then worse and worse. Everything she said might be true; perhaps the Jews were pulling their strings, but even to think of it was contrary to the demands of the hour. It was the language of the past. The Jews had defeated Germany; one had to come to terms with them.

"The young are against me," he said, taking no notice of what she had just said. "It has nothing to do with the Jews."

"Exactly," she said righteously. "That's why you must go to Frankfurt. You have been pictured to the young as the Devil incarnate. If you look in their eyes, resistance will melt."

"I must phone Munich," he said. He had had an idea.

He went out into the hall, shutting the door behind him. He waited till his house answered. He said all sorts of things to Joseph which his butler could not understand, pretended to be waiting for an answer, and could not help smiling at the thought of how often in the past he had carried on similar conversations in the presence of Gertrude, when he wanted an excuse to go out, to Hermine. His deception almost made him feel young.

When he came back he feigned dismay—he could still teach the actors a thing or two. What he had feared had happened: there had been an urgent call from the producers, they wanted to talk to him, in an hour at the latest he had to be in Munich. The idea had occurred to him just at the right moment. Hermine would want to show him that she put his professional interests above her own desires. Perhaps she really hadn't changed.

She said she understood, although she had been looking forward to the evening. "Won't you at least try a few oysters?"

The housekeeper brought the oysters and black bread with Cheshire cheese. He promised he would ring her that night, after his discussion with the Lohmeyers, and also that he would think over her suggestion that he should go to Frankfurt.

Then he was sitting at the wheel of his car. His gloved hands gripped the wheel firmly, almost convulsively. The dark woods, the lights of the villages and the filling stations flew past; the black lake lay behind him. He thought about the premiere and Christopher, but he no longer thought about the *Michael* house. He wouldn't ring Hermine and he wouldn't see her again. He was sure now that she had brought him bad luck.

Christopher hired a Volkswagen and drove to Frankfurt. Karl Melchior had confessed to him that after the first article, which had "burst like a bomb," his paper planned a real shocker, a series of articles on "The Life of Christopher Wendelin, alias Abraham Avni."

I must prevent it. Perhaps they only wanted a shocker. The press is free, but it is behaving like a released prisoner forfeiting probation. They seem to want to play me off against my father. Even I once dreamed that I was speaking at a mass meeting, thousands of people, I delivered a speech against my father; there were cheers from everywhere. I didn't come home in order to write stupid articles about swans and truck drivers, but I don't want to be paraded about as the stuffed hope of the future, either. "Millions of Germans would have made *Ritual Murder*—they didn't happen to be film directors." Am I merely trying to protect the name Abraham Avni, a pure name? The Jews will say I went to the kibbutz to put up a show. Let Bull and his friends go for my father if they want to—"go for," their favorite expression. Only I don't want any part of it. I don't want to be my father's son, not even the lost son.

He reached Frankfurt in the afternoon. He left the Volkswagen outside the hotel to make it easier to ask the way to the newspaper offices as he went along.

Near the Hauptwache he saw his name for the first time on a hoarding. The name Wendelin was printed in heavy type, five times, six times. The creator of the shameful film *Ritual Murder,* the "Führer's film director, the armchair murderer . . ." The poster announced a student protest rally, a protest march to the cinema.

The blood rose to his head. Was it anger at his father because he had done what he had done, or anger because he did not defend himself? Was it anger at his father at all? He saw his father's face. Was he sitting in a Frankfurt hotel room, or had he stayed at home? Was he an armchair murderer? A new expression, an apt expression. Did it only apply to his father? or was he, was Christopher, the only one who could accuse him? Truth as a family possession, protected by patent, made by Christopher Wendelin. It might be that his father was speaking the truth when he wrote in his letter about active repentance. The Jews had a right to revenge—but did the Germans?

He hurried on. Someone had hastily stuck a red notice on a cigarette poster. "Protest rally against the showing of the new Wendelin film in Frankfurt. Speaker: Dr. Wilhelm Gerhardt, Member of Parliament." The new feeling that he had discovered—pity for the hunted animal, anger at the hunters, more anger than pity, or perhaps more pity than anger—grew in front of every poster. Passersby were lounging outside the newspaper offices. The article which he had already read in Munich appeared on the third page, occupying five columns. "Like father, unlike son." Two photographs, father and son. Richard Wendelin, photographed at Göring's wedding, handing the bride a bouquet of flowers. Two dozen people in the photograph, but no names underneath. Who were they? My father is the scapegoat, and all the others go unmentioned. Guests at a wedding.

The secretary had been expecting him. You could always guess the spirit of the boss, mirrored in the faces of the secretaries, like under a magnifying glass. The elderly woman looked like a nurse receiving patients. The door flew open, and Bull welcomed him loudly and heartily. Welcome, patient, to our clinic! The most modern equipment at your disposal. Kidney stones, gallstones, abscesses removed neatly and painlessly.

In Karl Melchior's room two young men rose from their armchairs; two were standing by the desk. Thus protected, it was easier for Bull to apologize for his treachery, to explain his motives. It was true that he had checked up on Christopher's life in Israel—"I stayed on two days longer, especially"—but he had not published the material before, wouldn't have published it at all—"Cross my heart, Christopher, you know me." But then Richard Wendelin's comeback—"You must admit that" —was really the last straw. "You know better than anyone how hard it is to shake our dear countrymen out of their sleep. Something had to happen. We're all counting on your collaboration."

One of the young men pushed a chair across to Christopher. No one sat down. They all walked up and down; only one of them stood by the window. Two Germans make a club, five Germans a police station. In a minute one of them will offer me a cigarette; the police are kind to prisoners they want to soften up.

"What do you mean by collaboration?" he asked.

Bull sat down behind the desk. They were planning a series of articles; he had already hinted at it on the phone. They knew a great deal about the life of Richard Wendelin; they knew a little about Christopher's, but not enough. "Obviously we want to go for your . . . for the man who directed *Ritual Murder*. That's a foregone conclusion, but we are a serious newspaper, Christopher, everything has to be accurate." The telephone rang. "The hall is packed," he said, turning to his colleagues. "In half an hour they will march on the cinema. You've got two photographers on the job?" The man by the window nodded. "We're not after a scoop," Bull went on. "Your name is Wendelin, that's good, and you were in Israel. Nevertheless you've come home to fight against the old Nazis . . . I don't want to put words in your mouth. We'll print anything you say." Naturally it had to be done in a hurry; the series was to start the day after tomorrow. "If you prefer, Helmut can take it down on tape."

In half an hour they would march on the cinema. Perhaps they expect me to be at the head of the column. That would be something for the photographers! A rally is unnecessary, a tape will be sufficient. If my father could see me here—a fair-haired boy and a stooge! He would think I had come to Frankfurt because of the film, in order to be there when they "go for" him, the way all the good sons "go for" their bad fathers. But date of birth is no indication of a man's quality. If Kasimir Nessor could be here! I wonder where my father is, whether his friends are with him or if he is alone. For years he has lived on sleeping pills; he was taking them even when I was living with him; perhaps he was only trying to put his conscience to sleep. He is not the suicidal type, but a few extra sleeping tablets . . . Christopher rose. "Is my father in Frankfurt?" he asked.

"No," said one of the young men. "He simply didn't have the nerve to come."

"As I was saying . . ." Karl Melchior picked up the thread, but Christopher interrupted him.

"What do you think you're doing?" he said. "The Jews will say I was trying to get publicity from my stay in the kibbutz, and the way you make things look, they would be right."

"Oh, come, come!" protested Karl Melchior. "I'm beginning to think you worry only about yourself. What would the Jews say if we let a Wendelin film be shown in Germany less than ten years after *Ritual Murder?*"

The man at the window came closer. "I think you're wrong, Karl," he said. "Herr Wendelin isn't thinking of himself at all, and that's the trouble. If you don't raise your voice now, Herr Wendelin, it will be interpreted as tacit approval."

Now they are playing up to my vanity. In a minute they will say: "Richard Wendelin, the armchair murderer . . ." And then I shall say: "He's my father." I don't want to defend him. I merely don't want to go after him.

"I haven't seen the film," he said.

"The film has nothing to do with it," said one of the young men.

The editor came in; evidently he had heard about the visit. Not a word about the articles, not a word about the demonstration. "A cigar Herr Wendelin?"—"No thanks, I don't smoke." A jovial man, middle fifties, pink, chubby, innocent as a suckling pig. He had heard that Herr Wendelin was working as a reporter. Free-lance work wasn't really the best thing; why didn't Christopher try his luck in Frankfurt? There was a splendid working atmosphere—a youthful staff. "Let the young people show what they can do, I always say." The five young men nodded agreement; the editor shook Christopher's hand and left the young man to the young men.

"You see," said Karl Melchior.

"What do I see?"

"The boss genuinely means every word. With us you would have the chance of your life."

"Are you trying to buy me?"

"Christopher!"

A new feeling had become overwhelming; he didn't care what the five young men thought of him. The half hour was up, the protest march was about to start. Young people were marching to war with his father, but why with his father, why only with his father? He stood up. "I let you get away with this lousy deal, Bull, because it was too late to do anything to stop it." The calmer I remain the better. If any more articles appeared, he said, he would take the best lawyer he could find, even if it cost him his last penny. "Tell the 'boss' that a single photograph of me will be enough . . . I am myself and no one else. What I have against my father is my affair . . ." He was already at the door when he went up to Karl Melchior again. "Be careful, Bull, otherwise I really will break your neck. You were always nothing but a weakling."

He rushed past the astonished secretary and down the stairs. He was already out in the street, yet in his mind he was still upstairs in the newspaper office. He imagined them looking at each other as they had looked at each other all the time. "He's his father's son," one would say, and he is probably right, I am my father's son. "Why did he go to Israel at all?" asks another, and Bull can't give an answer; I can't give an answer myself. "He didn't need to come home to say what he just said," says one, and I don't know myself why I came home.

He walked straight ahead, in the direction in which he had started out. He might just as well have gone the other way, but the neon advertisements were illuminated signposts, forcing him in a particular direction.

He found himself standing outside the movie house. The title of the film was in huge letters over the entrance: *The Miracle Worker of Paestum,* a Lohmeyer production, and underneath it in small letters, a necklace of glowing green beads: Directed by Richard Wendelin. The box office was besieged. They were lining up to see the new Wendelin, *The Miracle Worker of Paestum.* They don't give a damn about the miracle worker— what they care about is Richard Wendelin, the director of *Ritual Murder,* recalling a glorious era; it's not the Führer they want back, only the memory. The crowd pushed slowly forward, lined up in a disciplined way, just as they had lined up for bread in the glorious era. There was not a single famous name among the actors—Marina Bertolini, who had ever heard of her? A comeback, Bull had called it. And since the past never comes back, let us at least celebrate the return of Richard Wendelin! Anger descended upon Christopher like a great black bird; he pressed himself against the wall, looking at the well-fed, disciplined faces. *I behaved like a fool up there.* He had to use all his strength to prevent himself from spreading out his arms and blocking the crowd's path to the box office. *Bull was right, his friends were right. Had they all come to see a new Ritual Murder?* They would be disappointed. *I know my father; I know Richard Wendelin. He will make you applaud your splendid new state, as he once spurred you on to persecute and burn the Jews.* But Christopher stayed against the wall, turned up his coat collar.

Because he stood against the wall, he did not notice the restlessness of the crowd until another crowd of people crossed the street toward the cinema. The traffic stopped. The cars stood still as though bewitched. The crowd came from the direction of St. Paul's Church, four abreast, carrying placards. The placard *"Will you permit . . ."* The young men planted themselves on the edge of the sidewalk, a few on the other side of the street, all of them dignified, all of them disciplined. *"A man who made anti-Jewish films must not be allowed to film any more in Germany"; "Put a stop to Wendelin, the man who made films for the concentration camps"; "We don't want Wendelin in Frankfurt."* A man near the box office said, "Impudent scum!" A woman pressed her handbag to her. "Bunch of bums!" Another, wearing a felt hat like a steel helmet, shouted, "Where are the police?"

The police were there, as always. The sirens of the radio patrol cars soon cut into the nervous hooting of the private cars. There they were in their neat blue uniforms, rubber truncheons in hand; they jumped out of the cars as though to charge an enemy. "Move along, there! Get going! Off the sidewalk!" The sidewalk obviously belonged to the good citizens who want to see *The Miracle Worker of Paestum,* the road to the good citizens who want to go home to their wives, children, and desk lamps.

The wall of students stood on both sides of the street. They did not move; only a few marched up and down, the placards above their heads. A red-haired boy passed Christopher, a child's face with a tiny nose covered with freckles—eighteen, nineteen at the most. Christopher worked it out: he must have been eight or nine when the "catastrophe" came, the "collapse." "Your generation must be an example to the next." What am I waiting for? I ought to take the placard from his hands, I ought to carry it against the police, I, Christopher Wendelin, son of Richard Wendelin. I ought to shout to the crowd who I am. A Wendelin doesn't get stoned in Germany, but I ought to shout out to them that I'm not standing in line, but rather carrying a placard: that's why I came home from Israel, that's why I'm at home. But between the crowd and the redhead, suddenly the face of Richard Wendelin appeared. Christopher saw the sad, dismayed face of his father, heard his father's sad, disillusioned voice: You too, my son Christopher?

He wanted to slip away, but it was too late. He didn't see what had happened, he only saw the effect of what had occurred. Someone, quite a long way away from him, had struck a placard out of a student's hand. The student had bent down, and a blow had hit him on the back of the head. Four or five of his comrades came to his aid. They found themselves facing a police cordon. The wall of students had broken up. The woman with the felt helmet was yelling, "Police! Police!" Cars were hooting, alarm sirens wailing, and amidst it all, the bell announcing the beginning of the performance was ringing. It sounded like a child crying.

Swinging their rubber truncheons above their heads, the police went for the demonstrators. "Placards down!" shouted one of them as he hurried past Christopher and knocked the placard out of the hands of the redhead with the freckles. Two policemen were dragging a struggling student to a car. One of them was holding him by the legs, the other by the head. The boy's behind was dragging along the tarmac; he was still kicking out with his legs, but then the kicking ceased. A third policeman had struck him on the head with his truncheon in passing, and now the boy hung like a sack of potatoes in the arms of the men in uniform.

The Miracle Worker of Paestum was up there in lights. It was not called *Ritual Murder,* or *We'll Die for You,* yet blood was flowing over the Frankfurt street. Glass was breaking; a man had gone head-first through the window of a radio shop; a policeman lashed out at another one, lying on the ground; the bell announcing the start of the film was still ringing. Why did you do it, father? Didn't you know this would happen? No, you didn't know, perhaps you really didn't know, you say you never knew, but what is the use of that? Blood is flowing and you have done it!

"Police!" screamed the woman, but it had long since become superfluous. The police were there, as always, dutifully carrying out their function. The placards lay on the ground. A few students still clinging to their placards were pushed away, farther and farther off, into the darkness. A man by the box office stamped on a placard, *"Will you permit . . ."* Only tattered remnants were left. A policeman dragged the redhead past Christopher; the boy's face was smeared with blood.

And I do nothing. They'll take the students to the police station; there it will continue. They dared to rise up against my father. Oh, yes, it was only a minor incident, it's all over. In the middle of the roadway stands a policeman regulating the traffic, the symbol of calm and order, the victor, because now the cars are slowly moving off again, first on one side, then on the other. The pedestrians are moving off, strolling past the movie house, and there is a second victor, also in a neat uniform, the man who is taking the tickets from the last of the audience. The show can begin.

Christopher crossed the street and looked up at the wall of the theater. The green lights had gone out. *The Miracle Worker of Paestum,* Marina Bertolini, a Lohmeyer production, the names of the actors. And where the name Wendelin had been there was a black hole.

He didn't want to see the film, didn't want to know anything about it. But when the film was shown in Munich, a week later, he went to see it.

The Munich premiere caused no scandal. It would have

been taking too much notice of the "potboiler," as the critics had dubbed *The Miracle Worker of Paestum.* The reviewers had scarcely mentioned the director's past. They called his technique out of date, his camera work old-fashioned, his realism outmoded. They had cast him on the scrap heap to rust like used cars; in such cases, no one asks about their origin.

Christopher purposely came late; the theater was already dark. At the appearance of the name Wendelin there were a few catcalls, but they sounded dutiful rather than heartfelt. Had the critics been fair? Neither fair nor unfair. They were bad graphologists, unable to distinguish the character from the handwriting. *The Miracle Worker of Paestum* was like minor works by great masters, which, even if they are unsuccessful, reveal the hand of the master in a detail, an expression, a color. Nor did they see that the new Wendelin, helplessly and despite himself, was the old one. Who else would have turned the peasant girl's brother into a Neapolitan Siegfried, a hero *sans peur et sans reproche*? He didn't wait until the lights went on in the half empty house. By the time the audience came out he was already sitting in the nearest tavern. They had not understood his father, either in good times or in bad: a sinner condemned for a crime he had not committed, accused of a crime of which he was not guilty.

The projected series of articles had not appeared in Frankfurt, but the first article did not go by unnoticed. An article which Christopher had written on pawnshops, and which he had delivered to the Munich editors, was not printed, and when, fearing the worst, he inquired about it, the editor sent for him.

It had been a breach of confidence, said the editor drily, for Christopher to have concealed his name, to have called himself Caesar Wendt. It was not a question of persecuting innocent relatives, as the Nazis had done; on the contrary, Christopher had made the paper a laughingstock in journalistic circles. "You write local chitchat for us and give the scoop to Frankfurt." It had been unfriendly, if not unethical, but not by any means irreparable. The paper would reveal to its readers in a brief note who "C.W." really was and why "C.W." had signed his article

on Israel Abraham Avni, and then Christopher Wendelin's autobiography could begin, half personal, half political. "It will be
sufficient if you just mention your father in passing. We see it as
a repudiation by the younger generation of the older generation,
as a demonstration on the part of a new Germany particularly
concerned about a reconciliation with the Jews." Christopher
said No, but he was wrong if he thought that his refusal would
be accepted without further consequences. "I understand you,
I understand you very well, Herr Wendelin," said the editor.
"But your name has become a symbol. Most of our readers have
not seen the Frankfurt article. If you're not anti-Wendelin, then
you must be pro-Wendelin. Five hundred indignant readers'
letters, two thousand regular orders cancelled—we can't afford
that."

April passed, the confusing month at the turn of the seasons.
Martha wrote that she had to take the place of an interpreter
in London who had fallen ill and would not be able to come to
Munich until mid-May. It was a cordial letter, but heartless,
friendly but showing no impatience, and it made him ashamed
of the impatient telegram he had sent her.

In accordance with his nature, he had lived frugally, had
saved some money; but he knew he might soon be a burden on
his mother again. He had to face the struggle of existence. After
each day of idleness, he felt more than ever that he must not
allow himself to remain paralyzed any longer.

So the paper won't print my "local chitchat." There are other
newspapers, there are publishers looking for books, there are
theaters looking for plays. Not unwritten ones of course. I lie
on my bed staring at the wall of the house opposite. Two or
three months after the war—my father was in prison—Uncle
Bertram introduced me to an American. "Wendelin?" said the
American. "That's a bad name." Perhaps he thought it was
funny, perhaps he expected me to say: "Richard Wendelin? I'm
no relation of his." A shock for a fifteen-year-old, the psychoanalysts would say; it's difficult to get over a shock like that, but
psychoanalysts don't know everything. At one time, when I was
sixteen, I suddenly was unable to write my name. Christopher
Wendelin, Lower Sixth. I used to write Wenelin and Vendelin

and Wennelin, and couldn't get it right. A gift for the psychoanalysts. But what if the shock becomes an excuse? That is the
stage in which I find myself today—can you help me by any
chance, doctor? I sleep till two in the afternoon, the effect of
shock—or out of laziness? I could tell a publisher my idea for a
play; that's enough to make money these days. But first I would
have to give the secretary my name. Am I afraid of secretaries?
Or of the sentence, "Oh, you're the son of the director of *Ritual
Murder?*" Or worse still, "You're the courageous young man
who was in Israel? A very good story, but why don't you write
your own?" No one who is afraid sleeps as well as I do. Yet out
of fear I sleep till two. Moreover, I have other suspicious excuses.
Money is everywhere; they call it the "German miracle," a nice
combination of words: if a German peasant girl sees a vision, it
is not the Mother of God she sees but the tax collector. I haven't
inherited your ambition, father, and what ambition I had I lost
in Israel. Eighteen pounds a month, board and lodging, two
stamps free. But I am twenty-five, and no longer living in the
world of the kibbutzim. Prove yourself, and that means more
than eighteen pounds a month. If you have no money you become a burden on your mother, and to borrow money from a
friend when you are in good health is immoral. So, the path to
morality is through money. Whether you put money to a good
purpose, or whether you drink it away, whether you buy inde-
pendence with it or spend it on whores, whether you refuse to
compromise because you have money or compromise all you
want because you have it—you can make all these decisions
only after you have earned money. The path of morality is
through money. If I were a Socialist I would have had to stay
in the kibbutz. Moshe Dzwonicki used to praise my diligence.
So I'm not lazy, I'm only afraid of responsibility. I hated being
a child, and because I'm scared of responsibility I am becoming
fourteen again.

Once more he thought of his father. "In all lotteries," his
father had said, "there is only one first prize. But if you haven't
a ticket you can't possibly win it." A good saying. He wouldn't
win the first prize. But he must buy a ticket.

* * *

Since his return from Israel he had avoided society; now he went out to meet people, stopped everyone who was selling lottery tickets.

The taverns and restaurants were packed and everywhere youth predominated. It was almost as though they had replaced the occupation troops, as though they had put the old to flight, as though the old had crawled into their holes. The young met one another on the dance floor, from table to table, at the bar counter; they didn't introduce themselves, they didn't ask names. Youth was the identification mark; they belonged to the same generation, that was enough.

Most of the young people whom Christopher met had heard of him. Because he had been Abraham Avni he was no longer Wendelin, he was Christopher Wendelin. They knew this, but they didn't care. They wanted to have fun; they talked little to each other; they sang and spoke little. Much had changed for the better. The longing for freedom had come out into the open, and if Christopher felt ill at ease because he thought his new friends confused a new freedom with free time, he blamed it on himself. He met some with whom he had been in the Naval Hitler Youth, and they talked of times past. But after such conversations, Christopher was never sure whether what his former comrades regretted were the years of evil or merely the lost years in which they had been forced to spend their Sundays marching, doing gymnastics, drilling. As he sat at the bar, he looked at the dancers and had a vision. The jazz suddenly broke off, the legs that had been contorted to the rhythm of boogie-woogie rested for a moment, the eyes that had been directed toward the dancer's own legs as though at a foreign body or a wriggling animal became fixed, the relaxed muscles tensed, chests were inflated, and then a march rang out. The floor went into motion again; now the legs were thrown powerfully forward, the tips of the toes shot up, hands were pressed to thighs, the boogie-woogie had turned into the goosestep, and youth was doing the goosestep once again. He was relieved that they were dancing boogie-woogie; he was relieved that the free, wild rhythms were echoing from across the free, wild distance; it was good that Negro soldiers were dancing with white girls and Negro girls were sitting at the bar; it was good that they had scared away the old people and that they did not remember—but wasn't it possible that only the rhythm had changed? Was political conviction a matter of music? And since it might well be only a matter of rhythms, wouldn't the old rhythm come back and suppress the new one again; how much security could boogie-woogie give you, after all?

There were conversations, sometimes, at Ferdinand's, in the bars, late at night, or when they went to the home of a young man or a young girl to drink Coca-Cola or whiskey. Sometimes they talked about the past, but Christopher was dismayed to find that although he was almost always in agreement with everyone and everyone with him, they met in the void of commonplaces, where people can agree without understanding each other. The son of an industrialist, in rebellion against his father, could talk against the nascent nationalism; but then he said that the nationalism of the Americans was in no way different from German nationalism—and what was Christopher to reply, since it was true, and untrue only in so far as no one had ever heard of an American Auschwitz. The son of a lawyer never spoke of his father other than as the "old Nazi," but he lived with the "old Nazi" and planned to inherit his practice. Once they took an older man along with them from a bar because everyone felt sorry for him. He had insisted on introducing himself as "stinking corpse Meyer," with good reason, as he thought, because when he came home from a Russian POW camp only two years ago he had found that his wife had meanwhile married somebody else. "Dead is dead," she had told the man who had been declared dead, and asked him kindly to behave like a corpse. But when they got back to the apartment, after a few whiskies, the corpse Meyer began to curse Russians, Jews and Americans and to sing the Horst Wessel song. They put him out in the street. Someone said, "His wife is quite right, he stinks." But they didn't waste another word on him, and it seemed to Christopher that his friends imagined the past could be simply put out in the street, where it would stink without poisoning them. There were discussions, but there were also red lights at which they stopped. In the middle of open roads

traffic lights sprang up from the ground, and the red light refused to go out. Someone said their fathers' regime had been a
regime of criminals, but it was a shame that the Americans had
not halted the Russian advance on Berlin. Someone said it had
started with Coventry and Rotterdam, but the Allies ought to
have spared Dresden. Someone said the whole of Germany was
responsible for the persecution of the Jews, but if they were
talking about bad parents, then the suppression of the Negroes
in America was the work of bad parents, too. Red lights came
on and the discussion ceased. Perhaps Karl Melchior had been
right, perhaps Christopher had been in Israel too long. The
world was as it was, Germany was as it was; he had to come to
terms with it.

He sought the company of young intellectuals—Ferdinand
knew a great many. "You will feel at home with them," he said.
"They can smooth the path for you." They read poems, unfinished plays, chapters from novels to one another; they called
all these "texts," as though on the one hand to emphasize the
fragmentary nature of these endeavors, on the other to under-
line their biblical finality. Almost everything Christopher heard
was unintelligible to him; he remained isolated among people
of his own age who seemed to understand everything. Did they
really understand? Did they only pretend to understand? Why
did they pretend? He couldn't help recalling the Indian language of children, put together out of meaningless syllables and
sounds from nature. Why did these earnest young men employ
such an infantile jargon? Children invent secret languages in
order to shut out adults from their circle. Now the language
had become so secret that the children no longer understood
each other. Or was this language really not so childish at all? Was
it an attempt to speak, write and read a different language
from their fathers? There was the healthy distrust of everything
smooth and conceited and accepted and sure of itself; but distrust implied doubt, and none of these young intellectuals
seemed to doubt, none asked, all answered. Was he being unfair? Not to accept any answer was as conformist as not to ask
any questions. Suspicion of every answer was just as German as

had been the demand to tolerate every answer. Intolerance of the finished raised the fragmentary to an imperative.

The young intellectuals asked him to read something of his own, but although he had meanwhile finished the first act of his play, he feared that everyone would understand it and ridicule him. When the word "conformist" was uttered, they all crossed themselves, but they almost all wore the same haircut—smooth and combed forward, Bert Brecht as a dictator of fashion. They almost all wore the same suits and the same glasses—rimless lenses with only a gold strip over the nose; and none of them liked what the others disliked. When you had heard the opinion of one of them on Beckett's *Waiting for Godot* you had heard all of them. Whoever was young was right, and whoever did not experiment was dismissed as a Grandpa. They all seemed intent on pleasing one another. All of them said they belonged to the "Left," but they turned up their noses when there was talk of the masses—out of arrogance, perhaps, but even that wasn't certain. Maybe they knew why they feared the masses and thought themselves "intellectual" when they really were exiles from their own people. In the cabarets which they visited and on whose programs they collaborated, they hit out at the "German miracle" with unfailing success; but outside the cabarets stood the authors' Porsches and Sunbeams and MG's. Christopher thought of the kibbutz and wondered why he wasn't a Socialist and yet didn't own a Porsche. The most successful of the circle, who had published a novel and a volume of short stories, had become famous through the story of the adventures of a deaf mute in the Third Reich. They resented Christopher's inability to join in the general applause—it was very funny to be a deaf mute in the Third Reich, but the deaf mute had been sent in error to a concentration camp, and millions had been sent to concentration camps not in error. No one felt responsible for the fate of a deaf mute, and they fought with irony against the living. It did not bring a single dead man back to life; mockery struck the objects of the present, but it minimized the past, and the past was not funny, and anyone who could laugh became an accomplice. Did they laugh? No, they only mocked.

They had irony without humor; the smile lay only around the corners of their mouths, and their hands were as heavy as their hearts.

Christopher grew more and more lonely. He longed for the kibbutz. He often thought it was more sensible to converse with the wall of the opposite house than with the people he knew. But in the studio next door Gertrude Wendelin received her friends. The glasses clinked; Wolffi, blind Frieda's dog, barked; or in the studio next door sat the wife of an industrialist and had her fat painted away; or in the studio next door there was silence. He fled into town, stood at bars, drank beer, danced boogie-woogie, felt electrified by the rhythm, opened his collar, imagined he felt at ease, clapped out the time, listened to incomprehensible poems, clapped applause, let himself drift, drank beer, drank whiskey, took off his jacket, discovered his own body in the rhythm, sweated, was almost run over, raced away from the police in the low seat of a low car, looked down a barmaid's bosom, saw pictures made of dabs of paint, danced till dawn, avoided conversation, felt old and tired.

Inge hadn't really been the most easygoing girl in the world; there were others who were even more easygoing. Many had one-and-a-half-room apartments, many had Volkswagens. They were easygoing and honest, they had the same desires as men, every man needs a woman, inhibitions were out. Why should they deny their desires? One took Christopher back to her apartment, the other took him in her Volkswagen, a third said in apology, "I can't take you home. I live with my parents." One was called Karin, the second Anneliese, he couldn't remember the name of the third. It was sordid to have ulterior motives, but then, no one really had ulterior motives, it was all out in the open. His friends said he was lucky with women. Once a girl spoke to him in a coffee bar and said she knew him, and he really did know her, but he only remembered that she had very small pointed breasts, like a lemon, though in the coffee bar the girl was wearing a loose sweater. They must be right, he was lucky with women. It was now May, and Martha had written from London that she was still busy . . . perhaps in June! Once he woke up in a strange flat. Beside him lay a note: "I've got to go out. You will find milk and eggs in the fridge. Don't forget to turn off the gas." One of his friends recommended that he take a coat hanger with him in the car—it was a pity to spoil his suit if he had to undress in a hurry. He didn't have a car. A girl with whom he wanted to sleep went to bed with some-one else, but Christopher wasn't angry with him, and the other didn't have a guilty conscience. He said, "Any time I can do you a favor in return."

"I don't mind if you talk about girls," said Ferdinand. "It doesn't worry me. All my friends tell me about girls."

There was nothing to tell. "It isn't true what people say. The girls do talk about love. It's just that they don't care whether you still talk about it next morning." They talked of love be-tween a bit of sentimentality, a bit of longing for Grandma, re-version to the Victorian era. Everything was brief, a quick reac-tion, a short, short circuit. Young men and young women loved past each other, like trains passing in the night. Sometimes a train stopped on the open track and waited for the train going in the opposite direction. But Christopher did not wait, and no one was waiting for him.

Indecision was part of his nature; decision was like a fever that came over him. One morning when he woke, he felt fever-ish. He looked at his watch, an object which for months had seemed superfluous to him. It was five to nine. The May sky was cloudless; in the trees in the front garden the birds were twittering. He went to the window, his eyes flew after them. He was seized with impatience; he didn't know what he had missed, and perhaps he had merely never stopped to gaze at the birds. They described meaningless arcs that seemed to him more meaningful than anything he had seen for a long time. He didn't notice that there was a house opposite. He did everything differently from the way he had been doing it for months. His mother was asleep. He tiptoed into the kitchen, made break-fast, did not eat it in the kitchen but took it into his room on a tray. He chose a light suit, a white shirt, looked carefully among his ties. All his money was in a box; he didn't know how much it was. Now he counted it; there was rather more than he had imagined. Among the notes he found an Israeli pound; among the coins, twenty Israeli agorot. He wondered whether to ring the big publisher whose name Ferdinand had given him, but decided to take a chance. He looked at his watch. At twenty past ten he set out.

When he went to see Ferdinand, in the early afternoon, the doctor was just leaving the house. "He isn't feeling well," said Ferdinand's mother. "No, no, stay just the same. I'm sure he would like to see you."

Ferdinand was sitting in his wheelchair by the open door to the terrace. His right hand was wrapped in a cloth; he stretched out his left to Christopher. "A boring mess," he said. "Paralysis in two fingers. But it will clear up. It was the same with my right eye, but it cleared up. Mother is too easily scared." He knew about his mother's bleak bulletins and began almost every conversation by reassuring his visitor. He laughed. "You look like the cat who has swallowed the canary. Have you been to see Ludwig?"

"I'm going away," said Christopher. He was not surprised that Ferdinand had guessed where he had been. Ferdinand lived his friends' lives; he always knew what they were doing. "I'm going away," he repeated, and as though he didn't trust his own good fortune he added, "I'm probably going away."

He burst out with his story. The publisher had received him at once—Ludwig Ludwig, also called Ludwig the Great. "I'm no longer surprised at his name, he is such a full personality his family name wasn't enough for him. He underlined it with a second 'Ludwig.' " Anyhow, Ludwig Ludwig had been enthusiastic about the subject of the play, had asked himself and Christopher why no one had ever thought before of dramatizing this heroic epic of the Jews. He had run through the first act in Christopher's presence. His readers were already on the job, but Ludwig the Great remarked that he trusted his own instinct more than his readers. They would draw up the contract by tomorrow, the day after tomorrow at the latest. However, Ludwig Ludwig had urged, indeed demanded, that Christopher should go to Warsaw and there hunt through the archives for further details not generally know. He should let the spirit of the place work on him and, if he thought it right, complete the play on the spot. It was splendid, he said, that Christopher had known a leader of the uprising personally, but the point was to present the tragic tableaux like a report. "I was impressed," said Christopher, "at how carefully he plans to handle the theme. 'Everything has got to be right,' he said. 'This is a subject which will make all invention appear frivolous.'" The publisher would pay Christopher's expenses. "He mentioned an advance that took my breath away."

Ferdinand remained grave. Christopher loved this calm and serene face with the transparent skin and the transparent eyes. Ferdinand did not look older than he was—twenty-eight—not tired and experienced, but rather like someone who has been born with wisdom and has remained pure despite his knowledge.

"Are you sure that Ludwig persuaded you to go to Poland?" he asked. "Wasn't it the other way round?"

"I don't know. It just happened." Christopher placed his hand on his friend's hand. "I shall be back soon," he said.

He wasn't thinking of himself, said Ferdinand. After all, it was he who had sent Christopher to Ludwig, the great Ludwig. "Will you get a visa?"

"Ludwig the Great has good contacts, and naturally my name will help me, as in Israel." But he missed the joy in Ferdinand's voice.

"You won't be back for a long time," said Ferdinand.

"You mean I'm running away."

"Perhaps."

"It's possible," said Christopher.

They looked out into the garden. Spring had suddenly come. Christopher was surprised that he had admitted the truth so readily. I don't often lie, but I don't always tell the truth, either. Ferdinand always tells the truth, almost the whole truth. Character is often a chameleon; it takes on the color of its environment. Perhaps there have to be two before either can take on his own character.

"In Poland you will have no excuse," said Ferdinand. "You're not going to Poland under a false name."

"Abraham Avni wasn't a false name."

"But it wasn't your own. You won't have the crutch of being looked at accusingly because of your father. Fathers' sins are very convenient, Christopher. Firstly, they are not your own, so you don't have to have a bad conscience. Secondly, they are nevertheless held against you, so you are entitled to feel offended. Self-pity is a fine excuse for anger. In Poland no one will care that you are German and that your father's name was Wendelin, because the Communists hold that society is responsible for the individual. To begin with, they will think that you are a product of a rotten bourgeois society. Then they will say that you can be redeemed by a Socialist society that has performed miracles."

"And perhaps they will be right," retorted Christopher. "In the kibbutz I thought too much about the Jews and too little about Socialism."

"With the Israeli visa you became a Jew," he said. "No sooner do you think you're going to get a Polish visa than you become a Socialist. Do you know the story of the goose girl who always sought the green grass on the other side of the river?"

Christopher said nothing. Is Ferdinand being unfair to me? Here I'm at the end of my tether. Here they don't want me, they only want my autobiography. The only other thing they're interested in is how I'm going to kill my father. Honor your father or strike him dead; there's no third way.

And because he was disappointed that Ferdinand did not respond to his enthusiasm with enthusiasm, because he wanted to give a reason for turning his back on his "beloved homeland," he talked of his disappointments. He had taken Ferdinand's advice and sought out the young—and then what? Only a restricted circle, naturally. People always say: You went to the wrong place. The others are the right ones. Don't go to the intellectuals, go to the workers! Don't go to the workers, go to the intellectuals! What do you expect if you look for youth in the nightclubs? What do you expect if you look for youth in the gym clubs? Had not Ferdinand himself talked about self-pity, angry self-pity? Did that refer only to him? "We weep so bitterly over our helplessness that anyone who comes around can rape us. Our fathers were Nazis, we aren't. What are we?"

"It won't be long before you start calling for the fostering of the positive element in German life," interposed Ferdinand. "Like the youth of the gym clubs."

"I expected opposition. I found scepticism, but no opposition. Everything offered to us we turn over ten times before accepting. We refuse to be deceived anymore. But then what?" Refusing to be deceived was a passive attitude; it meant letting the others try. Those who will try are the old ones. He strode up and down. "We stood in the streets and waved flags and saluted flags and let the Wehrmacht and the SA and the SS march past us. Young people were onlookers then; they are onlookers now. What's the difference?"

"The most important thing," said Ferdinand. "We neither wave flags nor salute them."

"Come off it," retorted Christopher. "We're still lining the streets. We don't wave flags and we don't salute them, but we still line the streets. Do you know what we are? Disgruntled. Skeptical. We've been betrayed! So we don't wave flags and we don't salute them—but do we pull them down? We're rebels without rebellion. It was never worthwhile, we say. Today's skepticism is as convenient as yesterday's discipline."

"You're forgetting one little thing," Ferdinand interrupted him. "A very small little thing. There was something after Nazism. The atom bomb dropped on Hiroshima."

"Of course," said Christopher. "The end of the world. But can we be so sure the world is coming to an end? Do we do anything to stop it? All we do is line the streets to greet the end of the world. No cheering this time, no flags. Only immobility. We haven't gassed any Jews, we didn't drop the atom bomb on Hiroshima. It's nothing to do with us, so we don't oppose it. We'd rather find things bad than make things good. We all think it would serve mother right if I froze to death, or father —and so on." He broke off. "But why are we talking about it?"

"We're always talking about it," said Ferdinand.

As though to excuse himself, Christopher said, "I only wanted to explain to you—in case I stay away a long time."

"You've met the wrong people," said Ferdinand.

"Do you know the others?"

"Some."

CHRISTOPHER AND HIS FATHER

Christopher heard the anger in his own voice as he said, "Why didn't you introduce me to them?"

"It wouldn't have been worthwhile. You would have run away anyhow. You should have got to know them yourself. Two girls in one week is too many."

"I didn't only go around with girls. Your magnificent intellectuals . . ."

"You got mixed up with a group of provincial snobs. The more class differences disappear, the greater snobbery becomes."

"So I got to know the majority," said Christopher.

"No country becomes tolerable until you discover the minority. The search is more difficult and more worthwhile. Moreover, even in the majority there is an invisible minority. You lined the street and let youth march past you. You didn't mix with the crowd. You expected opposition and forgot that skepticism is the basis of opposition. First, people don't want to see anything, then they want to see everything black. In the end the outlines emerge from the darkness. No one is responsible for your impatience but yourself." He smiled. "You might be right when you keep saying you're a seismograph. But you are a seismograph that is so sensitive that it breaks at the slightest tremor."

"Maybe," said Christopher without conviction. "To me it is no coincidence that you have remained my only friend."

"The others have less time to think," said Ferdinand.

They talked about their friendship. Christopher did not shy away from sentimentality. It even seemed as though from the very beginning he had only wanted to talk about their friendship. Ferdinand concealed sentimentality behind gaiety. He seemed to see no reason for an emotional farewell.

The cloth around Ferdinand's hand fell to the ground. Christopher picked it up, wrapped it around the numb fingers.

"You must try and get well," he said.

"I shall try to get my fingers moving again," said Ferdinand. He wouldn't get well, he went on after a pause, nor would he die. He talked like someone who lives outside his illness. Immediately afterward, he turned to Christopher, turned to another life, not necessarily more worth living, only more worth being concerned about. "Will you see Martha before you leave?" he asked.

Christopher blushed. "She has written again. She isn't coming. Later! She has had a lover for a long time. Bill, or someone else."

"Did you write that to her?"

"No, of course not."

"Why 'of course not'? You gave her up as you gave up Israel. You waited for Moshe Dzwonicki to press a gun into your hand." He spoke of Moshe Dzwonicki as though he knew him personally. "You condemn the others because they line the streets. And yet you always wait for someone to press the gun into your hand."

He felt that Ferdinand was being unfair to him, but what could he answer him? He hadn't told Ferdinand the whole truth.

With a sudden decision—it was time for a farewell and he was trying to defend himself—he began to talk about the night in the Jordan Valley. "I didn't sleep with her," he said. "I don't know why not."

He did not expect an explanation from Ferdinand; he already regretted having taken his friend into his confidence. Six years ago the first signs of the mortal illness had showed themselves in Ferdinand; for years he has been tied to his chair. He was not mistaken. Here was the barrier that understanding and friendship were unable to surmount.

"You should see her," said Ferdinand drily.

Quickly, not very skillfully, Christopher beat a retreat. "I'm not emigrating, you know. I'm not writing my play for Poland. The only thing is—Ludwig must have felt it—I can't write my play here."

"I'll believe all that when you have finished your play," said Ferdinand.

"You don't think I'll finish it?"

"I hope your Polish, Socialist experience won't prevent it. Like the experience in Israel. One has to start somewhere. Probably it is best to start with the past."

Christopher leaned against the open door. If only Ferdinand

were well! With Ferdinand I could have met different people, I would have seen them with different eyes. With Ferdinand I would have got to know a different Germany. I wouldn't have had to run away. Or Ferdinand would have come with me to Poland. There he sits in his wheelchair; a new center of inflammation has formed between spinal cord and brain, two fingers are paralyzed, and who knows what will happen tomorrow? He looks out into the garden into which I can run; I am six feet tall and can tear up a tree by its roots, yet I want to lean on Ferdinand.

"Perhaps I have no talent," he said. "Perhaps I don't finish anything because I know it won't be worth anything."

"I'm more inclined to think you tell yourself it won't be worth anything so that you don't have to finish it."

"The perfect picture of the dilettante."

"If it were a question of your talent, only your plays and your novels would remain unfinished. But Israel remained unfinished, and Germany has remained unfinished, and your love for Martha has remained unfinished."

Ferdinand wrapped himself more closely in his blanket. It was beginning to get cool. The wind was stirring the grass on the lawn, where winter had still left its marks.

"Shall I shut the door?" asked Christopher.

"Couldn't you take me for a little walk?"

They called it "going for a walk." Christopher carefully lifted the wheelchair up over the step. Then he pushed it to and fro on the terrace, four steps one way, four steps the other.

"Why are you so sure that I won't come back soon?" said Christopher.

"I don't know," said Ferdinand. "It's a feeling, no more." He laughed. "But although I have been hard on you, I have a good feeling."

"If I am homesick," said Christopher, "I shall be homesick for you." He didn't say: I shall be away a long time.

"Although I have been hard on you?"

"Far too little," said Christopher.

"Anyhow, you won't only be homesick for me," said Ferdinand.

*   *   *

In the doorway of his home the guide dog Wolffi jumped up at him. Gertrude Wendelin was painting her blind friend, Frieda. Frieda was sitting, whiskey glass in hand, in an armchair, calling angrily to Wolffi who, as a model, should have been lying at her feet but instead had walked out of the picture wagging his tail.

"Your father called up," said Gertrude Wendelin.

"Did you talk to him?"

"Yes. Just imagine, for the first time in ten years he deigned to talk to me."

"What does he want?"

"He has to speak to you urgently."

As she took a step back from the easel she observed Christopher out of the corner of her eye. He caught her distrustful glance; perhaps she was trying to guess whether he had been seeing his father in secret.

He took a bottle of milk from the refrigerator, poured out a glass, remained standing by the kitchen door.

"I've got good news," he said. "Ludwig Ludwig has accepted my play."

"Hurray!" cried Frieda, and drained her glass.

"You've only finished the first act," said his mother.

"I'm going to finish the play in Warsaw."

"You're going away?"

He heard the dismay in her voice. "Possibly next week," he said.

"How long will you be away?"

"Three months, perhaps four. First I shall work in the archives, then I shall write the play."

"Couldn't you have written it at home?"

He did not answer. In a minute she would say that he was running away as Ferdinand had. It was a good thing his father had only rung today; otherwise she would have said he was running away from him. She thought that anyway. She thought the Frankfurt premiere had upset him. Or the article on Abraham Avni. Since then she had treated him like a sick person. Tenderness? She had had urgent business in Nuremberg when he came back from Israel. He was being ungrateful. You could live your own life and nevertheless love others. She would miss him, but he did not want to be treated as if he were sick.

"You can pour me another glass of whiskey," said Frieda.

She held the glass out to him with a firm hand and looked at him as she did so, although she saw nothing. Her eyes were bright, as the eyes of the blind are, bright eyes in a small face.

"In your place I would stay in Poland," she said.

"Since when have you been a Communist?" Gertrude Wendelin snapped at her.

"I'm not a Communist," protested Frieda, and embarked on a long, confused speech. You didn't need to be a Communist to see that on the other side of the Iron Curtain they were getting things done. Maybe the future didn't belong to them, but they had mastered the past. "They have simply prohibited it. You're all blind," she said. "You see too much and hear too little. If a sign says 'keep off the grass,' then people keep off. That's so everywhere, not only in this country. People love the sign with *Verboten!* written on it more than grass, but that doesn't matter. If grass is to grow over the past, people must be forbidden to walk on it. For a young man . . ."

"Shut up," Gertrude Wendelin interrupted the blind woman. "In another ten minutes you can go."

There was silence. The dog had wandered off into the kitchen. The only sound was his tongue lapping against the bowl.

It's not Frieda my mother is angry with, it's me. I expected congratulations, joy, cheers. Instead, she is standing in front of the easel, slapping on the paint as though firing it from a revolver. First Ferdinand says I won't come back for a long time; then Frieda says I ought to stay in Poland; now my mother is going to say I'm running away. I'm writing a play that takes place in Warsaw and my publisher is sending me to Warsaw, but of course, in my case, that has a special meaning. When my father hears of my plans he will say: "So you're taking refuge behind the Iron Curtain? Is it my name you're fleeing from, my boy? Give my love to your mother. I know what I've done to her." Perhaps my dear parents have come to an understanding. We ought to help the poor boy to get on his feet; he is full of neuroses. We ought to prevent him from doing something as senseless as that Israeli adventure. He must simply get his bearings in our wonderful new Germany. Must, must, must.

Gertrude Wendelin put down her brush. "I'll take you down," she said to Frieda.

She kept her dirty smock on, took Frieda by the arm, pressed the dog's leash into her hand. At the door, Frieda turned around and waved to Christopher. "Take no notice of your mother," she said. "Be glad you can get away."

Gertrude Wendelin came back later than she usually did after taking Frieda to the bus stop. She peeled off her smock, cast an ill-humored look into the mirror, as though she felt like putting out her tongue at her reflection.

"Have you phoned your father?" she asked.

"Do you really think that his every wish is my command?" He bowed mockingly.

"You ought to see him before you leave."

"What has that to do with my trip?"

"Everything," she said.

She sat down beside him. The failure of *The Miracle Worker* was a misfortune, she said. If the attempt had been successful, if Germany had taken Richard Wendelin to its heart, Christopher would not be making speeches against his father. "Now you don't know what to say. You don't want to take his part, and you don't want to hit a man when he is down. Because you don't know what to do with your father, you don't know what to do with Germany." She didn't give him a chance to speak. She had suffered long enough because of his father, she said. "I was lucky. He threw me overboard like so much ballast. If it hadn't been Hermine Moellendorff, it would have been someone else, or no one. Then he made *Ritual Murder*. Don't think I would have left him because of *Ritual Murder*. He threw me out in time. That was my good luck. He thought I brought him bad luck, and he thinks you bring him good luck. To him the world is full of mascots."

When will she stop talking about him? The telephone conversation has stirred her up. The news that I am going to Poland has aroused her. The two things have nothing to do with each other, but she doesn't know that.

"I'm ugly," she went on, "but I could have married ten times. I sometimes think I didn't want to discard his name. He is like an earthquake which you still remember when the houses have long since been rebuilt."

"He is not an earthquake to me," said Christopher. "I've finished with him. You won't believe it, but I'm not going to Poland on his account."

"That's what you think," she said. "You went to Israel on his account, too."

"That was a different matter."

Darkness had long since fallen; only the gleam of a street lamp lit the room. They sat side by side in silence. Then she slipped her arm under his as though she wanted to go somewhere with him.

"I was a bad mother," she said. "All mothers are bad who are preoccupied by one single man." He mustn't imagine that she thought a lot of her own painting. It was no coincidence that she had only started painting after her divorce. "The flame of creativity first blazed up in me when I was alone." Then she had worked to earn a living, to feed herself and her son. It might have been better, who could tell, if they had gone hungry and she could have devoted herself to him. "I didn't write to you for weeks on end while you were in Israel, and I wasn't at home when you came back, and yet I made up my mind never to let you go away again." Egotism? Of course. But it wasn't egotism if she now didn't want to let him go away. It would be for more than three or four months, she knew. He would come back after one or two years, and then he would be twenty-six or twenty-seven, and everything would be much more difficult for him. "One thing I know about growing older. Happy coincidences become more and more rare." She knew he didn't want to take money from her, but that was nonsense. "You can earn money with dilettantism almost as easily by playing cards. Why should I paint if I can't help you with your work?" Israel had been a defeat; he wouldn't be able to stand another defeat. And again she talked about Richard Wendelin. "He is the pole that attracts and repels you. Believe me, I don't care whether you go to him or not, but if you want to create anything, you must get over him."

He stroked her hand, stood up and went over to the window. The light fell on the easel, and on the picture of blind Frieda with the guide dog.

He felt a warmth round his heart, and yet he was shivering, as though his heart did not belong to him. "You're all blind," Frieda had said. Immediately after his return from Israel, he had been ill—tonsillitis, a high temperature—and his mother had not left the apartment for five days. Then she had forgotten him, and he had thought only of the fact that there had been nothing waiting for him but a letter with Frau Winter. Once she had complained of pains in the breast, and although they didn't talk about it, they had both feared that it was cancer, and when the happy news came, he had drunk till the early hours out of sheer happiness. But since he didn't know that she loved him, he had also not noticed that he loved her. Ferdinand and mother, the two people who loved him, had one thing in common: they thought that he was a failure, and they had little hope that he would not fail again. They threw him a life buoy, but he didn't want to be saved. He wanted to swim or go under, but not to be saved. How was he to tell them that?

Now I really believe I am running away. This morning I still thought I had hit the jackpot; now, a few hours later, I feel as though the prize money had slipped through my fingers. If I let myself be convinced that I am running away, that the contract is only a passport which enables me to flee, that I shall not keep the bargain, shall not write the play, then I am the weakling who is bound to fail.

"I must explain to you," he said, and sat down beside her.

He took her hand in his hands. She had no handkerchief with which to dry her tears.

Shortly before his departure, Christopher visited his father. It was a warm June day. The front garden of the villa was in full blossom. Nevertheless, Christopher had the impression that the garden was neglected. The grass was tall and the rose beds dry.

Josef opened the door. He apologized for being in shirt sleeves. "The Herr Staatsrat is waiting for you upstairs, Herr Christopher," he said.

"Is he ill?"

"On Thursday night we had to call the doctor. He ordered him to stay in bed for at least a week."

Christopher glanced in through the open door of the study. The marble bust stood, lost, on the mantelpiece. A few rolled-up carpets were leaning against the wall. The venetian blinds had been let down; it was cold in the house. He went upstairs and knocked.

Richard Wendelin had grown thin. In the huge bed he looked like a sick child whose parents have put him in their bed. The bedclothes were of yellow silk—Richard Wendelin liked sleeping in silk; the silk was the same color as the skin of the man in bed. At the foot of the bed lay books, newspapers, magazines; files were piled up on a chair.

Richard Wendelin apologized for receiving Christopher in this way. He only casually mentioned the slight heart attack he had suffered five days ago, as though he wanted to avoid an appeal to his son's sentiments. He spoke quickly and in an undertone, as one speaks to a doctor whose time is limited, to whom one relates the symptoms of an illness, asking for advice but without believing that the diagnostician would be personally involved. He said, "Have you seen my film?" But although his son replied affirmatively, he did not ask his opinion of it. He seemed not to expect any favorable criticism and did not want to hear an unfavorable one. The "adventure"—that was what he called it—had proved to him that his acquittal meant nothing, was not accepted by the public or by those who, rightly or wrongly, represented the public. Now, for the first time, his vanity showed through like the warp of cloth. He seemed not to consider the possibility that the reviewers might be unprejudiced, that the public's rejection might be justified—the failure had nothing to do with the work, everything to do with his person. "My enemies"—this word, too, he threw into the conversation. Christopher knew all about that. For Richard Wendelin the world was divided into admirers and enemies. The man who did not admire him was an enemy; only enmity could cause the public, that is to say, the world, not to admire him. But there was no hint of revolt, or of rebellion, in his words. He was a man prepared to accept even the most unjust verdict, to come to terms with it. He was, of course, too young to resign himself, he said. He owed it to his name, his work, above all to the vital things he still had to say, to resume the struggle, even under the most unfavorable conditions. "It ought to be past, present, future. But in Germany it is present, past, future."

Christopher looked at his father. He thought of the marble bust in the study: a big head without a body, therefore twice as large. What does he want of me? He is frank, perhaps frankness is his final weapon—but why is he frank with me, of all people? He hasn't talked about me yet. Does he want to hold me responsible for his defeat?

Richard Wendelin was sitting upright against his pillows; his small, strikingly white hands lay on the sheet. Everything he said seemed to be frank; the only mystery was why he said it. He didn't want to claim, he continued, that he had been unjustly treated, or only insofar as he had been given a particular role. "I am a scapegoat who is guilty, but not more guilty than those who go free." He pointed to the newspapers. The second in command to the chancellor had once helped to frame the Nuremberg anti-Jewish laws; several ministers had been Party members; the widow of an executed war criminal had had restored to her the estate which her husband had obtained through robbery; a general whose hands were red with the blood of the innocent was drawing his full pension; colleagues who had contributed to the fame of the Third Reich were applauded. He laughed. "The Lohmeyers, it turns out, employed slave labor, but this hasn't harmed their career. After all, they changed horses, from potatoes to films. Perhaps I, too, would be forgiven if I changed horses, from films to potatoes."

Although the windows were open and the hot June afternoon was brooding outside, it was cold in the lofty, timber-paneled bedroom. Richard Wendelin looked around. "You are visiting me here for the last time," he said. "I have sold the house. I'm going to rent a house near town. Perhaps only an apartment.

I have given Rosa notice. Josef wants to stay with me, but I can't accept his offer to work for me unpaid. I'm at the end of my resources—but no compassion, please; money never meant much to me. I shall always find a roof to shelter me and my books. Frankly, poverty may have a rejuvenating effect; at times I feel like a student who still has everything before him." He looked old.

Even this renunciation of pity seemed honest to Christopher. It was true that money never meant much to him, unless as a confirmation of his importance. He sold himself for applause, not for money. Nevertheless, it was hard to picture his father in a rented apartment on the outskirts of town. His father had wanted to talk to him urgently—there was nothing urgent about all this. Even pity isn't urgent, and he is one of those people who want to be envied, not pitied.

Richard Wendelin pointed to the chair by the bed. "Can you hand me that, please?"

Christopher didn't know whether his father had meant only the topmost file of the heap; but with a gesture, Richard Wendelin indicated that he meant all the files—red, green, violet folders, two expanding files bursting with papers, and pocket files stuffed with newspaper cuttings. It was hard to find room for all the papers on the bed; the silk sheet disappeared under them. Like Indian braves, who are buried with their weapons, Richard Wendelin lay buried under files.

"My dossier," said Richard Wendelin.

He turned to the bedside table; laboriously his hand reached for a book. He opened it at a place marked with a strip of paper, sought nervously among the papers for his glasses.

"In a legal book, *The Continuity of the Dossier*, I found these sentences. I should like to read them to you."

"I should like to read to you." How often the boy had heard this sentence, how often it had been the introduction to hours of reading, to the best hours that he could remember. *Faust, Maria Stuart, Hanneles Himmelfahrt, Die Familie Schroffenstein,* read aloud.

Richard Wendelin read: "A cloud masses together, the tide

rises, a dossier accumulates. Woe to the mortal against whom a dossier accumulates! But woe too to the man not yet dead against whom a dossier ever has accumulated. Such a dossier holds him in check to the end of his days . . . When Adam and Eve were expelled from Paradise after they had been successfully enticed into eating the forbidden fruit, Satan started the first dossier on the subject. Since then Satan has been uninterruptedly at work, every time a machine-gun made up of statements, comments, findings, sheets of correspondence, and divided into page and file numbers, is discharged over the tormented human being . . ."

As he listened to his father—still the same voice, the same sure accents, the same glance over the top of his glasses that established contact with his listener—Christopher asked himself whether he ought not to spare him the pointless excitement. The old game: I'm innocent! I have done nothing against you, father. I didn't go to Israel to punish you. I didn't give my approval to the Frankfurt article. I didn't take part in the demonstration.

"You weren't present at any of my trials," said Richard Wendelin. "I'm not reproaching you for that. But perhaps it's not too much if I ask you to study my dossier."

"What good would that do, father? I'm leaving for Poland next week . . ."

"I know."

"How do you know . . . ?"

"I know."

Christopher shrugged his shoulders. "It may be months before I come back. No one is going to ask my opinion of you anymore, and if they ask, I won't answer. What I thought was never important to you. It shouldn't matter to you what I think now."

"It doesn't matter to me," said Richard Wendelin.

Now it was so quiet that they could hear a single birdcall. As though tired by the strain of honesty, Richard Wendelin sank back onto his pillows.

"What's the point, then?" said Christopher.

"I can't live without my work," said his father. "If I can't work, I don't want to live. It wasn't all finished after the war. It's finished now. They would have forgiven me for being what I was, but never for being the cause of losing money!"

"What has that to do with me?"

"Your opinion is important to me insofar as the opinion of the world cannot be a matter of indifference to me."

"I'm not the world."

"What would you do if my dossier convinced you that I had been unjustly treated?"

"I don't know."

"My enemies are your friends, Christopher," said Richard Wendelin. "I say that without bitterness. I envy you for them. I am a bad judge of men. All vain people are bad judges of men. If I had been less vain, I would have become a refugee. Not out of conviction, but out of a knowledge of men." He straightened up. "The father has to ask a favor of the son. It is my last chance."

Christopher lowered his eyes. He didn't want to see the little man in his paper grave. If only he had accused me! If only, vain and arrogant, he had accused the world! If only he had denied reality, as he did back in Hamburg! I don't want him to humiliate himself in front of me.

"You know men like Dr. Aaron Weinstein," said his father. "They trust you. Only men like Dr. Aaron Weinstein can rehabilitate me. If a single one of them spoke up for me . . ." His face had reddened. "My acquittal means nothing, because people say I was acquitted by men like myself. I mention Dr. Weinstein, but it could be someone else. If possible a Jew. A German Jew, a refugee, would be better than an American Jew."

"You are asking the Jews to do the impossible."

"No, no, I trust the Jews of all people to have the magnanimity, the willingness to take my part. I often feel like a Jew, Christopher. Probably everyone is a Jew once in his life. Only the Jews know what it means to be punished for belonging to a particular people."

He imagines he is being punished because he is a German, thought Christopher. He doesn't think about *Ritual Murder*, about the extras from the concentration camps; he doesn't think of the honors he received from the Third Reich. But Christopher thought this without anger. He looked into the sick, lined face, saw the small white hands and wished that he himself were small and frailer.

"A cloud masses together, the tide rises, a dossier accumulates," his father said. "I am suffocating under my dossier. I have never lived according to my convictions; you went to the kibbutz out of yours. I am not asking you to do anything against your convictions." He stopped. "I am not demanding anything, I am beseeching you. If these papers convince you that I am not worth saving, then forget this conversation. I won't remind you of it." He sank back onto his pillows again and gazed up at the ceiling. "It is no chance that of all Shakespeare's monologues the one I love best is Prince Henry's. I used to read it to you when you could scarcely understand it yet." His voice monotonous:

> So, when this loose behaviour I throw off
> And pay the debt I never promised,
> By how much better than my word I am
> By so much shall I falsify men's hopes;
> And like bright metal on a sullen ground,
> My reformation, glittering o'er my fault,
> Shall show more goodly and attract more eyes
> Than that which hath no foil to set it off.

I want to improve, Christopher. I cannot be prevented from trying."

"I wouldn't know who to turn to," said Christopher.

Richard Wendelin sat up and began hectically to sort out the files, placing them neatly one on top of the other, as though the important thing now was extreme pedantry. "So you will study my dossier," he said. "Take your time. Please don't skip anything. You will find someone. Only it mustn't be anyone with the slightest stigma. But," he laughed, "you don't know any of my friends, you only know my enemies. I'm going to give myself to your friends, to my enemies."

Before Christopher could speak, Richard Wendelin rang for the servant, ordered him to pack up the documents and put a string around them. When Josef had gone, he shook his son's hand. "Thank you," he said. "Thank you in any case."

Christopher went down the stairs. The house was as unfamiliar to him as if he had never lived here, as if his father had moved out long ago.

Downstairs the servant gave him the package of documents with the grateful look of an accomplice.

Christopher took the parcel under his arm. It was a heavy parcel.

IV

My Name Is Kristóf

*H*E wanted to go east and went west, instead. Immediately across the French frontier the landscape changed, became milder. Perhaps the Impressionists had really been Naturalists, French Naturalists. The green of the fields consisted of patches of color, the leaves of the poplar trees were transparent, the poppies in the plowed fields were out of a painter's fantasy, and the birches were of the same gentle white as the women's veils in Renoir's paintings or the ballet skirts in Degas's pastels.

I must make a clean sweep. Three or four months, though it may take longer. Martha didn't come in May, nor in June. She returned to Paris long before, but she had kept putting off her trip to Germany. One has to know not only what one has, but also what one has lost. I telegraphed her and didn't give her time to reply. Perhaps she would be waiting for me at the station, perhaps she wouldn't be waiting for me at all; or she might want to take me to a "little party" at her parents', to which I won't go. I'm no longer afraid to talk to her. Let them all believe that I am running away. I'm living a new and different life. People say you can't change your skin—a stupid cliché, since we change our skins all the time. Character is a question of age. If you still have the same character you had yesterday you are wearing a shabby suit.

He looked up at the suitcases lying in the luggage rack.

What if I find Martha as I left her in the kibbutz? Shall I then stay in Paris, or shall I go to Warsaw and write my play? Forty-eight hours is all the time I need. I don't want to go to Warsaw with false hopes that belong to the past. I could have done without the second suitcase, if I weren't lugging my father's dossier around with me. I shall leave the dossier with Kasimir Nessor in Paris, if he will see me. He should read the documents, though my father talked of Dr. Aaron Weinstein. Father still thinks it was the Jews who won the war; they are the victors who acquit or condemn. The Germans murder six million Jews and then expect the Jews to show tolerance. Jews are higher beings; therefore we exterminated them. And if they don't show tolerance, then they are lower beings and that's why we exterminated them. No mercy, but a demand for forgiveness: that is German logic. Kasimir Nessor is the man to help my father, but what will he say when I ask him to read the dossier? I'm not doing it for my father's sake. I want to travel light.

Martha was standing at the barrier. She embraced him, kissed him on both cheeks.

She was wearing a light summer dress. Her arms were bare and brown, as they were when she walked beside his tractor. "It's unbearably hot in Paris," she said. Tiny drops of sweat glistened along her hairline. He loved the little hairs that refused to be disciplined and were tangled by the wind. He had made up his mind to be different from what he had been in the kibbutz, and different from what he had been that unhappy evening in Paris. Perhaps he really was different, but it was terribly difficult to be different with someone who knew nothing about the change. If he spoke the language he had spoken in the past, he would become Abraham Avni or Christopher Wendelin, the old one, who in one night had gambled away his love. But if he spoke in a different language, forty-eight hours were no more than a fleeting instant, the new man was a stranger, and why had he come?

While they were still in the car in which she took him to his hotel, he told her about his trip to Warsaw, about the great good fortune he had to have his play accepted by a publisher, about the work in which he was now ready to immerse himself. He caught himself, not lying, but—contrary to his usual habit —exaggerating, and his gaiety seemed false to him. He was marketing himself as one markets a new product, and when he said he had come to Paris to see Kasimir Nessor—"I must talk to him urgently"—he thought she looked at him out of the corner of her eye, as if to say, "You expect me to believe you didn't come to Paris on my account?" Quite naturally, she said, "I thought we'd eat at my place, something cold. We can talk more quietly at home." His heart beat faster, and he was no longer so sure whether he had left his anxiety behind him.

Martha's apartment was on the outskirts of the city. They drove through the summer streets that were deserted and smelled of hot asphalt and tart wine. She would have liked to come to Munich, she said, but she had had to go to London. Then the American tourist season had started and there was no chance of taking a holiday. "By the way, my parents are in South America. I haven't seen them, either, since you left." Had he heard anything from Ani Omer? "Just imagine, Moshe wrote me a very nice letter." He said nothing.

The pleasant new apartment house in which Martha lived was on the edge of a small housing estate. There was no building in front to spoil the view. The garden ran out into fields, and through the darkness single lights were winking. The apartment consisted of two spacious rooms whose furniture contrasted with the modernity of the house: the secretaire from the time of Maria Theresa, the silver candlesticks and the portrait of a woman by Napoleon's court painter, David, must all have come from Misha Kohorn's various homes.

While Martha was busy in the kitchen—"Off limits," she said—he hadn't the patience to remain on the settee. He walked to and fro about the apartment, went out through the open door onto the balcony, gazed into the darkness, inhaled the heavy air, came back, started his wandering again as though looking for something. He was ashamed to think that perhaps he really was looking for something: a man's photograph, something that told him about her life, his own photograph, a letter, which he would have read without the slightest hesitation. On her bedside table there were only the photographs of her parents, the picture of a young man in an RAF uniform. Over a chest of drawers hung a framed snapshot from the kibbutz. He spotted himself in the background, between the gynecologist from Krefeld and the other Abraham—one small head among many. "May I make a phone call?" he shouted through the not quite closed kitchen door, like someone with urgent business to attend to. He dialed Kasimir Nessor's number, the housekeeper answered, he heard voices; at last Kasimir Nessor came to the phone. "Of course, my dear friend," said Nessor. "Come along, I shall be glad to see you." Thanks, tomorrow between three and four. His eyes ran over the bed, on which a silk wrap had been carelessly thrown. Through the half-open door of the bathroom he saw a bright blue bathing cap hanging on a nail. A pair of white gloves lay on the chest of drawers, and on the floor beside it stood white satin shoes. But all these everyday objects excited Christopher more than the sight of Martha had excited him; they were part of her existence which was closed to him. There had been days when he had not remembered her, weeks during which he had scarcely thought about her. This now seemed to him incredible, just as, when pain returns, it seems unbelievable that we were ever without it. He went back into the living room, sat down at the laid table, chatted with her through the kitchen door, and felt the intimacy of a conversation from room to room to be a lie in which they were both involved and which did not deceive either of them.

A hot pie introduced the carefully prepared meal. Martha put a bottle of Bordeaux on the table. They talked about Warsaw, about Nessor's new book, about Misha Kohorn's successes in Brazil, about Germany, about *The Miracle Worker of Paestum*. Although these were things that touched both of them, every word that might be considered personal came to a halt in front of a locked door. It was impossible to continue a conversation that had not begun; and every time there was a silence, one or the other would say: "Do you remember . . . ?" and both of them held fast to the lost anchor.

Later—he had drunk almost the whole bottle on his own and opened a second one—he sat down beside her; but he immediately rose again, went out onto the balcony, came back and sat down beside her again. He only listened with half an ear to what she was saying.

She is calm, she is watching me as children watch wild animals behind bars. How can they allow wild animals to live in such confined spaces, locked in? And yet it gives one a superior feeling, this freedom in front of the confined animal. Can I make amends? Is it right for me to think of love on a forty-eight-hour schedule, with a ticket to Warsaw? And do I love her? I only seem to love my vanity, or to be concerned about my ridiculous virility. The beginning of a love? In reality, it will probably be the end of a love, so that I can travel light. She is looking at me as though she knew. Feeding the wild animals behind their bars. You never know what might happen if you set them free. In Israel there were always too many words, and now there is too much silence. Why haven't I wanted anyone during these last months? Love and no trip.

Just as previously he had wandered about the apartment, so he now wandered about the room as though looking for something. He was circling round her and round himself, two focal points, but there was really only one. He had come to explain to her what had happened back at the kibbutz, but by now he had forgotten that. What he had to say to her could wait, but without words he could not find her body, without her body he could not find words. She mentioned names which he did not know; the unfamiliar names were offensive. It was offensive that she had been living and that time had passed. She talked about his play and about the Warsaw Ghetto and about his prospects, and it was offensive that she should speak of the future, as though all they had in common were the past and the future. "You're not listening," she said, and he thought that was the bridge. "Of course I'm not listening," he said. "I was lying just now. It was only because of you that I came to Paris." And he bent down and took her in his arms, and his body was as awake now as it had been dead before. She took his head in her hands and said, "You're leaving tomorrow, or the day after tomorrow." "I'll stay as long as you want me to," but he already knew that his treachery was useless.

He searched no more. She told him that she was not alone, that she had met someone. "It's not a great love and something different from what will always be between us." A commonplace—what else could she say? A whole flood of clichés, and she is expecting clichés from me. I'm not angry with you, don't be angry with me, I will always . . . I know you will always . . . and so on. If at least I could have explained to her why I couldn't love her that evening on the slopes above the Jordan Valley! The kibbutz, the eyes of the others, first love, the incomprehensible miracle, the infertile soil, hard hands, the harsh light, the false name, the long night. Too late.

He went out onto the balcony. Not a breath stirred; the night was merciless. When he felt that she was standing beside him and heard the rustle of her dress, he said, "If only it wasn't so simple." But he did not explain what he meant. He had looked for a bridge and had cut his way through the scrub. He had searched and searched, and in the end it had all been so ridiculously simple: the photograph of a man which by chance had not stood on the bedside table. By chance or not by chance.

"It isn't simple," she said, because she had not understood what he meant. "Back there on the kibbutz . . ." He tried to interrupt her, but she said, "Back there on the kibbutz, you knew nothing about yourself. Why should I know everything about myself today? I don't know, either, what will happen in three weeks or three months or three years . . ." He didn't want to listen. After the clichés the hopes would now come, but he had been hoping for months, and sometimes it is easier to live with hopelessness than with hope. He went back into the room, filled his glass, wandered up and down, passed the open door of the bedroom, slammed it shut. We agreed to be friends, she will tell the other man tomorrow, in bed, and he will kiss her breasts. Christopher only came to prove that he is a man. And he will take her, and she will sigh in his arms, and she will say, Poor boy, he's full of neuroses. Perhaps if he hadn't listened to me, if he had taken me without asking—but he is far too sensitive for that, a complicated, hypersensitive German. And I shall be sitting in the plane to Warsaw. "It was silly of me," he said. "I should have flown to Warsaw straightaway." There's nothing for me to do here. In a minute she will put up a bridge leading back to our friendship; then she will ask if she can give me a lift back to my hotel.

"I must go," he said.

"I'll give you a lift home," she said.

He could see himself sitting next to her in the car, the lights of Paris appearing, more and more dense, the windows open, it's sultry, we shall talk, when does your plane leave, actually we could see each other tomorrow, shall I give you a lift to the airport, the air is thick enough to cut with a knife, Paris is deserted around this time of the year, Paris is hot, the Seine, the hotel, I'll write to you, don't be angry with me, perhaps you will write, too.

"Please call a taxi," he said.

He got out at a small station on a local line. His suitcase was heavy. He was the only passenger to get off here. He asked the railway official the way to Kasimir Nessor's house. "It's only ten minutes by taxi." The afternoon sun was blazing down on the empty square. Two dogs were coupling. In the driver's seat of the one and only taxi slept an old driver with a mustache. "I'm glad you woke me," he laughed. "I have to collect a lady from Monsieur Nessor's anyway."

The Île-de-France lay in the summer heat almost as though this piece of earth really were an island, a big green island in the midst of a great sunny sea. Farmhouses alternated with châteaux, and it seemed to Christopher as though the farmhouses were even richer than the châteaux, for the rich, juicy earth seemed to belong to the farmhouses, while the châteaux were like backdrops that a troupe of roving actors had left behind. One thing the white farmhouses and the gray châteaux had in common: most of them were surrounded by little streams; bridges led to them. For the peasants and the masters, the Île-de-France was not enough; wisely they had built islands on the island.

The Sunday peace of the countryside affected Christopher, but he had been really calm since he awoke that morning. He was surprised that he had slept at all; it made him feel almost ashamed. It had been a deep, but not a peaceful, sleep. In his dreams he had continued his conversation with Martha, and while he made love to her, she had stretched out her hand to a photograph on her bedside table. It had been the photograph

of Bill, the young American at the little party in the Avenue
Hoche. She had put the photograph on her bosom; the picture
had lain there like the cross on the chest of a dead man; he had
hammered on it with his fists. His hands had become bloody
from the broken glass, and her breast had become bloody under
his hands. The dream did not pursue him into the sunny Sunday
morning. He awoke without anger, almost serene. Now he
looked out of the car window and began to understand. All that
had happened was part of a mysterious design; he had not just
traveled to some foreign country, he had left everything
behind. A divine hand, perhaps, had cut even the last threads.
If he traveled into hope, not hope but hopelessness must be
left behind. A sweet bitterness came over him, a happy obstinacy, the beautiful arrogance of resignation.

The taxi crossed a bridge thickly overgrown with wild
roses and came to a stop in the courtyard of a small château that
looked almost like a town house lost in the country. What happened then seemed naturally derived from Christopher's mood
of exaltation. Kasimir Nessor was in the act of saying goodbye
to his visitor, whom Christopher recognized as Frau von Benda,
the woman who at Misha Kohorn's little party had awkwardly
avoided shaking hands with him. Even before Kasimir Nessor
could greet his new arrival, she held out her hand to Christopher. "It's nice to see you again, Herr Wendelin," she said in
pleasantly muted Viennese. "Kasimir has told me a lot about
you." As Christopher bowed, embarrassedly, over her hand, she
said, "I'm sorry I have to go. Kasimir has promised to bring you
to see me next time you come to Paris."

"You see," said Kasimir Nessor as the taxi swung round and
out of the courtyard, but he only waved to his departing guest
and did not explain what he meant. "There are women like
that," he went on as he led Christopher into the house. "You
have probably never heard of Professor von Benda's mission.
Shortly before the war the Nazis sent him to the Refugee
Conference at Evian to offer the Jews for sale, I believe at two
hundred and fifty dollars a head. On the way back—although
he was a Jew, he intended to return to National Socialist
Vienna—he died of a heart attack, a very natural death for such

a brave man in such a cowardly age. Bettina comes of an old Austrian family. Although she was thirty years younger than the Professor, she never remarried. She couldn't leave Austria until the end of the war, but then she moved to Paris, and since 1945 she has never returned to Austria. Just as there are people who regret not having been Nazis, so there are late refugees, and they are not the worst. She lives entirely for her son, who is studying to become a doctor. Naturally, she is convinced that he will be great."

In the entrance hall Christopher put down the suitcase. "Don't be frightened," he smiled. "It only contains papers which I would like to leave here."

"Don't think I'm so easily frightened. Besides, you are a very welcome visitor. Since my wife's death—fourteen years ago, now —I have lived alone. I sometimes imagine that the walls are speaking to me."

The house which he showed Christopher was a bachelor's house, elegant to the highest degree, yet surprisingly neglected. There were the celebrated collections of Impressionist paintings, centuries-old carpets, Venetian mirrors; but a Manet for which there was no room was leaning against a door. Here and there the carpets lay one on top of the other or four deep; dusty mirrors stood along the walls. Christopher could not help thinking of his father's house. There the collection of bronzes was not merely displayed, it was displayed as though in a museum; niches had been specially made in the walls for the Gothic madonnas, and the Frans Hals—had his father sold it?—was lit day and night by a light cunningly concealed. Christopher was convinced that Kasimir Nessor had no manservant, an assumption which was immediately confirmed. A housekeeper, whom Kasimir Nessor introduced as his "pearl Marie," served tea. They sat by the fireplace with a door wide open, near the long Renaissance table that served as a desk. "I have never had a study. In studies one is safe from interruptions. Here I have the nice illusion that someone might come and stop me from working." Christopher had put down the suitcase beside his armchair.

Innate politeness, natural grace, prevented Kasimir Nessor

from asking Christopher the purpose of his visit. Christopher, in turn, felt it would be dishonest to deceive his host as to the reason for it. In Munich, when he had made up his mind to call on Kasimir Nessor, then on the train to Paris, later still, in the local train, he had carefully thought out the words with which he would introduce the matter, had memorized them. Now he seemed to have forgotten his prepared speech. Incoherently, without disclosing why he was telling all this precisely, he began to talk about his father, about the failure of *The Miracle Worker of Paestum,* about the bloody clashes in Frankfurt, even about Richard Wendelin's illness. Here he broke off, realizing that he had not yet said anything about his imminent trip to Poland, about the encouragement which Ludwig Ludwig had given him. Since his return to Germany, he continued, he had only seen his father once, and then to say goodbye. And now he repeated almost verbatim what his father had told him, what he had asked of him. He did not mention that his father had spoken about the Jews, the refugees, who could save him.

"The suitcase speaks volumes, to use an unfortunate metaphor," Kasimir Nessor interrupted him. "You have studied the dossier and discovered it not to be too light."

Christopher answered somehow, embarrassed, and, as he admitted to himself, at first evasively. Once more he caught himself quoting his father almost verbatim. The Under Secretary of State in Bonn who had helped to draft the commentaries to the Nuremberg Race Laws, the generals and admirals who were still strutting about, a famous economist acquitted at Nuremberg, who traveled the world as a much-sought-after economic expert, the wife of the chief war criminal upon whose steps gift parcels were heaped at Christmas and about whom a sentimental serial was now appearing in an illustrated paper . . .

"Other nations, too," interjected Kasimir Nessor, "glorify their criminals after a few centuries. There are statues of Nero in Italy. America, while honoring Abraham Lincoln, also honors the soldiers who fought for the slave-owners. We Germans go one better. We honor our criminals in our own generation."

He hadn't come to discuss his father's innocence, said Christopher. His study of the dossier had convinced him more than ever of German guilt. "The word 'scapegoat,' which my father is so fond of using, is incorrect, because they were innocent boys punished for the misdemeanors of young princes. My father is not innocent, he is merely no more guilty than thousands of others."

Again Kasimir Nessor glanced at the suitcase. "To know that," he said, "you didn't have to read your father's dossier."

"Oh, yes I did," replied Christopher. His hand was nestling on the handle of the suitcase. He hadn't known, he said, that Dr. Goebbels had requested his father to marry his, the Propaganda Minister's, mistress, who had been ordered to leave the country—to marry her *pro forma* only, of course—and that when Richard Wendelin refused he was given all the most thankless tasks. He hadn't known that his father had kept the concentration camp Jews and Gypsies busy in Hungary two weeks longer than necessary, possibly for no particular reason, yet, who knows, perhaps in order to prolong their lives. He hadn't known that several hundred meters of *Michael the Ancestral Farmer* had been destroyed, because they did not conform to Goebbels' orders, and that there had been three earlier versions of the *Ritual Murder* scenario—he pointed to the suitcase—even worse than the fourth, and that his father had had to apologize in a letter to Dr. Goebbels for having chosen the "mildest" script. "People talk about judicial murder," he said, "when it transpires that an honest man has been condemned to death. But if a housebreaker is condemned to death for a murder he did not commit, no one talks of judicial murder, although the injustice is no less. My father was not punished unjustly; only the degree of the punishment seems to me unjust." He stopped, looked at Kasimir Nessor almost in dismay, said, "You think I have changed a great deal."

"No," said Kasimir Nessor. "You have merely seen your father again. You love your father."

"I am trying to be fair."

"We only try to be fair toward those whom we love. Moreover, I'm not blaming you. It is a law of nature that we hate our fathers; it is a law of nature that we also love our fathers. Although made by men, history does not evolve according to the laws of nature. But since man evolves according to the laws of nature, he is constantly in conflict with history. If your father were not your father, you wouldn't give a damn whether justice was done to him. The young German's outlook is so hopelessly confused that every one of them plays the dual role of defense counsel and public prosecutor. Everyone accuses the other's father and defends his own. Thus my generation will be both acquitted and found guilty, and if you talk about making a clean sweep you are operating with a concept which no German understands."

"The Germans shouldn't have fought against the concept of collective guilt. I'm not sorry to be going east . . ."

"Because there, collective guilt is, so to speak, laid down by law." The wrinkles around Kasimir Nessor's eyes were dancing, heralding a smile. "You are asking the Western Allies to be too unjust. To begin with, the victors did pay lip service to the inhuman idea of collective guilt, but it was really kept alive by the Germans. After they had once adopted the humiliating and yet comforting idea of collective guilt, they could say to the victors—and not altogether unjustly—that the Germans were confident of being treated collectively but not too harshly. The comfortable solution arose of its own accord: a thoroughly bearable collective punishment, possibly with remittance for good behavior, and acquittal of the individual."

"We are masochists . . ."

"That's what the nationalist papers are writing now, but it isn't true. The masochist has a feeling of guilt, even if it is concealed. He wants to be whipped, not to watch the flogging of others. No German takes another German's guilt upon himself, let alone his own. On the contrary, it suits him very nicely that his nation takes upon itself the guilt of the individual. If there had been a Himmler in England, the English patriots would have said he wasn't an Englishman; the German nationalists say it's true he was a criminal, but, after all, he was a German, too."

Christopher noticed that as he spoke, Kasimir Nessor was

scrutinizing him attentively, and he thought he had to defend himself. "My father was no Himmler. Excessively vain, a ruthless opportunist, an amoral weakling—but no Himmler. You have noticed, I cannot deny it: I'm sorry for him. He repents nothing—I should be lying if I said he repented anything. At most he repents having backed the wrong horse. I haven't changed, I'm merely trying to draw up a balance sheet. He spent a year in prison. He wasn't allowed to work for seven years. You know him . . ."

"But now he has had his chance."

"Which was no chance at all. He was given the subject of a cheap film as one throws a lean bone to a dog. The critics scarcely reproached him with his past, but that wasn't magnanimous, only crafty. First the critics established their own objectivity, then they tore him to shreds. The students in Frankfurt were not demonstrating against his work, but against his existence. I feel partly to blame for that."

"You go to extremes . . ."

"Don't misunderstand me," said Christopher quickly. "I would go to Israel again tomorrow. If I feel partly to blame that is only because I drew attention to his name. I feel uncomfortable in the role of St. Paul. Every time my name crops up, people say: Paul, the son of Saul. My father's enemies have made a symbol of him, and I have contributed to that."

"Your father's enemies!" said Kasimir Nessor, and stirred his tea. "You hate your father—and the enemies of your father. You will have to decide. And not only you."

Christopher noticed that he had been holding on tightly to the handle of the suitcase; his hand was cramped around it. He let go. "If I hated my father's enemies, I would not have come to you."

"Does your father know that you have come to me?"

"No. I didn't mention you. He said I should go to Dr. Weinstein, ask Dr. Weinstein to study the dossier. Dr. Weinstein would rehabilitate him."

"Why didn't you?"

"I don't think that Dr. Weinstein would have seen me, after my desertion from Israel."

"Is that the only reason?"

"I remembered that you knew my father . . ."

"Is that the reason?"

"I didn't want to go to a Jew."

The shadows over the park were lengthening. A gardener was going to and fro outside, turning on the lawn sprinklers. A cool breeze was rising; the air in the living room was also growing cooler, but Christopher could feel that there were beads of sweat on his brow.

"Don't be afraid," said Kasimir Nessor after a long silence. "I don't misunderstand you. I know you don't fear that Weinstein, the Jew, would have had no understanding for you."

"I would have felt too ashamed," said Christopher gratefully.

"And with me you don't feel ashamed, because I'm a German."

"I have confidence in you . . ."

"Go on being honest, Christopher! You came to me because you think I speak your language. Perhaps your father's language, too, with a different accent."

"My motives are opportunist," Christopher hazarded. "You are the most famous living German abroad. Your word . . ."

Kasimir Nessor shook his head. "Without knowing it, you believe that because I am a German I might eventually be reconciled with your father. I'm afraid you're wrong. What your father did to the Jews is notorious"—with his long, narrow hands he indicated the suitcase—"but I should be surprised if there is a single word in that mountain of documents about what your father did to the Germans. I don't mean the reactions abroad. If, as seems to be the case, we Germans are only punishing the sins of the Third Reich in order to please public opinion, we might as well let the criminals go free. Your father has seduced not only his nation, but also mine."

"No other nation would have allowed itself to be led astray by him."

"That is quibbling. Every seducer tries to prove that his victim enjoyed what he did. I am not speaking of him but of myself." Now he was smiling again. "I am trying to make clear to you that my resentment is greater than Dr. Aaron

Weinstein's. '*Dieu me pardonnera, parce que c'est son métier,*' Heine is reputed to have said on his deathbed. Undoubtedly, he was thinking of the God of the Jews, who, did He not possess the capacity of infinite forgiveness, would long since have caused the world to go up in fire and smoke. I am not a Jew; forgiveness is not part of my métier."

Christopher's hand was resting on the suitcase again. Kasimir seemed to have noticed this, because he said:

"Nevertheless, leave the papers here. I shall read them. I shall read them, but I don't think I shall do anything about them. And yet, you might be right, it may be that your father's guilt is less than I suppose. If I were to feel that the world sheds daily tears over the fate of six million innocent, I might —so far as lay within my power—undertake the rehabilitation of one who was not guiltier than others. But it is not my impression that the world is shedding tears. I do not see Germany weeping."

Christopher rose, opened the suitcase, looked for somewhere to put the files; but the desk was so full that he wondered where there was room for a single sheet of manuscript. "Leave the papers on the floor," said Kasimir Nessor. "Marie will take them to my bedroom later."

While the housekeeper was telephoning for a taxi, Kasimir Nessor took Christopher by the arm and led him into the garden. Dusk was falling; Kasimir Nessor had not forgotten what Christopher had told him about his journey and his plans. He talked about Poland, where his books were much read. "The zloty," he laughed, "is a splendid currency. They reckon in hundreds of thousands." He spoke of eastern hospitality. "I used to go to Budapest once a year." He spoke of the publisher's sound judgment. "I belong to the old-fashioned school which still considers it important that every street name should be noted down accurately." Finally, he mentioned the possibility of the play's being staged in Paris.

Marie announced the arrival of the taxi. Kasimir Nessor accompanied his guest into the shady courtyard. "I've forgotten the suitcase," said Christopher, and ran back into the lounge to fetch it. When he returned, Kasimir Nessor said, "Let me know when you're in Paris again. But give me time. I'm a slow reader. Keep your trust in me, my friend. That means you mustn't imagine that I now think badly or even differently of you. If I had a son I would expect from him what your father expects of you. That is perhaps the German tragedy, that the fathers rely on their sons."

After the taxi had crossed the bridge and driven out into the evening that lay over the Île-de-France, Christopher continued for a long time to see the waving figure of Kasimir Nessor. He thought, I ought to have left the suitcase behind. What am I going to do with an empty suitcase . . . ?

"You won't come back for a long time," Ferdinand had told him. Christopher had intended to stay in Warsaw three or four months. Instead, he stayed in the east for almost two years.

He had not written his play. In the very first weeks, while doing research on the history of the Ghetto's rising, he had met a young official of the Polish Ministry of Justice, Piotr Rokowski, who opened up the "Brown Archives" for him, the MSW Archives, as the Poles called it.

The four-story building near the new skyscraper, the Palace of Culture and Arts, became his home, his gray and terrible home. In the morning he went in through the heavy gate and the sweat came out on his brow; in the evening he left the building through the heavy gate and was still bathed in sweat. He met only a few people: the silent archivists, who had taken on the yellow color of the papers; silent officers; silent students. The archivists looked in silence at the tall, fair-haired, blue-eyed German. What was he looking for here, among the dead? The dead needed little space. The murderers needed little space. Thin walls separated the murderers from the dead; they had to put up with each other. "A cloud masses together, the tide rises, a dossier accumulates." The dossier had accumulated. Dossiers on the horrors of the Ghetto and the concentration camps and the prisoner-of-war camps; dossiers on the execution of hostages and deserters and prisoners of war and resistance fighters and slave laborers; dossiers on men who once again possessed power and prestige and money; and next to them, figures: ten thousand murders, fifty thousand, a hundred thousand. Photographs like the enamel pictures on the graves in southern Italy, photographs like those in a rogues' gallery. Photographs of Jewish transports, of Jews digging their own graves, of Jews before the executioner's block, on the block, after execution. Photographs of dignitaries and camp commandants, male and female, and butchers in uniform or at a tavern table, with a wolfhound or with a canary. The stairs up to the attic, the stairs down to the cellar. Christopher ran up the stairs, Christopher ran down the stairs, under the silent eyes of the archivists, the officers, the students, a tall, fair-haired blue-eyed German looking for murderers and the dead.

The dead came to life, stepped out from the files, stood along the walls, sat on the stairs, sat at the tables. The murderers came to life—or were they still alive? "Morgue" was written over the door of one room. Behind it were the dead murderers—those who had been executed, those who had escaped earthly justice, damned to all eternity. "Disappeared" was written over another door. Murderers who had disappeared, victims who had disappeared. The room was small, they had to put up with each other. When Christopher stopped for a moment, stood by a window as though being trailed, he saw the skyscraper of the Palace of Culture and Arts. The Palace seemed to him small, and this four-story chamber of horrors like a skyscraper.

Why had the great accusation not been made? Why had an accusation been made against this one and not against that? Political motives, no doubt. For ten years bandits kept Europe in fear and trembling; no hiding place provided safety. Edgar Allan Poe's macabre story came to his mind. The lonely wanderer finds himself in a madhouse, where the doctors and nurses are languishing in the cellar; the madmen have set themselves free and put on the white coats of the doctors and nurses. There sit the archivists, the officers, the students; they are wearing white coats; the madmen are back in the cellar, but the house has been devastated.

"Have you found your father's dossier?" Piotr Rokowski asked. On the first day, I went to room U-Z. Like the last volume of an encyclopedia. Wendelin. *Ritual Murder*—see under R.

Ritual Murder trials, the first in 1494. Recorded by Antonius Bonfinius—see under B. *Ritual Murder* film—see under F. From room to room, from floor to floor, from archive to junk room, upstairs, downstairs. In my play the children's chorus sings: "A bird flew by, a bird that saw / A shoe that once my Momma wore. / The shoe was empty, the shoe was red— / General, who is it waiting for?— / Jewish child, your Momma's dead!" God knows that's not the trumpet of Jericho, that's not going to bring the walls down. They acquitted my father: "Justice has triumphed!" I enter this building in the early morning, and am the last to leave it. I am a hunter of men, avenging God, God and the Devil in one person, Abraxas, a self-appointed God and Devil. What am I looking for?

He did not know what he was looking for, but the hunt went on, with angry diligence. It must have been in reaction against the superstitious orderliness of his father; he himself was so disordered. Now orderliness degenerated into pedantry. He got his teeth into a name. From the files a man emerged. Christopher got to know him. Somewhere, deep in a chest in the attic, the names of the victims were to be found; the man's service paybook was filed away in a cabinet in the basement, along with a photograph. Out with the magnifying glass—one small head among many. The hunt went on, with angry diligence.

In the third month he received a long, warmhearted letter from Kasimir Nessor, a well-founded refusal. "It cannot be my task," wrote Kasimir Nessor, "to justify your father. Retribution, vengeance, for a lifetime? I've never wanted anything to do with that; today, having studied the dossier closely, I want even less to do with it. Only I cannot acquit an individual simply because I accuse the age. Moreover, it is not my place to acquit or condemn. The court acquitted your father; there can be no question of a judicial murder. I cannot make his peace with that mysterious authority known as public opinion; he alone can change it. Public opinion, sometimes overestimated and sometimes underestimated, is nevertheless a highly sensitive seismograph. It will only register shock waves if they come from the depth."

Am I looking for proof of everyone's guilt, so that my father's guilt may be submerged in the universal guilt? W. Wendelin, Richard—a single corner, a little bundle of papers in a house full of papers, a chamber of horrors, the comforting collective guilt. If that were it, I wouldn't have looked up the judge who tried my father and acquitted him. As my instinct told me, the man was a judge on courts-martial in Hitler's Reich. Where were the graves of the fourteen soldiers he had handed over to the firing squad for spreading alarm and despondency? A vain search. I was told there was "further information in the morgue," since he had lost his life in a train wreck shortly after acquitting my father, peace to his ashes. I won't be discouraged; I must prevent the corpses, like the body of the living corpse Meyer, from rotting in the open street and poisoning the air.

He wrote to Ludwig Ludwig, told him the truth, recklessly offered to pay back the advance. Ludwig the Great proved worthy of his name. There could be no question of repayment, he wrote. If Christopher could amass documentary evidence —"Never mind how much"—the publishing house was willing to meet the expenses of Christopher's stay for a year, and possibly even longer. "The book is to be called *Facts,* and that is what it must contain." It should deal in the first place with people in public life, those who "are floating on top again." Perhaps Ludwig Ludwig was out for a sensation, but never mind. Perhaps Dr. Aaron Weinstein was also out to prove that the God of the Jews is no avenging God. One could not search out motives, neither other people's nor one's own.

Meanwhile, he admitted to himself, it was not merely his work which kept him in the East. Piotr Rokowski had introduced him to a circle of young people: writers, students, working men and girls, actors, engineers, painters, doctors. Some spoke German, some spoke French; gradually, Christopher also learned a little Polish. They talked from dusk to dawn with no other purpose than to talk. They were not all Communists, but they all said the wheel of history could not be turned back. Some made an effort to convince Christopher, but he refused to be convinced. Here, too, there were the privileged and those who were discriminated against; there were idealists and profiters, even rich and poor, although the rich would have been accounted poor in the West. Here, too, even if it was with an ideological pretext, people claimed the right to do wrong. The circle of those who practiced free speech was like an Island of the Blessed, and here, also, there were traffic lights on the open road. They criticized and protested, but mainly against formalities, not against the form of government, for then the light turned red; they had gone out in the street and cheered the Hungarian rebels, but the rising was put down and the light turned red again; they talked about colonialism and self-determination and the nation's urge to freedom, but Russian soldiers walked past the windows and the red light went on. At times Christopher told himself that he felt at home because he was not at home, because all this did not concern him. But the green lights were more frequent than the red. No one put the words "war criminal" in inverted commas, everyone dared to utter the word "Jew," no one spoke shamefacedly or shamelessly of heroic deeds done during the war, no one was proud of having been a good fighter for a bad cause, and when they talked about the end of the war, no one spoke of collapse and catastrophe; they spoke of a beginning and the future. They were poor, at least according to the standards by which Christopher had grown up. This poverty was depressing, and the gradual liberation from its clutches took place in an oddly antiquated manner, so that the outlines of a bourgeoisie, which the regime claimed to be fighting and to which, who could tell, it might one day fall victim, stood out more and more clearly. The traces of atom-age Biedermeier were already appearing in architecture and living habits, in furniture and behavior, in careful speech and bureaucratic arbitrariness. But the poverty also had other sides. People communicated in words, not in sounds; they celebrated festivals as something rare and precious; a book, a concert, an exhibition became passionately discussed events; people walked about the country as though the automobile had never been invented; little things became big; because not everything was for sale, people gave gifts and knew how to value presents; people were satisfied but not

satiated; and Christopher thought of his father. "Poverty reju-
venates," he had said.

At dawn, as he made his way home to his furnished room
after long discussions in cafés or little apartments, and the city
in the early light looked like every other city—the night waiters
in their raglan coats and the milk-floats and the street sweepers
and the police patrols and the sirens of the ambulances and the
would-be suicides—he asked himself why here, where freedom
was suppressed, he could breathe so freely.

Have they convinced me? Of what? It may be that here they
are longing for a freedom that we have long possessed; it may
be that here they say progress and mean Biedermeier; but
among us they mock what they possess, and here they long for
what they do not possess. It may be that here they pursue false
dreams, but they have the courage to dream; among us, dreams
are scorned; when we say revolution we mean anarchy, when
we say progress we mean a faster sportscar. It may be that the
fresh wind that blows here in the morning is flying westward,
but in the West the wind stands still. Here people look westward openly; among us they glance eastward surreptitiously.
We love our fathers or hate them, but we all fear them; here
they do not fear their fathers, whether they love or hate them.
Fathers are old everywhere; among us the young are old, too.
Ferdinand was wrong—I do not feel homesick at all.

He forgot that he was not only in a new land but also in a
new landscape. It could be that he was confusing system with
country. He had never been east of Berlin before. The East
was a new region, a new world. The doors of strange houses
opened to the stranger, as though he were a long-awaited guest
emerging on the horizon of the steppes. The girls felt free of
the compulsion of bourgeois morality, but they did not consider the family a bourgeois prejudice. Christopher flew from
one warm nest to another. The women had remained women:
they expected chivalry and they received it. People wore their
hearts where they belonged: on their sleeves. No one was
ashamed of romanticism or of exaggeration. People said beautiful things to each other and did not demand tart honesty; they

judged uninhibitedly to the very limits of friendship, not beyond them; they avoided offense and did not ask for frankness;
they were passionate in anger and quick in forgetting, polite
out of tradition and humane out of instinct.

No one cared to mention his father. Ferdinand had been
wrong, and so had blind Frieda. It might be that he owed the
continual extension of his residence permit to the name Wendelin. The Party paper had also written a great deal that was
untrue about him, considering how short the article was, had
depicted the "persecution" to which he had been subjected in
the West in an inaccurate and highly colored way, had made a
convert out of him. The convert was welcome, of course, and
the director of *Ritual Murder* was "naturally" nothing but the
representative of capitalist corruption. But they went no further than rather threadbare propaganda, did not disturb him
at his work, let him do as he liked. No one expected him to
declare himself for or against his father. If the name of Richard
Wendelin was occasionally mentioned, it was as though they
were talking of a silent-film director who once, in a bankrupt
and liquidated past, had played a certain role. How strange
that he was still alive.

Again and again Christopher postponed his departure, but
he knew that he would have to go home soon. He was not
Abraham Avni; he had not deposited his identity at the frontier. Every day, at eight o'clock, it was handed to him at the
gate of the archives.

Thus summer of 1957 approached, heralded by a summery
spring. Over the walls hung lilac. The sky was blue and the
yellow houses of the Old City were like warm gold in the sun-
light. Children played in the narrow streets. The nights were
heavy with the scent of acacias. The trees threw off their
widows' veils and decked themselves in bright green summer
hats.

In the middle of June Christopher went to Hungary.

The task of collecting his material had taken Christopher
right across Poland and to Czechoslovakia. But this was his first
trip to Hungary.

With every mile that disappeared under the wheels of the slow express, his excitement grew.

Am I happily excited, or is fear dogging my heels? I ought to have gone to Hungary long ago. I should have spent months here, not the three or at most four weeks I plan to spend. This is where my father made *Ritual Murder*. *Ritual Murder*: directed by Richard Wendelin. I was at the German premiere, in a smart Hitler Youth Naval Cadet's uniform. How often have I seen the film? Five, six times? My father made a splendid job of it, I remember every scene, and if I didn't remember, the scenario is in the dossier, back in the archives of the assassins and the assassinated.

It is the story of the poor peasant's son, five-year-old István Balla, who on the third of June, 1746, was found dead in a barn. The village was called Orkut. I've known the true story for a long time. A naked boy, strangled, a sex murder, no doubt about it.

They wouldn't hear of this at the time. The Bohemian provincial painter Trtina András Kajetán lived in Orkut. He was given permission to paint the boy's corpse. A precursor of police photography, a deadly piece of evidence against those who were later charged. The search for the murderers proved fruitless. Traveling journeymen, artisans, beggars, vagabonds wandered the countryside—who took note of them? People see what they want to see, imagination is like prefabricated houses: you can transport it where you want. Anti-Semitism was directed from Vienna, a lightning conductor for the rebellious feelings of the Hungarians. In the scratches and strangle marks on the dead boy's body the villagers discovered Hebrew characters. No question of an exhumation: Kajetán's picture was sufficient. All the Jews of Orkut and its environs were arrested; only a few escaped to Bratislava, the secure Communitas Judaeorum Poseniensis. The chief among the accused, the innkeeper Jakab Lefkovics, did not live to see the trial. There were two kinds of interrogation. The accused who confessed was condemned and executed. The one who did not confess died as a result of the torture. Jakab Lefkovics died at the hand of the executioner from Eperjes. The court retrospectively vindicated the interrogation as "justified." The other accused were executed.

Why did my father reach so deep into the wastebin of history? My father or Goebbels or Himmler? Because the immorality of anti-Semitism seeks its justification in the morality of Christian doctrine. Racial hatred, religious hatred—both very good, but how much better the racial hatred that is coupled with religious hatred! The Christians in Germany still stood aside. How could they stand aside once they had been shown that Jewish ritual had a law which demanded the murder of Christians?

At the Hungarian frontier, his luggage and passport were checked. "Nothing to declare?" Christopher had nothing to declare. The young police officer returned his passport. Christopher Wendelin. A traveler from the German Federal Republic; a rarity, but the name Wendelin seemed to mean nothing to the official.

In *Ritual Murder,* the painter Kajatán, acted by the most popular juvenile lead in German films, is the central figure. A great artist, a fanatic for truth, a painting Sherlock Holmes, the avenging angel of the Hungarian peasants exploited by the Jews. At the beginning of the film, for long stretches, one saw the life of the Jews in Orkut. One might have thought Richard Wendelin was opposing the principles of the state. In reality he was drawing a parallel with the pre-Hitler era: the Jews adapt themselves to the host nation, ingratiate themselves with it— and only dream of drinking their host's blood. Richard Wendelin had forgotten nothing, including the famous scene of the bloody inquisition of Jakab Lefkovics. Brutal, naturalistic, what was the spectator to think but that even in the eighteenth century, indignant people rose in revolt against the impudent alien race?

Christopher was alone in his compartment. He let the window down. Although the train was now traveling faster, not a breath stirred. They had made *Ritual Murder* in the summer— the Hungarian season. The film could have been made in Germany, at Neubabelsberg or in Geiselgasteig, but Richard Wendelin was a modern director; he liked working on location, to capture reality.

Reality and truth are similar concepts, but this is a deceptive similarity. In my father's film the Jew Lefkovics does not die at the hands of the inquisitor. In his film the executioner of Eperjes is not a German, as he was in reality. The "honor" of the murder is given to the Hungarians! There are regular proceedings against Lefkovics, a Hungarian court condemns him, he is executed. My father even dragged the Empress Maria Theresa into it. Grand finale: "Justice has triumphed." Helene Westerthal played the Empress. I shall never forget her. It was my favorite scene.

He sat down, not wanting to see the landscape, wanting to forget that he was in Hungary. Four weeks, at most. Then the hunt would be finished, he could start writing it down. He had been at work half a year. I shall have to write the book in Germany, where Ludwig Ludwig wants to see results. Occasionally I have felt homesick. For my mother and Ferdinand. Sometimes I compared the Polish forests with the German. Sometimes I felt hungry for German cooking. Homesickness is a gastronomic affair. In any case I don't remember ever starting a sentence in Poland with "In Germany we . . ." In Germany —that was the chamber of horrors in the shadow of the skyscraper, where I spent ten hours a day. It seems that back home, several articles have been written about me. Now I am considered a Communist. When they find out what I've been working on they'll say, "A Communist, a fellow with no country, is fouling his own nest." It's not the murderers who fouled their own nest, but me. Must you stir up the filth again, Herr Wendelin? One shouldn't stir up the filth, one should let it lie. Naturally you found things that were wonderful behind the Iron Curtain. Naturally. They feel that anyone who doesn't spread the mantle of oblivion over our past is a Communist. Why "our" past? Yours, perhaps, not mine. You know yourself, Herr Wendelin, they make us responsible for the sins of our fathers. I didn't know our fathers were dead. Did our fathers die in 1945? All of them? And were we born in 1945? All of us? Are we not, perhaps, our own fathers? Do we not fake our birth date, like vain women? You are joking, Herr Wendelin. There must be an end to all this, eventually. What do you mean by "eventually"? In ten years, fifteen, eighty-two? Who decides when the end is to be? Every nation has a right to be proud of itself. Proud of the present—or of the past? Of both. We can't go on forever humiliating ourselves. What do you mean by "forever"? My father is fifty-six. You're a Communist, Herr Wendelin. Your only excuse is that you have a father complex.

The Hungarian villages lay in the hot summer sun. The sparks from the locomotive fell on burnt grass. A peasant cart was waiting at a level crossing; the driver seemed to be asleep. By a shallow pond, a chance piece of water, stood a little peasant boy in the middle of a flock of geese. He was barefoot, and the geese were so white that it looked as if he were standing barefoot in snow.

István Balla. Soon the bearded Jews would come and kill him. He was played by the most successful child star of the Third Reich. Straight from *Hänsel und Gretel*. I envied him. What was his name? He must be twenty by now. He is probably still playing a juvenile lead.

He stood up again, leaned out of the window. "Take care you don't get a spark in your eye," his father used to say. He thought of one of the attractions of Berlin's Luna Park. You boarded an old railway carriage; no sooner had you sat down than the carriage began to rock and shake, giving the illusion of traveling at high speed. And then, pictures of places were drawn past the windows. The Eiffel Tower, his father had explained to him, Piccadilly Circus, the Acropolis, the mosques of Constantinople. You travel as fast as that when you are a child.

Now the Hungarian landscape was being drawn past the window. Wells with long lifting arms, thatch-roofed houses, rack wagons, aimless roads, grazing horses, the sky, a mountain over the plain. The more Christopher felt he recognized the country, the more unreal it seemed.

And all at once he knew why he had put off the journey to Hungary for so long, why he had now come to Hungary. He had searched and searched and he had not found what he was looking for, because he had been looking in the wrong place. How wrong Kasimir Nessor was! For a time, perhaps, he had believed that he could drown his father's guilt in a sea of guilt. For a time, perhaps, he had believed that he could free himself from his father's guilt by disowning his father. But you seek in vain for guilt if you do not seek the sources of guilt. In his search for Jewish guilt, his father had returned to the sources, and since he found pure sources he had poisoned them. On his search for his father's guilt he must return to the sources which his father had poisoned. Here, in Hungary, was the home of his father's guilt. Here Christopher was at home.

Two weeks later, Christopher sat on the balcony of his hotel overlooking the Danube and wrote to Ferdinand.

"We can begin to count the weeks—in four weeks at the latest I shall be back in Munich. By then I shall have finished collecting my material, but I'm not sure whether I shall be able to start writing it down straightaway. Here I have found what I must write—a play. I think I shall be able to get it down on paper in a few weeks.

"I know what you're thinking. Something else in Christopher's life has remained unfinished. You're wrong. If the crates of papers arrive safely in Munich—I shall have to think up all sorts of dodges to prevent them from falling into the wrong hands—I shall assemble the documentation in a short time. I have confined myself to the past of those who still play a part in Germany today. Many of them are hiding under false names. Hiding? That is a chapter of its own. Just to take one example, there is the commandant of a concentration camp whose hands are smeared with the blood of tens of thousands of innocent people, who has built up a splendid life for himself under a false name in the selfsame town in which his family spent the war. Does no one know? The policeman at the police station knows, the grocer knows, the tailor knows, his drinking companions know best of all. A good, solid family man, they will say, who loves dogs, takes lumps of sugar home for his canary, and is a strict but loving father to his children. And it's quite true. He was always kind to the dog that tore the Jews to pieces. Perhaps he will now be brought before the court. But the policeman, the grocer, the tailor and his drinking companions certainly won't be arraigned. 'The greatest scoundrel in the nation / Is he who makes a denunciation.' Not the mass murderer. We couldn't eliminate guilt entirely from our judicial vocabulary. But we have eliminated complicity. A nation that was a silent accessory to Auschwitz is full of understanding for silent policemen, silent grocers, silent tailors, silent drinking companions.

"What about silent writers?

"But let me tell you what happened in Budapest.

"I was received here, if anything, even more affably than in Warsaw. On the one hand this is connected with the rising—a new sense of belonging to the world. On the other hand, of course, it is deliberate propaganda. But it also springs from a desire to work with all those who want to make a clean break with the past. The archives, however, are in a sorry state. The war did not inflict such devastation as in Warsaw, but last year's rising was like a second operation performed on a wounded body. During the first few days I asked why this house was not rebuilt after the war, why whole streets were still barricaded, whose statue stood where now only a plinth speaks of fallen heroes. I don't ask anymore. People go about with bent heads—a nation that is accustomed to holding its head high. If you hear laughter, it is the laughter of an ignorant child—a nation that is born laughing and dies laughing. The women look at you questioningly and sadly and reproachfully—a nation that has always served its women.

"But I am straying from the point. I must talk about the fifth day of my stay, the decisive day.

"Among the young intellectuals whom I have met here—I was given names and addresses in Warsaw—is the theatrical director János Varga. He is thirty-two or thirty-three, a dark little man who is hard to describe because he is made up of so many contradictions. If I say that he has piercing eyes, it isn't true, because sometimes they look at you so sadly, as if the arrows they have shot are sticking in his own flesh; if I say he is mercurially vital, it isn't true, because he can suddenly lapse into a silence from which he starts up as though waking from a nightmare; if I say he is a convinced Communist, it isn't true, because no sooner has he tried to convince you with Hegelian dialectic than you feel once again how deeply he is enmeshed in bourgeois culture.

"János Varga's mother was a Jewess. This is important, I must say it at once. On the fifth day he took me to the Jewish cemetery—because of my research; it had nothing to do with him and his mother.

"The cemetery is called Rákoskeresztur. Can you imagine a cemetery in which eight out of ten tombstones bear the same date? The date is 1944. The years of birth vary—1890 and 1910 and 1938—but the year of death is always the same. If there were a well-preserved medieval cemetery it would look like this one, and the year 1260, say, would mean that the plague had raged at that time and reaped a terrible harvest. The plague raged in Hungary in 1944, the German plague.

"At one of the gravestones, which stand in long black rows like black hussars, Varga stopped. 'That is my mother's grave,' he said. I thought he had made a mistake, because on the gravestone there was only a man's name, Ferencz Bertalan, I believe, 1872-1930. Then Varga led me around the gravestone to the other side, where there were fourteen or fifteen names with various years of birth and one year of death: 1944. His mother's name, Ilona Varga—or Varga Ilona, as the Hungarians say—was the fourth from the top. Varga looked out over the cemetery lying in the midday sun, a black sea in the sunshine. 'There are no dead lying in this grave,' he said. 'The bodies were thrown into mass graves in Auschwitz, burned in Buchenwald, flung onto rubbish heaps in Bergen-Belsen, rotted away in Polish soil. I don't know where my cousins died, my uncles and aunts, my mother. Their father keeps vigil here over those who have vanished.'

"I felt ashamed, Ferdinand, ashamed of something I did not do. It wasn't my father I felt ashamed of; you too would have felt ashamed. Your generation and mine did not share in the guilt, but it comes to share in the guilt if it does not share in the

shame. We betray Germany by not admitting to being Germans
—as Abraham Avni did—and we betray Germany if we do not
feel ashamed.

"There, among the graves, we began to talk about my father.
'Your father,' said Varga, 'went back to the origins. Anti-Semitism is a tradition. His justification is the injustice committed
by the fathers. The anti-Semite has to prove that the Jews
crucify Christ again and again, that the Christians revolt again
and again against the crucifixion of the Saviour.'

"We talked about *Ritual Murder*. In the evening we continued the conversation. And then, something I had long suspected suddenly became clear to me. The struggle I have been
carrying on for years, to the best of my ability, is senseless if I
do not wipe out the memory of my father's sin—not for his sake,
but for my sake and yours. It is not enough to punish hatred of
the Jews: it must be torn up by the roots. This—paradoxically,
but only apparently paradoxically—is a German task. Other
nations also entertained the barbaric idea of anti-Semitism,
but since we sinned not merely in thought, we must do penance
in deeds. Don't imagine that I think barbarity began with the
ritual murder trial or even with my father's *Ritual Murder* film,
but I should be overestimating my powers if I thought I could
master the whole problem. I am my father's son. All I can do is
this: I must cause him to be forgotten.

"It seemed to me like a sign when I found that János Varga,
like many Hungarians, of course, had been preoccupied by the
ritual murder trials, and one in particular. For years he has
wanted to see the ritual murder trial of Tiszaeszlár dramatized
or filmed. It was no coincidence that my father did not choose
for his film the most famous instance of unleashed anti-Semitism.
This case is recorded in the three-volume work by the greatest
lawyer of the day, Károly von Eötvös, *A nagy per—The Great
Trial*. I read the book, which Varga lent me, in two days.

"At that time—1882—there lived among the two thousand
seven hundred inhabitants of Tiszaeszlár, a wretched village,
on the left bank of the Tisza, twenty-five Jewish families. They
formed part of the community; no one bothered about them.
On the first of April, the Saturday before Passover, the Jewish

Easter festival, several foreign Jews came to Tiszaeszlár, because the religious congregation had advertised the post of preceptor and circumciser. On this day the fourteen-year-old peasant girl Eszter Solymosi disappeared in Tiszaeszlár.

"To keep it short, when no trace of the vanished girl was
found, anti-Semitic agitators from Vienna set up their headquarters in Tiszaeszlár. By word of mouth and in writing they
proclaimed that the Jews made a practice of killing a Christian
child, an untouched girl, before Passover, in order to mix her
blood with the kosher flour and bake matzos, the Jewish Easter
bread, with it. This nightmarish lie sprang from the words which
the rabbi says during the blessing of the unleavened bread in the
presence of thirteen Jews. 'Behold, this is matzos. It comes from
blood and is made of blood, and lies in blood and goes in blood.
Take it and grow and be fruitful and healthy and strong and
pure.' The poison of suspicion seized Tiszaeszlár. The suspicion of having committed the murder was directed against the
Jewish bell ringer József Sarf—that is what the synagogue servant is called here, although synagogues have no bells. First
with promises, flattery and gifts, then with threats the enraged
villagers—the whole press was now demanding retribution
for Eszter Solymosi's death—persuaded the synagogue servant's son, little Samu, who was not yet five, to testify against his
father. He described how his father had lured the Christian
girl into the house, how a 'Jewish uncle' had cut her throat—
'Her head fell on the floor'—how his brother Móricz had held
the bowl into which Eszter's blood had flowed. How the boy
of barely fourteen was likewise persuaded and forced to testify
against his father would be a drama on its own, though not a
specifically Jewish drama—Louis XVI's son was similarly persuaded and forced to testify against his mother.

"In a few weeks I shall tell you the whole story of the case.
You can also read Eötvös' book. The German press said that he
was a Jew and that his name was Goldschmied. In reality the
ancestors of the Eötvös family came to Hungary with Arpád, the
first Hungarian king. Today I will merely explain why my
father did not choose the 'great trial' as the subject of his film.
An immense scandal is attached to the name of Tiszaeszlár. It

transpired later that the examining magistrate, who took Móricz into his personal custody, had previously been convicted of robbery with violence. In the summer of the 'year of the murder'— and this is the important point—the body of little Eszter Solymosi was found in the reeds of the Tisza. Only after Eötvös had taken on the case for the accused was the corpse exhumed. During the great trial, Eötvös demanded a new examination, which ended with proof that Eszter Solymosi had not died a violent death. Moreover, she had fallen in the water long after the Passover festival. After Károly von Eötvös' seven-hour speech, all fifteen accused were acquitted on 31 July 1883, and the verdict was upheld by two higher courts.

"I must close.

"I shall write the play, and in honor of Károly von Eötvös it will be called *The Great Trial*. I shall go back to the origins. I shall show the conspiracy against the Jews and shall not conceal the historical fact that even then it was hatched by Germany and Austria. I shall not spare the Jews, of whom a terrible thing can be said—that they too are human. And I shall show that the human path forks at the Jews. They stand at the parting of the ways, dead and living symbols calling upon mankind to decide. This way, humanity and tolerance and understanding and love and justice; that way, stupidity and envy and hatred and apathy and inhumanity.

"I see you before me. You clap your hands above your head. Christopher is taking up his father's theme! Christopher is writing a drama based on *Ritual Murder*! People will say, 'He is imitating his father in reverse.' Worse still, they will say, 'He is exploiting his father's disgrace.' They will say, 'He is fleeing into the past in order to escape from the present.' People will say, 'Now it is clear, absolutely and unmistakably clear, that all his actions were dictated by his father fixation.' Do you know what I shall reply to that, Ferdinand? That I am glad of it. That a good conscience is no conscience at all. That is exactly what I set out to prove, that without our father fixation, we shall not be cured. That all we need for a cure is this: a father fixation.

"Tomorrow I leave for Tiszaeszlár."

Only a few more lines—then he sealed the envelope. Evening had spread over the Danube. The air was vibrating with heat. Before a Danube bridge an old steamer lowered its funnel like a white flag. Across the river, on the Danube quay, the lights went on—gleaming spots on the dark target.

Christopher felt light and happy, as he had not felt since his childhood.

From Budapest to Miskolc they went first northeast, then almost due east.

Christopher was sitting next to the woman who was driving the car, an old-fashioned vehicle which the Ministry of Culture had put at the travelers' disposal. The woman was young, dark-haired, with dark eyes above broad cheekbones and a large, angular mouth above a slightly projecting, almost straight chin. Her name was Eva Zátony and she worked in the Ministry. Because of her knowledge of languages, she was employed for the most part in showing the country to visitors, who now, after the rising and the "thaw," came to Hungary in great numbers. János Varga, who was sitting in the back of the car, had told Christopher that she had been divorced for a year, and had two daughters, aged four and five. Christopher had met her with certain misgivings, because in Warsaw he had had difficulty in shaking off the guides who confused Baedeker with Marx. But neither on the long journey to Miskolc nor in this second-largest city of Hungary, where they were going to spend the night, did Eva seem to want to convince Christopher of the blessings of Communism—either because she did not look upon him as a typical visitor from the West, or because of her friendship with János Varga. It was not difficult to perceive the fabric of this friendship; indeed, it would have been difficult to overlook it. Every word, every gesture betrayed János Varga's romantic passion for Eva, an emotion which he tried awkwardly to mask. She, on the other hand, emphasized her innocuous friendship for the young director, joked with him as with a comrade, disarmed him by her blind trust.

It wasn't easy for Christopher to travel with a couple whose relationship was on the one hand so simple, on the other so complicated. When he looked at Eva from the side he was aware that he hadn't desired a woman since that evening in Paris. Women had shared his bed, but he had not desired them. His friends had envied him the women in Warsaw, but he did not deceive himself. Since Martha had confronted him with the truth he had been homeless. Young women felt this; they gave him asylum, and he left them the next morning as vagabonds leave the flophouse. He answered Martha's letters, but answered them late. He threw so many drafts away, wrote them again, threw away, finally sent off, almost shame-facedly, letters about which the only genuine things were the versions which he threw away, letters that were smooth and cautious and noncommittal, that betrayed nothing but his hurt feelings and concealed nothing but his wounded vanity.

She reminds me of Martha, he thought, but there is no similarity. Her skirt has slipped up over her knees; she lets it do so. It's only in Germany that women have such long legs. Her feet are too large—curious that I like that, too. She seems to like me. Free and easy and coquettish—quite different from her comradely behavior toward János. I wouldn't like to hurt him. Nor would I like her to think me shy or standoffish. I won't look at her. János is watching me. He leans forward, his hand touches the back of her neck as though by chance.

"We are now entering a district which won't look to you 'Hungarian' at all," she said, lapsing into the tone of the professional guide.

To the left of the motorway the dense forest rose to the Zemplén mountains. "At least we call them mountains," jested Eva. "The highest mountain is two thousand three hundred feet." After the town of Bodrogkeresztur—"You'll never be able to pronounce that"—the road turned off to the right. Now they were in the midst of the Tokay wine-growing region. "Even 'your' Goethe," said Eva, "did justice to our Tokay. He mentions it in *Faust*. Schubert celebrated it in the song 'In Praise of Tokay.'"

"It's a mere tourist attraction," Varga interrupted her, rather irritably. "Tokay is overrated."

"The commander of the Benczur Hussars always ordered

his regiment to march as though on parade when it passed through here," she retorted.

"The Benczur Hussars were stupid serfs," declared Varga. "They had never tasted a Bordeaux or a Moselle."

"Since I don't know anything about wines," said Christopher, "I won't notice the difference either."

They passed through the little town of Tokay, bore right again, and now drove a few miles southward along a dusty road bordered by traffic signs, like premature heralds of the future.

Tiszaeszlár. They would scarcely have noticed the village, might perhaps have driven past it, if an unusual sight had not brought them to a halt. Four or five men in their black Sunday best and black boots were standing at the entry to the village, and although the sign on the first single-story house, *BOR, PÁLINKA,* disclosed that it was an inn, these were not lounging drinkers but rather the notables of the village who, notified of the visit from Budapest, had been waiting, no doubt for some considerable time already, to receive the guests. The visit began at the inn—Christopher did not understand a word of the juicy Hungarian that gushed out to meet the guests— where a six-butt Tokay was served, a rarity, as Eva explained, because normally only three or four *puttony,* the sweet soul of the choice berries, were added to a cask of 160 liters.

The heavy wine went to Christopher's head. As always, when he had drunk too much, he imagined that he could see himself more clearly than his environment. At such moments, too, disconnected images passed in front of his eyes, sequences linked together as in a film trailer that only shows the high points and promises more than the show will fulfill. He saw himself in the fort on the Syrian frontier, but he was sober enough to realize why precisely this picture had risen to the surface from his subconscious. A foreign language was being spoken around him, the woman was talking a foreign language with the men in black; they had come here on his account, yet he was isolated and excluded.

To these people the "ritual murder" of Tiszaeszlár is a historical event; it happened seventy-five years ago. To me it happened yesterday. Am I still searching, or have I found what I was searching for? Am I hunting the past because I want to exorcise the ghost of my father? What would my father say if he could see me now, in his hunting ground? The feeble second generation! Can't you do anything but imitate me? If you would only realize, father, that I have not suffered because of your name. I haven't been persecuted because of your name, or not for a long time—I could more readily reproach myself for the fact that people show me greater understanding on your account. Just look, he's a Wendelin, and not a criminal! I haven't suffered because of your name, but because of the applause you gained, because of the unjust acquittal and the unjust condemnation. But what am I doing here, at an inn among the Tokay vineyards?

They left the gathering and went along the main street, the only real street, because the side streets consisted of only a few houses and ended in open fields. The sun blazed down mercilessly upon the village street; the dust was so deep that walking through it was like wading in water; the shadows of the men walking in front of Christopher sank into the dust, the dust swallowed them up, they walked without shadows, like Peter Schlemihl. The acacia trees by the roadside also spread no shadow. They were acacias such as Christopher had never seen, poor little trees with poor little green crowns. The single-story houses were separated from the roadway by a ditch that ran the whole length of the village; tiny concrete bridges linked them with the roadway; but the ditch was dried out and the filth left by the last rain had dried as hard as stone. You could see from one end of the village to the other; the main street also ran out into open fields, the village ended in black earth, in a no-man's-land. There was no one to be seen, not a dog. In the houses the sliding shutters had been let down. The better or worse shutters, of metal or crooked venetian blinds, were the only indication of whether the house was occupied by the poorest or only the poor. A grocery, which was now shut, the inn, the headquarters of the Communist Party, the peasant collective and, for some reason, the village photographer were the only houses bearing signs. At last, from the other end of the village, came the policeman. He looked like a Russian soldier. He stopped outside the grocer's shop, pretending not to see them.

In front of a half-collapsed brick wall the man came to a halt. Behind it, gray grass grew wildly; a few blocks of stone lay about. This had been the synagogue, explained Eva. It had stood here until the last year of the war, then it was razed to the ground. The Party secretary, the chief spokesman of the group, gave some explanation. Eva did not translate it. Here, one April day seventy-five years ago, the Jews had gathered— Abraham Braun and Hermann Vollner, Ignacz Klein and Emmanuel Taub—to choose the preceptor and circumciser. His name was Salamon Svarz, age thirty-eight; his name had come first on the bill of indictment. The synagogue had survived the ritual murder trial, but not the year 1944. No tombstone spoke of the death of the synagogue.

The house next door was still standing. József Sarf, then forty-one, sexton of the synagogue, or "bell ringer," accused number five, disappeared after the trial, emigrated to America with his son Móricz, number one witness for the prosecution. The Party secretary walked ahead, knocked at the door. An old woman opened; an old man rose to his feet, also in his Sunday best; he had been sitting by the window. The room was spotlessly clean, although only planks lay across the mud floor. A bottle of Tokay came out and was put on the table. Yes, József Sarf's house. Some gentlemen from the city had made inquiries here some fifteen or twenty years ago, but what was there to see? At most the yard behind the house, a few chickens which were not bothered by the sun, a few pigs in a shed. Here little Samu Sarf had played, Sarf Samu, until the men from the city came and gave him chocolate, until the young peasant women brought him toys and told him his father had murdered the blond Eszter Solymosi and the "Jewish uncle" had cut off her head with a big knife. *"Egészségére!"* "Your health," the men drank to Christopher. They were sorry, that was all they knew; it was a long time ago, seventy-five years ago.

The spirit of the place, Ludwig Ludwig had said, had to be caught. So this was the spirit of the place. The Tiszaeszlár ritual murder trial had taken place seventy-five years ago, but thirteen years ago they burned down the synagogue. So it goes on, and it will continue to go on if nothing is done to stop it. The sons bore false witness against their fathers. It goes on, and it will continue to go on if nothing is done to stop it. Is there anyone still alive who remembers?

The men in their black Sunday best looked at each other. Six or seven Jewish families had lived here. They had been taken away in a truck in 1944. There was only one Jew here now, eighty-year-old Lajos Bukszbaum, who had been five years old at the time of the trial. Abraham Bukszbaum, teacher from Ibrány, accused number two, must have been his grandfather. He lived in the last house, on a side street. He was sitting in an armchair by the stove, in his black Sunday best. He liked Christopher; he was flattered by Christopher's attention. He thought that only Christopher spoke German, so he, who also spoke German, must be something special in Chrisopher's eyes. He talked about a policeman. He had seen the policeman beating his grandfather, his only memory. But one of the guides said to Eva that that was Lajos Bukszbaum's father; he was confusing his father with his grandfather. The old man teetered over to the kitchen cabinet and brought out a bottle of Tokay, Tokay Szamorodni, but the men slapped him on the back and said they had drunk enough already and he shouldn't open his Szamorodni.

The village is called Tiszaeszlár, but it is not on the banks of the Tisza. They left the village, walked in the direction of the sinking sun toward the river. The men strode along beside the narrow canal, János Varga with them. Christopher and Eva followed at a short distance. Christopher saw the black boots in front of him, four pairs of black boots. The grass bent under their boots and lay flat, trodden grass, a narrow path beside the narrow canal. "Eszter Solymosi must have taken this path," said Eva. Christopher reached out his hand to her, kept her hand in his. When János Varga looked around at them, he let go of her hand. She smiled. He said to himself that he was here to absorb the background in which his drama was to be set, that he ought not to think of anything else. But the wine and the sun had entered into his blood, and his eyes ran over

the thighs of the woman walking in front of him. So Eszter Solymosi had taken this path, and along this path they had carried the corpse, from the Tisza to Tiszaeszlár. The boots were
no longer moving. There was the river. "Down below, in
Csonka-Füzes," said János Varga. He was standing beside Eva.
"There, in the reeds, they found the body," The vineyards on
the other side of the river sloped gently down to the Tisza. The
reeds were still tall, as they had been seventy-five years ago.
The men in their Sunday best nodded, uncomprehendingly.
They were friendly people and hospitality was inborn in them,
but they did not understand why these people had come from
the big city to see where the boatmen had found the body of a
little peasant girl. Two world wars had passed over the land
since then; once the Emperor had held maneuvers here, and
then the war game had turned into real war; their own and foreign soldiers had descended on them, the Germans had come
and the Russians; the Jews had gone, Jews had come back, Jews
had been herded into trucks, the synagogue was no longer standing; the police had beaten people up, and one policeman had
been strung up on an acacia tree; and the Tisza still flowed
along its narrow bed, and the grape harvest always began later
than elsewhere, and the reeds were still tall—and what had
all this to do with a peasant girl who had fallen in the water, and
with a village whose name happened to be in learned books?
They didn't read books in Tiszaeszlár.

They walked back along the canal, through the fields that
had come to life. The peasants greeted and stared after them.
János Varga walked with the men in their black Sunday best.
Every now and then he looked around. Eva did not let go of
Christopher's hand anymore. "You could write your play in
Budapest," she said. "Perhaps," he said. "It's hot," she said,
and came to a stop. He dried her wet forehead with his handkerchief. She pressed her cheek against the palm of his
hand.

The village, too, had come to life. Two men on a cart shouted
something to the men in black. They laughed. The policeman
was walking to and fro. He pretended not to see them. The
children ran toward the group as it approached the inn out-

side which the car stood. In front of József Sarf's house the old couple were sitting on a bench.

They had to go into the inn once more. They drank wine, ate black bread and bacon. János Varga wanted to pay. The men wouldn't let him. When they went out into the street again, half a dozen children were standing admiringly round the car.

Eva sat at the wheel. Christopher insisted that this time János Varga should sit beside her. One boy, rather older than the others, swung himself up onto the running board. Eva drove at a walking pace. At last the boy jumped off. Christopher looked around. Tiszaeszlár had vanished in a cloud of dust.

They had planned to spend the night in Tokay, but they were tired from the wine and the heat, and stopped at an inn in the middle of the wine country, on the Bodrog. The single-story house, not a State undertaking but a leftover from the days of private property, had only two small guestrooms. The innkeeper arranged for a third bed at a nearby farm. Christopher and János Varga argued as to who was to sleep at the farm; each wanted to leave the room at the inn to the other. They could not agree and postponed a decision.

It was a long time before the food was brought in. They heard the frightened cackling of the chickens from the yard. The table stood among the vinestocks, which reached down to the river—green dancers holding hands. They drank Tokay and talked about the afternoon, the journey into the past. Dusk was falling.

We are sitting on the banks of a river whose name I have never heard before; we have ordered breaded chicken; Eva is looking at me; the wine sharpens or dulls my senses; János is watching us; we are discussing a trial that was forgotten for more than seventy years. I talk about Móricz Sarf and feel Eva's knee against my knee. It is true that I am carried away by enthusiasm, but I preen myself like a peacock. János or I—who will sleep at the farm? If I sleep at the inn, I shall sleep with Eva. János has crumpled up his paper serviette, now he is clutching mine. If he were capable of hate he would hate me.

But he is only capable of unhappiness; I shall insist on sleeping at the farm.

"Everything was lost before Eötvös intervened," said János Varga. "Two Jewish lawyers, Dr. Heumann and Dr. Flegmann, had been refused permission to see the Christian girl's body."

"The Jews are forbidden to defend themselves," said Christopher. "People say a Jew is never objective toward another Jew—and why should he be? A Frenchman may defend a Frenchman, a Protestant a Protestant—the Jew remains dependent upon the philanthropist."

Eva, who till now had taken no part in the conversation, said, "Justice ought to replace the philanthropist."

János Varga agreed. "The Christian doctrine has not fostered mankind's slow development to the knowledge and practice of justice, but abruptly interrupted it."

Christopher contradicted this. It was evident that János Varga was barely twenty-four when Hungary went Marxist.

The theater director flared up. Jesus Christ had been a good but impatient man, who refused to believe in the triumph of justice on earth. Therefore, instead of justice, he proclaimed love, and although there was no proof that mankind was capable of justice, it was quite certainly incapable of love. The question, retorted Christopher, was whether justice is possible without love. No, said János Varga, the question was whether love is possible without justice. "It is not a matter of order of precedence, but of chronological order," he went on. Love was a capricious impulse, justice an austere habit. It was, nevertheless, possible that people who lived in justice might learn to love one another. They might learn to love those who dealt justly with them; and they might learn to love those with whom they dealt justly. "There is no one we hate more than a person to whom we have been unjust." But love was arbitrary. "He who loves an individual does not yet love man, he who loves man does not yet love mankind, he who loves mankind does not yet love man." It was no coincidence that it was not until the third book, when he laid down the Ten Commandments, that Moses said: "Thou shalt love thy neighbour as thyself"—whereas he had presented the commandments of justice

long before. "Love is, at best, the eleventh commandment."
Even the Church spoke of the Last Judgment. Debtors in love
we remain always, Paul wrote to the Romans. The love of man
is not enough, even for the Church, nor is the love of God
enough for it; in the end there must be justice.

"The accused of Tiszaeszlár," replied Christopher, "finally
obtained justice. But what did that mean? The persecutions of
the Jews continued. The judges were capable of justice, not of
love."

He had turned away from Eva and was speaking only to
János Varga, and János Varga was speaking only to Eva. "That
is precisely what proves that love is an inhuman concept—inhuman because it was not made for man."

"I heard something this afternoon that I didn't know," said
Christopher. "It will influence my whole play. After the trial,
József Sarf took his fourteen-year-old son Móricz with him to
America. And if you want to talk about Paul's Epistle to the
Romans, there is a passage in it which I now understand for
the first time. *'Who against hope believed in hope.'* That's the
point. What could József Sarf expect from the son who had
accused him of murder, had hurled the terrible and unjust
accusation in his face and made common cause with the executioners? And what could Móricz Sarf expect from his father,
whom he had cut to the quick, whose blood he had denied, to
whom he had imputed blood guilt and whom he had very
nearly handed over to the executioner? Justice? Justice would
not have helped them, János, as they traveled steerage to America!" He noticed the look that János Varga and Eva exchanged.
"I'm not a sentimental German. I won't bring the story of
Tiszaeszlár to an end between decks on a ship to America,
nor shall I end it with love between father and son. But the
struggle for survival begins at birth, and how are we to survive if we do not believe that there is a hope against hope?"

The dark eyes of János Varga, which often looked as sad
as the eyes of a dog that has resigned itself to having to live
among human beings, flashed. Almost provocatively he asked,
"Why did you go to Warsaw?"

"What do you mean by that?"

He felt that Eva was about to intervene. Did she fear that the philosophical discussion would stray into the personal and therefore dangerous? Did she fear that it was happening on her account?

"You have wanted retribution of some kind," said János Varga. "You have worked for it, and thus for justice. You haven't been working for love, and you were right. Are you writing your play to escape responsibility? Have you discovered love in order to prove that reconciliation between father and son exists, even if one of the two has damned himself by his deeds to all eternity?"

"You mean I am József Sarf and Móricz Sarf is my father?"

János Varga did not reply. He lapsed into a brooding silence, almost as though he had forgotten that he had challenged Christopher. Eva touched Christopher's hand under the table.

Is he right? Have I turned from an avenging angel into the Good Samaritan? Am I fleeing from the present, am I fleeing into the past? Did I think that I would discover hope only in the past? Did I have to discover hope because we Germans have nothing else but hope? Why does *The Great Trial* fascinate me as it does? I must justify myself not to János, but to myself.

He tried to smile. "You uncovered Tiszaeszlár for me. Are you now going to deny your child?" He wrinkled his brow. "In the cemetary of Rákoskeresztur something strange happened to me. I found, if you like, something petty in myself. I no longer felt responsible for all fathers, only for my own father. If it is true that for millions of Germans *Ritual Murder* is still the truth, then before I can think of retribution, I must set truth in the place of the lie. The chronological order, as you say."

"Even without hope?" said János Varga.

Christopher couldn't answer. The meal was brought. Eva served it, praised the Hungarian chicken, asked jokingly whether the gherkin salad with red pepper wasn't too strong for Christopher, whether he had ever eaten cream *palacsinta* before. There was something intentional in the triviality of her conversation—but was it Christopher she was trying to protect or János Varga? Both seemed glad that they had been able to break off their threatening discussion. They went to work with a will on the Tokay, and the forced gaiety quickly gave way to the joyous sense of their youthful friendship. János Varga's mood changed more rapidly, more abruptly than Christopher's. He raised his glass, toasted the happy chance of their meeting, the blessing of the wine, the good day, the warm summer night. He drank to Christopher, drank to Eva, remembered her children—"The most enchanting creatures in the world. You must see them"—and yet, a sweet resignation echoed in his words.

Now Christopher, too, allowed himself to be carried away. He began to talk about Ludwig Ludwig, to whom he had not yet revealed the subject of his play, but upon whom you could rely—a good publisher, that was a big step forward, but now a theater had to be found that would dare to stage *The Great Trial*. "If there's no German theater it will have to be a Hungarian one," broke in the director, as though forgetting what he had said previously. No, said Christopher, there were enough theaters in Germany; they would find the right one. And more and more excitedly he cast the play, mentioning actors whose names his friends scarcely knew. "The most important thing," he said, "is to find a boy who can play Móricz Sarf. He can be fifteen, of course, even sixteen. We've got enough infant prodigies. They haven't become extinct since one of them played István Balla in *Ritual Murder*. Now they play more innocuous roles: the good child who brings his estranged parents together again. I don't want any of the angel faces. Anyway, that's your affair, János."

They both looked at him in surprise. "My affair?" asked the director.

Christopher wasn't sure whether, as he now said, he had really thought of it from the outset, whether it had seemed to him a matter of course that János Varga would direct *The Great Trial*. Perhaps it was gratitude, perhaps it was the sentimental mood induced by the wine; perhaps he wanted to prove that they were not so far apart from each other as had for a moment appeared; perhaps he even wanted to convict János Varga of inconsistency. With an enthusiasm that surprised himself, as though his wish was an accomplished fact, he spoke of their future work. He spurred himself on, talked himself into a state of confidence—guest directors were no rarity on German stages. Hungarians were doubly welcome in the West just now. Also, there was good reason to insist upon his friend's being employed: János' knowledge of the facts, his role as midwife at the birth of the theme, his connection with the Hungarian background. "If you didn't exist, you would have to be invented."

More speedily than he had anticipated, his enthusiasm spread to his friends. János' pale, sunken cheeks had reddened. No doubt he would be able to get leave from the *Nemzeti Szinház*; exit permits were issued more liberally now, and finally, his invitation would be regarded as a tribute to Hungary. "Don't you agree, Eva?"

Although she had drunk less than the two men, Eva joined in the chorus. She turned to Christopher and told him that she had been thinking of it for a long time. He didn't know what a fortunate choice he had made. It was a pity the theater was closed for the summer, so that he hadn't been able to see János' most recent production. *A néma levente* had been a triumph. "We have no one better in Hungary."

János Varga said nothing.

It isn't modesty, it must be something else. He doesn't expect from Eva the applause of the audience on the other side of the footlights; he is offended to see that in her eyes I am the giver. I shouldn't have shown myself so self-assured, so patronizing. Her eyes encouraged me. I am being considerate toward his feelings. She isn't. I shall deceive Martha. What the hell, she never loved me, and I have deceived her a hundred times. Has there ever been more between János and Eva than friendship? Has he lost her? She is free, like Martha, but Martha has obviously thrown off a burden, whereas Eva never carried one. Why doesn't János say anything? Is he thinking about *The Great Trial*, or about the fact that Eva and I might be left alone together?

The innkeeper put a candle on the table, protected by a globe, but even without this, the light would not have been blown out; not a breath stirred. They could hear the murmur of the Bodrog, a sleeping child talking about its dreams in its sleep. In the light of the candle the dust on the vinestocks was like costly glass. The innkeeper said something about going to bed, about trouble with the farmer.

"No, Christopher, it can't be done," said János Varga.

"Who's to stop us?"

"I haven't been in Germany since the war. The Germans in Hungary—I lived for a year in the cellar of the theater. The idea of working with German actors of whom I don't know . . ."

"But I know . . ."

"People would say, 'The Communist from Hungary! And on top of that, half-Jewish!' I'm not a coward, but I don't know whether my nerves would stand it."

"Leave it to me, Christopher," said Eva. "I'll persuade János."

"Eva is sure she can persuade me of anything," laughed János Varga. His expression had changed again.

The innkeeper hung about the table, and once again the argument started as to who was to stay at the inn, who was to follow him to the farmhouse. "If you can't decide, then I'll go," said Eva, but János suggested they should draw lots.

She took a coin in her hand, hid it behind her back, held it in one of her hands. Whoever picked the hand with the coin in it was to stay at the inn.

We are casting lots for Eva. Perhaps János suggested it in order to humiliate her. But she pretends not to notice; she never notices anything she doesn't want to. *You are not bad, only lacking in resistance. / You are not a liar, only eternally toneless. / You may have done the most terrible things / And will only be pretty and tired and quiet.* Who wrote that? She probably doesn't understand either me or János. She is laughing. János knows she won't belong to him—irrespective of whether I go or he does. János suggested drawing lots because he thinks he always loses. I hope he points to the right hand.

Eva held her clenched fists over the table. The candlelight played on her strong, beautiful hands.

"No, you choose, János."

"You're the guest," said János Varga.

One hand seemed to him a bit bigger than the other; the coin must be in that one. He chose the other. She unclenched her fist. The coin lay on the palm of her hand.

János didn't seem to have expected anything else. He acted his part badly. The gaiety with which he said goodnight was exaggerated. "See you at breakfast, not later than eight." He followed the innkeeper. The darkness swallowed up his thin, bent figure.

They waited for the innkeeper's return. They were alone; they moved a little farther away from each other.

"I almost took a coin in each hand," she said. "But I couldn't be sure you would be the one to choose."

"János is in love with you," said Christopher.

"After my divorce he wanted to marry me. It would have been a good thing for the children."

They talked about the children, but the conversation was like the capricious trilling of the birds on a telegraph wire. It makes no difference to the vibrating of the wires, or to the messages which the wires are conveying.

"You should write your play in Budapest," she said.

"Even then it would only be for a few weeks."

"We think in terms of weeks."

"I want to get to know you," he said.

"I am difficult to get to know," she laughed. "I always do what I want."

A sore feeling of happiness came over him. Two days at the side of a woman whom he desired, Tiszaeszlár, a heady conversation, the heavy wine, Móricz Sarf, the woman's hand on his cheek, the sultry night, a promise for which he had not had to fight. A good sore feeling—a wounded body that is healing and pants for life. Like all convalescents, he would have liked to have talked about the illness that he had overcome: the deceptions of his childhood, his father, the humiliations, the doubts, the aimless path whose aim had at last come into sight, the Warsaw hunt, the light that was coming nearer.

"We could drink brotherhood now," she said. "But then we would have to kiss. That's the custom in Hungary."

"Let's walk down to the river," he said.

She didn't move. "I'm going to call you Kristóf," she said.

"I suppose that's the same as Christopher."

"It's totally different. Kristóf is a fine Hungarian name."

"Did you ever know anyone called Kristóf?" he said, trying to imitate her intonation.

"An ugly dwarf with a humpback," she said.

To get a new name is as simple as that. Everything is perfectly simple, I just didn't realize. You can do what you like and you count time in weeks. You have two children and remain a young girl. Christopher has a harsh ring. You stress the second syllable and the name sounds almost like a command. I've never thought about it. Kristóf has a soft sound. János knows that we shall make love tonight. Is he thinking, she has gone to bed with the tall, blond German? I am thinking too much. My body is sore and young, and I desire her. There is no need for me to feel ashamed of my recovery.

The innkeeper returned. He took them into the house, showed them their rooms, but only in one room did he put the candle on the bedside table and light it. The room was freshly whitewashed, the bright blue peasant furniture was decorated with colorful Hungarian tulips looking like embroidery. There was a smell of fresh timber. Christopher couldn't help thinking of North Sea bathing huts.

The bed was narrow, the linen rough and slightly damp.

They made love as naturally as though completing a day that could not have ended in any other way. Her body was young and strong and had no secrets. Her body took him in as though they had made love a hundred times. She bore his burden and took the burden from him.

The red, bulging featherbeds fell to the floor. "They are meant for Siberian nights," she laughed, stretching her naked body. "The peasants are always cold. And also, they're always ill."

"I can't imagine that you were ever ill," he said.

"I've never been ill. I haven't had time."

She lay on his arm.

The two days they had spent together were their past, their whole common past.

"I wanted to go to bed with you already in Miskolc," she said.

"Do you remember how I wiped the sweat from your brow?" he said.

"Of course," she said. "I didn't want to go to Tokay. I knew why."

"Did you stretch out one hand further than the other?" he asked.

"Yes, the right one," she said. "I thought, I'll stretch out the hand with the coin, he will think I'm doing it so that he should think the coin is in the other hand, so he will pick the hand that's stretched out, the right one. I was right. That's how complicated I am. We shall say tomorrow that we drank brotherhood."

He took her in his arms. Beneath his body her face became serious. Nothing was as serious to her as the meeting of two bodies. She didn't say "I love you" and didn't seem to expect him to say "I love you." Her face was no different from that afternoon, in the village street of Tiszaeszlár.

"I'm thirsty," he said, and before he could stop her she had put on his jacket, which reached to her knees. She ran off, barefoot.

Martha. For the first time I am deceiving Martha. A sentimental German—of course I'm not deceiving her. I have no bad conscience. Nor do I feel any satisfaction in deceiving. *"Martha—c'est une fille merveilleuse."* Perhaps I really shall write my play in Budapest. It's a good thing I've saved up, I can stay six weeks or even eight. Where has she gone? It may all be chance, but one never meets a woman by chance. She has given me a new name, Kristóf! We will say that we drank brotherhood. As though I wouldn't give myself away! I must go and see where she has gone.

In one hand she held up the carafe, in the other the glass. He wanted her again. She shook her head, bowed deeply and said, "Hungarian women strike water from a stone when their lords command them!" As he stretched out his hand for the carafe and glass, she was in the bed with one bound; she hadn't time or didn't want to take off his jacket. He put his arms around her hips. The empty ends of the long sleeves played round his neck.

The sultriness of the night did not abate. The acacias were giving off their scent, the birds were silent, the crickets were cheeping—now it was their turn. The candle was burnt out.

"I can't see your serious face anymore," he said.

She sighed in his arms and said nothing. Then they heard nothing but the murmur of the Bodrog.

"At night, rivers speak more loudly," he said.

"I knew we wouldn't sleep," she said.

And they did not fall asleep until the rays of the sun poured into the room. Day had taken over from night like one sentry relieving another.

He wrote his play in Budapest.

The summer was hot; he hardly noticed it. In the tiny hotel room the books were piled high along the walls; there was scarcely room on the little table for his papers. There was no detail of the Tiszaeszlár ritual murder trial that he did not know.

It had been an abyss of corruption. Even at the preliminary hearing, the eighteen-year-old peasant girl Julcsa Vámosi stated that she had seen her friend Eszter Solymosi at one in the afternoon on the day of the murder. After the "blood ritual," in other words. With this, the case against the Jews should have collapsed at once. But two weeks later, Julcsa's mother laid a charge against her own daughter—of perjury. For this the punishment is five years' imprisonment. The mother sent her daughter to prison. Mother bore witness against daughter, son against father. Only one false witness? Christopher counted up to thirty. The peasant girl's corpse was identified, the accused was acquitted. But is that justice? The false witnesses should have been brought before the court, but not one was charged.

Christopher's room was filled with people long since dead. The lawyer Nándor Horanszky who gave up the defense. He was a politician, and a lawyer who defends Jews never gets elected to parliament. The teacher Abraham Bukszbaum, aged twenty-seven, who smiled during the whole case. "Why are you smiling, Bukszbaum?"—"An innocent man has no need to be sorrowful, Your Excellency." The deputy examining magistrate responsible for interrogating the Jews, Kálmán Péczely. In 1865 he and his mistress together had murdered and robbed an old man. A paradox of history: twenty-five years before the interrogation of Móricz Sarf, to the day, he himself had been condemned to fifteen years' imprisonment. The abyss.

Is that the only thing that motivates me, to combat the poison of hatred against the Jews? Is there nothing else? My father sinned against the Jews. I have a father fixation, I have a Jew complex. It wouldn't be surprising, but the one concerns me as little as the other. With every line I see more clearly. The Jews are the tree around which the serpent winds itself. He who speaks of Jews has no need to seek for symbols. They are the symbol. Tiszaeszlár. This is how a mass psychosis is bred, how terrible obedience is born, how authority wreaks havoc unchecked, how eyes see what they did not see, how the commandment of family loyalty breaks down, how politics smothers the heart. Death to the Jews! The cry never dies away unheard. Concentration camp guards, a never-ending supply of concentration camp guards. And Károly von Eötvös. *Who against hope believed in hope.* Against hope. The same Epistle to the Romans contains the statement, wonderfully new, new even in its cautious rhythm: *For scarcely for a righteous man will one die: yet peradventure for a good man some would even dare to die.*

Ten hours, twelve hours. Every day János Varga came to see him, or they met in a park, or Christopher visited his friend in his little house on the hills of Buda. But János Varga stubbornly refused Eva's invitation to meet Christopher at her flat.

If he were invited, the director said, he would come to Germany. A definite promise? Nothing János Varga said was definite. Christopher felt a great liking for him, but he didn't think that he knew him. János Varga's soul resembled the house in which he lived. Scrupulously clean and yet neglected, a thousand books and a broken-down camp bed, as though to emphasize that it was not a man who lived but a disembodied brain that worked here. At the same time there were countless pictures of his mother, paintings, photographs, framed, unframed.

The house was full of flowers, then of dead flowers that were not taken out of the vases for days on end, so that a smell of rotting vegetation and cemetery met you even on the staircase. János Varga never spoke of himself, as though his watch had long since run down. Christopher thought of Ferdinand. Had he once more chosen a cripple for his friend?

Every day he read aloud to the director the scenes that he had written. Justice, love—no quarrels, there was a fine, quiet unanimity. János Varga advised him, stressed dramatic effects, discarded rhetorical dialogues, helped Christopher to polish a part, encouraged Christopher when he failed in his efforts. Where his profession was concerned, János Varga was another man—joyful, self-confident, often ruthless. There were scenes which Christopher wrote four, five times. The weaker the scene was, the more passionately Christopher read it. János Varga's face remained cold. During a good scene he might spring to his feet, clap applause. "Never mind what people may say. That's good, very good. Móricz is alive, that is enough. The poet is a god, not a tailor. He doesn't worry about the clothes which his creatures wear."

And yet, they talked a great deal about the form in which Christopher clothed his thoughts. At times he feared that he had not been able to free himself entirely from what he had heard, seen, read. "Don't strive for originality at any price," said János Varga. "You have something to say." Wasn't a writer original when he had something to say? "If you have something to say, you don't think about originality. Everything has been said before. Because it has not been said correctly or intelligibly or convincingly, you have to say it again."—"My own handwriting . . . " said Christopher. "Don't think about your own handwriting," János Varga snapped. "We have made an idol of manner. No one is more unmistakably recognizable than the French newspaper caricaturists. Yet they're no Velázquez or Munch." Right at the beginning, Christopher had introduced a narrator, a man of today. "That's a crutch for the lame," said János Varga. "Let the lame stay outside." They had long conversations, apparently theoretical, but connected with the work. Man in the atomic age—what does he care about Tiszaeszlár? "The atomic age," said the director, "is the safe conduct of the dilettanti. Man in the atomic age has to become rather more human, that's all." Is it still possible to portray reality? "It was never possible to portray reality." Is it possible to convey *hubris* in words? "The poet's mission is the portrayal of *hubris*. He writes the story of the illness; he doesn't vomit in the marketplace." Won't *The Great Trial* strike people as too humanist? "What if it does? I admit that the human face is ugly, but it is ours. The artist is not a child who holds his hands over his eyes and imagines he can't be seen." When Christopher accused his friend of doing homage to an imposed and outdated Socialist Realism, János Varga said, "I am a Socialist, but I don't know what Socialist Realism is. Is it the invention of a party secretary or a man of letters? Realism does not tolerate any adjective. All writing is abstract—except abstract writing. Abstract writing is an insult to writing, Socialist Realism an insult to realism. To Socialism, too, incidentally." At times Christopher rebelled against the director's theatricality. Indeed, he looked upon it with suspicion, because János Varga's sincere relationship to his craft seemed to contradict his artistic intransigence. "Why do you write, if you don't want to make an effect?" said János Varga. "In our thoughts we all write. You write in order to communicate something. Everything else is intellectual vanity. There is no humanist literature, because all literature is humanist, and there is no egotistical literature, because no literature is egotistical. We all erect monuments inside ourselves, but only artists unveil them. Literature is the unveiling of monuments."

Christopher did not follow all of János Varga's advice. Because with each page he grew more sure of himself, he grew increasingly doubtful of what he had written before. He knew more and wrote more slowly, turned back the pages, started all over again. One morning, János Varga telephoned to say he could not meet him. His eye trouble had got worse, he had to lie in a dark room for two or three days. Almost roughly he refused a visit from Christopher. When they met again, János Varga said not a word about his absence. "It's the best thing you've written," he said, after hearing the finished scenes.

If you could see me, Ferdinand, you wouldn't recognize me!

I doubt what I wrote yesterday, but not that I shall finish the play. Probably I left everything else unfinished in order to be able to write *The Great Trial.* I was never so happy as here, and for the first time I am homesick for Germany. Homesick for the German forest, homesick for a street out of my childhood, even homesick for the language. I know why homesickness brushes past me now like the swift wind. I dare to feel homesick because I think I can improve something at home. Probably we are at home where we can improve something.

He made few acquaintances here, unlike Warsaw. Official Hungary seemed not to bother about him. Hungary was licking the wounds of the 1956 uprising. The longing for life was stronger here than the instinct for politics.

He often worked in the early morning when the air was still cool, the new day full of vigor. The tiny steamers crossed to and fro between Buda and Pest; around midday he could hear the beating of their wheels. Work was being done on a damaged bridge. The din of hammering and boring forced its way into his room. He didn't hear it. He walked for an hour through the old streets of Buda. On the stone benches of the Fisher Bastion, where once menservants waited patiently for their masters, students now sat in the sunshine. King Mátyás, who had besieged Vienna, rode into the blue sky. Christopher's footsteps echoed on the cobblestones between the little baroque palaces.

He almost never worked at night. In the evening, when he took a shower and put on a clean shirt, he felt like a peasant after a day's work of sowing, plowing, tilling. He discovered that of all passions, none is greater than work; it satisfies without satiating. To begin with he believed that Eva's constant, uniform serenity had passed into him, but it might also be that his serenity had passed into her.

In the evening he went to her place. She had a small apartment in a narrow side street of the Váci utca. Neither the gray house nor the apartment with its jumble of old furniture suited her. The walls of the house opposite forced their way into the rooms. The children were spending their holidays in the country, with Eva's sister. Eva drew the curtains. She cooked Hungarian dishes for him. Gradually he got to know them all—

paprika chicken and gherkin salad and *tarhonya* and *fogas* and cabbage strudel. He read to her. They sat till late at night in little garden restaurants, under limes and chestnuts, drinking Hungarian wines, Kéknyelü and Szürke Barát. They went back to her place and made love until day took over from night. It happened that he walked home through the clean-washed morning, sat down at his desk, worked. "You stick to your day of rest on Sunday like a bricklayer," she said. He did not work on Sunday. They fetched the children, drove to Lake Balaton, bathed, climbed up to the church of Tihany, crossed the water by ferry, rowed among the reeds, lay in the sun. She was born by Lake Balaton. She showed him her birthplace in Balatonboglár. He played with her children. Adél was four, Bianca five. Both were pale blond; passersby often took them for his children. He was not worried that his life often appeared to him bourgeois, not free from coziness and sentimentality. Coziness, sentimentality? He was counting the time in weeks.

They never talked about the future. Once, as he was reading her the first scene of the last act, she said, "Now you could write more slowly." But she laughed as she said it. When he took her in his arms her face became serious. He no longer believed that she became serious because she took nothing seriously but the meeting of two bodies. He saw that she had a second life which was closed to him. He said, "You must come to Germany for the premiere." She replied, "You know that's impossible."

At the end of August he wrote the word "Curtain" for the last time. It was a Saturday. "I'm like a bricklayer," he said. They did not fetch the children, did not drive out into the country. On Monday morning she drew open the curtains. He walked across the Danube Bridge to his hotel, packed his bag. He had left the second bag in Warsaw. He only intended to spend one day there.

His train went in the evening. Eva had borrowed a car from the Ministry of Culture. Two hours before his departure she was with him. They kissed. They drove to János Varga's house. On the way they didn't utter a word. János Varga climbed into the car. He sat at the back, reclining in the seat. They talked uninterruptedly.

Then Christopher was standing at the window of his railway compartment. The window was down. Through the broken glass of the station dome the sun blazed down on the dirty platform. The train moved off. János Varga walked for a long time alongside the train. Eva had remained where she was. He could make her out in the crowd. She didn't move. She didn't wave.

V

My Name Is Christopher

ALL day long Richard Wendelin had been restless. He sat down at his desk, which now stood in the lounge, rose again, straightened a book, tidied his colored pencils, looked at his bronzes, switched on lights, switched them off again.

It was quiet. During the last few months the telephone had rarely made its presence felt, a silent companion who only speaks in order to say something unpleasant or indifferent—almost the same thing. The banker wanting to know whether to sell or buy; the little fortune brought in by the house in Bogenhausen had to be invested cautiously. The gallery trying to find a purchaser for the Frans Hals. Dealers, the nearby garage, the bookshop, collections for the war wounded or refugees from the East. From time to time, people with crazy schemes. Wouldn't you like to buy a ranch in Argentina, Herr Wendelin? Don't you think it would be possible to secure the release of your old films for Egypt? Every now and then, producers would ring up whose names he had never heard. One ought to do something, Herr Wendelin. We ought to arrange a South American tour, Herr Wendelin—Chile, Paraguay, Venezuela. Okay, if you say it can't be done . . .

And then, yesterday morning, the call from Düsseldorf. "I'm putting you through to Herr Dr. Gereke." A bad joke, a mistake? Experienced in caution, he was about to say that he would ring back when he recognized the President's voice. It really was the Palace of Industry, it really was the President. A miracle that he recognized the voice. Before the collapse they had seen each other frequently—at state receptions, balls, premieres. He had spent a weekend with Hermine Moellendorff at Dr. Gereke's house; Dr. Gereke had been to dinner with him. In autumn 1943—or was it the previous year?—they had hunted with Göring in Hungary. Was Gereke already "Dr." Gereke at that time? Certainly, at least one honorary doctorate. At least two or three honorary doctorates since then. When he had thought of those who, unlike himself, had survived the catastrophe, the honorary Dr. Gereke had often occurred to him. Now, in conversation, his anger melted. Which American was it who said, "I hate everybody, until they say 'Hello' "? It was the same with him now. He hated everyone, until they raised their hats. One was dependent upon everyone who raised his hat. And now the honorary Dr. Gereke, President of the Industrialists Union, was raising his hat. He saw him in his mind's eye. A slim gentleman of fifty. His photograph was in the paper recently. An underexposed photograph, or an underexposed face. The captain said that Dr. Gereke flew to London in a private plane for every fitting of every new suit. A pity you couldn't land in Savile Row with a helicopter. A pity that Dr. Gereke confused the fashion drawings in the *Tatler* with the English. Could he call on the Herr Staatsrat, asked Dr. Gereke. He happened to be in Munich. Happened to be? For the first time in twelve years? But Richard Wendelin only said, of course, with pleasure. Would Dr. Gereke perhaps prefer it if they met in Munich? No, no, a confidential discussion. Dinner? Thank you, but I'm afraid that's impossible. Nine o'clock sharp.

Richard Wendelin looked unbelievingly at the instrument from which Dr. Gereke's voice had echoed like a message from a vanished world. It was almost nine. The little villa, which he had rented two years ago, was twenty-five minutes from Munich by car. No, imagination had not played a trick on him. Since yesterday, nothing was impossible. Human beings were chess pieces and moved according to the rules of the ancient game of the Persian kings. Lethargic pawns that moved stolidly forward, step by step, useful, but fundamentally cannon fodder. Bishops that raced across the whole board, but only the white or black squares, light-footed, but incapable of progressing in a straight line. King, queen, castles. He himself was a knight. His path ran neither straight forward nor diagonally; he came out of ambush, described a rectangular L. Perhaps he only dominated four squares, but of both colors, and in his movement he was superior to castles and bishops and pawns, even to the king and queen; he could leap over other pieces. He moved rarely, and then with one leap over the others' heads. A famous film director fell down dead in the studio, a heart attack. Richard Wendelin carried the film to completion and to triumph. Great men had stood in his way. Then the Reichstag burnt down, the Jews fled, their friends emigrated—one jump and he was in the middle of the board. Naturally, this would have been of little help if he had not been a brilliant director, the best of his generation. A single production in Berlin, *A Midsummer Night's Dream,* in the presence of the Führer; by pure chance the King of Afghanistan was visiting Berlin. A bishop jumped over, a castle taken.

Richard Wendelin's heart was beating irregularly. The heart replied to joyful or sad emotions with the same restlessness. He opened the drawer of the desk: a single nitroglycerine tablet would do no harm; it would calm his heart without dulling his wakefulness.

Twelve years since the catastrophe, two and a half years after the unsuccessful experiment of *The Miracle Worker of Paestum,* what did Dr. Gereke want? The film industry was in a gigantic bankruptcy. In the midst of the economic miracle, closed studios, bankrupt financiers, not even enough to bring in the costs for the negative. Ruined amateurs! Herr Lohmeyer had done six months in jail, not because of his political past, but for issuing bills of exchange with no cover. If heavy industry was at last planning to take over the film industry, even the most shortsighted and foolish layman could not help thinking of Richard Wendelin. But why all this secrecy? They might be considering placing the inconspicuous, and hence all the more powerful, medium of the film in the service of politics. No more soldiers, the victors had proclaimed. Now a military airport was being constructed near Richard Wendelin's villa, near the entrance to the city there were barracks to the right and barracks to the left, orders were being given once more, troops were marching once more. Without Germany they couldn't wage a war, not even a cold one. There were better countries, but none more necessary. Only the youth of today wasn't willing, they were difficult to bring up to scratch, they had boogie-woogie in their legs and nonsense in their heads. "Without us," they said, and "We've had enough." Perhaps the authorities remembered that earlier, too, the young had had enough and later had marched to a hero's death.

Richard Wendelin put away *De origine et situ Germaniae*. He had been reading Tacitus. Tacitus would not look good on his desk. Anyone who had time to read Tacitus, in the original Latin, was not coping with reality. It was a good thing he had rented this small but elegant house, had not sold the finest pieces of furniture and the collection of bronzes, had not dismissed Josef, had at least not abandoned appearances. The time was ripe for the knight to jump.

He wondered whether to accept the offer. "I am an artist, Herr Doktor, politics has never done me any good—as you know better than anyone." He could not spare his visitor this reproach. At the time when they had arrested him, prepared the charge against him, put him in the dock, Dr. Gereke had long been in the saddle again. He only needed to lift his little finger, but he didn't. All right, we'll say no more about that, but only a fool makes the same mistake twice. "What guarantee have I that my efforts on behalf of the national cause will not be turned into a noose for me again?" Had he not enjoyed the protection of the other regime, and who had protected the regime? It wasn't the same, fortunately. The fallen regime had declared its aims, had disregarded the rules of the game, had gone too far. They should have threatened, not marched. With the Sudetens everything went well, with Czechoslovakia everything went well, with Austria everything went well, with Alsace and the colonies everything would have gone well, too. They should have elbowed the Jews out; instead, they did them in. But now there were men like Dr. Gereke at the helm, in his captain's uniform from Savile Row. In any case, there was still time to think it over!

The light from the headlamps fell on the narrow forest track leading from the main road to the lonely house. Richard Wendelin drew the curtains. He would sit down at his desk, not rise until Josef announced his guest.

As Dr. Gereke entered he rose and went to meet him. "You haven't changed a bit, Herr Doktor."—"You haven't changed a bit, Herr Staatsrat." Brandy, whiskey, champagne? He wouldn't say no to a glass of *Sekt*, declared Dr. Gereke. German champagne? Richard Wendelin had had a few bottle of Taittinger 1949 put on ice. When had they last met? Dr. Gereke conjured up memories. "Well, you were never a mighty hunter before the Lord, my dear Herr Staatsrat." They laughed. Hunting memories, polite conversation in the best of spirits. Don't at any price betray curiosity, don't show impatience! "Delightful bronzes," said Dr. Gereke. Well, yes, you could still pick up antiques in Munich. "I've just come across a beautiful little Goethe manuscript—only four lines, but unpublished. If only one had more time!" Now they had come to the favorite topic: lack of time, rush, the managerial disease, heart attacks. "Have you heard? Oskar Schimmel is in Bühlerhöhe, following a heart attack." Richard Wendelin hadn't heard. Humiliatingly enough, he lived outside the world of heart attacks. Dr. Gereke: "Well, I've survived my first heart attack." He spoke of it modestly, as though not wanting to boast; after all, it was only the first. "Times have changed," said Dr. Gereke. One only had to study statistics, "a genuine sensation"—he was very fond of the word *genuine:* the higher the income, the higher the blood pressure. "I should like to be one of my workpeople. Your health, Herr Staatsrat."—"All the best, Herr Doktor."—"Delighted . . ." —"Thank you . . ."

Richard Wendelin shivered. Ought he to have had the heating turned on? Or was the cold rising from within him? Dr. Gereke hadn't come to make him an offer. Was the time not ripe for the knight to jump, or had he long ago been swept from the chess board, into the mass grave of the lost knights, bishops, pawns?

Immediately afterwards his heart began to warm again. What was the Herr Staatsrat working on? Dr. Gereke inquired. He hadn't seen his last film, *The Miracle Worker of Palermo*—he said Palermo—"You know, one has no time for anything"—but his wife had been full of enthusiasm for it. "It's a shame, putting a man like you on the shelf. I hope you're working on a new project."

Richard Wendelin looked around. Did this house look like the home of a man who was working on a new project? He had put the Tacitus back in the bookcase, but even the collection of bronzes was steeped in the petty bourgeois atmosphere of life in retirement.

"No, I'm not working any more," he said, like someone who feels it isn't worth lying.

"That must be changed," said Dr. Gereke. "It will be changed, my dear Herr Wendelin." A new wind was blowing through the homeland, he went on. "To be German has been a reproach long enough." The German people were tired of representing the scarecrow in the European field. No nation could exist without pride, no youth could grow up without a national consciousness. For twelve years the Germans had had nothing but their shameful deeds listed to them. The past was dug up on every suitable and unsuitable occasion. "It's time this came to an end, don't you agree?"

Yes, he agreed, said Richard Wendelin. Now his guest would at last come to the point, he thought. He had simply been trying to find out whether Richard Wendelin could still be counted upon. "Another so-called war crimes trial," he said with the zeal of the star pupil. "We're ceaselessly made to run the gauntlet—as though anyone still wanted to know about that. Our own press makes hay with everything that speaks against us. It's inexplicable." That's enough, he thought. At the same time his resolve to make conditions, to demand time to think it over, melted away. Now Dr. Gereke would make his offer, and he would grab it.

Dr. Gereke had not yet finished his discourse. It was all the fault of the Americans, he stated. He was in a position to judge: in the last year alone he had been "over there" four times. Jews and refugees were still in the saddle in America, still stirring up feeling against Germany with impunity. The Americans had wasted their time on the famous reeducation, instead of march-

ing against the common enemy. "In so doing, the gentlemen
are cutting off their noses to spite their faces. The young Germans are supposed to stick out their necks, while their fathers
are damned forever more. Rearmament, well and good, but after
all, we're not mercenaries. You hit the nail on the head, Herr
Staatsrat, when you mentioned the war crimes trials. Day after
day the German uniform is defiled. They reproach us with having done our duty and yet demand that we do our duty again."

"Another glass of champagne, Herr Doktor?" asked Richard
Wendelin.

"Half a glass, Herr Staatsrat."

They drank to each other. Then, almost as though it were
part of his discourse, Dr. Gereke asked, "What news have you of
your son, Herr Staatsrat?"

Richard Wendelin put down his glass. His hands were ice
cold, the sweat broke out on his brow. So it was all about Christopher. Since the letter from Warsaw informing him of Kasimir
Nessor's refusal, he had heard nothing from his son, had only
read the newspaper articles. "The son of the director of *Ritual
Murder* behind the Iron Curtain." It would be wrong now to
stress family connections, equally wrong to deny his son.

"You know," he said, "the boy prefers to live in Poland."

Dr. Gereke quickly assured his host of his friendly feelings.
His feelings did not remain unknown. And since he "happened"
to be in Munich he had been asked . . . in the interest of both
parties. Who had asked him? In whose interest?

Dr. Gereke's thin, pale face had reddened with the purple
of high blood pressure. "Seven crates," he said. Seven crates filled
with material dangerous to the state had been seized. The
sender: Christopher Wendelin. The addressee: Ludwig Ludwig. "A notorious man, one of the notorious left-wing intellectuals." There could be no doubt about it: sender and addressee
had intended to publish these subversive documents. No doubt,
either, of what lay behind it: defamation of the Federal Republic, an attempt to undermine the authority of the state, a
cunning revival of the past. The idea was to prove that in the
Federal Republic, "the old Nazis" were once more at the helm.
"A massive initiative of Communist propaganda!"

"Where is my son?" asked Richard Wendelin.

"That's just the point. According to what my friends tell me, he arrived in the Federal Republic on Friday, coming from Poland and Hungary."

They've arrested him, thought Richard Wendelin. He suppressed a laugh. They were keeping the Wendelin's place in prison warm. The father, an old Nazi; the son, a young Communist.

"Hasn't he been in touch with you?" asked Dr. Gereke.

"Not so far," replied Richard Wendelin cautiously.

He was a step ahead of his guest. He no longer felt as small as previously, when he was hungrily waiting for an offer. A strange farce! They had stirred up the son against the father, and now they came to the father to assuage the son's anger. "A cloud masses together, the tide rises, a dossier accumulates." His own dossier had long since been closed; he had long since been condemned to gaze at the wallpaper and read Tacitus. "Well, you were never a mighty hunter before the Lord, Herr Staatsrat." Hunting with Göring in Hungary. And where had the others hunted, the friends of honorary Dr. Karl-Heinz Gereke?

That the matter did not concern him personally, said Dr. Gereke, he hardly needed to state. He was acting out of genuine friendship, nothing else. Well, then, the seven crates. The matter had to be looked at politically. So-called incriminating evidence, got together any which way. But naturally, the Bolsheviks were not after small fry. They were after eminent economic leaders, leading politicians and military men, men of art and science. "The Reds' plan is perfectly obvious. On the one hand, our will to resist is to be broken, on the other, a wedge is to be driven between the German and the American armed forces. It is a real threat to the state . . ."

In what way did it threaten the state? Richard Wendelin wanted to ask. It is supposed to be "the old Nazis" who are a threat to the splendid new state. "Yes, there are still a few fine antiques in Munich." Perhaps from the Wendelin collection. Perhaps it would have been more intelligent to have thrown the "old Nazi" Wendelin a life buoy in good time. Perhaps he would then have shot a great film and his son would have joined

in the general applause, as he had joined in the applause for
Ritual Murder and *Michael the Ancestral Farmer*. The magnificent new intelligence service. "They" obviously knew Christopher's every move in Poland and Hungary—had Christopher
also been in Hungary?—but they knew nothing about relations
between father and son.

"You want me to prevent the documents being published?"
he asked.

"That has been prevented by the seizure. I told you: our
interests are the same. I mean my friends' and yours."

"I'm a has-been, Herr Dr. Gereke. I have no interests."

"I can understand your bitterness—by God, it is justified. But
as I said before, a new wind is blowing through our land."

"Seven crates from Warsaw will make no difference to that."

"Think of your son, Herr Staatsrat!"

"The papers have been seized—what now?"

"Nothing now, I can assure you, if your son does not allow
himself to be persuaded by his publisher and other Communists
into making a big to-do about it, going to court, creating a scandal. Two years behind the Iron Curtain, crates of subversive
documents—the suspicion of high treason cannot be lightly dismissed." A certain emotion crept into Dr. Gereke's voice. "You
not only have a genuine opportunity once again, as you always
have done and always will do, to serve our country—you can also
come to the aid of your son."

More and more, Richard Wendelin felt himself emerging
from the senile comfort of his armchair into the fresh everyday
world that had come with Dr. Gereke into his hated house of
retirement. There had been no offer yet, but it would come.
The all-powerful President and himself, the scapegoat—now
they were shipmates. Past, present, future—no, present, past,
future. One of them saved, the other just escaped with a whole
skin, the third fished out of the water as a bloated corpse. Here
were two old men in a room, millions of old men throughout
Germany, the fishermen, the rescued, the dead, all in one boat.

"I see my son very rarely," he said. "When I was in prison,
my ex-wife took him to live with her."

Dr. Gereke seemed to understand the reproach. "He was incited against you. A genuine test case, my dear Herr Wendelin. I meet this phenomenon everywhere. The destruction of morality and respect and family—we have had our share in it, we cannot acquit ourselves. But if you will permit me, we will talk about your own case. We allowed a man whose only crime was to have served Germany with absolute loyalty—forgive me, Herr Staatsrat—to be thrown into jail; allowed a world-famous name, under foreign compulsion, of course, to be dragged in the dust— and then we wonder at youth's lack of respect. We are merely reaping what we sowed. Cowardly Communists, most of whom don't even dare to run off to the East, boogie-woogie dancers, a spineless generation of innocents."

"Quite right, Herr Doktor," said Richard Wendelin. "But isn't it too late? Your fathers are criminals, the young Germans have been told. How can they respect their fathers, how can they grow up without examples? Of course I can speak to my son, but do you imagine that I can give him orders?"

That was not the point, replied Dr. Gereke. On the one hand, he reiterated, the matter must be looked at politically; on the other, humanly. The state was in the process of reestablishing paternal authority, to the benefit of fathers and sons alike. But this was also the historical moment to stretch out the hand of reconciliation to the sons. Dr. Gereke was moved. He must put in a word for the young Wendelin, he went on. He was twenty-seven, and that was a particularly unfortunate age, because this generation was marked by the sudden collapse of all values, Germany's humiliation, the phrases of the occupation dictatorship, the masochistic renunciation of national feeling. "I'm lucky," he said. "I have a son of fourteen." The youngest generation once more gave grounds for splendid hopes. During their military service, in particular, the young men were taught discipline and national pride and respect for age. It was high time. "Nevertheless, we cannot write off those in their twenties." He drained his glass. Richard Wendelin had forgotten to fill it again. "I appeal to Richard Wendelin the German, but I appeal, above all, to Richard Wendelin the father."

"I thank you for your confidence, Herr Doktor," said Richard

Wendelin. "I shall talk to the boy—with what result, I cannot say. Shall I telephone you?"

"If I may, I will telephone you."

Dr. Gereke looked at his watch, rose. Although he had already taken a step toward the door, Richard Wendelin hesitated to accompany him. He became aware that the whole evening he had been waiting for an attempt at bribery. Perhaps at the last moment—no, there was no sense, he was waiting in vain. Attempted bribery was a compliment; you do not lead into temptation a man without power. A little touch of blackmail, but that, too, was directed solely at Christopher. High treason. The gun wasn't loaded, otherwise Dr. Gereke would not have come to him. "I'll ring you." At least that. Ought he to have displayed greater confidence in his abilities, to have promised the President that he would perform the disagreeable task? Suppose his attempt failed? The sons were merely accused, while the fathers were condemned.

In the entrance hall, Dr. Gereke took leave of his host. "I know what you are feeling, my dear Herr Wendelin. But the matter is more serious than you imagine. They are our children. If we can, we must save them. We must show them that we are capable of forgiving and forgetting."

Outside a door banged shut; between the black pines the lights moved away.

Richard Wendelin had drunk little. He filled his glass, emptied it. Taittinger 1949, something less good would have done. The champagne tasted flat. Success can be forgotten, like charm. I'm afraid he has aged terribly, Dr. Gereke is thinking now, on his way to Munich, he is a broken man. Who broke him, Herr Dr. Gereke? A dead man is not a good shipmate, Herr Dr. Gereke.

He was thirsty, he poured himself another glass of champagne. As he walked up and down the room his glance fell on the Tacitus, which he had hurriedly put back in its place. The book was still sticking out a little. With an abrupt gesture, he took it and laid it on the table.

And suddenly, it was clear to him what he ought to do, what

he would do. Perhaps it was too late to win back his lost kingdom. But it was not too late to win back his son. He would talk
to Christopher, but differently from the way in which it had
been suggested to him. Christopher—a Communist? Probably
not. No more than I was a Nazi, my boy. A sweet feeling of satisfaction came over him. People are very reckless with their ac-
cusations—a Nazi, a Communist. You can see for yourself, my
son. You have pushed me down even deeper—that won't prevent me, Christopher . . . Would Christopher understand?
Probably not. But one thing he would understand: that the time
was past when Kasimir Nessor could have come to the aid of
Richard Wendelin. Richard Wendelin could save Christopher
Wendelin. Even if the honorary Dr. Karl-Heinz Gereke had
only remembered him because his anonymous friends feared
the young Wendelin, in one respect he was right. While Richard
Wendelin, forgotten by the world, had raged against himself,
Germany had remembered itself. They had thrown him overboard, but they had not betrayed his inheritance. You didn't
want to live with me, my boy; you will have to live with the
Gerekes. "They have reproached us long enough with being
Germans." You have reproached us long enough with being your
fathers. I was on my deathbed when I asked you to do something
for me. I survived it. Now I can do something for you. The day
that belongs to the fathers has dawned, Christopher.

Christopher's first visit was to Ferdinand. The garden gate
was bolted. He knew the little estate: at one point the hedge
was low; he jumped over it. All the doors from the garden were
locked, too. On the terrace stood the empty wheelchair.

The man living in the house nextdoor called out to him. He
had often seen Christopher going in and out. "Ferdinand has
been in the hospital for a week," said the man. "He's very ill."

At the hospital they refused to let him see Ferdinand. Nor
could he speak to Ferdinand's mother. The doctor told him,
"He is putting up an admirable fight."—"Is there any hope?"
asked Christopher. "Nature sometimes works wonders," said the
doctor.

Christopher was no longer living with his mother. Ludwig

Ludwig owned a spacious house in Grünwald, only half an hour from the center of the city, in turn of the century style. It looked as though it had not been tidied since then. Here the publisher was in the habit of putting up foreign visitors, authors who needed peace and quiet, young writers. All that Christopher could call his own was one large room with an unimpeded view of the nearby forest, but now he was alone in the house. Also, his first impression had proved false. Twice a week a cleaner appeared, who, apart from the vice of accompanying everything she did with a commentary—"I'm cleaning the stove," "I'm dusting the books," "I'm beating the carpet"—seemed only to have virtues.

Ludwig Ludwig read Christopher's play in one night. His enthusiasm was honest, and because it was honest it was infectious. Christopher allowed himself to be convinced that with *The Great Trial* he had succeeded. "The fact that things won't be easy is another matter," said Ludwig Ludwig. "But we'll find a theater—even if I have to buy one."

Next day the great Ludwig—and Ludwig the Great was great in more than one respect, a huge man with a huge double chin, a huge belly, huge hands and a huge asthma—was in a terrible mood. The publishing house, as addressee, had been notified of the seizure of the Warsaw consignment. "We can't let them get away with that," Christopher flared up. They must make a public protest, arrange a press conference, demand the immediate release of the documents. Meanwhile, Ludwig Ludwig's anger had died down. He had spent the war in voluntary exile in London, but he had risen to prestige and wealth in the new Germany, and although a controversial figure, he had been able to smooth the path for his young authors. He believed in the new democracy. "Every government," he said, "is out to dodge the laws with which it governs its citizens. Power ruins character. The question is only whether the government is stronger than the law, or the opposite. Democracy means correction, going on all the time. In dictatorships the law yields to the government, in democracies the government yields to the law." Not that he was prepared to take this arbitrary abuse of power lying down— far from it. The firm's legal adviser had called in two lawyers, the most famous attorney in Munich, a terrifying swashbuckler, and the equally famous but more cautious professor of law at Bonn. "If we kick up a fuss," said Ludwig Ludwig, "those fellows will quietly destroy the most important documents, especially, of course, those that incriminate the former Gestapo agents now in the ranks of the new Secret Service. The charge we have laid gives us a guarantee that the documents of the case will remain in the custody of the court. At the trial, the state has to prove that the material is a danger to the state. Where one can bring a charge against the state, nothing is lost. Besides, the lawyers are agreed that we have won our case before it opens." Ludwig Ludwig was not to be shaken in this belief, even when various papers carried a report that the son of the director of *Ritual Murder* had returned to the West "after trying in vain to gain a footing behind the Iron Curtain." "We'll save our ammunition," he told Christopher. "You can see for yourself, not a word about the seizure of the papers. Those fellows are still more afraid of us than we are of them."

Christopher was not sure that his publisher had chosen the right path, but the constant worry about Ferdinand paralyzed him. When the news from the hospital sounded more encouraging, he worked on the corrections of the play; when hope vanished, he hung about the clinic, thinking death would not dare enter the gate on which he was keeping his eye. On one occasion he strayed into a church, sat down on a pew at the back, folded his hands. He prayed to a God in whom he did not believe. Like children, he made promises to the stranger, offered him a bargain. With the foul argument of the living, he tried to console himself that a merciful end would be a release for the sufferer. It was no consolation. There was no one who loved life more than Ferdinand. Ferdinand's gay laugh echoed through the church.

Christopher mixed little with people. Without admitting it, he had hoped for two years that the cripple would one day take him by the hand and lead him. He had become a stranger in his homeland, where he now wanted to make himself at home. No one took him by the hand, and he waited as one waits in the courtyard of a castle for the next conducted tour. He longed for

János Vargas and Eva, and wrote them long letters. János Varga answered briefly and cordially. He received long letters from Eva that described her life, told him about her children, seemed to accompany his footsteps and avoided the word "love." His departure had not opened up a chasm, as his departure from Israel had done; only the veils between himself and the last few years fell more and more thickly. Not an Iron Curtain, but just as opaque.

In the evening he often went to his mother. With her he could talk about his work and about Ferdinand. Her ironic attitude to her own work cheered him up. "I only paint abstracts now," she said. "Firstly, secondly and thirdly in order not to starve, and fourthly because in one's old age one must go along with youth. Young men with serious expressions and hair over their eyes come along and tell me what I thought and felt while I was painting my daubs. What people say to me on Monday I give out as my own on Tuesday. They tell me I have at last fought my way through to experimentation, therefore I am accepted into their circle. They distrust everything, because they don't trust themselves and confuse the final with the irreparable, and at the same time they regard the fragment as final. It's true that their superstitious worship of the latest fashion is provincial—only the rag trade takes what *haute couture* says literally— but it is also infantile. Children like everything which later on good taste forbids them. And so, as time passes, I am becoming happily infantile. My studio is my beauty salon. I have always spent very little on lipstick and rouge. Now, no hairdresser ever sees me anymore. Don't be surprised if before long I am taken for walks in a pram." She liked Christopher's play enormously —"I'm not a doting mother"—but she was by no means sure of its success. "But I may be wrong. You are young, and don't have to worry about being considered old." When Christopher called to say he was coming, she cooked his favorite dishes. Since she described herself as a "trance cook," her meals were not always crowned with success. She was delighted when a meal turned out all right, and laughed when soon afterward the same dish was burnt or was as hard as stone.

One night when he returned from his mother—that evening

the voice of the nurse at the hospital whom he was in the habit of calling had sounded cheerfully hopeful for the first time—he found under the door a telegram from his father.

He made his way from the little station on foot. The yellow rust of autumn lay over the trees. The smoke rising from a hidden gabled roof became a tiny cloud in the cloudless sky. There was a smell of pines and resin. He had enjoyed the beauties of nature everywhere; here he breathed them in. Was he, however, at home?

Richard Wendelin's hair had turned snow-white. Even more domineering than before, the big head ruled the thin body. Just as snow covers everything, so the white hair seemed to cover not merely the head, but also the face. The furrows of the face disappeared beneath it, the scorn of the lips, the watchfulness of the eyes.

His heart had given him all kinds of trouble, he said, six weeks in the hospital. But he mentioned it as though casually, merely adding, "While you were in Warsaw." A mild reproof: his son hadn't written, he hadn't written his son—how could Christopher have heard about it?

Josef brought the tea. They talked as though two years were but a day. Richard Wendelin did not mention the telegram.

Christopher was surprised how well informed his father was about everything that was happening in the arts. He praised a play, lamented the closing of a gallery, made merry over a successful author, illustrated an event with an anecdote which Christopher did not know, and hit the nail on the head again and again. He was even able to speak without bitterness of the crisis in the German film industry. "They're simply tackling the wrong subjects. If a lover with a German name appears, foreign audiences ask: Whom did he murder fifteen years ago? On the other hand, you can't have all the parts played by children, any more than we can promote recruits to generals. They're scared of German subjects—the only ones foreign audiences would accept without suspicion." Like Baron Münchhausen, who pulled himself out of the water by his own hair, Richard

Wendelin seemed, as it were, to have pulled himself out of the morass by his own brain.

"You must see the garden before it's dark," he said, and walked through the small, well-kept garden at his son's side. "Beyond the fence the forest starts, and I can pretend to myself that it belongs to me. You have inherited the modesty of your mother's demands on life. I have acquired it in old age."

What part is he acting now, and is he acting a part? Perhaps his demands have become modest; but he hasn't stopped acting. He didn't send for me merely to see me. He is warming up his audience. He scarcely listened when I talked about Poland. Only when I mentioned Hungary did his face twitch. He has become his own stage designer. He is working on the backdrop, on the wings. The performance cannot start until they are up.

Richard Wendelin showed his son over the house. Christopher noticed the absence of this and that, but he said nothing, gave hesitant approval. The heavy furniture, which he had always disliked, looked like big toys placed in a small doll's house. "But I have got hold of a few copperplate engravings," said his father. He said "but" as though answering Christopher's mute question. "Better good engravings than bad paintings." He opened a portfolio. "An original by Michael Wening. The siege of the citadel of Buda by Max Emanuel's troops in summer 1686. The parallels between the present and German baroque are striking." In a few sentences he proved his theory. They went up the narrow stairs. "The photographs are in the cellar," said Richard Wendelin. "So is my bust. One day, when I am forgotten, it will be exhibited—because of the sculptor." He laughed. "One should only surround oneself with the immediate past when one has a future. I have never understood people who display photographs of their dead. Every time the good Josef says 'Herr Staatsrat,' I feel a shock in every limb. A hundred times I have forbidden him to do so, but it is easier to forbid masters to use their titles than to forbid servants to address them by their titles." They were standing by the window of the small bedroom with the sloping ceiling, looking out into the evening that seemed to be rising up out of the forest, as though the black firs were growing into a sky full of black firs. Richard Wendelin turned and pointed to his bedside table. "I'm reading *De origine et situ Germaniae* again. It is curious how impressed Tacitus was by the 'barbaric freedom' of the Germans. Evidently our virtues were already overestimated two thousand years ago. That is why people fear our vices."

I could do with an elderly friend like him—if only he wasn't my father! I wouldn't have thought of visiting him, but now that I'm here, I am overcome with admiration—and annoyance. Am I annoyed because in reality I would like to talk about myself? Why doesn't he ask whether I've written anything, what I'm living on, what my plans are? He hasn't even mentioned my visit to Kasimir Nessor.

In the living room Richard Wendelin asked, "Would you like a whiskey? I don't drink anymore." He poured Christopher a glass. "I have heard about your play," he said. And, as though he had not noticed Christopher's almost startled expression, he went on: "It's a magnificent subject. I remember the district very clearly from the time when I was working on *Ritual Murder*. I also possess a copy of Eötvös's book, from which you have taken your title."

"Who told you my title?"

"Anyone who has lived long enough in a dictatorship learns the value of accurate information. In those days we had to be informed of the enemies' plans in advance."

"Do you think my play is the act of an enemy?"

"On the contrary." And he went on, evasively: "Perhaps you don't know that I really wanted to film the story of Tiszaeszlár"—he pronounced the name of the village as correctly as any Hungarian—"but naturally, that wasn't possible. The Jews' innocence was all too evident."

Christopher looked at his father as though seeing him for the first time. He had expected anger, horror, indignation, had thought that the telegram might be connected with the play. He had expected an appeal to his filial heart, a mixture of sentimentality and blackmail. You can't do that to me, my boy. Nothing of the sort. Is he a step ahead of me again? As though to say, You think you have liberated yourself from me, but meanwhile, I have long since liberated myself from myself. Cynicism —the life belt with which he crosses the most raging torrent. To him, world history is nothing but raw material for artists. That's what he meant just now, when he said the Germans should concern themselves with their own problems; Auschwitz is easy to turn into a film. And then this jargon, as though between accomplices: a "magnificent subject." I didn't take *Ritual Murder* seriously; naturally, you don't take *The Great Trial* seriously. Or is he making concessions now, in order to gain a greater concession later? He didn't call me just to slap me on the back.

"I hope my play will not be compared with *Ritual Murder* and stir up what has been forgotten," he said.

"It certainly will be," said Richard Wendelin, carefully tying up the portfolio containing his copperplate engravings and putting it away. "And why not? 'Son, behold, take now my spear—/Too heavy for my arm, I fear,' Count Stolberg makes the Swabian knight say to his son. People will say the son is trying to make good his father's sins. That's nothing new. Is it so bad?"

"I came across Tiszaeszlár by chance," said Christopher weakly.

Richard Wendelin smiled. His lips were almost as white as his hair. "You are lying to yourself about your motives, just as I did. Your motives are noble, even if your endeavors will meet with little success. You can pray for the salvation of the sinner's soul, but only the sinner himself can make good his sins—if it can be done at all! 'To make good' is a silly expression—it should be 'stop doing bad' or 'do differently.' And here, too, the sons can do very little. If you try to serve your father's sentence, you do not confirm the sentence, you identify yourself with the sin. Instead of making *The Miracle Worker of Paestum*, I should have remade *Ritual Murder*. You find the idea macabre, perhaps worse—frivolous. You think to yourself, 'Such opportunism is typical of him.' If that were so, every active repentance would be opportunist. Is the drinker who stops drinking and preaches teetotalism an opportunist? Is the adulterer who goes into a monastery an opportunist? If you think about it, every act of repentance is frivolous—and if you think about it, it isn't."

"It isn't opportunist if it springs from conviction," Christopher interrupted him.

"Nothing is more overrated than conviction. The whole of human society, indeed, the whole of ethics, unlike religion, rests on a justified distrust of individual conviction. I didn't make *Ritual Murder* out of conviction, but my actions would not have been better if I had been convinced of the Jews' blood guilt. We are continually confusing human and divine justice. Divine justice judges according to motives—or so we hope, at least, because we credit a higher power with knowing human motives. Since we ourselves certainly don't know them, the man who appeals to his conviction is a witness for his own defense. If I say that today I would make *Ritual Murder* with its premises reversed out of conviction, my own son may believe it or not, but that proves nothing, because you can't know whether I ever believed in the accusation of ritual murder. It would be better for me to act correctly today from the wrong motives than to have acted wrongly yesterday for the right motives. Incidentally," he said, with no change of intonation, "I would like to read your play. Can you send it to me?"

"I'll send you a copy," said Christopher. He immediately regretted his promise.

"Perhaps I may be able to give you one or two pieces of advice," said his father. "I'm sure it's excellent. The theater is in your blood. Moreover, it can't be chance that you have finished the play."

Christopher was about to rise. With a gesture, Richard Wendelin held him back, and at the same moment, Christopher knew that now, at last, his father would disclose why he had sent the telegram.

"One more thing," said Richard Wendelin. "Contacts of which I am not proud have made it possible for me to prevent criminal proceedings against you on account of the Warsaw documents."

"Contacts? With old Nazis?"

Richard Wendelin smiled. "Old or new. They place their trust in me and don't know that I do not deserve it."

Christopher went red in the face. "I should have welcomed criminal proceedings. Only Ludwig Ludwig restrained me from bringing the dirty business out into the open."

"He gave you the fatherly advice which you wouldn't have accepted from me. Not that you're wrong. The very fact that they made representations to me has convinced me that you are right to be indignant about the restoration. But you won't prevent it, any more than we were able to prevent it in 1933."

"You didn't try."

"On that point the books are not closed. You condemn the old, and fundamentally, you are condemning only those Germans who at the time were as young as you are today. It worries me that I was able to help you. It cannot be a good world when you need my help."

"I can manage without it."

"That's what you think." He laughed. "I'm a specialist in remand prisons. The walls of remand prisons are the same to prisoners on remand as those of ordinary prisons are to prisoners who have been condemned, and you can learn from my example how little an acquittal means. And I am not mentioning it because I expect gratitude . . ."

"I am not grateful to you. Or, only because you have shown me that your friends still rule Germany."

"Did you doubt it? Every new generation lives with the one before, and by the time it is ready to wrest the power from the hands of its predecessors, it is already as corrupt as its predecessors. It is the lot of the fathers to corrupt their sons." Now he, too, rose. "If you are going to condemn me again, I beg you to note that I have not tried to dissuade you from staging *The Great Trial*. In fact, I have done the opposite. More than that, I hope you will have the documents which you gathered together in Warsaw published one day"—there was a half-cunning, half-merry twinkle in his eye—"at the risk that my own dossier is among them. But the publisher who would publish this sober collection under the name of an artist would be doing you a disservice. Concentrate on *The Great Trial*, my boy, that's where

er 224
s lies. God knows, I have been wrong often enough,
but never in matters of art. Don't forget to send me your manuscript."

Josef had thrust a flashlight into Christopher's hand. Darkness
had fallen. The dim ray of a flashlight fell upon the bumpy
ground of the forest.

He had prevented criminal proceedings through contacts of
which he was not proud? When I sailed in the *Admiral Hipper*
he was proud, but he prevented me from dying a hero's death.
He holds his hand over me. He doesn't want to be reminded that
he is dead, but he holds his hand over me, the safe hand of the
dead. He likes quoting—why doesn't he quote the *Erlkönig*?
The most German of all German poems. "The Alder King with
crown and train." And swastika banner. "My mother has many
a/golden robe," and all you need do is join in the German miracle and you will have one too. "Be quiet, keep quiet, my child."
Don't kick up a fuss, my child, then everything will be all right.
"And if you're not willing, I'll have to use force." Gestapo Alder
King. "The father shudders . . ." Oh, no, the father doesn't
shudder. "In his arms the child is dead." When children rely
on their fathers, they all die. Suddenly he calls me an artist. He
despises the art which he praises to the skies. Nothing but the
certainty that a play is still more innocuous than a list of murderers and their victims. Jews on the stage—oh, well, they're
only actors, policemen's boots from the wardrobe, the bloody
judge wipes off his makeup, after ten he becomes a good citizen.
Or the audience leaves the theater "mute with emotion"—is it
emotion? It is impossible to be quite sure. When you discuss a
play, there is no need to discuss its subject matter. You wanted
to make *The Great Trial*; you made *Ritual Murder* instead.
You didn't even have the courage to tell a great lie; you chose
the easiest way out. *Ritual Murder* was nothing but a minor
deviation from your good intentions, a slight mistake. He had
to sell the house in Munich, but the contacts of which he isn't
proud were sufficient to save me. "It cannot be a good world
when you need my help."

He had to wait for the train. He was hungry; his stomach ached. He pushed a coin into the automatic machine and devoured a chocolate bar. As he threw the silver paper away, the station official, the only one at the little station, emerged as though from a dark hole. "Haven't you ever heard of a waste-paper basket?" the man snapped at him. "Pick it up, if you don't like it," said Christopher, fully aware of being in the wrong. They stood facing each other, Christopher and the man with the shaven bull neck and the shaven skull surmounted by a uniform cap that was too small. "You must have grown up in a pigsty," said the man. "I'm Richard Wendelin's son," Christopher wanted to say. "I grew up in a neat brown house," and, "Take care, my father has contacts." But he said, "Anyhow I've forgotten what I learned in your Nazi state." This was a second injustice, but he didn't care, he didn't care that the same thing could have happened to him in a Swedish or a Dutch suburban station. Or not. Must, must, must. The proper place for silver paper is in the wastebasket; for gold teeth in a neat pile. "You see too much and hear too little," Frieda had said. It depended on the tone. Keep off the grass. He was seized by a senseless rage; he wanted to grab the official by the collar. "Why are you wearing a uniform? Don't lie, no one wears a uniform if he can earn a living any other way." "But railway officials wear uniforms everywhere." "Shut up, you're a German, your uniform sickens me, your wastebasket sickens me." "I'm only doing my duty." "Exactly, you were only doing your duty when you set the points for the train to Auschwitz." He thought of bundling the official out of his uniform. Then there will at least be criminal proceedings; my father won't be able to prevent that. But he merely stood in front of the official with clenched fists. The official defied his gaze, but Christopher could feel that the man was measuring his strength against the mad passenger's, and he had to suppress a laugh. Retreat was already legible in the official's eyes. Of course, if the official had not been alone in the nighttime station, if the fellow facing him had not been fair-haired and blue-eyed and had not hands that looked as though he could push a railway carriage off the lines on his own—"I shall bring a charge against you," said the official, and it was almost as senseless as Christopher's outburst, since he had no means of knowing who was standing in front of him.

Christopher sat down on the bench in front of the single-story building and observed almost lustfully the silver paper lying by the lines and gleaming in the light of the arc lamp. It was an idyllic local station. In his childhood he had always loved stations like this. Evening had set free all the wood scents; from all sides they streamed toward the station. In the windows of the peasants' houses on the encircling hills winked isolated lights. But Christopher stared only at the glittering silver paper. He no longer thought that he was at home.

On the way home his feeling of malaise grew. He did not go out to Grünwald. He rang the hospital from a telephone in the station.

In the afternoon, at four-thirty, Ferdinand had died.

Ferdinand was buried in the Forest Cemetery. The little white-tiled room in which his coffin lay resembled a bathroom in a suburban bathing establishment. The fresh flowers were withered. Two black-clad men stood in a corner. Their impatience was evident; they wanted to close the coffin. The relatives were fussing around Ferdinand's mother. Christopher didn't know any of them; they were probably relatives who only appeared at funerals. "Believe me, Hilde, it's better for him." Tomorrow, other relatives would be saying the same thing to another mother. Or to a father, or to a wife. When Ferdinand's mother caught sight of Christopher, she burst out sobbing. When you shared sorrow, it became greater. "He lived to read your last letter," said Ferdinand's mother. "We didn't know you were at home," said one of Ferdinand's uncles apologetically. "Now we have already decided who is to carry the coffin." Did it matter who carried the coffin? They were dragging the wreaths from the bathroom. Impatient men wiped sweat from their brows. Through an upper window, no larger than a hole in a prison wall, the sun was blazing down.

Couldn't you have waited, Ferdinand? I had so much to tell you. Do you know, I've finished my play. Your friend Ludwig

Ludwig found a theater yesterday. Believe it or not, I've finished something. It may not be very good, but the word "End" is written at the bottom of it. The Warsaw material has arrived, too, but it has been impounded. We carried on a one-sided correspondence when you could no longer move your hand. No, I no longer hear from Martha. They say it is better for you to lie in the coffin, which they are going to close in a minute. You would have laughed at that. How can I understand what happened here while I was away? You never left your wheelchair, and yet you always knew everything. I'm going to find things pretty difficult without you, Ferdinand.

When Christopher stepped out into the light, there were so many people standing outside the mortuary that Christopher stopped in amazement. In one group there were forty or fifty young people, possibly more, young men and young women. They wore dark suits, dark dresses, and all the young men looked as though they had just come from the barber. They looked at each other, they did not speak. They stood in the blazing hot afternoon, waiting for Ferdinand.

The funeral procession moved off. Christopher stayed behind, joined one of the rows toward the back. They walked in threes, all in threes. A girl on Christopher's right, a young man on his left. The girl was young, barely twenty, nevertheless a picture out of his grandmother's time. The young men walked along tidily, in threes, like boarding-school children. When Christopher looked up he saw young, strong, unlined necks, young, strong, straight backs. The young people were walking too fast; a cemetery official in a morning coat hurried alongside them and whispered to them to walk more slowly. The light burden danced on four young, strong shoulders. They were carrying the coffin too high, but the cemetery official left them to it. The birds were singing in the trees. Visitors to the cemetery crossed the path of the procession, gazed after it in astonishment. It passed old graves and new, it passed fresh and forgotten sorrow.

For an instant Christopher felt jealous. Had Ferdinand had so many friends? Why had he not introduced him to them? Perhaps they were not friends, but only occasional visitors to the wheelchair. Perhaps they were friends and he, Christopher, had always run away from them, to Israel, to Poland. The jealousy passed away and Christopher was seized by a strange, inexplicable gaiety. For two days he had wept as he had not wept since his childhood. Now Ferdinand's coffin was dancing above their heads, and he was gay. He wanted to run along the procession and call out to the mourners: Don't go away, let's stay together! I must know who you are, we must get to know each other. You knew Ferdinand, you were Ferdinand's friends, so we belong together. Perhaps there are only forty or fifty of you—forty or fifty is a lot. The old people gaze after you, for a moment they mourn the young man who is dead. They shake their heads because you are walking so fast. Walk fast, friends! "It worries me that I was able to help you," my father said. We don't need his help. "Your generation could become a model for the next," Kasimir Nessor said. "If I could be certain of that . . . It isn't certain, but at least it's a hope." I wondered how I was to get you to the opening night, Ferdinand. You read my last letter. You know that I didn't leave you in the lurch. Your friends won't leave me in the lurch.

The coffin swayed above their heads. It seemed to Christopher as though Ferdinand's friends were carrying the coffin like a banner, like a narrow, proud, firm banner. Then they put down the coffin and stood around the grave. They stood in two rows, shoulder to shoulder, hand in hand, young men, young women. Only a few older people were weeping. Two men supported Ferdinand's mother. Over the dug grave, Christopher looked into the faces of his friends. He was standing with his back to the sun; the others were looking into the sun. Their faces were grave but not sad. They were faces he had been looking for, in the Schwabing night clubs, in the homes of intellectuals, in lecture halls and taverns and in the streets. "You haven't met the right people," Ferdinand had said.

Had only Ferdinand known the right people? Forty, perhaps fifty. Forty, fifty—that was a lot. The earth swallowed up the coffin. The sun was blazing down. The birds were singing in the trees.

At the cemetery gates, the young people said goodbye to one

another. Some looked for their cars, some for their bicycles, some walked to the bus stop. Many knew each other, others had seen each other for the first time. They nodded to one another, went their separate ways. Christopher walked alone.

He could not remain alone. He took a streetcar into the city, went into a tavern, drank beer, walked along the Leopoldstrasse, sat outside a café. The autumn was mild. Long-legged girls were sitting outside the café, young artists with portfolios under their arms strolled past. The streetcars rang their bells, cars hooted, people laughed. He moved on. Evening was falling. He drank beer and schnapps. He went into the first jazz bar. He sat at the bar and looked up, startled, when a barmaid recognized him. Like an automaton his feet moved in rhythm. The rhythm was new. He thought of Ferdinand and the dancing coffin and the dark-clad young people by the open grave. He went into a second bar, a third, drank beer, drank schnapps.

It was almost two when he stepped out into the street. Schwabing was an odd district. The life of the city flowed right through the middle of it, cutting it in two, an alien river. Sleeping houses, garages, shops, the daytime world mixed with the world of night. A fancy white car stopped beside Christopher. "Coming home with me?" Then a cry: "Well, I'm damned, it's Christopher!" It was Christa. "How are you?" he asked. "You can see for yourself," she said. And, "You can still call me." Through the lowered window of the car she handed him a visiting card. She did it like an estate agent touting for clients. Don't forget me if you want to buy a home. He put the card in his pocket; the car swept off.

I can't help laughing. At the October carnival I laughed, too. Every time I come home I meet Christa. Only this time it's a different Christa. In a chic dress, in a chic convertible, with a chic visiting card, no doubt with a chic apartment. She has probably kept the whips, and by now they are chic, too. "You can do it even without whipping," she had said. Why did I come home? Why don't you answer me, Ferdinand?

The great Ludwig had found a theater. It was called the Neue Bühne, the New Stage, and it was a new theater, even if in an old building. It was to open with *The Great Trial*. The manager was young and had big plans. He seemed to have considerable means at his disposal, for the rebuilding of the theater, and in particular the modernization of the stage, had cost a small fortune.

The auspices were favorable. A Hungarian film directed by János Varga had won a prize at the Cannes festival. There was little objection to his directing the play. On the other hand, Ludwig Ludwig had to exert all his influence to convince the theater that the part of József Sarf must be played by the famous actor Heinrich Kahn, who had returned from exile. Heinrich Kahn enjoyed great esteem, but he was said to be too old for the part, to have difficulty in learning his lines, and also to be a difficult man, hard to get on with. Christopher, who had seen Heinrich Kahn in the part of József Sarf as long ago as the nighttime conversation beside the Bodrog, suspected anti-Semitic resentment; but there was no question of this. In a paradoxical way, it was almost the opposite. An author suspected of Communist sympathies, a publisher known for his "Leftist intellectual" leanings, a director from Hungary and now an *émigré* Jew as one of the main actors—they had to think of a certain section of the public, a certain section of the press, who would say it was too much of a good thing. Not without irony, Ludwig Ludwig reported to his author that he had succeeded in jumping this hurdle, too. "We have a quota system, you know," he said. "People have nothing against the Jews, only there mustn't be too many of them. But I have beaten them with their own weapons. We have got rid of the ghettos, but the spiritual ghettos remain. You only have to look at the newspapers. When a book by a Jewish author appears, hard as it is, in nine cases out of ten a Jewish critic is found to review it. If he praises the book, then one Jewish hand is washing another, if he damns it then how bad the book must be! It works out either way. 'Let the Jewish principal part be played by a Jewish actor,' I told the gentleman. I used the argument that a Jew can best feel his way into the identity of a Jew. They understand this at once, since they are profoundly convinced that the

Jewish heart is quite different from ours—not necessarily worse, perhaps even better, but in any case, different."

Christopher was waiting for the arrival of János Varga. The director had received an exit visa, but he had to complete a job he had started at the National Theater.

During this time, the newspapers paid increasing attention to Christopher Wendelin and the play that was about to be presented at the Neue Bühne. "All publicity is good," said Ludwig Ludwig. "All publicity is welcome," said the young theater manager. Christopher had no understanding of this new, evidently generally accepted morality, which seemed to rejoice in one's running the gauntlet as though it were a successful hurdle race. No one knew the play, but everyone seemed to want to make commentaries on it. Ex-soldiers, including members of the Waffen-SS, now had their own newspaper, which accused Christopher of trying to capitalize on his father's film *Ritual Murder*. Not a word was said against the film itself. The paper merely said that the young Wendelin, who "denies his father" —and how could a son "sink lower than that"—"is fouling his own nest" and was out to reawaken memories of certain "lapses which have, of course, been grossly inflated by our enemies." What Christopher Wendelin was after was not hard to guess. While the German nation had been striving by the sweat of its brow to build up a country that had been "destroyed by Allied bombers," Richard Wendelin's son had become "the darling of Israel and the countries behind the Iron Curtain"; these countries naturally had an interest in destroying "Germany's regained status in the world"; for this purpose they were making use of a young man "to whom all patriotic feeling is alien." "Are the Bolsheviks financing *The Great Trial?*" the newspaper asked, "or has the Neue Theater been rebuilt with Israeli money, which is, of course, the German taxpayer's money?" Another weekly, known for its liberal views, put Christopher's father complex under the microscope, regaled its readers with a detailed description of all the ritual murder trials in history, in which, owing to unfortunate circumstances, the innocence of the accused Jews had not always come unequivocally to light, and then demonstrated its learning further by discussing the father and Oedipus complexes discovered by the "Jewish doctor" Freud and gave a brief exposition of both Richard and Christopher Wendelin's private life, not omitting to publish photographs of Christopher's mother and Hermine Moellendorff—"the young author never got over his parents' divorce." An illustrated paper said it with pictures. Christopher was shown in the uniform of the Hitler Youth Naval Cadets; in one picture—in which his head was tiny and scarcely visible in the crowd, but indicated by an arrow—he was seen at the premiere of *Ritual Murder*; the caption, "The Transformations of Christopher Wendelin," spoke volumes. The daily papers either attacked Richard Wendelin's son or defended him; there were two distinct camps. But most of them trained their sights on János Varga. Obviously no German director, and there were plenty of them, had been prepared to direct *The Great Trial*; a "well-known Communist" had had to be specially imported from Hungary!

After a few weeks the sensation wore off; Christopher Wendelin's name disappeared from the newspaper columns. "The calm before the storm," said Ludwig Ludwig, and Christopher didn't know whether his publisher lamented the calm or feared the storm. He had collected the newspaper cuttings, but he wasn't sure whether he would show them to János Varga. His friend was high-strung. He had lived in a world in which people were ordered to keep off the grass. There were similar notices in Germany, but not everyone obeyed them. One had to be a German in order to understand this country's *hubris*: Germans put up monuments in the concentration camps, and Germans said the past must never return, and Germans winced when one spoke of the past; Germans condemned Hitler's henchmen, and Germans condemned the "traitors" who had fought against Hitler; ministers dissociated themselves from the past and sat beside ex-Party members on the front bench; a non-Jewish emigrant who lived in America was considered a "German-American," a Jewish emigrant remained a "refugee," even after his return; many were liberal but few were color-blind; people felt sorry for those who had suffered, and accused them of resentment; they demanded the "overcoming" of the past and imagined they were overcoming it with harmless jokes from the Third Reich; Germans thought with pride of the men of the 20th of July, and Germans spoke of the "stab in the back"; Germans made pilgrimages to Israel, and Germans waited for the surviving Jews to leave; Germans looked upon the Allies as liberators, and Germans hated the British and the Americans. What was it Kasimir Nessor had said? "They look back on a concentration camp past, of which the majority are ashamed, and on a war past, of which the majority are proud." Would János Varga understand?

It was chance that brought Christopher his leading actor.

They were sitting in the theater canteen—Christopher, János Varga and the literary director, Dr. Gerhart Strbrny, an East Prussian of professorial appearance, highly educated, conciliatory, quiet-mannered, a scholar manqué. The play had been almost completely cast. Heinrich Kahn was going to play József Sarf, Walter Einsiedel Károly von Eötvös, Ludmilla Lackenbach little Eszter Solymosi's mother, Anton Eich the examining magistrate and murderer Kálmán Péczely. The Jews of Tiszaeszlár, the Jews in the dock? The Jews didn't actually have to be played by Jews, but why shouldn't they give a few Jewish actors a chance? argued Strbrny. There was Fritz Eppstein, who had failed to leave Germany in time and had miraculously survived seven concentration camps in eleven years—really a comedian, small, bald, matchstick thin, but a great artist, who would be able to act the preceptor and circumciser Salamon Svarz. There was also István Gerö, whom János Varga had proposed and who had just arrived from Budapest, a blond giant in his late twenties, from the same family of Jews Christopher had met in Israel—just the right man to play the accused, Abraham Bukszbaum, the pure fool who cannot defend himself because he cannot understand what he is accused of. And finally, there was Immanuel Steinhardt, the son of a Berlin banker, now an American actor, who had come to Munich to appear in a film and had stayed there—not a great actor, but not a bad one either, a useful craftsman and just right for the

part of Amsel Fogel, the Jewish boatman who is the first to discover Eszter Solymosi's body and is brought before the court as
an accomplice in her murder.

But who was to play the main part, Móricz Sarf, the fourteen-
year-old? All the well-known child prodigies of the German
theater, the German cinema, had passed before János Varga.
Each time he had merely shaken his head. He had told Christopher the story of the famous pianist Misha Kohorn—he
had no idea that Christopher knew him—who had listened to
the child prodigy of an enthusiastic family and afterward said
to the dismayed parents: "He may be a genius, but he certainly
has no talent." The geniuses were no use for the role of Móricz
Sarf. They had to find a young actor of talent. "Children and
dogs," said János Varga, "are a plague in any case. They can
act everyone off the stage, they're certain of applause, yet there's
nothing behind it." Nor was a human parrot any good to him,
the director had added. The play stood or fell with Móricz Sarf;
the boy had to understand what it was all about, must feel at
home in Tiszaeszlár, must not be a whimpering milksop who
merely breaks down under the inquisition, gets drunk on the
unaccustomed alcohol; he must hate his father, must hate his
own poverty and his Jewishness, must be in love with the world
of Hussars, carriages, hunting parties and violin-playing Gypsies,
in the feudal Hungarian world of the nineteenth century, from
which nothing separates him but the misfortune of having been
circumcised in a synagogue instead of baptized in a church.

They were sitting in the canteen discussing the matter, when
one of the theater's actors approached them, Hermann Lambrecht—a relatively unknown name and an actor of whom
they had not thought at all for *The Great Trial*. Lambrecht
apologized for the fact that he could not help overhearing
the conversation at the next table. Gerhart Strbrny politely
offered him a chair, and Hermann Lambrecht hesitantly sat
down. The man was timid by nature, but it was a timidity
that affected Christopher unpleasantly; a servile character who
began almost every sentence with an apology, seemed to be
justifying his existence, stressed his own insignificance on every

possible occasion, fidgeted on the edge of his chair and dared not raise his eyes.

So they were looking for a boy for an important part, if he had understood correctly, a fourteen-year-old. Well, his son was fifteen, born 1943—"I was back home already then, shot through the lung"—but he was not too tall, extremely bright, intellectually developed beyond his age, a definite acting talent. "Don't judge by me," he said, turning to Dr. Strbrny. "He doesn't get his talent from me. His mother was an actress. She would have become a great actress if she hadn't been killed in an air raid." It hasn't got much to do with heredity, replied János Varga. Where and what had he acted? Nothing, except in school plays, admitted Hermann Lambrecht. Adam —that was his name—was at high school, and although no genius, he was vastly superior to his schoolmates. "And he thinks of nothing but the theater."

Dr. Strbrny wanted to get rid of the doting father, and Christopher also found the idea absurd, but before either of them could open their mouths, János Varga said, "Bring the boy to Grünwald. I'm living there with Herr Wendelin. This evening at seven, if that suits you." He thought it over, changed his mind. "If possible, send him alone. He will be less inhibited . . ."

Adam Lambrecht came on the dot of seven. More accurately, this was when he knocked at the door; a good half hour before the appointed time, Christopher and János Varga had seen him prowling around the house. Christopher would have liked to send him away. Hermann Lambrecht had doubtless been telling the truth when he said his son looked no older than fourteen, was a well brought up, intelligent boy, but the pale blond hair with its careful parting, the big pale blue eyes, the pink complexion—no, by no stretch of the imagination could Christopher see Adam Lambrecht as Móricz Sarf from Tiszaeszlár.

It did not seem to worry János Varga. "So you want to be an actor?" he asked the boy.

"I want to play the part," said Adam.

"What do you know about the part?" asked Christopher.

CHRISTOPHER AND HIS FATHER

"It's like this," said Adam. "When my father came home in the middle of the day, he told me he had spoken to you. Immediately after lunch I went to Fräulein Holzhauser, that's Dr. Strbrny's secretary. She lent me a script."

"And you've read the play?" asked Christopher in astonishment.

"Unfortunately, only up to the point where my father—I mean, where old Sarf—is left alone with the lawyer. I didn't get any further. I didn't want to skip anything."

"Do you like the play?" asked Christopher, more and more surprised.

"That's hardly the right expression," said Adam almost reprovingly. "I think it's incredible." He blushed, explained with a stammer, "Not in the sense that I don't believe it. You write: 'Based on true facts . . .' I only mean . . ." He groped for the right words. "It's terrific."

"Do you know anything off by heart?"

"Oh, yes, a lot. A few quite long poems. For instance, 'The Cranes of Ibicus.' "

"I learned that at school, too," said Christopher. He was thinking of Ani Omer. The last evening. The grammar school teacher and the goatherd Pollack had recited "The Cranes of Ibicus."

"That's a bit too long," smiled János Varga. "But it isn't really necessary, anyhow. We'll do a reading rehearsal."

He went to the desk, took out the duplicated script of *The Great Trial*, began to leaf through it.

Christopher watched the boy. He was sitting upright in a big, torn armchair; his feet barely touched the floor. His whole body was tense and attentive. At the same time he seemed neither excited nor constrained, curious rather than ambitious.

He looks like a swimmer on the diving board. He knows he has to swim, but he doesn't necessarily have to win. I have prejudices. I imagined the Jews as dark, with piercing eyes and hooked noses. Until I went to Israel. No sooner do I meet a German who looks like me than I think: Hitler's dream of the Aryan, good riddance! Why shouldn't Adam Lambrecht be able to play Móricz Sarf? If necessary, we can put a wig on him.

"Do you remember the scene in which Móricz Sarf first drinks a glass of wine?" said János Varga. "Just before the interrogation. We'll read through this scene. Don't worry about getting the right intonation. We'll read it like a passage from a school reader."

When the reading was finished, János Varga began to explain the situation, Móricz Sarf's personality, the boy's relationship with his father. Christopher admired his friend, who did not fall into the mistake adults make: he did not try to talk to the child as though to a child, didn't worry about what Adam would or would not understand. But the boy's ability to listen and to absorb what he heard also astonished Christopher. Before János Varga started to act the scene with allotted parts, Adam said:

"I'd like to know what happens afterward. Generally I look at the end, but I thought . . ."

"You want to know whether the father is acquitted," said János Varga.

"The Jews are innocent, they must be acquitted. I thought perhaps Móricz takes back everything he has said against his father before it's too late."

An unusual boy. Or is he, perhaps, not so unusual? I don't know many boys of his age, and those only fleetingly. Innocent, so they must be acquitted. Have new concepts, new ideas of right and wrong, come to be accepted while I was away, and I haven't noticed? The idea never occurred to me that somebody must be acquitted because he is innocent. When I was as old as Adam, the People's Courts dispensed injustice. Then came the occupation, "automatic arrest," a grotesque combination of words. Then they acquitted my father. Perhaps Móricz takes back everything he has said against his father in good time! He can imagine Móricz, under pressure, bribed and drunk, committing perjury; he cannot imagine that he would not, in the end, change his mind.

"The play takes place almost eighty years ago," said Christopher. "In a world which today we can scarcely understand.

If you play the part, I shall explain to you; we shall have to talk about it a lot. You will understand why Móricz Sarf does not retract his false statement, can't retract it."

Adam nodded.

And then, before Christopher's eyes, Adam Lambrecht changed into Móricz Sarf. He muddled the words, blushed, asked permission to repeat two or three sentences, lapsed into the pathetic tone of the school declamation. His drunkenness was for a moment involuntarily comic, but this seemed to Christopher unimportant beside the eruption of mysterious, natural talent. A parrot? János Varga only occasionally spoke a sentence to him, as though no longer concerned about individual sentences. Hate and fear, terror and servility were in the boy's words and gestures, in his eyes. Christopher caught himself watching the actor and the director with the same attention. He feared the director might overlook the flickering signs of talent; he hoped the director would notice them.

János Varga put down the script. "I can't promise anything," he said. "Perhaps I chose a scene that particularly suits you. I don't want to tire you now with another." Adam, who was standing there with red cheeks, was about to reply, but János Varga didn't give him a chance. "In any case, we shall have a lot of work to do. Read the play through to the end"— "Today," said Adam—"and I'm sure Christopher will also explain a great deal to you. We'll give it a try. Tell your father to come and see me tomorrow."

Adam started to go. He was about to make a little bow and leave, like someone who is afraid the others might change their minds, take back their vague promise. "If you can, stay another few minutes," said Christopher.

It turned into a good hour. Christopher sat with his legs crossed in front of the cold fireplace; János Varga lay, half reclining, on the sofa. Adam sat between the two of them. He had made himself comfortable in the armchair and forgotten that he wanted to look bigger than he was. The two men's questions were cautious. The conversation must not look like an interrogation, but out of the loose stones of the replies a mosaic composed itself.

Adam had been born in Berlin, two years before the war came to an end. "I don't really remember Berlin. I never went back there. I don't remember my mother, either." Cologne, Frankfurt, Vienna—up to four years ago, he had moved about a great deal. "My father acted on various stages." Had his father been able to look after him? "My father had a wife—that's to say, she wasn't his wife. They were going to marry, but it came to nothing." Finally they settled in Munich, a real bachelor household. "Twice a week we have a charlady." He spoke of his father with an esteem that did not sound quite genuine, as though he feared that the others did not think much of his father and he had to stand up for him, although they might have good reason for treating Hermann Lambrecht with distrust. More than once he mentioned the shot through his father's lung; this injury was supposed to excuse everything, but he did not say for what he was forgiving his father. True, he did not boast, or merely boasted of minor matters with a childish pride, but it was clear from his words who was the adult in the Lambrecht bachelor household: it was the fifteen-year-old, not his father. "And now I must go," he said. "My dog is alone at home; my father is acting in *Caesar* tonight."

"I could have listened to him for hours," said Christopher.

"I may be wrong," said János Varga, "but I think we've found our Móricz."

"I hope so," said Christopher. "Something very strange happened to me today . . ."

"I know," laughed János Varga. "I was watching you. You've become an old man."

Adam Lambrecht got the part. Rehearsals began.

By now it was January. The snow lay deep in the street, the roadway glistened, the men on the monuments wore white Russian caps. In the snow the big city became a small town again, the modern city became as old as in Michael Wening's engravings.

Christopher was in the habit of having breakfast in a café near the theater. By this time, János Varga had already been at

rehearsal for quite a while. After breakfast, Christopher
walked slowly toward the theater. The air was raw; this morning, one could feel that the city was in the mountains. Suddenly
he caught sight of a man walking along in front of him. He
was walking along the wall, with a bent back, an old man in a
fur coat. He was bareheaded, the snowflakes were settling on
his white hair. At first the man attracted Christopher's attention because the fur coat did not go with his decrepit appearance. A poor old man in an expensive fur coat with a mink
collar. Then Christopher recognized his father.

He addressed him. At the sight of his son, Richard Wendelin's back straightened, his neck stiffened; it was as though he
were growing up toward his son.

"What are you doing about town so early?" asked Christopher.

"I sleep badly," said Richard Wendelin. "I like the town in
the morning." The snow settled on the son's fair hair. "Are
you going to rehearsal?" Richard Wendelin asked.

Christopher nodded.

"How are the rehearsals going?" asked his father.

"At the moment, very well."

"When is the first night?"

"On the eleventh of February, I think."

Richard Wendelin nodded. "The difficulties are still to
come," he said. "But I have heard very good reports of János
Varga."

"He has totally immersed himself in it," said Christopher.

His father said, "It's good that you were able to get Kahn
for old Sarf."

They were standing outside a jeweler's window and did not
know how to say goodbye.

Perhaps he was prowling around the theater. Perhaps not for
the first time. He used to take me to rehearsals. *Faust* and
Florian Geyer. The horrible *Schlageter*, too, of course. The
doors flew open when he came. The stage-door porter was
said to hurry on ahead of him to tell the actors what mood the
Herr Staatsrat was in today. The Third Reich was not his kingdom; the theater was his kingdom. He can't sleep, he goes in to

town in the early morning. At midday he goes home again, by the local train. Josef looks at him questioningly; Josef knows why the Herr Staatsrat went in to town.

"Well, then," said Richard Wendelin.

"Wouldn't you like to watch the rehearsal?" asked Christopher.

Richard Wendelin's face went red. Christopher stretched out his hand to him; he was afraid his father had been taken ill.

"It would attract disagreeable attention," said Richard Wendelin, but he quickly added, "But I need not be noticed at all."

He seemed unaware of the humiliating meaning of his words. He walked along with a springy step beside his son. Obviously he was still afraid that Christopher might retract his over-hasty invitation. He said no more about the play, no more about the rehearsal. He praised the fresh air, said his house was drowning in the snow.

The porter was a young porter; he didn't recognize Richard Wendelin. The theater was dark. Only the stage was lit up; only on the director's desk was a small light burning. Richard Wendelin stood still at the rear trapdoor. Like someone entering his own house, where he knows every room, every cupboard, he whispered to Christopher: "The best would be a box, in the dress circle."

The empty stairs echoed with their footsteps. Richard Wendelin walked in front. At times he took two steps at once. At the top, in the bar, he stopped, gasped for air, smiled as though apologetically. At the two ends of the foyer stood the marble busts of two dead theater managers. "One day, when I am forgotten, my bust will be exhibited—because of the sculptor," said Richard Wendelin. Dead actors looked down out of their gilt frames at the empty glass top of the bar. "You'll catch cold," said Christopher. His father shook his head.

Christopher sat by the balustrade of the box. Richard Wendelin quietly peeled off his overcoat, squeezed into the uncomfortable seat in the background. From the stage rose the smell of dust, the white smell of stages in the morning. Christopher could hear his father breathing deeply.

János Varga was rehearsing a courtroom scene. Christopher turned to the back. "The first confrontation between father and son. Ordinarily the stage is full."

"I know," said his father. "I've read the play."

"János is rehearsing with Adam and Kahn on their own. Yesterday, something went a bit wrong." Richard Wendelin put his finger to his lips. He nodded, as though he knew all that, as though he knew the play by heart.

Down below, on the stage, József Sarf said:

"Don't you care if they hang me? Don't you care if all these old people are hung?"

"What do I care about the dirty Jews?" said Móricz Sarf.

"Do you pray every day? Show me, do you wear the zitith?" said József Sarf.

"I'm not a horse. I don't need anything round my neck," said Móricz Sarf.

"Why do you hate our religion?" said József Sarf.

"I just hate it," said Móricz Sarf.

"But you must have a reason. If someone jumps into the Tisza or hangs himself, he also has a reason," said József Sarf.

"Everyone hates the Jews," said Móricz Sarf.

"Not everyone hates the Jews," said József Sarf.

"Everyone hates the Jews. Even the Jews. You know that perfectly well," said Móricz Sarf.

"You said that it is written in the Jewish law: the Jews need the blood of a Christian girl. Where did you read that?" said József Sarf.

"I didn't read it anywhere. I know it," said Móricz Sarf.

"Who told you?" said József Sarf.

"Everyone told me. Because everyone knows it."

From the director's desk came the voice of János Varga. "That's still not right. I hope you won't mind my saying so, Herr Kahn, but you're saying all that much too aggressively. You're not the defense counsel, you are the father. You don't need to prove that there is nothing about ritual murder in Jewish law—everyone knows that. You don't care whether you are hanged . . ."

Heinrich Kahn had come forward to the footlights. A gray-haired man, massive, with small, deep-set, flashing eyes, a fleshy, hooked nose. "Do me a favor, Herr Varga," he said. "You're talking nonsense. Everyone cares whether he is hanged."

János Varga ignored the rudeness. "Of course you care, *but* that's not the point in this scene. If he can't convert his son now, then József Sarf doesn't care whether he has to die. His son's statement is his death sentence." He turned to Adam, who was standing at the back of the stage with downcast eyes, as though he did not want to be a witness when an old man like Heinrich Kahn was corrected. Now he came quickly forward, as though to be lectured in his turn. "Adam, you did it far too passionately again," said János Varga.

"Of course," Heinrich Kahn agreed. "He speaks like a public prosecutor. That's bound to stir me into making a speech for the defense."

Up in the box Christopher turned to his father and said, "Kahn is a disquieting person."

"A great actor," whispered Richard Wendelin.

"When you say 'I hate you,'" said János Varga to Adam, "it sounds as though you had always hated the Jews. Or when you say 'I know,' it sounds as though you really did know. I told you yesterday, you are a talking machine into which a penny has been put. The audience must feel that it has been repeated to you over and over again, and you are repeating it once more because you've no alternative."

Richard Wendelin bent forward to Christopher's ear. "He is explaining too much to the boy. He ought to act it for him."

Meanwhile, János Varga had left the auditorium and hurried up onto the stage. They couldn't hear what he was explaining to Adam, but they could guess from his gestures.

"I must go down for a moment," said Christopher.

He went down to the first row of the stalls and attracted the director's attention.

He is sitting up there at the back of the box, breathing in the air of the theater. In front of him the lit-up stage, the director. Who knows, perhaps he would really do it better. He is convinced that he would do it better. Did he wince when János Varga spoke of ritual murder? I have avoided the word throughout the play. It wasn't easy. I avoided it on the audience's account, not on his. The word means nothing to him. He switches off memory like an electric light. I hope János doesn't call a break now. I can't leave my father sitting in the box. I shall have to introduce János to him. I must have been mad. If Kahn hears that my father is in the theater, he will stop the rehearsal. When he came back to Germany he said in an interview: "The only thing I regret is having to breathe the same air as Richard Wendelin." Or something like that. I must have been mad. Fortunately, the rehearsal is continuing.

"We'll start again at 'Don't you care . . .'" said János Varga.

When the scene came to an end—the director interrupted it twice, but he nodded his satisfaction to Christopher—Christopher left on tiptoe.

He went back into the box. The door was open. His father was gone.

When he went with János Varga to the café where they were in the habit of eating lunch, Christopher realized at once that the news of his father's presence in the theater had got around. Someone must have noticed Richard Wendelin leaving the theater. The Espresso was frequented mainly and in democratic confusion by the generals, the officer corps and the infantry of the surrounding theaters. Often, events in the theaters were known here earlier than in the theaters themselves. The Espresso was a club of people with the same outlook, the same frame of mind, the same interests; people talked loudly and rarely in small groups; they shouted news from table to table, communicated in half-sentences; rumors were served along with beer and coffee. Someone had left his part, another had quarreled with the director, a third was already flirting with television. The café was a club, a stock exchange—reduction in wages, star salaries, stocks rose and fell.

Christopher could feel that his stock had fallen sharply. "My father," he said to János Varga, when they were still alone after ten minutes. He had admitted to his friend while they were still in the theater that Richard Wendelin had been present at the rehearsal in the protective darkness of the box. "Even the waiter seems to know," he said now, wiping the gravy from his trousers. "It was not a good idea," said János Varga, wrinkling his brow. "The situation is explosive enough."

As though events were only waiting to confirm his pessimism, Heinrich Kahn came toward them from the door. The aging gentleman was rarely seen in the Espresso, which was mainly frequented by young actors. People gazed after him curiously as he strode across the room with heavy steps, a booming herald of himself. His face was red, even his small, dark eyes seemed to be colored with the red of his face. Without waiting for an invitation, without taking off his winter overcoat, he sat down at Christopher's table.

"How did your father like it?" he said.

"I don't know. When the rehearsal was over, he was no longer there."

"I should like to know how he got into the theater."

"I invited him."

"I thought you were no longer in touch with your father?"

"I think that is my affair."

"Not when you smuggle your father into the theater where I am acting."

Heinrich Kahn made no attempt to lower his voice. What he had to say was not intended for Christopher's ears alone. The bigger the audience the better. With a large, imperious gesture he beckoned to Fritz Eppstein who, undoubtedly not by chance, was hiding behind a newspaper.

"Herr Eppstein," said Heinrich Kahn, "Richard Wendelin was at the rehearsal today. Hidden, of course."

"I know," said the little comedian who played the part of Salamon Svarcz in *The Great Trial*.

"Is that all you have to say?"

"Herr Wendelin's presence did not disturb me," said Fritz Eppstein.

"Which concentration camp were you in?" The Grand Inquisitor asked him.

"You can take your pick, Herr Kahn," answered Fritz Eppstein.

"Then you must also have been in a concentration camp where *Ritual Murder* was shown. Isn't that enough for you?"

A smile passed over Fritz Eppstein's pale, bony face. "If you made the effort, you could also see the matter from another point of view. Perhaps Herr Wendelin should be forced to see his son's play from beginning to end."

More and more customers had been attracted toward the center of discussion. Some sat down round the table, others remained standing by it.

"Do you know something, Herr Wendelin," said Heinrich Kahn, turning back to Christopher. "I don't believe a word you say anymore. You go to Israel, take a Jewish name and drop it again, go to the East, ostensibly to collect evidence against the Nazis there, come back, and not another word is heard about this evidence, you write a play on the subject that made your father 'immortal' . . ."

"You didn't find all that out for the first time today, Herr Kahn," said Christopher.

He had turned pale, was controlling himself with difficulty. Kahn is a Jew. Kahn is a Jew. He has suffered, people hate him because he has suffered. I can't answer him. That fellow over there, Gert Seebold, is looking at me encouragingly. I don't need your approval, Herr Seebold. You were in the Hitler Youth, Kahn is a Jew. I can't stand him any more than anyone else, but I won't answer him.

"I didn't know that you were in touch with your father, Herr Wendelin," said Heinrich Kahn, emphasizing the name. He did not look at Christopher, spoke to himself, but just as one speaks to oneself on the stage, he was also speaking to the audience. "I believed the opposite—that is why I agreed to act in lin. The sons ought to have the right to turn away from their fathers."

"Quite right," said Werner Schaal, a young actor in the

background. "As a German, I agree with you completely. If Richard Wendelin is smuggled into the theater . . ."

János Varga touched Christopher's hand appeasingly. Christopher glanced sideways at his friend; he was pale and his hand was trembling.

The applause encouraged Heinrich Kahn. "Yes, smuggled into the theater. And you will permit me to take that symbolically as well, Herr Wendelin. You are trying to smooth your father's path into the theater. After all, Richard Wendelin has already been allowed to make a film in this country . . ."

"A terrible potboiler," interjected Helmut Bang. Christopher didn't know him personally, but knew that he was the most successful caricaturist of the younger generation. "If it had happened to be a good film, Richard Wendelin's yelling would long since have been heard in the studios again."

Why are my fingers itching? Bang is only saying what I have thought a hundred times. Am I allowed to say it and not he? Didn't I hope at one point, that everyone else would think it?

"I took the part," said Heinrich Kahn, "because I wanted to give you a chance, Herr Wendelin. I thought one ought not to live in this country if one is not prepared to give its youth a chance."

The old give us a chance. We don't take it, they give it to us. Heinrich Kahn has no idea what an affinity he has with my father.

"And you"—Heinrich Kahn leaned forward and looked Christopher in the eye—"misuse the chance you have been given."

"I can understand your agitation, Herr Kahn," said Christopher.

"Don't slap me on the back," Heinrich Kahn interrupted him. "When you were in the Hitler Youth, I . . ."

Christopher pretended not to have heard. "You're seeing ghosts, Herr Kahn."

"The ghosts of millions of murdered Jews, for whose death your father was partly responsible."

Kahn is a Jew, Kahn is a Jew, Christopher repeated to himself. "I didn't smuggle my father into the theater. It happened by chance. I met him in the street, outside the theater."

"I thought you didn't know him anymore."

"I had the feeling he was prowling round the theater. He's an old man . . ."

Heinrich Kahn had turned his back on Christopher. "Please take out your handkerchiefs," he said to the others, who were gathering in ever denser ranks around the table. "None of it's true. Even the remark about his old age isn't true. When I was playing King Lear, Richard Wendelin was a young assistant director. With his wretched talent he would never have got anywhere if we hadn't been thrown out."

"I know your quarrels with my father," said Christopher. "I admire you, but that doesn't alter the fact that my father is a great artist." This time he would not allow himself to be interrupted. "He no longer works as a director, but he has the right to see my play . . ."

"If he buys a ticket," said someone, and most of the bystanders nodded approval.

This country is better than I thought. They want nothing to do with the old Nazi Wendelin. That's what I wanted, that's what I hoped for—and yet I'm disappointed.

He, too, leaned over the table. "I didn't smuggle him into the theater, Herr Kahn, but he hid. He wanted to hide, it wasn't I who hid him. He wanted to see his son's play, but he had the tact not to offend you by letting you see him. What more do you want?"

Heinrich Kahn turned to Christopher again. More calmly, but all the more effectively, emphasizing every word, he said, "It's not a question of your father, Herr Wendelin. I should be kept very busy if I troubled about every armchair murderer . . ."

Fritz Eppstein interrupted him. "You are letting yourself get carried away, Herr Kahn," he said gently. "For my part, I refuse to be an accomplice in your family arrest in reverse."

Heinrich Kahn gasped for air. That the counterattack came from Eppstein's side disconcerted him. As though Eppstein were not there, he went on: "I am concerned about you, Herr

Wendelin. I believed in this play. I believed in you. When I came here, I was resolved to speak my mind and leave it at that. I thought"—he laughed—"that you would apologize for your outrage. Instead of that, you are defending your father . . ."

"I'm not defending him . . ."

"You are not only defending him, you are glorifying him. You have probably already reserved the stage box for him. He doesn't need to buy a ticket, his son will give him one. Perhaps Richard Wendelin will take a bow alongside his son. Without me!"

Repulsive old man! Was Nessor right when he said: "You hate your father and—your father's enemies"? I don't hate all my father's enemies, I only detest this intolerant old man.

"I cannot act in a play in which I do not believe," Heinrich Kahn went on. "Several things struck me as suspicious from the outset."

Christopher noticed that János Varga was about to say something, but the words died on his lips.

"Several passages stink of restitution," said Heinrich Kahn. "Confess your misdeeds without suffering for them! But I said to myself: No, you're already accused of resentment as it is" —he turned around with an accusation in his eyes that seemed to be directed against everyone—"your hearing is not merely acute, you hear things that were never said. I spotted something in the language, the Nazi jargon, but Herr Varga wouldn't change a word. Now it is confirmed once more— my suspicions of yesterday are the facts of today. It means nothing to you, Herr Wendelin, that the concentration camp butchers were egged on by showing them *Ritual Murder*. Perhaps you're not a Nazi, or don't know what you are, but there's the Nazi in you, Herr Wendelin." He stood up, reached with nervous fingers into his overcoat pocket, took out the script, threw it on the table in front of Christopher. "Without me! Give my part to an old Nazi! There are plenty of them around, waiting to take it!"

Christopher had risen. I'm standing, facing him as I faced the railway official the other day. A man from the past. A second man from the past. A Jew? Hell—that's the mistake we make. Jews in the concentration camp. Jews on reservations. Jews in ghettos. There they all stand behind Kahn, thinking: He won't dare . . . He won't dare to answer a Jew! Jews are different, one doesn't answer Jews.

He said, "You're a vicious old man, Herr Kahn. You never gave anyone a chance but yourself. You could never understand that József Sarf forgave his son. I'm glad you're not playing the part. If you had the courage to look in the mirror, you would discover how closely you resemble my father."

Heinrich Kahn heard the last words on his way to the door.

No one spoke, no one moved. Only when Christopher dropped onto the seat did the tableau break up into individual figures. People stood up, sat down, argued together. Quickly two groups formed, characters came to the surface: the zealots, the enthusiasts, the compromisers. A few crept away—we weren't there, we didn't hear anything. Some said, "You had no right to say that, Herr Wendelin." Some said, "Kahn's indignation is very understandable." Some congratulated Christopher: "It had to be said, sooner or later." And Christopher sat there, pale, exhausted, worn out, not knowing which pained him most, the reproaches or the applause.

The theater was in an uproar, the publishing house was in an uproar. They telephoned Heinrich Kahn; Ludwig Ludwig went to see the actor personally. They could do nothing to budge him. They telegraphed to Berlin, Hamburg, Frankfurt. They tried to get Otto Stuckenschmidt, who had played fathers' roles during recent years with uncontested success. In a film portraying the disintegration of the family in the Third Reich, Stuckenschmidt had made a profound impression. In the Third Reich, Stuckenschmidt had appeared only on provincial stages. His views, not articulated, but unambiguous, had stood in his way. The actor asked for the script to be sent to him in Berlin. Then he agreed. In two weeks he would be in Munich.

Meanwhile the rehearsals continued. Christopher was present at every one. He was worried about János Varga. The better he got to know the director, the more strongly he felt his friend's seismographic sensibility.

As though borne by a swift wind, and tangled by the wind, news of the incident at the Espresso had been carried into the newspaper offices. From the cultural section of the papers the news flew into the other sections. A Hamburg paper spoke of a "brawl" in the Munich Espresso; a mass-circulation newspaper attributed "anti-Semitic remarks" to Christopher and did not fail to mention that he was "the son of the director of *Ritual Murder*"; another paper came to Christopher's defense, praising his "humane attitude" toward his father and remarking with hypocritical benevolence toward the Jews that "men like Heinrich Kahn, with their intolerant resentment, however understandable it may be, are doing their own people a disservice." János Varga was also mentioned in one or two articles. His silence was interpreted in whichever way the reporter pleased. "The Hungarian," said one account, "must have had his own thoughts when he learned through Kahn of the presence of the 'shadow director.'" While Christopher was annoyed to be told that "any scandal is useful," János Varga winced under the unaccustomed publicity as under a whiplash. "I pictured things differently, I pictured things differently," he repeated, and when Christopher, forced into defending the press against his will, said that in a democracy everyone was entitled to express his opinion, Varga only said, shaking his head, "It's too complicated for me. I pictured things differently."

One day, a Saturday, they rehearsed without a lunch break, and when Christopher was leaving at four o'clock, Adam asked if he could go with him. Christopher had some shopping to do in town; that was all right, said Adam, he had to pick up his father, who was doing a matinée in another theater, around six.

"You got it dead right today," said Christopher as they set out. "I have the feeling that you find it easier with Stuckenschmidt."

"I don't know. I quite liked Kahn. He used to yell at me

pretty often, but he yelled at everyone. Once he took me home with him after a rehearsal. He has three grandchildren, two boys and a girl; one of the two boys was having a birthday, and we stayed till ten in the evening."

"Yes, it was probably my fault," said Christopher. "I lost patience."

"No, no," protested Adam. "I would have lost patience, too." He redoubled his pace to keep up with Christopher. "I wanted to ask you something."

"Well?"

"But you won't take offense?"

"Come on. What is it?"

"What was it your father did that makes people speak so badly of him?"

Christopher came to a stop. "You don't mean to tell me you know nothing about my father?"

"Yes. What is in the newspapers. And what my father has told me."

"What has your father told you?"

"He says your father made wonderful films. But what my father says isn't necessarily right." And, as though to console Christopher, he added, "He was a Party member. After Stalingrad he wanted to leave the Party. He wanted nothing more to do with politics."

"Have you heard of *Ritual Murder*?"

"It's supposed to have been an anti-Jewish film."

Christopher went into a druggist's. Adam preferred to wait outside. The shop was full. Adam is standing outside. He doesn't understand why they speak so badly of my father. Since we have got to know each other better, he no longer speaks all that well of his own father, but it doesn't occur to him to feel responsible for his father. Two bars of soap. They made soap of Jews' fat. Adam doesn't know that, and it doesn't concern him. Does he speak his part like a parrot? Does it mean nothing to him that my father made an "anti-Jewish film"? Old Lavender, Yardley, Arpège. Heinrich Kahn yelled. That's the point, not that he is a Jew. I should have thought to myself:

Heinrich Kahn is yelling. Nothing else. "These two bars of soap," he said, "ten razor blades, a tube of toothpaste."

Adam stood outside the window. He seemed to have thought over exactly what he was going to say, for he spoke fluently, without pausing in the middle of a sentence. "I believe you upset yourself a lot. I don't know why you upset yourself. Stuckenschmidt may not be as good as Kahn, but he isn't bad, either. Or you upset yourself because your father isn't allowed to come to the rehearsals. I think that's very silly. What he did can't have been all that bad, otherwise they wouldn't have acquitted him. Naturally he's interested in your first play. If he could, my father would come to every single rehearsal."

"Just a minute! Just a minute!" said Christopher.

I must interrupt him. In a few sentences he has said so much that it would take me as many hours to explain to him how little he knows. The Jews of Tiszaeszlár had to be acquitted because they were innocent. For Adam the outcome was never in doubt, he didn't need to read my play to the end. And because they acquitted my father, it couldn't have been so bad. You're wrong, Adam! Sometimes courts dispense justice, sometimes injustice. Your father and my father—that's not the same thing. My father couldn't leave the Party, neither after Stalingrad nor before, because my father was never in the Party. He didn't need to be; instead, he made *Ritual Murder* and *We'll Die for You*. Or is there a similarity? After Stalingrad your father thought, Now it's all up, this is where I jump off. He was an opportunist, like my father, but he was more clever. It's true he thinks my father's films were marvelous, but he got you a part in *The Great Trial*. My father sits at home and can't understand why Heinrich Kahn doesn't understand him. "It's too complicated for me," said János Varga. How can I explain to you, Adam? Shall I explain to you? Isn't it better for you to retain your purity? Are only those pure who do not understand?

"You know," he said, "that my father made an anti-Jewish film. Not only one, by the way. In his *Ritual Murder* film, things were portrayed as though . . . as though I were to say the Jews really had killed Eszter Solymosi. He didn't only lie, he knew that he was lying. If I had written a play like that, for example, and it could be put on today, would you want to act in it?"

Adam thought it over. "No, not if I knew you were lying," he said.

"And how could you know?"

Adam's face brightened. He looked up at Christopher, who had begun to walk more slowly. "I know you can't lie," he said.

"That honors me. But are you sure you can judge?"

"Certainly," said Adam. "I know you."

He knows me. Therefore, the Jews didn't kill Eszter Solymosi. And suppose he didn't believe in me, but in someone else? Someone who says the Jews did cut off the Christian girl's head. Would he then believe they did it? Innocence hangs by a thread.

"Listen," he said. "It's not so simple. You know what atmosphere is . . ."

"Of course."

"People can create an atmosphere. In a family, for example, in which the parents are continually quarreling, or the brothers fight, or one is jealous of the other's success—in such a family, there is a bad atmosphere. Right, that is perfectly understandable. But now it becomes more complicated. Guests arrive. They haven't created the atmosphere, but before they're aware of it, they have been infected by the atmosphere. At first they merely feel uncomfortable, then they take sides, in the end they quarrel with each other. They don't say, There's a bad atmosphere here—they're not even aware of that. Although it is created by men, the atmosphere becomes stronger than men. Do you understand?"

"Naturally."

"In a state the situation is even more complicated. The family's guests can't leave. If there isn't a bad atmosphere in their own family, they realize next day that they behaved foolishly. In a state, family and guests are identical. Everyone is responsible for the atmosphere, even the one who suffers under it. We are now living in a particular atmosphere. It isn't the best possible, nor is it the worst. Therefore, you believe me when I tell you that neither in Tiszaeszlár nor anywhere else did the Jews ever kill a Christian girl in order to bake matzos with her blood. If the atmosphere changed—and many people are doing all they can to poison it—you would suddenly stop believing me. In the year in which you were born there was an atmosphere in Germany in which intelligent boys like you accepted the malicious nonsense of the ritual murders as naturally as you accept that H_2O is the chemical formula for water. And if the atmosphere deteriorated today, no one would know tomorrow who had created the atmosphere and who was merely its victim." He came to a stop. "Come on, we've got to go to the tobacco shop. I promised János."

Outside, the cold of the January evening came at them again. "I'll walk with you to the theater," said Christopher. "Button up your coat, you'll catch cold."

"I've been thinking over what you said," said Adam, obediently buttoning up his coat. And as though he wished with the sure hand of a child to lead the conversation back from theory to reality, he said, "You should not be upset over your father. I don't upset myself over my father. If what you say about the atmosphere is right, your father lived in a bad atmosphere and Kahn was wrong to keep him out of the theater."

"No," said Christopher. "He was right. There are millions of people of whom we don't know whether or not they created the atmosphere. In my father's case, we know."

"Then why did you quarrel with Kahn?"

Because my father is my father, Christopher wanted to reply. I can't anwer like that, because then I should have to explain to him that I don't mean "Honor thy father and mother . . ." What do I really mean? The letters in colored pencil, the director's script of *Faust,* reading aloud from *Don Quixote,* that he saved me from a hero's death, perhaps even that Dr. Goebbels gave me the electric railway? That I couldn't stand the injustice that was done him, because it did not make the injustice he had done any the less? That I wanted to be his sole judge and that they snatched justice out of my hand by acquitting him, then by condemning him?

He said, "I'll explain that to you another time. You're coming to see me next Sunday, a week from tomorrow. Then we can talk in peace and quiet. Only if you want to, of course."

"You bet I want to," said Adam.

They stopped in front of a men's clothing store near the theater.

"Your tie isn't very snappy anymore," said Christopher. "I think I'd like to buy you a new one."

Adam protested, but Christopher had already opened the door. The boy made straight for the rack on which the cheapest ties were displayed. He immersed himself so busily in choosing that Christopher sat down, wearily. It was hot in the shop. He unbuttoned his coat and watched Adam, who, with red ears, picked up one tie after the other.

I am twenty-eight and have never thought of marrying. Martha, Inge, Wanda, Stefanie, Marushka. And the nameless ones. I could have a son, or a daughter. Rather a son. Adam's mother died under the bombs, and his father left the Party after Stalingrad. I am buying him a tie, and in a minute I shall cry. Outside in the street I suddenly had the feeling I was turning into Kasimir Nessor. I must write to him, perhaps I can persuade him to come to the first night. I shall write to Martha tomorrow. I talked to Adam as Nessor talked to me. It can happen without marrying; you don't actually have to produce children. They are delivered to the house and you buy them ties. Pure silk—eighteen marks. "You are my son, not your father's son—there's nothing unusual about that." Something like that, Nessor had said. "No inherited disease is as virulent as one we have acquired ourselves." If it takes Adam any longer to make up his mind, his father will be waiting in vain at the stage door. Three bachelors go home—two in one direction, one in the other. Adam was two when the collapse came, the catastrophe. Let's hope he couldn't talk much yet. Anyhow, he didn't understand much. János is right, I've grown old.

After *The Great Trial* I shall write a novel. And I shall finish it. Adam was born in a good year.

"What do you think of this tie?" asked Adam.

"I think it's splendid," said Christopher.

That evening, János Varga was in such a depressed mood that Christopher suggested they should go into town, to a cabaret and have a drink.

They went first to a cabaret that had once been a student hangout; the students had turned it into a great success and the place was still flourishing. Christopher had merely wanted to take János Varga's mind off things, but suddenly he saw himself in the role of those guides who in Warsaw had extolled the achievements of the people's democracy to him. The fact that the young people on stage mocked conditions in the country with bitter irony, and often with wit and humor, that they used taboos as targets and struck the government when they aimed at William Tell's apple, would not in itself have made Christopher feel more confident. It was the applause to which he drew János' attention, the laughter at the right places, the occasionally demonstrative approval. True, he asked himself whether he had grown older, had joined the ranks of the satisfied and contented because *The Great Trial* was shortly to be staged; whether he was secretly preparing to come to an understanding with the "dear gentlemen," as Heine called them; whether he felt in Germany like the master of the house who praises what he possesses; whether they were merely joking here because the thing to do was to poke fun at what could not be changed; and whether the jokes were tolerated precisely because they did not change anything; but he also asked himself whether in his absence a new generation had come to maturity and had reached for a new broom. János said that there were political cabarets in Hungary, too; they were also tolerated. The thing must not be looked at ideologically, but in terms of contemporary history. All over the world the mighty had realized that wit does not kill, nor mockery; like the caricature it contributes, on the contrary, to the victim's popularity. The clown who runs after the attraction and makes fun of it merely increases the attraction's attractiveness, and he, the clown, is eventually carried out of the arena, rolled up in the carpet.

They went to a second bar, sat down at a small table, talked, as always, about the play, the actors, the prospects, the dangers. They came to speak of Tiszaeszlár and the evening by the Bodrog. Although Christopher had been almost continually aware of János Varga's homesickness—German food did not appeal to him, the noisy traffic irritated him, the foreign tongue, which he spoke perfectly, nevertheless filled him with feelings of inferiority—he did not imagine that János' depression was due solely to homesickness; nor did his political outlook, which had actually stiffened now that he was abroad, explain his disturbed frame of mind. That morning there had been two letters from Eva in the letterbox, one to Christopher and one to János Varga, and if each told the other the contents of his letter, neither showed his letter to the other. Jealousy? Christopher wanted to tell János Varga that something strange had taken place in him. Since he heard nothing from Martha and did not see Eva, he had become clearly aware of his feelings, of their varying degrees of warmth, strength, intensity— here a comforting memory, there a painful one, here the thought of something joyfully complete, there of something disturbingly incomplete, here a mellow glance backward, there a forward gaze into turbulent hopelessness. Yet he fought shy of telling János Varga the truth, because that would have sounded as though he had lightheartedly renounced something he possessed, while the other was raising to the heavens which he could not possess. They talked about Eva, but what remained unsaid stood between them.

Young people joined them, spoke to them encouragingly, seemed to have been informed about their difficulties, slapped them on the back, promised to "be there." Strangers recognized Christopher from photographs, shook his hand. Christopher could not suppress a certain vain delight in his new celebrity, but it moved him less than the proof that he was not alone. He thought of Ferdinand's funeral. Perhaps there were more than forty or fifty.

In a third nightclub, a spacious jazz cellar, they sat at the bar. János had complained of a headache and had followed Christopher only reluctantly, but beer and schnapps had put Christopher in an exuberant mood. Munich was celebrating Fasching. All over the city costume balls were taking place, and the further the hour advanced the more people in fancy dress streamed into the bar, so that Christopher and János Varga in their everyday clothes gradually came to feel out of place. The bar turned into a ball. Beautiful, half-naked girls, dressed only in a tiny corset and black stockings, knights and apaches, a young lady in a flowing robe—obviously Mary Queen of Scots, because she was carrying a papier-mâché head under her arm—Kaiser Wilhelm in a pointed helmet, Charlie Chaplin, not yet forgotten, a girl in a slouch hat—general applause for the successful costume of the murdered *fille de joie* Nitribitt—a Schweik uniform from the First World War, a bearded Existentialist, a flapper, cowboys, a young man in a doctor's white coat bearing the inscription "Gynecologist."

"One could make some interesting psychological studies," said Christopher. "Once a year they slip into an alien skin. Most of them are walking daydreams. Just look at that athlete, in private life a bookkeeper. The girl dressed up as Nitribitt is unquestionably a virgin." János was sitting with his back to the room, staring at the wall; he rarely looked around.

A girl, so naked that it was hard to say what she could have represented apart from nakedness, recognized Christopher, claimed to know him personally, took him by the arm. In a flash they were among the dancing crowd. The girl's breast pressed against Christopher, he let his hand glide over her back, pressed his knee between her hard thighs. They scarcely moved, it was scarcely a dance, but the hot rhythm passed over into their bodies. The smoke divided up the room into small, hot islands, the drums pounded, the place was sweating. The girl's tongue played with Christopher's ear. He thought: I'll put János Varga in a taxi and send him home. It's Fasching and I forgot it because I'm busy with *The Great Trial*, but Fasching will soon be over, and I'm not a little boy with spectacles. He was angry with János for having made him forget Fasching. One can save the world and still enjoy oneself. He kissed the girl on the mouth. Helen of Troy was sitting on the stairs with a cowboy's head in her lap. An old jockey lay half stretched out on the stairs with his hand in a bulging sweater. János is sitting with his face to the wall, grumbling, because the bourgeois world is rotten, or because I have chased away Heinrich Kahn, or because the newspapers write lies, or because he doesn't like German stew, or because Eva went to bed with me. "Have a good time, Wendelin," said a Roman senator beside Christopher. "Chin up," said a Cossack. And all the time Christopher kept looking over the heads—a lettuce field waving in the wind—for János Varga. He had disappeared. Had he gone home? All right, if he wants to be sulky and morose tonight. Then the slow wave carried Christopher to the bar. János Varga had only disappeared from view because he was no longer sitting on the high bar stool. He was standing, facing a big, square-built man; the square-built man was holding János by the jacket, and János Varga was as white as the wall.

Christopher left the dumbfounded girl standing and hurried up to his friend.

In the next few minutes everything happened with the grotesque suddenness of old silent films. "What's going on?" asked Christopher, and from János Varga's incoherent, stammering reply he learned that the man, who was not in fancy dress and had been sitting there earlier—Christopher remembered him—had spoken to him, had asked him if he was János Varga, the man who had something to do with the "Jew play," and when János Varga had protested at the expression, the man had said something about "Jewish swine" and told the director to "go back double quick" to where he had come from "uninvited."

Christopher was seized by the icy calm which he knew and which boded no good. He grabbed the man's hand, twisted his wrist, let go of it and said, not very loudly, "Now get out, and quickly."

"Oh, it's you," said the man. "You're the traitor." And he pushed Christopher in the chest.

Christopher stumbled back. The man was as big as he was, about forty, a hulking fellow with a face that was not ugly— only the nose was ugly, squashed flat between the brows like a boxer's. Christopher brushed János Varga out of his way and was about to leap at the man, when the man grabbed a glass of whiskey from the bar and threw the contents into Christopher's face.

Then it came, the blind rage which his icy calm had heralded. He struck the man in the face with his fist, but the man barely swayed and struck back just as hard. He caught Christopher over the eye; the blood spurted over Christopher's face, ran down over his shirt and into the open collar. He had only one thought: to bring the man to his knees. This time he caught him on the chin, hit him so hard that his own knuckles bled. The man fell backward, bringing down a Pompadour with him who had been sitting at the bar behind him. The man bent forward and spat out a tooth; blood poured over his mouth and chin. Christopher only waited a moment. He didn't feel like leaving it at one tooth. He went at the man again with raised fists, but his fist was seized in mid-air. A man had come from among the dancers—the enemy's friend, Christopher thought. The second man held Christopher's arm behind his back. The first had recovered and struck Christopher with all his force on the nose. Meanwhile, Christopher had jabbed the second man in the stomach with his elbow. He now seized the first man's hand with both hands and squeezed it so hard that he let out a yell. But Christopher didn't care about that; he pressed the head down over the bar and began to smash the square skull against the bar as though the head were nothing but an insensible hammer.

Blood and whiskey were running down over his eyes, and he saw what was going on around him as though through a veil. An apache had dragged the man away from him, evidently less to protect him than to prevent a homicide; two other men, no doubt from the man's group of friends, hit out at the apache; the white wig had fallen from the Pompadour's head; a young man in evening dress had lifted up the second, who had grabbed Christopher's arm, and was giving the bewildered man one slap in the face after the other. Women were screaming, men yelling, János Varga was pushed up against the bar; a waiter shouted "Police!" a woman yelled "Flying Squad!"; a cowboy—the comic nature of the situation flashed across Christopher's mind—was hitting one of the fighters on the head with the butt of his wooden pistol, and a second apache had begun to undress, but couldn't undo the knot of his red handkerchief, so that instead of taking part in the fight he was merely tearing his handkerchief to pieces—harlequins, Chaplins, cowboys, clowns, dominoes, hussars, civilians, Martians.

And while hats were being knocked off heads, glasses shattered, while someone screamed hysterically for a doctor, blood and beer ran over fancy-dress costumes. While a man reduced a bar stool to firewood, and the head of Mary Queen of Scots was trampled underfoot, and a girl dressed as a cat crawled behind the bar, while he himself punched a second friend of the square-built man over and over again in the stomach, Christopher suddenly had the feeling that it was all a senseless and uneven fight. "Give it to him, Wendelin!" yelled one, and another said, "Make mincemeat of the swine," and a third shook an unknown man and repeated monotonously, "Nazi swine! Nazi swine!" None of them had been at Ferdinand's funeral, and there were more than forty or fifty.

Christopher wiped sweat and blood from his brow. There was really no one left for him to hit. He thought of jumping onto the bar and calling a halt to the bloody turmoil, but it was too late for that. Harlequins and Pompadours and Nitribitts and dominoes shrank back. With rubber truncheons in one hand and the other on their revolver holsters, the police crowded into the bar.

"Stick with me," said Christopher to János Varga. "Are you hurt?"

"No, no," said János Varga.

Last time I got away before the police came. Tomorrow there will be headlines in the papers. Ludwig Ludwig, the theater,

The Great Trial in danger—because of a barroom brawl, a fight in Schwabing. Ferdinand had said, "Blows are no argument." Then what is an argument? The letter I wrote yesterday. Couldn't Kasimir Nessor come to the first night? The author is unfortunately unable to be present: he is in jail for causing grievous bodily harm. The letter to Martha. The rehearsals are coming to an end, first performance, I have finished something. More accurately, I have banged a head on the bar until the man was half dead. Or dead. Mitigating circumstances: it was done in defense of a friend. Of a Communist from Hungary? "An acquittal means nothing. I know better than anyone." Now the music stopped; it only occurs to me now that they went on playing through the whole fight. The mood—as always after a scrap. Everyone is standing in well-behaved rows, uninvolved spectators at a street accident. A stretcher. The man with the inscription "Gynecologist" has a bloody coat; he has turned into a surgeon. Behind the bar the fight is about to flare up again; someone still has an itchy fist, two men hold him back, belated heroism. "Who started it?" Ten people talk to the police officer at once, among them two clowns, indistinguishable from each other except that one is bleeding from a wound on the forehead. By a curious telegraphy, everyone seems to know what happened.

"Disappear," Christopher whispered to János Varga. "For heaven's sake, don't stand there—disappear!"

"What's your name?" asked the police officer.

"Christopher Wendelin."

"Don't cause trouble, come along voluntarily."

"I'm not causing trouble."

"Make way! Make way!" shouted the police.

On the way to the door, four or five men slapped Christopher on the back.

As he was going up the steps he swayed. He stopped, leaned against the wall. "Go on!" one of the policemen shouted into his ear. He went on. As the cold night air struck him, he heard the jazz band that had begun to play again.

* * *

"You've been lucky," said the police surgeon who sewed up his wound. "It might have been quite an eyesore, in every sense of the word." The police surgeon was a wit.

"Anyone seriously injured?" Christopher asked cautiously.

"No one's going to die," joked the police surgeon. "Hazards of Fasching. There ought to be a special insurance available during Fasching." He went to his desk, glanced at his papers. "If you count the stitches, it comes to a pretty fair number. You're a good average with eighteen."

"Can I go?"

"You can, all right, but I'm afraid you shouldn't. The Inspector has an irresistible urge to have a word with you. Have the stitches taken out in five days' time. That can't be done at the cost of the state."

In the Inspector's outer office seven sinners were waiting. Four—two men, two women—were sitting on one bench, three men on another. Here there was order: people were sorted out according to categories. Christopher had no difficulty in guessing where his place was. On one side of the room, under the barred window, sat a clown, a bear and a man in evening dress. The bear was sweating in his bearskin. He had put the bear's head down on the bench beside him.

As Christopher entered, the three men rose. "Walter Tuttwitz," said the man in evening dress. "Sigi Säckel," said the bear. "Glad to meet you, my name is Franz Mösbauer," said the clown.

"Have you seen my friend?" asked Christopher.

"The Hungarian?" said the bear. "He was one of the first. He's waiting for you downstairs. He wanted to stay here, but they threw him out."

Across the room, on the other bench, the two whores were quarreling. They were arguing about a wallet. Both protested their innocence, but they could not agree as to who had stolen it.

"I'm sorry you got in this mess on my account," said Christopher.

"It was a pleasure," said the clown, who had two strips of sticking plaster over his nose.

"Who is inside?" asked Christopher.

"He's not one of us," said the bear.

"We're the last of the Mohicans," said the man in evening dress. His shirt was red, his right hand bandaged.

"Does anyone know the name of the man who started it all?" asked Christopher.

The clown stood up, shook hands with Christopher, brought his heels together, mimed a screwed-up face with a monocle. "Jochen von Sitzberg." He sat down. "Doesn't the name mean anything to you? Can't you just see that fellow in uniform? Left, right, left, right. He can't do much marching at the moment, I'm afraid. A broken nose, two gashes, one molar in the Lost Property Office. Tell me, Herr Wendelin, where do you do your training?"

"I'm afraid we were ten to one."

"Not all at once," said the bear apologetically. "I personally was severely handicapped. Idiotic idea, this bearskin. And I can't even take it off. All I've got on underneath is a pair of pants. Besides, I was dead scared all the time of losing the head." He lovingly stroked the bear's head.

"For someone worried about his head, you did pretty well," said the man in evening dress.

"You know each other?" asked Christopher.

"We're both medical students," said the bear.

"What about you?" Christopher asked the clown.

"I have a very manly trade. I'm a saddler."

One of the two men on the other side of the room, an unshaven old man, had laid his head in the lap of one of the two whores and was snoring. The office door opened; a policeman entered and decided to wake the sleeper. "He was the last one to be brought in," one of the whores protested. The snoring man was woken and led away.

"What's this play you've written, Herr Wendelin?" asked the bear.

"A 'Jew play,' as Herr von Sitzberg would say. It deals with the persecution of the Jews in the nineteenth century."

"A pity," said the clown.

Christopher pricked up his ears. "Why a pity?"

"I thought it was something topical."

"And you know, the fellow wasn't even drunk," said the man in evening dress.

"Who do you mean?" asked Christopher.

"Herr von Sitzberg, of course. I was sitting on the other side of the bar, facing him. That makes me a first-class witness. He had been shooting off his mouth about one thing and another for half an hour already. About teaching the young people decency, and that sort of thing. I wonder why he goes to a place like that at all."

"That's obvious," said the bear. "He wants to get angry."

"Then he got what he wanted this time," said the clown drily.

"I thought his friend was even more repulsive," said the bear. "I mean the one with the bald head. He almost swallowed his false teeth. It wasn't fair of Paul"—he turned to Christopher—"a friend of ours, studying geology. But people shouldn't wear false teeth that look so genuine. A real SS face."

The policeman brought out the unshaven man, looked around, signaled to the whores to follow him. Only one man was now sitting against the opposite wall, a man in a shabby navy-blue suit wearing horn-rimmed spectacles. He had ostentatiously turned away from the other three. "At last," he said, lighting a cigarette with a precious gesture.

Christopher's throat was tight. This could be the happiest day of my life. I go into town to cheer up János, we talk about Eva, I feel sorry for János, I feel angry with János, I dance with a naked girl, I wish János were gone, I knock a tooth out of the mouth of a Herr von Sitzberg, I think to myself, There isn't going to be any first night, they sew up a wound in my forehead, I'm waiting to be interrogated by the police, and it could be the happiest day of my life.

"Herr . . ." He turned to the bear, who was ceaselessly wiping his brow.

"Säckel," said the bear.

"Herr Säckel, I want to ask you something that may sound very odd."

"Go ahead, Herr Wendelin."

"I have spent the last few years abroad . . ."

"I know," said the man in evening dress. "You were in Israel."

"And behind the Iron Curtain. I only came home a few months ago." How easy it suddenly is to say "home"! "I had a friend. He was a cripple. Soon after I got back he died . . . But that's not what I wanted to say. The rehearsals, my play . . ."

The three looked at him as though to say, You're right, that certainly does sound odd, Herr Wendelin.

"I mean . . . are there a lot of people like you?"

"I think I know what you mean," said the bear. "You see, I watched you. You went to work as though you meant to clear the bar. What did you think? Did you imagine the whole place was going to side with that swine and go for you?"

"Something of the sort," said Christopher.

The room was quiet. Through the barred window filtered the gray morning light. All they heard was the coughing of the man fidgeting restlessly to and fro on the bench opposite.

"You're right and you're wrong," said the man in evening dress.

"What do you mean?" said the bear. "Herr Wendelin is wrong."

"No, not entirely," said the man in evening dress. "In nine out of ten bars he could have talked about Jewish swine till dawn, and he would still have all his teeth. Not that anyone would have agreed with him."

"Anyhow, not more than a handful of idiots," said the bear.

"Forget about the idiots," said the man in evening dress. "The others would have sat there and let him talk. Someone has to hit out. In nine out of ten bars and in ninety-nine cases out of a hundred, no one would have hit out."

"In Germany, revolutions take place in bars," said the bear.

"In case of bad weather they are canceled," said the clown.

"Moreover, they don't even take place in the bar," said the man in evening dress.

"And if they do take place after all," said the bear, "they take place too late. On a twentieth of July, for example."

"Since we don't even revolt when we are repressed," said the man in evening dress, "you can't expect us to revolt before we are repressed. Everyone imagines that a man like Sitzberg —I beg your pardon, Herr Mösbauer, Jochen von Sitzberg!—is a lone wolf. Unless someone comes along and knocks his nose even flatter than it is anyway. In which case you can count on us."

"In which case . . ." repeated the clown. "Furthermore, that isn't quite true. Herr von Sitzberg could have whined on till the day after tomorrow about national honor and fellows with no country—no one would have so much as listened." The man opposite cleared his throat. "Something wrong?" the clown asked.

The man did not answer.

"Well, then," said the clown.

"In fact, quite a lot of people would have agreed with him," said the bear. "He has to use a phrase like 'Jewish swine.' Then we remember something we don't remember. Provided someone raises his fist, of course."

"Provided someone raises his fist," said the clown.

The door opened once more; the two whores were towed out; a bucket-load of obscenities was poured out over the gray room; the policeman led the whores to the exit and handed them over to a sergeant.

"Is there a Christopher Wendelin here?" said the policeman.

Christopher stood up. "I was the last to arrive," he said politely.

"Go in," said the policeman.

The small office was in twilight. A few electric light bulbs, exhausted by a hard night, were battling with the morning. Behind the desk the inspector was sitting with a *l'état-c'est-moi* expression. Apart from this, he bore little resemblance to the Sun King. The sergeant who had brought Christopher in sat down at a typewriter.

The inspector looked at his papers. "So you started it," he said.

"No," replied Christopher. "Herr von Sitzberg started it.

First he called my friend a 'Jewish swine,' then he threw a glass of whiskey in my face."

"But you struck the first blow." His eyes moved to and fro between the papers and the stickingplaster on Christopher's forehead. "Without you, there would have been no brawl."

"If a few young people hadn't been outraged, Herr von Sitzberg and his friends would have killed me."

"Your friend comes from Hungary. He is a guest here, in the West."

"Do we describe our guests as 'Jewish swine'?"

"So you deny all guilt?" He signaled to his colleague to take down Christopher's statement.

"Christopher Wendelin," said the colleague. "Born 10th December 1930 in Berlin. Residing in München-Grünwald, Perlacher Strasse 149. Your father's name?"

"Richard Wendelin."

The Inspector's eyes remained glued to the plaster. "Richard Wendelin?" he said. "Are you related to the famous film director?"

"My father."

The Inspector leaned back. "Your father will be pleased when he hears of your heroic deed."

"My father couldn't care less."

The sergeant was moving his fingers impatiently on the keys of the typewriter. At this point the official interrogation had been interrupted in a manner contrary to the regulations. It was true that the Inspector's last sentence had sounded disparaging, but disparaging in a kindly, familial, almost fatherly way.

"Your father isn't so . . ." said the Inspector.

"So what?" asked Christopher.

"I mean . . . he isn't a man to get upset over every trifle. He would be kept busy if he was. He has been through a lot, your father." He pushed a packet of cigarettes toward Christopher.

"I don't smoke," said Christopher.

I don't smoke. The official at the Israeli immigration office offered me cigarettes too. You're lucky, Herr Wendelin. In five weeks your passport would have run out. But my beautiful

German passport with the imperial eagle hasn't run out. A bit battered, but better a tattered eagle than none at all.

I'm lucky again. Richard Wendelin has opened the doors! When is your father going to make another of his wonderful films? My father doesn't bother about such a little thing as "Jewish swine," and why should he? There remains the possibility, a possibility worth considering, of shoving the wastepaper basket over the Inspector's head. If I don't shove the wastepaper basket over the Inspector's head, they will ride roughshod over the bear and the clown and the man in evening dress. Somebody has to start. Otherwise, the revolution will come too late. Or it will take place in a bar. Or not at all.

"In any case," he said, "my friend Herr Varga is completely innocent. And the gentlemen waiting outside are also innocent. If you wish, you may write that I alone am guilty of everything."

"How much had you drunk, Herr Wendelin?" asked the Inspector. "It must have been a good bit. I mean, it is Fasching."

"Yes. I had drunk a bit," said Christopher.

"There you are, then," said the Inspector, signaling to his colleague. The typewriter started clattering again.

"We shall have to take proceedings, of course," said the Inspector, looking as though hypnotized by Christopher's forehead. "But don't do it again, Herr Wendelin. You spring from"—he actually said "spring from"—"an honorable family." His eyes assumed a dreamy glitter. He seemed to be seeing a miniature cinema screen in the plaster on Christopher's forehead, because he said: "I can still remember many fine films your father made. Wasn't one of them called *Michael the Ancestral Farmer*? I saw it in the military hospital. You're a writer"—he looked at his papers—"you're an intelligent man. An intelligent man doesn't do things like that. Prove yourself worthy of your father. He rose. "Sign this!" He accompanied Christopher to the door.

Outside it was light, as light as it can be in the outer office of a police station. Outside, the bear, the clown, the man in evening dress and the man in the shabby navy-blue suit were still waiting. Christopher stopped in front of the Fasching group, winked at the three men and said: "I need your addresses. I shall send you tickets for my play."

The sergeant waited patiently until the proceedings were finished.

It had started snowing again. There was nothing to recall the street during the night; the ghost of Fasching had flown. Thank God, thought Christopher, János has gone home. He was about to call a taxi, when he caught sight of János Varga. He had waited in a café across the street.

Questioningly, uncomprehending, János Varga looked into Christopher's cheerful face.

"There are more than forty," said Christopher. "Perhaps more than fifty."

But János Varga only looked at him in even greater bewilderment.

The rehearsals were broken off. Although the afternoon papers already carried whole columns reporting the "violent brawl in Schwabing" and displayed Christopher's photograph on an appropriate scale—one or two commentators asked whether the author of the play *The Great Trial* was not merely after "free publicity"—the rehearsals had not been broken off on account of the scandal. János Varga had been lying for two days in a darkened room. His eye trouble, he said, but although he could see practically nothing, Christopher knew that János Varga's illness did not have a physical cause.

On the third day, he told Christopher that he had decided to give up directing the play and return to Budapest. Christopher implored him, but in vain.

"I know how ungrateful I am," said János Varga. "You overcome all your resistances to me, and now I'm leaving you in the lurch."

"That's not what matters," replied Christopher without conviction.

"It would be worse ingratitude if I stayed," said János Varga. "My nerves are in pieces. Of course, my eye trouble is psychosomatic in origin. The psychoanalyst, I'm afraid, is a watchmaker who can take a watch to pieces very skillfully, but cannot put it together again. It is not yet too late to find another director. If I went blind ten days before the first night, I would jeopardize the performance." He had been unable to settle down in the West, he went on—he avoided the word "Germany"; Christopher must have noticed that long ago. Like someone who is prepared to take the whole guilt upon himself, so long as he can thereby free himself from an intolerable compulsion, he avoided accusing the West. Curiously enough, he said, there had not been such hard fighting in the West as in the East, but in the East they had fought their way to a certain calm, and perhaps for that very reason they had become sensitive, perhaps hypersensitive. "You will say we have suppressed the voice of the opposition. Maybe, in any case, we have also suppressed vulgarity. You will say our system is imposed by force—maybe, in any case it has eliminated violence." He couldn't bear the sight of blood, he said; he had seen too much blood. In the darkness of the last few days, the eyes of the man at the bar had stared at him. "They were the eyes of the men who took away my mother. I see everywhere the eyes of murderers." It was unfair, he knew, but you were only at home where you could distinguish between one pair of eyes and another. The police had treated him politely. "But I can't face the police. I have been interrogated too often, Christopher." He could not endure the thought that there might be bloody clashes on the opening night. He should have resigned earlier, he confessed, at the time when the first blaring newspaper reports appeared, when the simple fact that Christopher's father had been inside the theater exploded into an uproar that stirred the whole intellectual world. Now he had no alternative but to pack his bag. "Think what you like," he said, like a deserter abandoning his comrades under enemy fire, and with a bitter laugh he added: "I am fleeing into the lukewarm comfort of a dictatorship. One needs stronger nerves than I've got to live in a democracy."

Christopher took János Varga to the airport. He was sad, but he could not be angry. He thought of the cemetery at Rákoskeresztur, where János Varga had first spoken of Tiszaeszlár. It was not the same thing whether you suffered from your father's guilt or from your mother's death. János Varga had spoken of East and West, of Hungary and Germany. He had said nothing about his mother. "Give my love to Eva," Christopher said. "Perhaps I shall see her today," said János Varga.

Ludwig Ludwig was in one of his terrible moods. This time he did not spare Christopher, either, so that by comparison with the publisher's rage, the consternation in the theater made little impression on Christopher. On the other hand, by comparison with the helplessness of Martin Mommert, whose vacillating character did not inspire much confidence, by comparison with the theater manager's hectic disquiet, the great Ludwig's busy activity was almost reassuring. The new theater had no resident directors, so one had to be found. The directors from the other Munich theaters refused. Ludwig Ludwig telephoned to Berlin, Hamburg, Frankfurt. Everywhere he was met with refusals. "It is hard to believe that really no one has time, everyone is already booked up," said Ludwig Ludwig. "It seems to me that they are afraid to grasp the hot iron. Kahn has walked out, Varga has walked out, and then the hostile press—they're all scared stiff." The theater's demands grew more and more modest, but an opening night under a provincial director seemed out of the question. A few film directors who had a good name and seemed not disinclined "to pull the cart out of the muck," as Ludwig Ludwig put it, had to be discarded after more mature consideration. One had made *And Tomorrow the World*, the other *Black, White and Red over the Cameroons*, the third *Hitler Youth on the March*. None of them could be compared with Richard Wendelin, none of them had become a Staatsrat, and now, none of them were symbols of the half-forgotten past, but they would have become symbols of the forgetful present if *The Great Trial* had been entrusted to them.

Three weeks before the first night, it seemed as though it was the law of Christopher's life that even what he had finished should remain unfinished.

Christopher looked out into the snow-covered forest. The white fingers of the moon were touching the white fingers of the fire. The forest was like a defeated army retreating out of the besieged city, white soldiers resting after the battle. He had put on two thick sweaters, because the heating had broken down. He thought of opening the window; rather the biting cold of the winter evening than the cooled breath of the house.

You wouldn't have left me in the lurch, Ferdinand. Or did you, too, run away? Perhaps the waves were rising too high and you, too, sought peace in the silent, the final dictatorship. János didn't understand: the eyes of the murderers are not a compulsion but a challenge. I don't run away anymore, Ferdinand. I don't know whether Ludwig has forgotten the seven Warsaw crates. I haven't forgotten them. I shall remain here till they are opened: Pandora's box in which all sufferings are caught and all atrocities, all plagues and all tormentors, and all the plagues of the tormentors, the box from which all the sounds and smells of hell escape and which in the end contains nothing but the grubby dregs of hope. *The Great Trial!* It wasn't vanity that made me dream of the evening on which the curtain would rise on *The Great Trial.* József Sarf's house. From the left: the wife of Jankel Smilovits. József Sarf's wife has been dead for years. Terka Smilovits wants to talk to Sarf about the preparation of the matzos. Moshe Dzwonicki told me there were matzos in the Warsaw Ghetto. They were starving; no bread. The baking of unleavened bread was forbidden, yet there were matzos on Passover. Móricz Sarf enters, right, sits down by the fireplace, sinks into sullen silence. Adam has learned to tell a whole story in silence, the story of a fourteen-year-old Jewish boy in Tiszaeszlár. Every day Adam comes to me, walks with me, waits for me, hours on end. His eyes ask, but he asks no questions. He consoles me. I can't give in.

He heard a bell ring, thought it was the telephone, a sound from the street. It rang again: it was the doorbell.

With red cheeks Richard Wendelin entered the room. He took off his fur coat. "Haven't you any heating here?" he asked, instead of any explanation of his sudden appearance. "Something has gone wrong with the heating," said Christopher. "You're alone?" asked Richard Wendelin. "Of course," said Christopher.

His father dropped into the ragged armchair, in which a few weeks before, Adam had sat. "Can I get you something to drink?" asked Christopher. "I don't drink anymore," said his father. "Strong drink is bad for my heart, and champagne upsets my stomach. I won't stay long."

Richard Wendelin looked around. "Have you found a director?" he asked.

"No. It looks pretty hopeless."

"That's why I've come. I don't think you lost a lot when Herr Varga left. I watched him." He gave a low laugh, rubbed his cold hands together. "I know that lot. Cerebral directors. They think too much. Intellectual means 'only spiritual.' The theater is not only spiritual, it is spiritual only secondarily. Besides, actors are a stupid lot. They don't understand the intellectual director. It's useless explaining to them what they are supposed to think or feel. You have to show them how to act, speak, gesticulate as if they were thinking or feeling such and such a thing."

What is he after? Has he come in the middle of the night to give me a lecture on the art of directing? He must have taken the local train, then a taxi; he doesn't drive anymore himself. Or is he going to recommend a director, one of those who made *Black, White and Red over the Cameroons?* Or . . . he dared not think the idea through to the end.

"Furthermore," Richard Wendelin went on—he seemed more relaxed, younger and in better health than Christopher had seen him for a long time—"furthermore, the director is the most overestimated man in the world. Max Reinhardt— and none of these amateurs ever got near to surpassing him— once called himself a glorified stage manager. He was speaking in jest, but there's a lot of truth behind it. It's luck for directors that authors don't know their own value. Any author with some experience of the theater can replace a glorified stage manager."

When his father uttered the name of the genius whom the Third Reich had driven into exile and exile had driven into death, Christopher winced. My father's lack of inhibitions is astonishing. Reinhardt had gone and instead Wendelin staged *A Midsummer Night's Dream,* in the presence of the Führer. And the King of Afghanistan. Then Christopher smiled with relief. He knew now why his father had come to see him.

Richard Wendelin wrapped his fur coat more closely around him. "One rarely thinks of the most obvious thing," he said. "A cliché, but true, like most truisms. Why doesn't it occur to the theater to let you direct the play? You have been watching Herr Varga at work for weeks. Unless I have misjudged that weakling, you influenced him more than he influenced you. You know your own play better than anyone. You discovered the Lambrecht boy . . ."

"We discovered him together."

"I'm sure it was your instinct. That boy is a find. Not an infant prodigy—they're more stupid than actors. And"—he smiled —"there's no denying that you're my son." He made a dismissive gesture. "No, it has nothing to do with blood. I know your theory—the only blood you see is when you cut yourself shaving. It has to do with our discussions since you were so big. You spent more time in the studio and at rehearsals than at school. It's amazing how often missed lessons add up to an experience of life. I can still see you sitting, bent over my director's scripts."

"I know," said Christopher. "The director's script of *Faust*."

Richard Wendelin pretended not to have caught the significance of Christopher's remark. "One must take opportunity by the forelock." Even his diction seemed to have changed; it took his thoughts by the forelock. There was nothing left of the unctuous pathos that he had acquired after his fall, after the collapse, after the catastrophe. Language had come back to itself and to Richard Wendelin. "Not that I imagine your career is guiding you toward the director's desk. You were born to be a writer. I always suspected it, now I know." He buried his hands in his large pockets, took out the duplicated version of *The Great Trial*, put it in front of him on the low table. "I bet they're only waiting for you to set to work. It's the natural solution, against which even the hyenas of the press can raise no objection. It simply had to occur to somebody." In his small, red eyes there was a crafty gaiety.

I understand. You want me to tread in your footsteps. Across all boundaries, your vanity bridges everything. Watch out! I don't need to take his advice just because he is my father. I don't need to reject it just because he is my father.

"Perhaps," he said. "Perhaps it really would be worth considering."

He stretched out his hand toward the script. With a quick, imperious gesture, Richard Wendelin placed his own hand over it. For an instant their hands touched—the young, strong hand of the son, the frail, tired, white hand of the father. Thus, their arms outstretched, their hands on the script, they sat facing each other, and their eyes met—the bright, hard, innocent eyes of the son, the pale, watchful, tested eyes of the father. Who would be the first to lower his eyes, who the first to take his hand from the script? Richard Wendelin did both first, so sure did he seem to be that his son would open the script.

With the magnanimity of the victor, he said, "I have worked through the script. I felt"—he laughed again—"like Emil. You remember Emil?"

"Of course," said Christopher. Emil had been the old stage-door porter in Berlin.

"Emil always stole the first casting script. He sat for hours in his lodge writing direction notes in it. One day I caught him in his secret. From then on, Emil always used to say to me after every first night, 'Just how I pictured it, Herr Staatsrat.'" Richard Wendelin was no longer shivering. He had thrown his overcoat wide open and crossed his legs. "I was sitting out there, completely snowed under, with nothing to do. You will find my notes in the margin." He picked up the script, put on his glasses. "For example. For example, scene nineteen. That's where Eszter Solymosi's body is carried onto the stage. No doubt Herr Varga directed that according to your stage direction. But it was all far too solemn. At this point the actors must speak in the language of newspaper reports. It's a piece of local news, not an obituary. Eszter Solymosi is not yet in her coffin, the stranded body has only just been fished out of the Tisza. The people themselves have no idea that this is going to be the great turning point in the trial. They have recovered the body of an unknown young girl, that is all."

He jumped up, and as he did so the cold room in the neglected, sparsely furnished house became a stage. Richard Wendelin became the ferryman, Amsel Fogel, carrying the dripping corpse over his shoulder. He moved the chair from its place, intentionally put it in his way, almost tripped over it, almost fell with the corpse, got rid of the invisible burden with a sigh of relief, rested his right hand on the small of his back, sat down on the edge of the sofa at the foot of the corpse as though it were not there, actually pushed the invisible feet aside with a little gesture, as though to make more room for his seat, turned to Dávid Herskó, the second ferryman, and said angrily, "It was lying in the reeds, the hair was caught in the reeds." He knew the text by heart.

He has only one idea, thought Christopher. He wants to direct. He has always had only one idea. *Michael the Ancestral Farmer* and *We'll Die for You* and *Ritual Murder*—always only one idea. Now he wants to direct through me, the cured alcoholic for whom there is nothing left but to get drunk on other people's drunkenness. The play, my work; and me, his work. Of course the scene is right; that is the only right way of doing it. János saw it wrong. If Fogel and Hersko make too much fuss about finding the body now, they can't be surprised in the next scene, when the peasant woman Borbála Boros cries out: "That's Eszter!" He doesn't care whether *The Great Trial* is ever put on. He wouldn't care if he couldn't make me his tool. Nevertheless, it's a good idea, a very good idea. "No provincial director, rather a discovery," Ludwig said. Perhaps he was only waiting for me to volunteer. It depends on me whether I become clay in the potter's hand.

Richard Wendelin remained sitting on the sofa. Now he was Richard Wendelin again, an old, shivering man in a fur coat. "The theater will agree," he said, "If you're clever. The slightest suspicion that I've got anything to do with it, and your play will never be performed. You yourself must forget that I ever held the script in my hands. I give it to you. I enjoyed the illusion, that's all. If you need advice—as I said, I'm unemployed. You've got my telephone number. You can come out to see me or I'll come and see you here, in the evening. Incidentally, I've been feeling much better lately. The doctor is satisfied. My blood pressure is two hundred and ten, still too high, but it was up to two hundred and twenty-five." There was a slight tone of reproach in his voice; his son had not inquired about his blood pressure. His son said, "I could see that right away—you're much better."

Christopher ordered a taxi. While they waited, Richard Wendelin avoided speaking of the play, the difficulties, the direction. Only once did he say, "Try to get on with the press. You don't know how to handle the press. Answer when the journalists ask you a question. You don't necessarily have to tell them the truth. They simply want to fill their columns."

Christopher walked with him to the garden gate. It was snowing; the snow in the roadway was up to the level of the snow on the sidewalk.

Back indoors, Christopher poured himself a large glass of whiskey. He sat down in the worn armchair and began to read his father's directions.

I wanted to be more clever than he; he is more clever than I. He is the master, I am the dilettante. Experience outweighs conviction, experience is stronger.

Ludwig immediately fell in with the idea of letting me direct the play. Strbrny was delighted. "A natural talent!" It meant nothing. During the first week I had to back out of one or two scenes; I didn't know what to do with them and didn't want to reveal my uncertainty. "Of course you've got stuck. The scene is far too long, and the beggar stands around far too long without speaking. In the theater, minutes are hours. It's not worth having him for the sake of a single sentence. It looks as though he is only waiting to say a single sentence—leave him out. There's no need for Vollner to come in here at all." Of course, perfectly simple, I should have thought of it myself: scrap the beggar. Some scenes drag. When directed by János, the scene between Móricz and Samu Sarf took two minutes; as I do it, it takes three. That's three hours. I'm gradually learning—from him, of course. Stuckenschmidt sticks to the stage. Pause after his entry, pause before his exit. My own uncertainty—as over my poems, which no one knows except Martha. I can judge poems—other people's, but not my own. I can judge the play, but not the stage. I sat down in the stalls, tried to slip into the skin of the audience. At times it was as though I heard nothing, saw nothing. Blind and deaf. I had always been an onlooker; now I could no longer be one. "It's difficult to tell from a distance. If I could be there—for five minutes." Casually, as though dropped in passing. I should have guessed. He had already planned it when he came to see me. He didn't merely want to direct the play through me, he actually wanted to direct it himself; the intoxication of others leaves him cold, he reaches for the glass. One scene corrected. But is it better now? I am satisfied—and alone. "I have to see the second act as a whole." Slowly, gradually, he disclosed his plan. The hour of truth, chosen by himself.

Seven days later he slipped past the porter's lodge, as he had done once before. The more blatant his intention, the more humble his words. "You go on ahead. When you give me a sign, I will run past the porter's lodge." Or: "Now they're all onstage. As soon as you have started, I shall come in. You yourself are not to know where I am." I became his accomplice without noticing it. He ran into an electrician, pressed an enormous tip into his hand. A bribe—now there are three accomplices.

At night in my house, the first clash concerned the final scene, which he had seen in the morning. "You must take this scene away from Eötvös. József Sarf must say it." No longer a suggestion, it was an order. I: "The speech is far too rhetorical for József Sarf. Perhaps József Sarf has an inkling that he is going to be acquitted, but he has been through humiliation, prison, torture. And the torments inflicted upon him by his son." He: "That's all wrong. The sense of innocence lends the father self-confidence." I should have foreseen it. He sees himself in the role of the unjustly persecuted father. Next day there was open conflict. It concerned the behavior of the Jews during the trial. He: "One can't hear Bukszbaum at all. He mumbles to himself. The man is innocent. He must shout out his innocence." I: "Innocence does not shout out." He: "On the stage it does." I: "It doesn't shout out on the stage, either." A conversation about the Jews of Tiszaeszlár. I: "They are poor little Jews. They haven't murdered Eszter Solymosi, but they are not snow-white. Lázár Weiszstein has been to prison several times for embezzlement. Eötvös is not defending them because they are splendid people, but because they are innocent." He: "That is intellectual claptrap. If these Jews didn't break down while they were remanded in custody, then they are splendid people." I: "They were able to stand firm because they were innocent. And by the way, Fogel and Herskó broke down." He: "You didn't write the piece merely to entertain the audience, but because you want to say something, because you want to achieve something. If the Jews do not win the sympathy of the audience, you might as well have them condemned." I: "I am not pleading for sympathy, but against injustice." Here, on the eighth day, I should have known that he was spoiling everything. He cannot slip into my skin, because he first has to slip out of his own. His ideal remains the SS. This time it's a Jewish SS. Black and white—those are the only colors he knows.

On Monday of the second week, Eppstein remarked, "People say there is someone hanging about during rehearsals." And he looked at me with his sad comedian's eyes. Perhaps he already knew who was hanging about the theater. I told my father. He said, "We must be more careful." The language of the accomplice. Why didn't I bar him from the theater? "Once we've got the last scene right, I can disappear." Why did I weaken? Werner Schaal came to me. "Listen, Herr Wendelin, there's a rumor that your father is directing the play behind the scenes. I don't care, but remember Kahn. The Jewish actors, the press . . ." I lied craftily. Don't deny everything, don't admit everything! "He watched one rehearsal. It might just as well have been a friend. He has nothing to do with the direction, you can see that for yourself." That evening I went to my mother. I told her the truth. Ferdinand is dead; one has to tell someone the truth, almost the whole truth. She showed no understanding. "It's impossible. He can't understand the play. It's difficult for me to understand it. You didn't write the play for us." I answered, "It's my play, my direction. He merely points out technical mistakes to me." "First they let Nazi engineers repair the canals, now they're regulating the channels of our brains." "He isn't a Nazi, he is an opportunist." "He is an expert. If you persist in your error, he'll be telling people in the end that he directed *The*

Great Trial. He knows no other voice but that of vanity." I should have known that it wasn't hate speaking from her, that she was only worried about me. Without vigor; she doesn't think her worry through to the end. "And don't imagine," she said, "that it can remain a secret. First one will speak, then two, finally everyone will known. And even if no one saw him, your direction will give it away. He advises you to use a gesture which is theatrically right, you carry out his suggestion, and the gesture changes the meaning. That's theater. I lived with him long enough. He is stronger than you."

Why did I let him have his way? Weakness, uncertainty, obsession with the theater, respect for the expert, gratitude, obstinacy, pity? Perhaps pity, too. How well he understands this terrorism of the heart! "So I'm not allowed to creep along the wall anymore?" The hand reaching for the nitroglycerine pills. Surreptitiously—but so that I can't help seeing it. The sons are responsible for their fathers' heart diseases. No, it wasn't pity. One evening I wrote the words "ritual murder" in two places in the manuscript. Only later did I realize why I had done it. There he sits, somewhere in the darkness, I myself don't know where, in a box, in the gallery, and hears the words "ritual murder." My mother is wrong: I wrote the play for the Wendelins. In 1945, I remember that somebody was indignant because an American general made the population of Dachau go every day to the concentration camp. Even then I praised the general. A general—it wasn't easy for me. I should have had nothing against it if the Wendelins were made to enter the auditorium of *The Great Trial* every evening. By compulsion, if necessary. But Richard Wendelin has to watch *The Great Trial* every day. On the day on which you came home in triumph—"I have been acquitted" —I felt the injustice that had been done to you. I had known about your own injustice for a long time; now they had cheated you out of repentance. "Can't I creep along the wall anymore?" I didn't want to, didn't plan to. But I have opened the gates of Purgatory to you.

The first day of the third and last week. Perhaps the great and final controversy would never have come about if my father had not felt weak in the morning, if he had come to the re-

hearsal, if Ludwig Ludwig, for the first time since I started
to direct the play myself—"I don't want to confuse you any
further"—had not spent almost the whole day in the theater.
Ludwig hesitated, as though he feared it was too late. Then he
said, "That is no longer your play, Herr Wendelin." Does he
know about my father? I don't think so. The great Ludwig is not
a man to keep things to himself. "The play is now so philo-
Semitic that it seems anti-Semitic." "I've barely changed ten sentences." "No, it's not what they say, it's how they say it. The Jews
have become an arrogant gang who think every one of them de-
serves a Knight's Cross because they didn't cut Eszter Solymosi's
throat. The wonderful first scene between József Sarf and Károly
von Eötvös has gone completely by the board. József Sarf if I remember rightly, says: 'We didn't do it,' and that means: 'Good,
kind Herr von Eötvös, please take our part, we really didn't do
it.' But the way Stuckenschmidt says it now, it sounds as though
he were calling upon Dr. von Eötvös to do his duty. 'Well, you
know we're innocent, so kindly get to work.' "

It's not my imagination; Ludwig has merely confirmed my
feelings. In the evening there were snowdrifts in the forest. I
could hardly get through to my father's house. I wanted to tell
him that now, in the last week, I must act entirely according to
my own ideas. I also wanted to tell him that the risk of discovery
was too great—accomplices' jargon, he would understand that.
But he began straightaway to talk about the scene that had
given us the greatest worry. Eszter's mother's hysterical accusa-
tions have distracted the attention of the police, so that the Jews,
herded together, have an opportunity to exchange a few words
before being led to the slaughterhouse. József Sarf speaks words
of courage to them: "Fear ye not, stand still, and see salvation
of the Lord, which he will shew to you to day: for the Egyptians
whom ye have seen to day, ye shall see them again no more for
ever. The Lord shall fight for you, and ye shall hold your peace."
Again my father spoke with the voice of József Sarf, and it was
not the voice of József Sarf, Jew and bell ringer at Tiszaeszlár;
nor was it the voice of my father, Richard Wendelin; it was the
voice of a Führer, the only voice the generation of my father,
Richard Wendelin, understood. That very afternoon I had spent

two hours on this scene alone, had actually shouted at Stucken-schmidt for the first time—probably because he was right when he said I had given him exactly the opposite instructions the previous day. "That's the way it is, that's the way I want it," I said. "After all, it's my play and I'm the director." I had liber-ated myself. In spite of my youth, in spite of my inexperience, Stuckenschmidt had yielded, and afterward, along with Ludwig, we had drunk a brandy together. But my father went back to his original conception. "If the Jews had nothing to cling to in József Sarf they would confess to everything, even to what they hadn't done. Just because they are little, oppressed Jews, they need a great Jew." And after repeating all the arguments I had already heard *ad nauseam*, he also appealed to the Bible. "Moses led the Jews out of Egypt. Without Moses they would have per-ished miserably." But I didn't want to hear it all over again, didn't hear it. Only a week, one single week, that was all I could think of, a bare week in which to wipe out the terrible mistake.

It's a good thing I didn't say any of this to my father. It would have sounded like ingratitude. It would have been heartless and senseless. I should have had to say: You can't help it. You can't help seeing uniforms; even the caftan turns into a uniform for you. You can't help it. Only the Germans were right, and now only the Jews are right; out of the mouth of the Jews speaks the German who is right. You can't help it. To you, Moses is a Füh-rer, and he led the Jews as another Führer led the Germans, to the Danube, the Seine and the Don. You can't help it. The ser-geant major is your secret hero, and in the end the Jews of Tiszaeszlár wear the ugly mug of the sergeant major. Your world is peopled by heroes and cowards. You have no idea how much heroism it takes to be a coward, and how cowardly the heroes are. I was wrong to stretch out my hand to you, for if I saved you, I would go under. You shouldn't go under for my sake, but I am not going under for yours. Stay on the bank, father.

It's a good thing I didn't tell him that. I lied, I said Ludwig Ludwig was going to be present at every rehearsal from now on, and that the manager and Strbrny were going to be present at every rehearsal, that we would be staying in the theater till late at night, that now I had to take all the responsibility myself. I don't know whether he believed me. I spared his sensibility, I deceived him. As I left, he gave me some more advice. I have one week left.

Christopher spent the next two days between hope and apprehension. It had been a pretext when he spoke to his father of Ludwig's presence, but the great Ludwig turned the lie into truth: he was at the theater all the time. His terrible mood switched to gaiety and soon increased to enthusiasm. "I'm gradually getting to be afraid," he said jokingly, "that you are a better director than a writer." On the other hand a gutter newspaper printed a "sensational" report of Richard Wendelin's "shadow direction." It asserted that the Hungarian director János Varga—the same man the paper had previously violently attacked—had refused to act as "a front for the director of *Ritual Murder*." Fritz Eppstein took Christopher aside and told him that a certain uneasiness was disturbing the actors; they knew now why valuable rehearsal time had been lost. "If your father were to appear in the theater again, we would all stop working." A protest against "the star director of the Third Reich," but at the same time other protests. "Today's mail," said Dr. Strbrny, showing Christopher three anonymous letters. One spoke of "high treason," the second one stated that they would "put a stop to the activities of the misfit," while the third openly threatened that "nationalist circles—they still exist!" would "turn the New Theater into a sea of flames." Even more disquieting were letters addressed to Christopher personally and signed with the writer's full name. Here the "war generation" took the floor. A sixty-year-old—"I was never a member of the NSDAP or any of its organizations"—demanded paternally that the young author should "think of his inheritance and his duty." Another one admonished: "You are probably not aware that you are fanning the understandable resentment in our people to white heat; the Jews, of whom you are apparently so fond, would have to ascribe the consequences to you." A third spoke in the name of those "expelled from their homeland" and asked with irrefutable logic why "a German should take the part of the Jews after hundreds and thousands of Germans have been deprived of their entire property by Soviet criminals."

When Christopher arrived home late in the evening on the third day of that week, the telephone rang. It was his mother.

"They called me," she said, "thinking you still lived here. Your father had a severe heart attack in a taxi. You must go to him at once." She gave him the name of the hospital to which Richard Wendelin had been taken.

The medical superintendent met Christopher at the door. "Your father is fully conscious," he said. "He insisted on seeing you. I beg you not to stay more than fifteen minutes, although . . ."—he interrupted himself—"I am afraid there is little hope."

Richard Wendelin lay motionless in his bed, but his eyes, which greeted his son with a smile, were so lively that Christopher began to doubt the medical superintendent's words.

"Thank you," said Richard Wendelin. "Sit close by me."

Only a lamp with a milky glass shade was burning above the door. A gale had blown up and was rattling the windows.

"Other people call the priest," said Richard Wendelin. "I called you." He was breathing quietly. "I have nothing to confess," he said. "Everything I have done is on record. I could say: I am a wretched creature. But that too is on record."

"Don't worry," said his son. "It isn't your first attack . . . You'll see . . ."

Richard Wendelin gently shook his head. "I am thinking of all sorts of lovely things," he said. "When you had had your tonsils out, I sat by your bed and praised you for not complaining of the pain. You couldn't speak, but you reached for a piece of paper and wrote on it: 'That comes of playing football.' A little while before, I had forbidden you to hang around the football field." He gave a low laugh.

"You shouldn't strain yourself," said his son.

"I have no pain," said the father. "I knew Boderode was conspiring against us. That's why I sent you to him."

"I know," said the son.

"Tell your mother I never loved Hermine. That, too, was

only opportunism. Tell your mother: Portofino. She will remember."

"Try and sleep. I shall stay here."

Richard Wendelin smiled. "I shall sleep long enough." He said in English. " 'Good night, sweet prince; / And flights of angels sing thee . . .' How does it go?"

Hesitantly the son said, *"Weswegen naht die Trommel?"*

" 'Why does the drum come hither?' Why?" said the father.

The wind was hammering on the windowpanes.

"Is it really so windy?" said the father.

"Yes, a violent winter gale," said the son.

"The taxi driver recognized me," said the father. "You wouldn't have liked him. He was one of my friends. By the way, I should like a quiet funeral. Naturally I would have preferred a state funeral. It would have been more in keeping with my life. Since that cannot be . . . Give me your hand."

Christopher took his father's hand and knew that his father was dying. The little white hand was already dead.

"Do you remember *Game in the Morning?*"

"Yes," said Christopher, although he only vaguely recalled the title of the film.

"You were still too small," said his father. "No one talks about that, although it was my best film."

They heard footsteps outside.

"What's the time?" asked the father.

"One-thirty."

"Don't put off the first night," said the father. "People wouldn't like it."

"Why should we put it off?" said the son.

The father's fingers closed convulsively. For the first time the son became aware of the battle which his father was fighting. Richard Wendelin let go of his son's hand, but immediately grasped it again. This time the son's hand was resting in the father's. It was strange that there was room for the big, strong hand in the little bony one.

"You couldn't know," said the father, "that there were worse people than I. You shouldn't have thought so much about me."

He stared up at the ceiling. "It was a pretty bad storm that time on the Chiemsee. We were a long way out. If I hadn't been such a good yachtsman . . . Admit you were frightened."

"Yes," said the son. He didn't remember.

"I made two suicide attempts," said the father. "But it was all play-acting." Richard Wendelin had closed his eyes. He said, "Tell Josef to lay the table for two. He may still come."

"What are you talking about, father?" said Christopher.

Christopher was afraid that his father was rambling. He was afraid his father might speak the truth. He had never heard his father speak the truth. Cautiously he took his father's hand and laid it on the blanket. Richard Wendelin was breathing heavily.

Outside the door Christopher met a doctor, introduced himself. "I know all about it," said the doctor. "Wait here." He went into the room.

Christopher sat down on a bench.

I often wished him dead. I never admitted it to myself, but I often wished him dead. But I was never thinking of him, only of his name. I wished the name dead. But a name doesn't die. My name will always be Wendelin. He is dying. I ought to have told him that he didn't need to die. My name is Christopher. When did he attempt suicide? Was it really only play-acting? I shouldn't have kept from him that I have thrown his direction overboard. We were clinging to each other, and one of us was bound to go under. Pain and bitterness came over him. He didn't know which was the stronger, the pain or the bitterness. You needn't worry, Herr Kahn, he won't be creeping around the dark gallery anymore. You need not creep along by the wall anymore, father. Portofino—I shall give my mother the message. I shouldn't have taken him into the theater with me when I found him prowling about in the street. He clung to me, therefore he was bound to go under. I couldn't live with him—how shall I live without him? The doctor is in the doorway; he is shaking his head. No, he doesn't want me to come in. Two nurses hurry away, whisper together. Had he really nothing to confess, or did he consider me unworthy to receive his confession? He won't be coming to the first night, don't worry, Herr Ludwig. I ought to have told him that I haven't forgotten everything he taught me during the past two weeks. We are acting the fifth and sixth scenes in the same set. An obvious idea, obvious to a master. When they move the tree right up to the front, I shall think of you, father. The nurses at the end of the corridor. They are bringing the oxygen tent.

He rose and went to the door. "Stay outside," whispered the doctor. "He is quiet now."

The clock showed three o'clock.

It was close to five when a great coming and going began. Two doctors, several nurses, entered Richard Wendelin's room. Soon afterward the medical superintendent appeared. Christopher was pushed aside like a bothersome stranger.

The clock was showing five-twenty when the medical superintendent came out. "I'm afraid I must tell you that your father has just died," he said, and squeezed Christopher's hand.

"Can I see him?"

Only the dead man was in the room. One side of the oxygen tent was raised. Richard Wendelin's little white hands were crossed on his chest. A crucifix had been laid on his chest. He seemed to be smiling in mockery.

Christopher went to his mother.

She opened the door immediately.

"I'm sorry," said Christopher.

She shook her head. "I couldn't sleep."

"He is dead," said Christopher.

They went into the studio. The central heating growled angrily, as though woken from sleep.

Gertrude Wendelin ran her hand over her son's hair. She had to stretch to reach his head.

"Shall I make you some coffee?" she said.

He sat down on the sofa. Light was slowly beginning to dawn.

His mother brought the coffee.

"He talked about you," he said. "He said he never loved Hermine Moellendorff, it was only opportunism. He said I was to remind you of Portofino."

* * *

Richard Wendelin was buried in the Forest Cemetery. When Christopher stepped out of the mortuary, the cemetery was black with people.

He had asked his mother to come to the funeral. He had done it impulsively, because he believed that his father would have wanted it. He was glad about it. He knew almost no one—Josef, two of his father's colleagues, two or three actors. And even these were standing on one side, with the vast concourse of mourners. As Christopher left the mortuary, they acted as though they had not seen him. They turned away, whispered together. A big, black, hostile crowd. Since he was an adult, Christopher had rarely felt fear. Sometimes at Baron Boderode's, when they had listened to the BBC. Now he was afraid.

A man in black, an employee of the undertakers, came up to him. "We have made all the arrangements, Herr Wendelin," he said. "I hope they will meet with your approval. You and his faithful servant in front, and two friends."

From the waiting multitude emerged two figures. They were two men around fifty; side by side they came toward Christopher, their eyes on the ground. That's not out of reverence, passed through Christopher's head. They take care not to get out of step.

"Von Ultitz," said one of them. He had a face like a death's head.

"Dr. Käfer," said the other.

Christopher knew the name. The man with the bull neck and the cynical eyes was a member of the Bundestag; people said he would hold an important office in the next cabinet.

"Josef and I will walk in front," said Christopher. "Apart from us, I should like two employees to carry the coffin."

"As you wish," said the man in black. He turned to the two waiting men with a look that said, He who pays the piper calls the tune. Then he had one more try. "Herr Bundesabgeordneter, Dr. Käfer would like to speak a few words at the grave."

"No one will speak at the grave," said Christopher.

Herr von Ultitz and Dr. Käfer returned to their places. To be sure, they had turned their backs on Christopher, but it was as though they had eyes in their backs, as though they were keeping their eye on him even during their retreat.

It had not snowed for days, but the snow was still deep. An icy wind swept across the cemetery. The sky was covered by snow clouds. It was not snowing; it was too cold.

A car came forward in a curve from behind the mortuary. Wreaths were piled up high on top of it. Christopher had not noticed the wreaths. As the car drove past him his eyes fell on the inscriptions. "To the Master of the German film," "To the Magus of the German theater," "In gratitude for unforgettable hours," "In indestructible loyalty," "When all others prove untrue." Hardly a wreath that did not bear the word "Staatsrat."

Christopher stood alone with his mother on the top step of the mortuary. He was not thinking of his father. His hands were clenched into fists. I ought now to raise my hands and speak. "Get out!" I ought to say. "Go to hell, you gang of criminals and criminals' accomplices, of executioners and executioners' assistants, go to the devil, you corrupt, corrupting, bribed, bribing, marching, commanding, obeying, trumpet-blowing, whipping, whipped, intimidating, cringing brown and black moles that have crawled out of your holes to stand to attention, to glorify yourselves and deprive my father of his dignity!" Oh, how they would run, that cowardly rabble who are only masculine in a mass, powerful in a chorus, clever in cunning, brave at a word of command. Hell, in a minute the funeral cortege will form, the mourners will march to the grave, a splendid funeral —and there are more than forty or fifty.

The coffin was carried out of the mortuary, still borne on the shoulders of four men in uniform.

A sob in the black crowd. Christopher seized his mother's hand; he couldn't believe his eyes.

There, in the second or third row, concealed till now by the cordon of mourners in front, he caught sight of Hermine Moellendorff, all in black, beneath the big black hat the tragedy-face of the girl violated by the Jews in *Michael the Ancestral Farmer*, the heroic daughter from *We'll Die for You*, the suffering Marie-Louise from *L'Aiglon*. "Tell your mother I never loved Hermine. That, too, was only opportunism . . ." "I would have preferred a state funeral . . ." You are having your state funeral, father.

Some of the men in black had turned to Hermine Moellendorff, were speaking comfortingly to her. Over there, on the other side of the little square, was the mainland, and Christopher was standing with his mother on an island.

As though he had sprung up out of the ground, Josef was standing beside him. He had crept up to him silently, as he used to creep silently through the Wendelin house. He pressed Christopher's hand, not too firmly, with an almost apologetic side glance at the crowd. Lift up the coffin, you served my father. I am bound to walk the path to the grave beside you, to share the burden with you. I hope your narrow underling's shoulders don't break under the burden of your master.

As the four men, with Christopher and Josef in front, passed the crowd with the coffin on their shoulders, it seemed to Christopher that they stepped back slightly. He saw an old student's face, with dueling scars; one of them had nicked the mouth, making it a half mouth. A square skull—it could have been Herr Sitzberg, Jochen von Sitzberg. A woman with a steel helmet of felt, a Nazi Woman's League leader, the face that told you she did not smoke, did not use makeup. An underling's face, blue with cold, bold yet servile. In all eyes he felt the same reproach. You are not worthy to be your father's son. Your lot are not worthy to breathe the air of this winter's day.

The two undertaker's men were tall, Josef was short; the coffin tilted, threatening to fall. Once Christopher tried to turn around and look at his mother, who, as he had told her to, was walking immediately behind the coffin, alone. Behind her, the pursuers. He walked so slowly because an old, well-known feeling rose in him, well known like an illness that one recognizes, even when it only knocks softly at the door. He wanted to run away! To drop everything and run away; "Who against hope believed in hope." There was nothing to hope for. And nothing to believe.

As the coffin was being lowered into the earth, Christopher tried desperately to think of his father. The white face, the dead hands, the voice that had become gentle. He couldn't manage it. He thought of Ferdinand. There were forty or fifty who had stood beside him then, behind him, facing him. And Ludwig the Great would say: "Be sensible, don't worry about the little group who eternally belong to yesterday." And Ferdinand would have said: "You didn't meet the right people." The cemetery was black with people, the moles were everywhere, it slowly began to snow, and it was impossible to distinguish between the piles of dirty snow and the white graves.

When he got to the theater the next day, Hermann Lambrecht came to meet him at the stage door.

It was about Adam, said the actor, after expressing appropriate condolences to Christopher. He would like permission, he brought it out, stammering, to wait in Adam's dressing room the day after tomorrow, the first night, to wait behind the scenes; but today and tomorrow he would like to fetch his son from the theater; therefore, he wanted to know when the rehearsals would be over. Of course, said Christopher, why not? But something in Hermann Lambrecht's voice had caught his attention —had Herr Lambrecht any special reason for his request?

Now it was Hermann Lambrecht's turn to look surprised. Hadn't Herr Wendelin seen the front of the theater?

They left the building, turned the corner. The front of the theater was painted with swastikas. In two places someone had written in clumsy letters: "Perish Judah!" and "Germany awake!"

"Of course, it's only kids," said Hermann Lambrecht. "But I'm a bit worried about Adam . . . You understand."

"Of course," said Christopher. "Today I will take Adam home as usual. But if you'd like to come along tomorrow . . . I'm very grateful to you."

Everyone in the theater already knew about the swastikas. Opinions were divided. "I'm a bit worried," said Stuckenschmidt. "A few diehards, obviously, but so far they confined themselves to knocking down Jewish tombstones. Now they dare to attack the living." A young actor who was playing the assistant to the lawyer, Dr. von Eötvös, suggested organizing a

vigilante patrol; he just felt like teaching one or two of those
youngsters a lesson. Dr. Strbrny had telephoned the authorities
and announced to the cast that during the first night's performance a special police guard would be on hand. "It has its
advantages," said Ludwig Ludwig. "It will make our splendid
democratic press, which has been giving us such a rough time,
something to think about." Fritz Eppstein shook his head and
said nothing. "Anyhow, we won't let them spoil our rehearsal,"
said Christopher.

Nevertheless, the nervousness of the final rehearsal was increased by a certain disquiet which Christopher found hard to
master. He wanted to run straight through the play without
stopping, but he had to interrupt the performance two or three
times. He sat down in the front row, moved to a box, tested the
acoustics from the gallery. He was satisfied; at times he actually
believed that the "silly kids' prank" had lent the actors wings.
In the dock sat the bearded Jews, József Sarf and Salamon Svarz
and Abraham Bukszbaum and Adolf Junger and Jankel Smilovits, but now they seemed like public prosecutors, and accused
were the murderers of the Jews, were the silly kids who had
learned nothing. The cries of pain of the tortured József Sarf
sounded more agonized than usual today, and when Károly von
Eötvös had ended his speech for the defense, Ludwig Ludwig,
the literary adviser, the manager of the theater, the stage designer and many of the stagehands broke into applause.

Late in the evening the rehearsal came to an end. Adam had
put on his winter overcoat and was waiting for Christopher.
The publisher had given him a small car; Adam got in beside
him.

They drove past the main entrance to the theater. In the
light from the street lamps the swastikas and the slogans were
more distinct than before. "Why do you think kids did that?"
asked Adam. All day long he had been hearing about them.

"I hope they weren't silly kids," said Christopher. He hadn't
wanted to talk about it in the theater, he said, but a "silly kids'
prank" would have been worse than anything else, because that
would mean that the poison, reproducing itself again, was giving
birth to evil. He talked about his father's funeral, without senti-

mentality, trying not to appear to the boy like a pious son. Cold
rage had seized him at the sight of the risen ghosts who had come
from their graves to stand in the snow-covered cemetery. Later,
on the way home, he had told himself that it had been thought-
less of him to let himself be so carried away. He had not seen a
single young person, only the dead who had marched behind
his father's coffin. Of course, nothing would be more dangerous
than denying the ghosts. The whole of Germany was haunted by
them, they clutched at the living with their bony fingers. There
were rooms in every German house where you could not sit
down, because ghosts were sitting in every chair, on every sofa,
at every desk. Nor should you dismiss the ghosts as stupid;
people were far too ready to believe that all they did was turn
tables, throw plates and rattle chains. In reality the ghosts used
the usual sharp or explosive weapons: national and racial arrogance, blind obedience, false pride, anti-Semitism, uncritical
respect for authority. In the schools—"You know best about
that"—the atrocities of the Third Reich, while not passed over
in total silence, were spoken of as a family affair that really
didn't concern anyone outside the family. Germany's enemies,
especially in their air raids on German cities, were presented as
though it would be the same whether you were the aggressor or
fought aggression.

They had reached Adam's house, but Adam made no move to
get out of the car. Yes, he said, he understood. Something very
strange had happened to him. When he was a little boy and had
asked about his mother, his father had told him that English
bombs had killed her, and although for the most part his father
was always talking about the Russians and their brutality, he
himself had hated the English because they murdered his
mother. Ever since he had gotten to know Christopher, however, he had thought differently, in fact had begun to think for
the first time. "If we hadn't attacked Poland, the English
wouldn't have attacked us, and if they hadn't attacked us my
mother might still be alive."

That was another chapter, said Christopher. Its title might
be "The Great We." On the one hand, it was good if Adam said:
"We" attacked the Poles, for if only the Nazi party had marched

on Warsaw that September day, the Poles would quickly have put it to flight and the war would not have lasted a week. But that little word "we" held secret dangers, because what "we" had done, in the end "we" must stand up for; he who shoots also defends himself, and he who defends himself considers himself innocent, and the word "they" fuses with the words "I" and "we." "Of course, it is painful to accuse our fathers. We cannot dispense with the word 'we,' no nation can. We are 'we Germans.' But if we want to be 'we Germans' we must realize that our 'we' has nothing in common with the 'we' of our fathers. If we want to love Germany, we must dig a moat between ourselves and them, so deep that no bridge can cross it. For if a bridge crossed from their Germany to ours, the ghosts would march over it. The ghosts are the first to march across bridges."

They sat in the car for a while. Christopher left the motor running; it was bitter cold outside. They returned, as in all their conversations, to the play, to the first night. Christopher, who had often found fault with Adam, now praised him, strengthened his courage, though this seemed to him quite unnecessary. He wished some of the other actors had Adam's calm confidence. "Since you have been directing the play," said Adam, "I like it twice as much."

"I've liked watching you act in it," said Christopher. "After the first night I will miss something."

Almost anxiously, Adam said, "I will still go on seeing you afterwards—won't I?"

"Of course," said Christopher. "Do you think that it is only as an actor that you matter to me? I must confess that most directors have little respect for actors; that's why every actor wants to become a director. And I'm afraid most actors have little respect for themselves. Hermine Moellendorff, who acted in my father's worst films, excused herself before the court by saying that she was 'only' an actress; she would willingly have accepted any good part. I was afraid you would only be a parrot, would simply repeat the words of the script mechanically. I spent all that time on you so that, from the very beginning, you wouldn't think that the part of Móricz Sarf was just an ordinary part.

Now I can feel your conviction. Believe me, you can't fool the audience."

It seemed to Christopher that Adam was scarcely listening, and he understood why when the boy said again, "I will see you often afterward—you promise me?"

"Word of honor," said Christopher.

As he drove along the ice-covered streets he thought, as so often after his conversations with Adam, of Kasimir Nessor. He wasn't surprised to find an express letter from Kasimir Nessor in his mailbox.

There was a letter and a telegram. The telegram was from Martha. It read: *Shall be in Munich for the opening. Unfortunately have to fly back next morning. Looking forward to seeing you. Fondly, Martha.*

He read the telegram twice, three times. The happiness that came over him was so violent that he hesitated for a long time before opening Kasimir Nessor's letter. He read:

"Dear Friend,

"A few days after I received your letter, and before I had found the time to answer you as fully as I wished, news of your father's death reached me. Today I must write you a different letter than the one I had planned, for just as your life was overshadowed by your father's life, so now it is marked by his death. Here I must ask you to forgive my brutal frankness, without which our relationship, however, would be meaningless.

"I said *overshadowed*, but I really should retract the word. You should consider yourself lucky to have been your father's son, should thank the shadows that fell upon you from your childhood on. Every day I see people passing my house in search of sunshine. Every day the papers speak of the hunger for sunshine and the cult of the sun. But now that, as you know, I am a gardener, I am becoming increasingly aware of the role that nature has given to rain and to shadows. Don't think, though, that from those sunny heights that always appear to the people in the valleys much higher and much sunnier than they really are, that I am about to extol the merits of darkness. The heavy burden of guilt which your father took upon himself did not weigh more than the guilt of others, but the shadows that it cast were longer and more visible. It is this visibility for which you should be grateful. Thousands upon thousands ruined Germany's name during those terrible years. It is not unintentional that I use such pathetic words, because your name preoccupied you in a way best described as pathetic in the English sense of *touching* and *moving*. If your name had been Müller or Meier, which, if I am not mistaken, you have often wished it was, you would never, or to only a limited degree, have been aware of your father's guilt, although it was not the Wendelins alone, but the Müllers and the Meiers, who pushed our nation down in guilt.

"I know the relief you are now feeling, are bound to feel. Not that you did not love your father—I was convinced how much you loved him by our most recent conversation, and it was this love which made me think for a long time. Relief however, because subconsciously you feel that that offensive designation, 'son of the director of *Ritual Murder*,' that has been repeated to you *ad nauseam*, will gradually wear out and be discarded. My dear friend, do not become a sunny character! Already the German papers I have seen report in the most sentimental fashion about the deathbed reconciliation between your father and you, tactfully leaving it to their readers to conclude whether the dying man asked for absolution or whether in the end the confessor confessed to the dying man. If your struggle during those nighttime hours when your father died were over, your struggle would have been vain from the outset. His struggle came to an end, not yours. A father fixation is pathological, but the father's complexes are historical. You will feel relief, but also emptiness. You are no longer struggling against your own father—but do not stop wrestling with the shadows of all the fathers! You were fortunate that, because his name was Wendelin, you could not forget your father. This embittered your youth, not least because you had sight among the blind—it is harder to see among the blind than to be blind among those who see. But just this has lifted you above those Germans who do not see their fathers and remain blind among the blind. The burden you carry has not become less. Your struggle, it seems to me, has just begun.

"Do not let yourself be discouraged. You have many enemies and I shouldn't be surprised if now, on the occasion of the first night of your play, they make themselves heard. There are many who will accuse you of treachery toward those 'ideals' in which your father himself never really believed. Others will say you should let the dead rest in peace, as though the dead slept better if their injustice was buried with them. If you fail, people will compare your failure with your successful father. If you succeed, they will call you an opportunist. Most Germans can't believe that anything other than opportunism ever wins laurels.

"Let me once more, today of all days, talk to you like a father. Do not join the growing crowd of disappointed young Germans! In the course of a long life I have learned that true love consists in the renunciation of being loved at any price. There is something exceedingly commercial about the phrase *reciprocated love*, reminiscent of reciprocal trade agreements, of a barter deal in which each tries to get the better of the other. The temptation to hate Germany because I am not loved there has come to me often in the last twenty-five years—half a lifetime. For much longer than I shall live, and probably for longer than you will live, Germany's shame will be a compulsory subject in the schools everywhere. Will the children learn to hate Germany? They will probably only feel distrust. You had the good fortune—good fortune, I repeat—to read in others' eyes the question: Is he like his father? It is not enough for young Germans to condemn their fathers—they must erase the similarity from their hearts and faces.

"Don't let yourself be discouraged, and don't make things too easy for yourself! Skepticism is no guarantee against false enthusiasm, and a clear conscience is unworthy of an intellectual. If you only worry about your own conscience, you cannot speak of a clear conscience, no matter how clear it may be. The intellectual, as I understand the honorific title, should be distinguished from the traveling salesman by the fact that the latter only has to live with his own conscience, but the former has to live with all our consciences. And they would not be good intellectuals who, out of disgust or self-satisfaction or fear of infection, flee from the sick after having diagnosed their malady so accurately.

"This long letter, my dear friend, must lead you to fear the worst. Only now do I come to the answer to your own letter. I wrestled inwardly for a long time as to whether I should be untrue to my own resolution and come to Germany after all to celebrate *The Great Trial* with you. I admit—don't reveal this to anyone—that I was tempted. But now I have weakened, in a physical sense as well—a severe cold followed by pneumonia sent me to bed, and although the miracle drugs have not failed in their effect, I now have to pay for the miracle with a prolonged period of rest. I shall not be up to the strain of a journey for several weeks, least of all the strain of a German *Winter's Tale*. Thus, you see, the trivial brings our finest plans to naught.

"My thoughts will be with you on Friday evening. You have many enemies, but also many friends. Your enemies are noisy, your friends are silent: that is the nature of things. But if you think that my telegram will not do more harm than good, as might well be the case, you may by all means hand it over to the press. It is the fate of fathers to see their sons going to war. Today I feel doubly that I feel you are my son.

Yours,
Kasimir Nessor."

Martin Mommert, the small, volatile manager of the theater, came to meet Christopher in a state of excitement. "When I came in," he said, "the stage was littered with swastikas. Like rain." He was holding one of the paper swastikas in his hand. "I'm having the theater searched."

Dr. Strbrny, normally calmness itself, seemed no less worried. He had received a letter in which "Adolf Schicklgruber" announced that this evening his friends would throw a bomb. "I informed the police, although with some reluctance. In the end they might forbid the performance."

More and more stagehands appeared who had found swastikas on various parts of the stage. In Otto Stuckenschmidt's dressing room a death's head had been painted on the wall. A towel in Fritz Eppstein's dressing room had been painted with the word "Jew." "The worst thing," remarked Martin Mommert, "is that it must have been someone from the theater. Nobody else is allowed in."

"Do the actors know about it?" asked Christopher.

"Not yet," answered Dr. Strbrny. "But word is bound to get around."

The actors heard about it at the stage door. Instead of giving them final instructions, Christopher had his hands full calming the disturbed crowd. He assumed a cheerful expression, joked, took refuge in the mild phrase "silly kids' prank." Speaking to Otto Stuckenschmidt, at whom the indelible death's head stared out, he recalled similar incidents, referring to them as "silly pranks," none of which had led to serious consequences. He felt he had to apologize to Fritz Eppstein. The comedian laughed: "I insist on using the Jew towel." He called the stagehands and electricians together, assured them of his confidence, and gave them instructions about what to do in the event of demonstrations. In Adam's dressing room Hermann Lambrecht sat, looking as though he regretted the day he had come to Christopher's table in the canteen. Christopher snapped at him. Then, as though nothing had happened, he conducted brief, factual discussions of individual scenes. When the audience began to stream into the theater, which was sold out, it seemed to Christopher that he had at least partially mastered the situation.

He watched the audience through the hole in the curtain. Critics and a select first-night audience in the first rows; behind them, men and women in strikingly simple clothes—a gray mass. "Every nook and cranny in the theater has been searched," Dr. Strbrny whispered to him. "We didn't find anything." Martin Mommert took Christopher aside. "It's disturbing," he said. "There are too many people one doesn't normally see at first nights.

"That's pure imagination," said Christopher, shifting a chair on the stage.

The stage manager was trying to get the actors who had noth-

ing to do there out of the wings. It seemed as though everyone wanted to be huddled close to the others. The bearded Jews
were standing in the wings, talking in low voices and gesturing.
No one spoke about the causes of unrest, but irritation spread in
all directions, a seething anthill. Anton Eich, a mild man who
was playing the cutthroat and examining magistrate, shouted at
a bit player. The porter approached, holding a roll of paper
wrapped in cardboard. "Mind the bomb!" cried a wit as Christopher took the roll. He did not open it. He went into Adam's
dressing room to make sure that Adam's makeup was sufficiently
pale. Turning away from Adam, he undid the package. It contained an old, tattered poster for *Ritual Murder*, showing five
or six bearded Jews surrounding and clutching a fair-haired
boy.

A few minutes late, the curtain rose.

What did the great silence mean? Christopher's heart was
pounding. It meant nothing, at least nothing bad. Stuckenschmidt is a bit unsure of himself; his pauses are too long, as
though he were thinking of something else. He felt Ludwig Ludwig's huge paw on his shoulder. They smiled at each other.
Adam was standing next to the stage manager. Christopher
gestured to him that he was keeping his fingers crossed. Adam
showed no sign of excitement. He made his entrance; there was
a certain restlessness as he entered—the worst might be over.
József Sarf said to Abraham Bukszbaum: "We need a good circumciser. And one who isn't too expensive." Laughter here and
there. I should have cut the second sentence, Christopher
thought. They are laughing because they think it's meant as a
joke: of course, the miserly Jew. Or do they find the word "circumciser" funny? Am I addressing an audience that finds the
word "circumciser" funny? Another silence, not a good one, this
time; it is hostile or indifferent. How can one distinguish between one silence and another? József Sarf to Salamon Svarz:
"Do you know what the policeman thought?" Salamon Svarz:
"A Jew always knows what a policeman thinks." At this sentence
there should be a movement in the audience. Nothing. Each
sentence falls dead to the ground. Between the stage and the
stalls the orchestra pit yawns like a chasm.

The curtain fell. After the first act there was only a brief interval. Christopher listened. The applause was thin—polite approval, it might be called, almost as in a living room in which the son of the family has been giving a private audition. Ludwig Ludwig, who had been hovering between his box and the stage, came back, panted for breath. "Don't worry," he said. "The audience isn't quite sure yet what it's all about. Just wait till the courtroom scene . . ." The courtroom scene was another fifteen minutes at least, or rather, fifteen hours. And the audience had scarcely reacted to the arrest of the Jews at the end of Act One. "Stuckenschmidt is on edge, try to calm him," said Dr. Strbrny. "Adam is saving the situation," said Mommert. So the evening had to be salvaged.

Christopher went over to the curtain. In the twilit auditorium he recognized Martha, in the front row, almost exactly in the center. She was wearing a pastel blue dress. In the kibbutz, everything had been so much simpler. Eighteen pounds a week, board and lodging, two letters a week. She should have come to a later performance. There won't be many later performances. He congratulated Adam, hurried to the dressing rooms. The author was allowed to despair, not the director. The change of sets took place without incident. A glance at the time: the performance was running on schedule, at least that's something. Fritz Eppstein touched his arm. "The audience is always reserved after the first act." Again he looked through the hole in the curtain. Only two or three men in the stalls were standing up; everyone else had remained seated. He remembered Budapest. He had finished a scene, he read it aloud, listening to his own voice, he was satisfied or dissatisfied, he was alone. And one day, suddenly, you speak in the same voice to a thousand people, but you haven't called them. Suddenly they are there, they are silent, and in silence they call you to account, and they are not people; there is a dark mass, a thousand heads on one body. That's not how I meant it. I wanted to finish something! I haven't finished it, it's a mistake. I wanted to judge, not to be judged; I'm not in the dock; you are in the dock; for twenty-eight years I haven't finished anything, it is not my nature to finish anything. "Act One was simply too long," he heard Martin

Mommert's voice saying behind him. "I don't like the look of the gallery," he heard Ludwig Ludwig's voice say. "Too many old people." He hurried into the wings. "Just remember that in reality you never believed there had been a murder," he said to Ludmilla Lackenbach, who played Eszter Solymosi's mother. "Just as at the last rehearsal." "We're starting," said the stage manager.

The first incident occurred when Anton Eich, the murderer and examining magistrate Kálmán Péczely, began beating Móricz Sarf. Out of the silence came a catcall, but it did not come as a surprise; the restlessness in the audience had been felt before, a rustling of paper and clothes, and the whistle too, though it was a whistle like any other, as though it came from lips that had long been pursed to whistle. "Quiet!" called out someone down below indignantly, but it sounded like the shout of a troublemaker. At the back of the gallery a high-pitched, shrill voice cried: "Stop it!" but it was not certain whether the shouter meant that people should stop disturbing the performance, or that the performance itself should be stopped. Christopher's eyes were fixed rigidly on the stage. The blows were beating down upon Móricz Sarf, but he could hear neither the crack of the whip or Adam's whimpering, and Anton Eich was shouting far too loud, trying to drown the sounds in the auditorium. Adam was standing, with his back bent, quite close to the wings. Christopher's eyes met the boy's. Christopher tried to look reassuring, but Adam was the Jewish boy Móricz Sarf, and between him and the auditorium stood the wall of the prison; he heard neither the whistling nor the shouts.

The performance continued, on schedule, undisturbed.

Perhaps it's all a misunderstanding. I wanted to whip up people's nerves and here I am, surprised that I have whipped them up. An organized demonstration? It could be that someone's nerves couldn't stand it, that someone couldn't bear the sadistic torture of the boy. We are like alcoholics, the blood is high, and one more drop means intoxication. A murderer who can't bear the sight of blood on the stage—quite understandable. Or maybe it had been a humane protest. "Stop!"—it had perhaps been shouted to the torturer. And the *Ritual Murder* poster? And the swastikas and "Perish Judah!"? A minute's darkness. Shuffling, swaying, shadowy figures: a change of set on the open stage. That's Walter Einsiedel. It's good to see him stride onto the stage as calmly, with as firm a step, as Károly von Eötvös did, seventy-five years ago. Dead silence. What was his mother thinking? It was too late to get Martha seated next to her. Two critics with their wives are sitting between them. What is Martha thinking? They are catcalling me, and I feel responsible for them. I apologized to Fritz Eppstein for the swastikas. What would Misha Kohorn think, and Kasimir Nessor? My father! He never looked for the fault in himself but always blamed the critics, the public. It never occurred to him that *The Miracle Worker* might be a bad film, that he might have spoiled it. Big, strong, vain father! Perhaps my play is a failure. József Sarf was saying: "We are always merely tolerated, Doctor von Eötvös." The sentence sounds wooden, even Kahn couldn't have spoken it any better. I should have heard that in rehearsal and changed it.

József Sarf: "Where are we to go, Doctor von Eötvös?"

The name Eötvös was inaudible. On the left of the gallery someone shouted: "To Israel!" On the right of the gallery a woman's voice: "To Bonn! For restitution!"

Laughter spilled through the theater, but not many laughed, perhaps only seven or eight. In the theater, the individual, disguised and made up, can only speak on the lighted stage. Down below, in the darkness, a thousand thoughts, a thousand moods and a thousand voices are fused into a mysterious unity which must remain silent. Here where it is forbidden, a single laugh becomes a rebellion of the pupils against the teacher. From everywhere, sounds of "Ssh" rang out admonishingly, angrily, indignantly. But although silence returned to the auditorium, the few who were dissatisfied had achieved their goal: the audience had turned to the gallery and forgotten the stage.

Darkness again, a change of set, longer this time, but this time, too, a perfectly functioning mechanism. In a minute the courtroom scene would begin, the first, but also the most dramatic courtroom scene, that would last till the second curtain.

An asthmatic panting, barely suppressed, warned Christopher

that Ludwig Ludwig was standing behind him. "Only a full-fledged theatrical scandal," he said, "can help us now. You must definitely take a bow."

"It isn't over yet," said Christopher.

During the courtroom scene he walked up and down on tiptoe behind the set. He became aware of his superstitious fear: as a child he had often believed that something bad could be averted if he turned away from the source of his anxiety. He had too often dreamed childish dreams in the last few months. Everything had been within reach. Ludwig based his hopes on the courtroom scene. Ludwig should have drawn his attention to the mistakes. Why else did a theater have a literary adviser? They knew nothing. One mind thinks like this and another mind another way, and a thousand minds think a thousand different thoughts. He heard the words he had written, as if they were muted. Many had sounded strange to him at rehearsal, unrecognizable. Perhaps the fault lay with the director. If only János Varga had carried the rehearsals through to the end, or if only I had taken my father's advice! My father knew his public. Abraham Bukszbaum is making his statement. Softly, softly, for he's a pure simpleton. But what do they know about a pure simpleton? In *Ritual Murder* there were no half sentences, no half thoughts that the audience had to carry to a conclusion. Now the witness Móricz Sarf is being called. I must look for Adam.

As always, Adam was standing beside the stage manager. He said nothing. He almost pushed his wig askew, he pressed himself so close to Christopher. A little black-haired Jewish boy in a brand new blue suit, the reward for being Judas. They have baptized the boy, they have bought him a blue suit, they have brought him here in a coach, his hair is pressed flat to his temples; Móricz Sarf doesn't look very different now from Adam Lambrecht. In a moment he will be standing in front of his father, screaming, "You killed her!" "Don't be afraid!" Christopher whispered to the boy, and Adam said: "Not me," and the stage manager had to take his arm, because it was time for his entrance.

There was not a sound in the theater. Out of incomprehen-

sion, indifference, reverence? Then the curtain came down for
the second time.

The applause was restrained, but no voice was raised in protest. How clearly the crowd was able to express itself! When the
actors bowed the applause swelled, the demonstration was loud
and silent at the same time: the clapping showed that the applause was for the actors, not the play. As Adam came onto the
stage the applause was doubled, trebled. He is saving the evening, thought Christopher, and an inexplicable, exuberant
gaiety came over him.

Martha came back-stage, then his mother. He almost forgot
to introduce Martha to his mother. It seemed to him a matter
of course that they should know each other. Martha kissed him
on the cheeks. "The play is magnificent," she said. "Everything
will be all right," said his mother. "I shall have to stay with the
actors for half an hour after the performance," he said to Martha.
"Will you wait at the hotel?"

"Don't hurry, I'll wait," she said.

News kept coming in all the time, news from the intermis-
sions, news from the lobby. The critic of a big Hamburg paper
had taken his overcoat, but perhaps he only wanted a breath of
air. A critic had winked at Ludwig Ludwig. There were very
few people at the buffet—had the play spoiled their appetite?
One police officer had kept a group under observation: they had
their heads together like conspirators. There might still be a
"full-fledged" scandal. Hermann Lambrecht said he had recognized a wartime comrade who had later become a *Sturmbann-
führer* in the SS. Dr. Strbrny reported that people were compar-
ing *The Great Trial* to *Ritual Murder*; he didn't know how the
comparisons were working out. Mommert said that everything
now depended on the critics. Christopher was holding Martha's
hand. He stood between the two women—the beautiful, tall
girl with the long hair and the little woman in the black dress,
who had been to the hairdresser and whose curled hair was like
a wig. It seemed to him so strange and so soothing not to be
alone that he spent too long with the two women and left them
late to hurry along the corridor to the dressing room. Otto
Stuckenschmidt apologized for his first-night nerves. Ludmilla

Lackenbach said: "It's a fiasco." Anton Eich said it had gone surprisingly well. Fritz Eppstein was drying his forehead with the towel on which "Jew" was painted.

The storm broke when, in the middle of the last act, the boatmen came onto the stage carrying Eszter Solymosi's body. There was a catcall, as in the first act, but immediately afterward came a second catcall, then a third; people were catcalling from the back, the last row of the stalls, and then someone blew a blast on an alarm whistle, and immediately afterward the auxiliary troops of disorder were on the spot. "Stop it! Stop it!" was shouted from several quarters—isolated voices still, but as though beginning to form a chorus. Amsel Fogel and Dávid Herskó, the two Jewish ferrymen, did not move. Herskó should have spoken long ago, but István Gerö, the Hungarian, who at the best of times had to struggle with the language, had dried up completely. Amsel Fogel, played by an old favorite of the public couldn't answer, couldn't put the dead girl down on the bench; he stood there, forlorn, with his burden that was gradually becoming too heavy for him, the blond girl's hair hung down almost to the ground and she was blushing, the corpse was blushing, the audience couldn't fail to notice. Catcalls, "Stop it!" and the gaiety spread. In despair, Christopher signalled to the Hungarian from the wings to speak; but Gerö did not see him. Christopher ran around the stage. At last the man with the body saw him, skipped a few lines, dropped the body onto the bench.

The majority in the stalls had meanwhile triumphed. "That could be Eszter," Gerö repeated twice. The performance went on.

After the set had been changed, the last courtroom scene began. Károly von Eötvös rose to make his speech for the defense.

It's not the play, it's the people in the auditorium, it's the country, the fatherland that Kasimir Nessor loves. I was three years old when he left it, that's twenty-five years ago. He has suffered a great deal and forgotten a great deal. A minority? Rubbish! In the lobby they compared *The Great Trial* with *Ritual Murder*—the comparison worked out in your favor, father! Don't become a sunny character! There's no danger of that, Herr Nessor. Bloody clashes during the Frankfurt premiere of *The Miracle Worker*—you didn't want it, father, and I didn't want it either. Shall I wait for the end of the performance? I must stay; the author can run away—not the director. "You never finish anything." What's the point, Ferdinand? "You have talent; everything you have written is highly gifted, I'm not a doting mother." Perhaps you are a doting mother. "It's no use running away." Is it any use staying, mother? Silly kids' pranks. Of course. It was all silly kids' pranks. Violated cemeteries, the burning of the Reichstag, Warsaw, Oradour, Lidice, Oranienburg, Buchenwald, Auschwitz, and then violated cemeteries again and then swastikas again and then lining the streets again and uniforms again and then Warsaw and Lidice again—silly kids' pranks. But, Herr Wendelin, you're exaggerating, you're looking at things too personally, you're exaggerating again, you're sensitive, Herr Wendelin, a few catcalls, a few interruptions, after all, we live in a democracy, people must be allowed to catcall, after all, you don't object to applause, I mean, you could have picked a different subject, after all, people haven't forgotten the war yet, the shortages and the atrocities and Dresden, and they haven't forgotten your father's beautiful film, either, after all, you could have trodden in his footsteps, the Inspector said so himself, you simply have to understand democracy properly, freedom of expression, that's democracy, Herr Wendelin, even if it doesn't happen to suit you just at the moment, just admit, you laid it on pretty thick, after all, the Jews aren't all angels either, if you have to look at those bearded Jews all evening, and then the dripping wet girl who isn't even properly dead, you can't expect the impossible, Herr Wendelin.

Károly von Eötvös had sat down. Christopher stood motionless in the wings. The play was running like a film strip whose end is blank. Christopher heard the words of József Sarf and Móricz Sarf, but he felt as though he had never heard them before, and he felt as though a strange director was standing in the wings. The man in the wings was a stranger to him—the author sends his apologies, he has gone home, he is packing his bags. His dress shirt was soaked through, but now the collar was beginning to dry. It wasn't the cool wind from the rigging loft;

only, he had nothing to do with the man to whom everything had been so important, The man to whom everything had been so important had already gone home, had packed his bags.

József Sarf: "Will you come with me, Móricz?" Móricz Sarf: "With you? Where to?" József Sarf: "Away from here." Pause. The last word. Curtain.

Suddenly there were people around Christopher, a lot of people.

Applause, catcalls, boos, applause. The cheers grew louder and louder. The curtain went up. The whole company, then individual actors. Finally, Adam, Walter Einsiedel, Fritz Eppstein, Otto Stuckenschmidt. Shouts of "Bravo!" Adam alone on the stage. "Bravo, bravo!" Ludwig Ludwig wheezed: "You must go onto the stage!" It had been agreed that he would appear first with the whole company, then alone. When Ludmilla Lackenbach stretched out her hand to him, he shook his head. "You can't back out," he heard Martin Mommert say behind him. "No," he said. He hadn't meant it like that. Fritz Eppstein stood in his way. He pushed the little comedian aside, the curtain rose, he went onto the stage alone. The way to the center of the stage was miles long, many miles, it took hours, many hours. There they were again, the boos, the catcalls. He stood still, raised his head, gazed into the audience, his neck stiff, he did not bow. Nor did he bow as the applause grew louder and louder, groups crowded round the banister of the orchestra pit, the dissenters fell silent.

"Curtain?" asked a stagehand. "Do what you like," said Christopher.

They stood around him, the great Ludwig, the manager, the literary adviser, the bearded Jews and the policemen, the peasant women, the peasant girls, the judges in their robes. A young man brought him telegrams. Dr. Strbrny opened them. Kasimir Nessor, Misha Kohorn, János Varga, Piotr Rokowski, Eva. "The foes are noisy, the friends are silent; that is the nature of things." The friends are silent, yet they send telegrams. Ludwig Ludwig said, "The critics are no longer important—we shall do the play a hundred times." Christopher embraced his mother.

"Don't run away, you're coming with me." He went quickly to
the dressing rooms, thanked the actors, came back to the wings,
thanked the stagehands. Sets were carried past him. He had a
feeling that there was a smell of fire. But it was only the dust.

Outside the stage door stood ten to fifteen young people. A
girl asked him for his autograph. It wasn't cold, it was snowing
in large flakes. Someone took him by the shoulders, said: "We
came as a bodyguard. But it isn't necessary. The cowardly
bastards!" It was the man in evening dress, from the police station. Behind him stood the bear and the clown. He had difficulty in recognizing them. They looked like boarding-school
students at the dancing class. He shook their hands.

"Thanks for the free ticket," said the bear.

"Thanks for the free ticket," said the clown.

He stayed in the bar for an hour, then took his mother home,
"I'm proud of you," she said. "You're a doting mother," he
laughed. "The play will be acted twenty years from now," she
said. "You went to the hairdresser," he laughed. "The critics
can't be unjust," she said. "There's no need to console me." She
said, "Hurry up, Martha is waiting. She was delighted." He
kissed her and drove to Martha's hotel.

As to success or failure, he knew less than he had known in
the theater. The actors, down in the bar, had bathed in their
success. The first night was over, few of them thought about
the play. Ludwig Ludwig had been in high spirits—maybe
the performance hadn't been as good as the dress rehearsal, the
play had rough spots that must be eliminated, but apart from
the first act, no one could say it had met with a lukewarm re-
sponse. Martin Mommert had already spoken to the big news
agency, informing them about the swastikas. "We shall continue to be talked about, that's the important thing." They
had picked up a hot iron. If they had burned themselves a little,
that was understandable. Dr. Strbrny quoted Hebbel after the
posthumous performance of a play by Kleist: "This is a play in
relation to which only the audience can prove a failure." "A
topic of conversation, that's the great thing," the great Ludwig

kept repeating. And next week there was the court case concern-
ing the Warsaw material. "We shall continue to be talked
about." On this everybody could agree.

The hotel lobby was empty. It was a big, chic hotel, recently
redecorated, the turn of the century minus plush. The marble
walls, the Venetian vases and the bronze statues dated from an
era when people had believed in eternity. By this time, shortly
before midnight, most of the guests had already gone to bed.
They too dated from the turn of the century.

In the bar adjoining the lobby, three gentlemen were still
sitting over a bottle of champagne. Martha was sitting alone in
an alcove. She rose, came to meet Christopher, put her arms
around his neck. The three gentlemen nodded to them benevo-
lently.

"It was magnificent," she said.

"You can't be serious."

"I mean the play, the author, the director, the actors. Not the
audience."

"I thought of you," he said, "and I felt ashamed."

"That could have happened anywhere."

"It would have happened differently elsewhere. But let's
not talk about that now."

"That's the important thing now," she said.

He looked at her forehead, her hair, her skin, and thought
that she was more beautiful than he remembered her. Time
had lulled his love to sleep; time had been kind to him, he could
not have lived with his love. During this time of deceptive sleep
his love had not aged.

"Do you really have to fly back tomorrow?" he asked.

She nodded, but she didn't seem to change the conversation
quickly. "I was proud of you when you stood on the stage alone,"
she said.

"I failed, but my mother says the same thing."

"All those who love you must say the same thing. You stood
there, alone, and you faced them all. You offered them your
forehead, as we say in German."

He laughed. "That's a good expression, to offer one's forehead. When I first saw you, in the kibbutz, it was your forehead

that first struck me. She offers her forehead to the world, I thought. And I tried to offer my forehead to you, because I was furious that you had disturbed my peace. Afterward I sat at my window half the night. I thought, they have smuggled a Trojan horse into the kibbutz, and the Trojan horse is full of beautiful Helens."

She laughed. "Shouldn't I have come today?"

"This isn't the kibbutz," he said.

"No. Here I cannot disturb the peace."

He ordered a brandy.

She said, "What are you going to do now?"

"That depends upon a court case. The Warsaw documents, about which I've written to you, have been seized. We are demanding their release. If we win the case, I shall set about finishing the book. I'm probably not a writer, but only a collator of documents."

"If you let yourself get discouraged, the barbarians will have won. I think I ought to come to Munich and tell you every day that you are a writer."

"You shouldn't make promises like that, frivolously," he said.

It wasn't frivolous, she said. Next month she had three weeks' holiday. "We could go to the mountains, we could ski, and you could work."

He looked at her as though he didn't understand what she was saying. She was saying what he could not say, and as if it were the most natural thing in the world.

"Don't you want to?" she said. "Just say so."

"There's nothing I want more," he said.

The waiter brought his drink.

He asked, "Why haven't you married?"

"That's a crude question," she laughed. "I don't want to marry, and it isn't what you want to know either. You want to know whether I have been disappointed, like before Israel. And whether it is over. I haven't been disappointed, if that makes you feel happier. Your trouble is that you don't understand the simple things."

"And what are the simple things?"

"For example, that one can't live alone when one is my age.

For example, that one doesn't have a great love every year. But also, for example, that one can't get attached to a man who is going off to Poland next day for two years."

"You couldn't know that."

"You were in flight. And if you had stayed on my account, you would have fled from me later."

"Did you think all that over soberly?"

"I don't think much of drunken decisions."

"And suppose I had forgotten you in the meantime?"

"I had to risk that. But . . . see above."

"What do you mean, see above?"

"One doesn't experience a great love every year."

"I really don't understand the simplest thing," he said.

The three gentlemen had drunk each other's health once more and left. The room was empty. The bartender stood behind the bar, yawning. It was growing cold.

Christopher began to talk. He felt he must tell Martha in one hour what he had wanted to say in all his letters. He talked about the letters he had written and thrown away. "I removed the heart from every letter; only then did I mail it. I ought to write a short story about a man who carries a communicating vessel in his chest instead of a heart. And seeks desperately for a woman like himself. What he carries in his chest instead of a heart only functions when he finds someone in whose communicating vessel the fluid is at the same level." He took her hand and remembered the night when they sat outside his house in Ani Omer. Now he did not wait for an answer either. He talked of the silent library in Warsaw and of the paper coffins in which the murderers and their victims lay, of the journey to Hungary, the country that had seemed so familiar to him, as though he had been there with his father, of the cemetery in Budapest and of the village on the Tisza, of the intoxication of creation and of the sobering up that comes with completion, of Ferdinand's death and of the forty or fifty at Ferdinand's grave, of his father's death and the rats and the moles, of his longing for her and his betrayal of her, of his happy homecoming and the betrayal of his homeland.

Then she spoke of her work, of which she was tired and which she was about to exchange for a job with the United Nations, of her father, who was still traveling around the world, of her mother, who didn't understand why her daughter did not want to marry and present her with three or four grandchildren and who secretly pulled strings that were visible to everyone, of her own longing for London, where she was at home, because one is at home where one has schoolmates, of Christopher's letters, which she had understood, and of her silence, because it is difficult to talk to a deaf man, of her doubts as to whether she had acted rightly in Paris, and of the certainty that it had been right.

"I shall be here on the seventh or eighth of March," she said. "I hope there will still be snow in the mountains."

"If I don't come to you before that," he said. "I don't know whether I can stand this country. I don't know whether there are more than forty or fifty."

"And I don't know whether it depends upon the number," she said.

They talked about *The Great Trial.* It seemed unbelievable to Christopher that three hours ago he had been standing on the stage, hoping, filled with misgivings, waiting for the bravos and the catcalls from the gallery. "My father," he said, "used to like quoting Goethe: 'The gods, the eternal ones,/To those they love give wholly:/Joy without end they give/And endless sorrow too.' In spite of everything, he must have been loved by the gods. The gods deal more harshly with me—or more mildly."

She had not let go of his hand. "Goethe meant it quite differently," she said. "He wasn't talking about such commonplace things as a first night and a rendezvous in a hotel bar. He must have meant that those whom the gods love feel everything completely, sufferings and joys. I suspect that you are loved by the gods. In fact, when you stood there alone on the stage, I was sure of it."

Then they talked of such mundane things as her flight to Paris. She didn't want him to take her to the airport in the morning, in only five hours' time, and he insisted that he would be at the hotel punctually. He prepared to go, and she insisted on getting her fur coat and going with him to his car.

It was still snowing. The car was standing alone in a side street. He brushed the snow from the windows. "I'm sure there will still be snow in March," she said. Then they kissed. She ran back into the hotel and he waited till she had disappeared around the corner.

He had packed his bag.

Tomorrow morning I shall go to my mother and tell her that I am going away for a few weeks, she doesn't need to know why. I shall come and visit her occasionally, but this time I'm leaving for good. I won't call Martha, I'd rather surprise her. After all, there's skiing in France, too, and you can work there. Maybe now I shall turn to the story of the man who had a communicating vessel in place of a heart. I won't write the *Facts* now that we lost the case. The public was excluded from the court throughout most of the trial, because of "security risks." It's a danger to security to reveal how many monsters are running around loose. The evidence was not conclusive and might possibly have laid innocent people open to public contempt or even deprived them of their livelihood. Livelihood is not life, nor do you lose your life because you lose your honor—and what is honor, after all? The judge said, "Herr Wendelin, as we shall assume in mitigation of his offense, was the unsuspecting victim of Eastern propaganda." In mitigation of my offense, for I was being accused. Perhaps I ought to go to Warsaw and find out who the judge, Dr. Heribert Kammelohr, is. Unfortunately, though, the Kammelohr file would be seized, and it could not be released, because, Herr *Oberlandesgerichtsrat*, Dr. Kammelohr is innocent, "possibly," and it would endanger his livelihood. The publishing house has appealed. In one year the case will come up before the first appeal court, in two years before the second. One must examine one's motives, for I might want something personal out of all of this. With the critiques of my play, for instance. Would you like to hear a few quotes? "The young author must be credited with having perhaps had the good intention of consigning his father's disgraceful film *Ritual Murder* to oblivion. As the reactions of the first-night audience showed, he achieved the opposite. Many remembered Wendelin's tendentious film with a shudder, but an artistic comparison worked out to the son's disadvantage." Or: "Things are not quite as simple as the opportunist Herr Wendelin imagines. Since people have come to accept the idea that *Mea culpa* has to be printed on every page of the German dictionary, Herr Wendelin imagined that he had to glorify the Jews on an equally all-embracing scale as his father had maligned them." Or: "This piece, completely old-fashioned in language and dramatic structure, does the cause of liberalism a disservice. The society which the author accuses is long since dead; it is almost impossible to understand why a young author in the atomic age should step aside into the realm of social problems that were solved long ago." And finally: "The son who, so long as his father lived, could not shout 'Kill him!' loud enough, has proved a worthy son of his father as far as opportunism is concerned."

There were attacks from Right and Left, from progressives and conservatives, but the notices were very detailed, several paragraphs long, and there was the splendid scandal, in some papers actually on the front page, which caused Ludwig no complaint. The theater sold out every day. There were offers for the film rights, by the dozen. The great Ludwig is a great man. His instinct is infallible, so is his judgment of the market. I am corrupted by prejudice, by contentment. One has too small a heart, the other too large a belly.

He looked at his suitcase. He owned more now than when he ran away to Israel. I'll get the rest in a few weeks or months, for my mother's sake if nothing else. Two suits, skiing trousers, sweaters. Books and papers I can buy in Paris.

It was almost eleven o'clock at night. I won't sleep well tonight. I sleep worse when I'm happy than when I'm unhappy. In the evening I shall be in Paris.

The windows were iced over, every window as though of double glass. At least no bathroom windows. It hasn't been so bad. The long discussions with János through the night. The reading audition with Adam. The corrections, the beautiful, lonely struggle for words. The trees tinted by the frost. A good autumn, a good winter.

His thoughts were interrupted by the ring of the front doorbell. Ten past eleven. A cold shiver ran down his back: he thought of his father's visit. Perhaps someone from the theater. On the way to the door he worked it out. Half an hour after the end of the performance, probably something had happened that they wanted to tell him about personally.

"I just wanted to see you," said Adam. "Am I disturbing you?"

"No . . . of course not . . . come in!" He looked at the car standing outside the door.

"My father," said Adam. He was carrying a small parcel. "He doesn't want to come in. I'll only stay five minutes."

They went into the living room.

"How was the performance?" asked Christopher.

"Packed. A very good audience. In the middle of the second act I was applauded. Stuckenschmidt was pretty sore."

"Sit down," said Christopher.

Adam was still holding the parcel. "Are you really going away tomorrow?" he said.

"Yes." Somewhat uncertainly he said, "I told you—I have to get back my breath."

Adam shook his head. "I don't think you will ever come back."

"What an idea!"

"I think you're fed up." He was fighting back tears; therefore, he stood up and held out the parcel to Christopher.

"Is that for me?" asked Christopher.

Adam nodded.

Taking great care, Christopher opened the long, narrow package. He knew what was in it. It was a tie, a dark blue silk tie, with a single red stripe.

"Magnificent!" said Christopher.

"Do you really like it?"

"Just what I needed. But you shouldn't have spent so much money."

"I'm earning a fortune. I wanted you to remember me."

"What nonsense! First of all, you're acting as though I were going away for good, and secondly, I couldn't possibly forget you."

Adam was standing in the middle of the room; Christopher stood in front of him, holding the tie in his hand.

"Well, then . . ." said Adam, but he made no move to go.

And at this moment it seemed to Christopher that he had done something which he had never done before, which he would not have thought himself capable of doing: he had lied to a child.

"I'll come and see you very soon," he said. "Perhaps you will still be playing *The Great Trial*. But you're right. I am fed up."

"Is it because of the row in the theater?"

"That too."

"What else?"

"You know about my court case. There was no time to tell you about it in detail. I can no longer speak the truth here, and if one can't speak the truth there's no point anymore."

Adam nodded. He looked at Christopher. His eyes were wet. "You always told me the truth," he said.

"Was that so important to you?"

"Oh, yes," said Adam. "Very."

Christopher sat down. He could hear the motor of the car running outside. He put the tie on the table.

You always told me the truth. Was that so important to you? Oh yes, very. And suppose he didn't believe in me, but in someone else? Although it is created by men, the atmosphere is stronger than man. Do you understand? I shall see you often. Word of honor? Cross my heart. Thanks for the free ticket. We came as a bodyguard. No need, friends—the man you wanted to protect has run away. Perhaps there are only forty or fifty. Then it would be thirty-nine or forty-nine. And then twenty-one or eleven or three or none at all. None who can tell Adam Lambrecht the truth.

"You'll think now that I'm crazy," he said.

"Yes?" said Adam.

"I'm not going," said Christopher.

A smile came over Adam's face, and the smile was so bright that it dazzled Christopher.

"How do you mean?" said Adam, as though he couldn't believe what he had heard.

"Just that," said Christopher. "I'm not going."

Adam took Christopher's hand.

"Go, now," said Christopher. "Your father is waiting. I'll see you tomorrow." He laughed. "Do you want to keep the tie?"

"What an idea," said Adam and ran to the door.

For a moment the noise of the motor grew louder, then it moved away.

Christopher went up the stairs.

He began to unpack his case.